THE
FOUNTAIN

A LAST RESORT NOVEL

BY

NATHAN BIRR

Published by BEACON BOOKS, LLC

Cover Images Copyright ©
Sean Pavone/Shutterstock.com

ISBN: 978-1-7321373-8-7 (hc)
ISBN: 978-1-7321373-9-4 (sc)

This novel is a work of fiction. Names, characters, businesses, places, events, and incidents are either the products of the author's imagination or used in a fictitious manner. Any resemblance to actual persons, living or dead, or actual events is purely coincidental.

www.nathanbirr.com

To those seeking life abundant . . .

May you find It.

CHAPTER ONE

Cameron Leigh looked up. The turquoise water above her seemed to glow, imbued with the cooler wavelengths of light that managed to penetrate some fifty feet beneath the ocean's surface. She watched the bubbles from her scuba regulator as they ascended toward a massive loggerhead turtle that glided through the iridescent water. Cameron's eyes followed the turtle for a moment, then turned downward to the ocean floor.

Littered with dark, decaying scraps of three-hundred-year-old wood, it was in stark contrast to the water around it. Three centuries and change ago, the scraps of wood had been a 104-foot-long Spanish frigate called *Descubridor*. Until Hurricane Matthew in 2016, the *Descubridor*, believed to have been sunk by pirates in 1705, had lain at the bottom of the Atlantic, her precise location unknown. Matthew had paralleled the East Coast of the United States, churning up the shallower waters around Cape Canaveral and depositing the dismembered wreckage of the *Descubridor* along a wide swath of ocean floor approximately two to three miles offshore.

No one had known at first. In the wake of Matthew, all manner of flotsam and jetsam had washed ashore from West Palm Beach, Florida, to Cape Hatteras, North Carolina. Most of it was unidentifiable or uninteresting junk, but several pieces had been relevant to those who knew what to look for. Cameron Leigh was one of those people.

A decayed but still recognizable figurehead of a woman, clinging to a cross, was found on a newly formed sandbar off Melbourne Beach. Some believed it to be Mary the mother of Jesus or Mary Magdalene, but most experts agreed that it was a representation of Saint Helena Augusta, the mother of Constantine and, traditionally, the discoverer of the alleged "True Cross." She was thus named the Patron Saint of Discovery, and her likeness was chosen as the figurehead for the *Descubridor*—the *Discoverer*. Several pieces of dinnerware, shards of cups, three forks, and a knife were found along the coast north of Melbourne Beach, and a gold pocket watch inscribed with the name of one of the *Descubridor's* believed passengers was recovered by a beachcomber on Cocoa Beach.

Even so, not many people had an interest in the *Descubridor*. It had been sunk en route to the New World, not returning laden with gold. In fact, it was something of a mystery why it had been set upon by pirates in the first place, unless it was simply for bearing the wrong colors. Nevertheless, it had been lost to history once submerged beneath the Atlantic, and evidence pointing to a location south and east of Cape Canaveral stirred only a select few in the salvage world.

Cameron had learned of the figurehead and pocket watch from separate sources, and had spent nearly two years raising funds, securing approval, convincing partners, and arranging expeditions. Then had begun the tedious start-and-stop process of locating the actual wreck. Numerous passes with side-scan sonar and fish finders, photographs taken by remotely operated underwater vehicles (ROVs), and hours of scrutinizing depth charts and tide tables had led to several false positives but nothing in the way of actual results until the previous spring, when a sport fisherman on vacation from Maryland had reeled in a stern lantern from a seventeenth-century Spanish frigate. Cameron had been notified via several contacts, had spoken to the angler to pinpoint the location, and had concentrated her search efforts on a patch of ocean two and a half miles offshore and about five miles south of the restricted waters off Cape Canaveral. She and her then partners had discovered the debris field, made numerous dives and sent ROVs to the ocean floor, and confirmed they had indeed found the wreckage of the *Descubridor*.

Even that hadn't panned out. Although she had found her quarry, Cameron had been unable to locate the object the old frigate had allegedly been carrying. The money ran out and her partners lost interest, and Cameron had temporarily called off the search. Six weeks ago, she had secured new funds and begun procuring a skeleton crew. Six days ago, they'd arrived in Florida again and started scanning and diving, this time expanding their search beyond the main debris field. Knowing it was possible *it* hadn't actually gone down with the *Descubridor*—or that if it had, three centuries and numerous storms, including Hurricane Matthew, could have carried it miles away—or that it could have been found by a treasure hunter or another fisherman or swallowed by an undiscriminating shark—Cameron was determined to leave no underwater stone uncovered.

2

On day four, with just minutes of air remaining in her oxygen tank, she had spotted a glimmer. It had faded as quickly as she'd seen it, and she'd used up the rest of her air supply searching to no avail. She'd marked the spot and returned the next day with an underwater metal detector and a camera. She had been about to give up when she'd spotted it again, mostly submerged beneath the sand and rock and seaweed that blanketed the seabed. Her heart had raced, and she'd taken a few moments to calm herself and regulate her breathing before confirming it was the object she'd long been seeking. She'd documented the find with a few photographs and marked the spot with GPS. Now, she was back, again diving solo, and prepared to excavate the discovery of a lifetime.

Cameron hovered in the water just over the seabed. This time she'd had no trouble honing in on the object, even without her dive light glinting off its bronze surface. That in itself was shocking—after three centuries, the bronze should be covered in a green patina, but it was nearly perfect. Then again, perhaps it hadn't been exposed to seawater until just recently, in Matthew's wake.

Using her gloved fingers, Cameron carefully brushed away the sand, revealing more and more of the round object, roughly the size of a large dinner plate. Only this plate was inscribed with a variety of letters in two rows around its circumference. She rubbed her fingers gently over the surface, able to make out some of the letters. They were somewhat crude and caked with sediment, and tiny, and she didn't take the time to decipher them further.

A shadow passed overhead, and Cameron quickly looked up, hoping to see the turtle again. She saw nothing, and warily looked a moment longer. She'd had a scary encounter with a great white off the coast near Miami a few years back, and was always on edge when underwater. Content that nothing was stalking her, she resumed her work of freeing the circular object.

When it was loose, she again studied it with the eyes of a scholar, noting its smooth rim, flat—other than for the inscriptions—surface, and heaviness. After a moment, she decided she would wait for serious analysis until she was out of the water. Letting the bronze disk rest in the sand, she reached for the belt at her waist and unclipped and unfurled a small airtight pouch. It was just large enough to fit around the disk, and when she had zipped it closed, Cameron reached for the belt again and retrieved a fifty-pound lift bag. Working quickly but not hurriedly, she connected the lift bag to the pouch.

Then, using her regulator, she inflated the bag just enough that it began to rise. Holding onto a tether line attached to the bag, scanning her eyes from her surrounding to the pouch holding the disk, Cameron ascended with it.

She had not been deep enough or submerged long enough that she needed to make decompression stops, but she took her time nonetheless. Gradually, the water began to lighten, the red and yellow wavelengths now shining through. With a few more kicks of her fins, Cameron's lithe body broke through the surface. She spat out her mouthpiece and removed her mask to look around.

Everything was still blue—the pure sky, the cobalt surface of the Atlantic, and the hull of the research vessel that had been her base of operations for the last week. It was some thirty feet away, and none of her crewmates were expectantly leaning over the side waiting for her to surface. Then again, they were hired hands, not partners dedicated to her cause.

Cameron exhaled several times, drawing in deep replacement breaths of fresh, natural air. She turned her face to the warm afternoon sun, feeling as if it was shining down specifically on her. She would have basked a little longer, but her scuba gear was cumbersome, and she wanted to get busy examining the find she'd been seeking for years.

She turned and swam toward the *Eternal Sun*, a vessel aptly named for its purpose, if not for its condition. Older than Cameron, the *Sun* had the rust stains and scuff marks to testify to a life at sea. So too did her crew, an old, abrasive captain named Sully (seriously, what else would he have been named?) and his son and nephew who managed the equipment. Despite their gruff appearances, salty language, and the fact that they drank on the job, Cameron had to admit that the trio knew what they were doing, and her initial fears had been unfounded—they had treated her with nothing but respect, and she'd actually grown to sort of like "Sully and the boys." Plus they were the only crew she could afford.

Johnny—the nephew—met her at the dive platform and extended a hand. His blond hair had almost been bleached by the sun, and he wore a bandana like a headband, allowing the hair to blow in the breeze. He was the quietest of the bunch, and also the hardest working, so it was no surprise that he was the one to assist Cameron out of the water.

"You've got it?" he asked, taking Cameron's mask from her.

"Uh-huh," she said, unable to contain a smile. She held up the pouch as proof.

Johnny said nothing, but nodded down at her scuba tank. She set the pouch on the bench seat beside her and unsnapped her harness, then turned around so Johnny could take the tank off her back. Free of the encumbrance, she exhaled again and unzipped the neoprene wetsuit she wore over her swimsuit. She removed her gloves and reached up to undo the ties holding her blond hair at bay, then forked her hand through it several times. Then she stepped out of her fins and removed the belt around her waist, handing both of them to Johnny as well. "Thank you," she said.

He nodded in reply. "Want me to take that?"

Every day, a pattern had developed. Cameron would surface, shed her gear with Johnny's help, then head below deck for a quick shower in the cramped cabin before joining Sully and Marty, his son, on the bridge to analyze data and discuss strategy while downing a cold one. Today, however, she was too eager to further examine the disk she'd found.

"No thanks, I've got it," she said, then grabbed the pouch and headed for the near steps toward the bridge. She quickly ran her eyes to starboard, north over the open water to where the launch platforms and water towers at Cape Canaveral were visible on the horizon, before twisting the knob and opening the door to the bridge.

"We did it, Sully. We fin—"

Sully and Marty stood with their backs to the boat's controls. They were not alone.

A man and a woman stood to the left, across the navigation charts table from Cameron. They were dressed like casual boaters, shorts and a plain T-shirt for him, Bermuda shorts and a tank top for her. He wore an Atlanta Braves baseball cap. Her bright red hair was in a tight ponytail. To their left—Cameron's right—on the other side of Sully and Marty, was another man, decked in board shorts and a polo shirt. Aside from everyone's stiff posture, they looked perfectly natural. Only they were strangers who hadn't been aboard the *Eternal Sun* when Cameron had begun her dive.

That, and they held guns.

Redhead and Board Shorts both carried pistols. Cameron didn't shoot guns, didn't know much about them. These were black and scary, and while they weren't aimed at anyone, the message they conveyed was loud and clear.

"What's going on?" Cameron asked.

"Do you have the disk?" the guy with the Atlanta Braves hat asked. He had taken a step forward, now directly across the table. He was big—not overly tall but taller than average and not overly heavy but heavier than average, and the combined effect was big. Intimidating, even without a gun. Cameron placed him at forty or so, dark hair, a goatee. His eyes were slits, black as coal.

"Who are you?" she asked.

Barely perceptibly, the man nodded. Cameron's eyes flicked to her right as Board Shorts approached her. He grabbed her arm with one hand, brandishing the pistol with the other. Marty stepped forward, but was stopped by a glance from Redhead and a slight raise of her gun.

"What's in the bag?" the man asked.

Cameron said nothing, trying to process what was happening. Who were these three? Where had they come from? Did they know about Johnny, or he about them?

Braves Hat nodded, and Board Shorts let go of Cameron's arm and snatched the pouch away from her. He took a step back and set the pouch on the table with a clunk.

"Careful," Braves Hat said just before Cameron uttered the same word.

Board Shorts said nothing as he backed against the wall, his gun still aimed at Cameron. Redhead had Sully and Marty covered. Braves Hat approached the table as movement to Cameron's left drew her attention. Johnny, at the door. He opened it slowly and held his hands at shoulder height.

"Over there," Braves Hat said, nodding toward Sully and Marty.

Johnny shuffled behind Cameron. "I'm sorry," he said.

"You knew?"

"They came aboard while you were under," Sully growled. "Said they'd shoot us if we warned you."

"Quiet," Braves Hat said. He opened the pouch and gently eased the disk out. His eyes studied it carefully for several minutes while nobody moved or spoke. The *Eternal Sun* creaked, rocked slightly. Cameron roved her eyes from Sully and the boys to the three infiltrators, resting on Braves Hat as he began to put the disk back into the pouch. He turned over his shoulder to Redhead and nodded out the bridge window. "Signal Charlie."

She turned over her shoulder and rapped on the window.

"The keys?" he asked.

Marty, who was closest to the ignition, turned and reached for them.

"Easy."

He used his thumb and forefinger to remove the keys

6

"Who are you?" Cameron asked. "Who are you working for?"

"Shut up."

Board Shorts extended his hand, and Marty tossed the keys to him. Intentionally or not, they came up short and clattered to the floor. Board Shorts bent down to retrieve them, and Braves Hat yelled. He was too late. Marty charged forward into Board Shorts, knocking him off balance and into the starboard window.

Cameron jumped out of the way. Redhead brought her gun down and around, but before she could get off a shot, Sully drove his weight into her arm. It—and the gun—swung around, first at Cameron, then at Braves Hat. He recoiled slightly, and Cameron saw her chance. She grabbed the disk with both hands, hefting it off the table. Braves Hat instinctively lunged forward, swiping at the disk but just missing it.

Clutching the heavy disk to her chest, Cameron turned for the door. She fumbled with the knob and practically crashed through when it opened, just before several pistol shots rang out. She bounded down the steps, ducking and screaming as two more shots sounded.

Reaching the deck, she looked to her right and saw a small powerboat had pulled along the portside of the *Sun*. A man with a cap low over his face was at the helm, and as he turned her way, he reached toward his waist. Cameron didn't wait to see if he indeed came up with a gun. Instead, she did the only thing she could.

Still holding the bronze disk, she stepped onto the gunwale and leaped over the starboard side of the boat and back into the ocean.

CHAPTER TWO

Mitch Owens felt the exhilaration—and the salt spray—as he blasted across the open water on his Jet Ski. It had taken him a few minutes to get reoriented to being aboard a personal watercraft, and to get used to even the relatively gentle swells of the ocean compared to the docile Colorado River back home. But once he'd done that, he'd cruised up the coast, "raced" a good-looking brunette on her Sea-Doo, and caught some air riding the wake of a cruise ship headed out from Port Canaveral. Now it was all about speed as he shot out toward sea as fast as the Jet Ski would take him, nearly sixty miles per hour.

After a blast, he gradually slowed and brought the craft back around, toward shore, cruising at half open. His eyes were half scanning for other boaters, half drinking in the late afternoon sunlight that danced off the surface of the water. His mind drifted toward nightfall. His first day in Cocoa Beach he'd laid on the sand and scoped bikinis, crushed some food truck fish tacos and a few beers for lunch, killed some of the afternoon on the Cocoa Beach Pier and wandering through local souvenir shops, and had dinner at an all you can eat seafood buffet. Today, after golf in the morning and satisfying his need for speed in the afternoon, he was in the mood for some good surf 'n turf while he plotted his future. Maybe another day on the beach, fishing off the pier, watching those bikinis. He also had a visit to the Kennedy Space Center in mind, sometime. His itinerary was free and infinite, and just the thought of that caused him to rev the throttle. He turned parallel to shore and gunned the Jet Ski again.

Mitch checked his fuel consumption, then turned and headed farther out to sea. The sky was perfect and clear, not a cloud in sight. And even though sunset was still hours away, already the eastern sky and the water near the horizon had taken on a slightly darker shade of blue.

When he turned around, Mitch found that a few other vessels were in his general vicinity, so he angled around a couple sailboats and a pleasure cruiser and back in the general direction of shore. Eventually, he eased off the throttle and coasted to a stop. With one hand, he removed the aviator sunglasses that guarded his eyes and the worn, faded, and now soggy University of Texas baseball cap he wore backwards over a mid-length mop of blondish-brown hair. He raked his other hand through it, then fit the cap snugly back in place. He turned his head north, toward Cape Canaveral, and imagined a powerful rocket igniting an enormous cloud of smoke as it launched a shuttle into space. Yeah, the Kennedy Space Center was definitely on the agenda.

Another cruise ship, this one bearing the distinct red, white, and blue "whale tail" exhaust funnel of the Carnival line, was just steaming out of the channel, and he thought about going to catch some more wake. Before he could, two sharp cracks echoed across the water.

Mitch turned his head, trying to trace them, as another two cracks—gunshots, he was pretty sure—sounded. His eyes settled on a medium-sized boat to his left, over a quarter of a mile away, aimed at the shore. It wasn't moving, but someone aboard was. He couldn't make out much detail at more than a thousand feet, but he was able to see a flash of blond hair behind a woman who made her way astern. As Mitch watched, she suddenly leapt over the side of the boat and disappeared beneath the surface.

He waited, his brain going into high speed as it processed what he was seeing and tried to determine if it fell within the parameters of normal. The matter was settled when he saw more movement near the bridge, and two more figures emerged, one going astern, one headed for the bow. The sun reflected off the bright red hair of the one headed forward, and then off something metallic. A gun.

Mitch was a good Texan, which meant he generally minded his own business. And he had no interest in involving himself in trouble. But the fact of the matter was, a woman had dived over the side of the ship after being shot at, and as a subconscious clock ticking in Mitch's head neared sixty seconds, she had yet to resurface.

*　　　　*　　　　*

9

As she hit the water, Cameron nearly lost her grip on the disk. The sudden buoyancy jostled it from her arms, and it slid up and bumped against her chin. She grabbed it tighter, then dove downward, kicking deeper under the water.

She was neither reckless nor impulsive, but she wasn't about to give up years' of work without a fight. Not that diving underwater without any scuba gear was much of a fight. She could hold her breath for a minute, maybe, and then what? Swim to shore unseen? With a twenty-pound weight?

First things first, she angled back under the hull of the *Eternal Sun*, then used one arm and her legs to guide herself toward the bow. As her lungs were starting to burn, she emerged slowly up against the hull, protected from view by its concave shape, and astern of the powerboat that had come along the starboard side.

Scenarios went through her head. Try swimming for shore, mostly underwater and surfacing to breathe, hopefully unnoticed? She'd never make it without being spotted, if she made it at all. Drop the disk to the depths, swim unencumbered, and hope to come back for it later? She'd still never avoid being spotted, and Braves Hat and gang had the scuba gear to go back after the disk once they realized what she'd done. Try to climb aboard the powerboat, overpower "Charlie," and race off to safety? How? And what about Sully and the boys if it worked?

No, they weren't a concern, and not because they were merely hired hands. Braves Hat's crew wanted the disk, and with it gone, they had no use for Sully, Marty, or Johnny. Besides, the trio could take care of themselves. After all, they were the ones who had initiated her escape.

Cameron looked left and right, spotting no sources of help but a sailboat at least a mile south. She heard voices, particularly a shout from Redhead, and feared she'd been discovered. She quickly ducked back underwater. She dove to about ten feet, turned over, and floated on her back, easing out from under the hull. She peeked up, saw no one looking over the starboard gunwale, and surfaced.

She gulped in air and looked up. She spotted a man in a baseball cap turning her way, and quickly sucked in more air and re-submerged. She nearly scraped her back on the bottom of the hull this time, hoping to come up under the powerboat, on the far side. Keep them guessing, for who knew how long or to what end. Maybe Charlie would come aboard the *Eternal Sun* and give her an opening to grab the other boat.

Instead, the powerboat began moving forward, and Cameron had to turn to avoid its propeller. She kicked to get out of its pull and to reach the bow of the *Sun* before her lungs gave out. She made it just barely, but knew the jig was up. There was no place to run, no place to hide. Charlie would bring the powerboat around and find her, probably shoot her. Even if she could avoid him once or twice, there was no hope in it. She was already exhausted, and could barely hang onto the disk any longer.

She pulled it away from her chest, about to let it go. Dropping it might buy her some time, and would keep it out of Braves Hat's hands at least for a while. But she couldn't do it. She couldn't let it go. She couldn't give up after all she'd been through.

And then she heard another shout.

*   *   *

Mitch had developed something of a knack for sizing up situations, and he quickly reached a couple of conclusions. The blond woman was in trouble. The other two figures—a redhead and a guy in a hat—were neither authorities nor pros, judging by the way they were dressed and how they operated. They were helter-skelter in their movements, scrambling around the boat. Besides, he'd heard four shots. Pros didn't fire and miss four times.

He turned the Jet Ski toward the boat and accelerated. Moving targets were hard to hit, and he weaved slightly instead of making a beeline. He was also unexpected, not necessarily a threat. And just because they had shot at the woman didn't mean they were willing to shoot at anyone and everyone. Mitch figured he had a one in three chance of avoiding a bullet. He'd survived worse odds.

Halfway to the boat, he saw the blond woman surface under the bow. A moment later, she was gone again. The hat and the redhead were scrambling again, and either hadn't noticed Mitch or didn't care about his presence. He took advantage of that, aiming for the bow of the boat. He slowed a few seconds later when he saw the blonde pop up midway back on the starboard side. The hat saw her too, and then the redhead saw Mitch. They gestured and yelled frantically, at each other mostly, not the work of pros. The blond woman had disappeared again.

Mitch aimed again for the bow. It provided some shelter, and he had to believe the blonde was out of options and doing her best to stay undetected as

11

long as possible. She'd surfaced by the bow, then starboard side. Going to the stern would be too prosaic, so if she was thinking like he was, she'd head to the far side or back to the bow.

He heard the roar of a motor. As far as he could tell, the boat in front of him was stationary. Then he saw the sleek white hull of a powerboat circle around the stern. Friend or foe? All foes, unless otherwise identified.

The blond woman surfaced again, just in front of Mitch and to his left. He took a quick glance up at the redhead, who now had a gun trained his way. He hunched down and coaxed the Jet Ski forward, then turned sharply around the bow of the boat. He looked down into the startled eyes of the blond woman. They were scared and desperate, but not panicky. She was youngish— thirty?—good-looking, not unathletic. He sized her up in a second, then reached his hand for her.

She was holding something, just below the waterline, and shifted it to her other hand so as to grab his. Neither of them said anything as he hoisted her and her possession—a round piece of solid metal—onto the back of the Jet Ski.

"Hold on," he said over his shoulder. She wrapped one arm around his torso, just under his life jacket, and he gunned the engine. Instead of turning toward shore, he accelerated toward the stern of the boat, and made a hard left turn to port, slingshotting around the boat and racing north. As he'd guessed, the powerboat had spotted him and come around the bow of the larger boat to investigate, and was now pointing in the opposite direction.

Mitch heard the report of several gunshots, and glanced over his shoulder once. He saw the man with the hat and the redhead standing by the starboard railing, shooting at them. He zigged and zagged a few times, then opened to full throttle, the woman's arm tight around him and her mysterious metal object pressed against his back.

CHAPTER THREE

Cameron was terrified.

They were shooting at her. They weren't likely to hit at this range, she didn't think, but they were shooting at her. And they had a boat. Charlie would be on their tail in an instant. She didn't dare look back, and she didn't know which was faster, a powerboat or a personal watercraft, but she surmised the boat.

And speaking of the personal watercraft, that's what really scared her. It felt like they were going a hundred miles per hour, and Cameron's one-armed grip on some strange man's bare torso felt tenuous at best. At any moment, she expected to hit a wave and be launched from her seat like a pilot ejecting from a fighter jet. Or worse yet, to lose her grip on the disk and have it be lost again. So she held it tight, held him tight, and stared straight ahead at the longhorn cow depicted on his faded orange baseball cap.

They turned, marginally, angling toward shore. It was a few miles to their left. The Cape Canaveral promontory—the cape—was a few more miles north. A cruise ship was ahead and to their right. Several boats of different variety dotted the water, likely oblivious to her and the stranger's plight. To everyone else, they probably looked like pleasure seekers with a death wish.

They turned a little more, and Cameron chanced a look to her left, toward the *Eternal Sun*. She saw it, now several miles off. The powerboat was coming their way, but had lost time having to circle the *Sun* and reverse direction.

She turned back, wanting to tell the guy with the longhorn cow on his cap to keep the pedal to the metal, so to speak. But she doubted he could hear her and, besides, the wind had dragged hair across her face and into her mouth.

They kept going, angling closer and closer to shore. Buildings lining the beach had taken shape—condos and hotels and apartments. In front of them, the beach was dotted with brightly colored umbrellas and speckled with swimwear of vivid pinks and blues and oranges—and plenty of skin tone.

"Hang on!" Longhorn yelled over his shoulder, and Cameron saw that they were rapidly approaching a breakwater of broken rocks and boulders. It extended a couple hundred yards out from the beach and guarded the entrance into Port Canaveral. And the reason for his warning became apparent as they banked left, toward the end of the breakwater. A fishing pier ran beside it, and several anglers shouted at them as Longhorn cut the corner like a slalom skier. Cameron looked back again and saw the powerboat farther back but coming at them.

Separating Cape Canaveral Air Force Station from the cities of Cape Canaveral and Cocoa Beach, the channel was about a thousand feet wide, with three turning basins on the north side, and lined with docks and wharves on both sides. Several cruise ships were docked on the south side of the channel, and a containership was chugging deeper into it. A few yachts and pleasure cruisers were also navigating the tranquil waters. Longhorn had eased up slightly, but they were still racing along. They dodged an oncoming yacht, then zipped around the containership.

They slowed down some more, and Longhorn took a look back. His face, as when he'd lifted her out of the water, was masked by sunglasses and a blond beard. A trimmed one, not some wild mess. He was a bigger guy, maybe not as big as Braves Hat, but well-built. That was evident in the muscles of his bare arms, and gave Cameron a measure of comfort. Well-muscled arms wouldn't stop bullets, but she'd rather have a guy built like a linebacker come to her rescue than a pencil-neck.

They veered left, accelerated past a commercial fishing boat, and then coasted toward a small, square-shaped marina. Wooden docks rimmed three sides of the marina, and extended out into the middle, forming a block M. Sunlight glinted off the fiberglass hulls of thirty or forty personal watercraft moored at the docks. Behind them, a single story building with a pyramid roof—a pavilion more than a building—flew a bevy of flags, topped by the Stars and Stripes. It too brought a measure of comfort, although Cameron didn't know why.

Deftly, Longhorn steered into the marina and coasted to a stop in the crook of the M, gently tapping the dock as the craft's engine quieted. As he turned the key, it was as if Cameron reentered the world around her. A guy in swimming trunks and a graphic tank top approached them from the pavilion.

Two girls in their late teens apprehensively straddled smaller personal watercraft on the other side of the M while a woman in a sundress and a baseball cap gave them instructions. Fiberglass bumped against wood and creaked against mooring ropes, hip-hop music played over loudspeakers hidden somewhere, and seagulls cawed.

The guy in the baseball cap slowly turned around. He looked at Cameron for a moment, and she looked at herself in his sunglasses. Then he said, "You can let go now."

*   *   *

Mitch smiled.

The woman was attractive, aside from a smudge of something on her chin. Dried blood, he realized, and the smile faded. Who was she? And what had he just saved her from?

A dude in a tank top depicting George Washington on a horseback and wielding an automatic weapon walked up and extended a hand to the woman to help her off the Jet Ski. "Whoa, what's that thing?" he asked, eyeing the metal disk she was holding. "Did you find that floating out there?"

"Uh, sort of," she said, swiping hair out of her face with her free hand. She looked around pensively. That made Mitch think of the powerboat. He'd last seen it aiming for the channel, and now turned his eyes east, toward the inlet. His view was mostly blocked by a fishing trawler in the foreground and a containership in the distance.

He got off the Jet Ski and unbuckled his life vest.

"She not have one?" the guy in the tank top asked as he took it from Mitch.

"No."

"Policy for every rider."

Mitch took off his cap and tousled his hair. "I actually picked her up. She had fallen in the water," he said, making eye contact with the woman.

"Oh, wow. Really?" Tank Top's eyes flicked to her. "Hey, are you all right?"

"Yeah, I'm fine." She looked out toward sea, probably searching for the powerboat too.

"We all good, man?" Mitch asked. He returned the cap to his head, facing forward.

"Yeah, bro."

Mitch nodded as Tank Top said something about checking the fuel and stepped onto the Jet Ski. Mitch and the woman headed toward the pavilion where Mitch's clothes and personal items were stashed in a locker.

"Are you really all right?" he asked as they walked.

"Yeah," she said and exhaled. "Now. Thank you."

Mitch looked at the disk she was holding. It had what looked like some kind of Egyptian hieroglyphics etched on it. Something out of a *Tomb Raider* movie. "You're not some kind of marine grave robber, are you?"

"No. It's a long story."

"The good ones always are. You need to call somebody?"

"Um . . . maybe." She slowly ran her hand through her hair. She started to speak, then stopped.

They'd reached the lockers, and Mitch retrieved a key from a zipped pocket in his swim trunks. He withdrew a small duffel bag from his locker and pulled out the top item, a towel. "Here," he said, handing it to her. While still clutching the disk with one arm, she dried her hair with the other. Mitch, meanwhile struggled into an old Nike T-shirt, then pocketed his wallet, keys, and phone.

A blur of motion out in the channel caught his attention, and he leaned around the far side of the bank of lockers to see a white powerboat—maybe the one that had been following them—cruising slowly through the channel.

"What?" the woman asked. "Is it them?"

"I couldn't tell. Who are they?"

"I don't know. I didn't hang around long enough to find out," she said, peering around the other end of the lockers. "Um, do you have a car here?"

He nodded.

"Could I trouble you for a ride?"

He looked into her eyes. They were blue and vivid, and full of urgency, but as when he'd rescued her initially, there were no signs of panic in them. He nodded again. "It's no trouble." He lifted the duffel bag, pulling out an old pair of tennis shoes, sans laces. "You want to stash that in here?" he asked as he stepped into the shoes. "Easier to carry and less conspicuous."

"Yeah, thanks."

When she had placed the disk in the duffel and he'd zipped it, they started toward the parking lot behind the pavilion.

"I'm Mitch, by the way."

She turned from looking over her shoulder. "Cameron."

"Nice to meet you, circumstances notwithstanding."

"Thanks again. If you hadn't come al—" She winced as her foot touched the faded asphalt. Mitch looked down at her bare feet. Bare legs to the knee, then a skin-tight, two-piece wetsuit, shorts and a top. Had she been diving? He'd seen scuba gear on the back of the blue-hulled boat, and it would explain what looked like a relic from under the sea.

"You want me to bring the car over?"

"No, I'll be okay."

"Right over here," he said, fishing his keys from his pocket. He beeped open a black two-door Porsche convertible, then reached for the passenger door for her.

"Thanks. Nice wheels."

"It's a rental."

He walked around the hood and cast a look back toward the water. Too much pavilion, palm trees, and Jet Skis prohibited him from seeing if the powerboat that had slowed in the channel was doing more than idling—say, approaching the marina.

Mitch placed the duffel containing the disk in the backseat and got in. He quickly started the car and opened the roof.

"Um, you mentioned a phone call," Cameron said. "Do you mind?"

"Not at all. Where are we headed?"

"Away, for now."

He handed her his phone. "Pin's one-four-oh-six."

She took the phone, and he looked at her hand long enough to see her ring finger was bare. Then he started the car and whipped out of the parking lot. While he drove, Cameron dialed a number and waited wordlessly. Apparently getting no answer, she tried again.

"Calling your people on the boat?" he asked as he turned onto a street leading back toward the main highway, the A1A.

"Yeah." She lowered the phone again. "How'd you know I had people on the boat?"

Mitch shrugged. "Big boat for one person, especially if you were diving."

"How'd you know I was diving?"

"Wetsuit."

"Oh, right," she said, looking down. "Sorry, I'm kind of scatterbrained right now."

"Not at all."

"They're not answering. I'm going to call 9-1-1."

He nodded. While she spoke to the dispatcher, he got them headed south on the A1A. It ran the entire length of Florida, from north of Jacksonville to Key West, and functioned as the main drag of Cocoa Beach. He tried to piece together details of what had led to Cameron dodging bullets in the ocean while also keeping an eye on the rearview mirror. He didn't spot anything suspicious, and didn't expect to.

Five minutes later, they were at a stoplight in the midst of tourist sprawl, and Cameron disconnected her call. "They're sending the Coast Guard out to the *Eternal Sun.*"

"*Eternal Sun?*"

"Our boat."

"Ah. You want to go to the police station?"

"No."

He looked at her. "That's a suspicious response."

"Sorry, it's just . . . I'd rather not have anyone else know what I found, and with the Coast Guard going to make sure the guys are safe . . ."

Mitch smiled. "Relax, it's okay."

Cameron exhaled and reclined her head back against the seat.

"Look, it's your business," he said, "and it won't change anything, but I have to say I am kind of curious. What exactly did you find?"

She rolled her head to look at him. "You promise not to laugh?"

"No," he said, grinning. "Not if it's something ridiculous."

After a moment, she grinned too. She swiped some hair away from the side of her face. Blond tinged with brown strands, still a little damp and wavy. Had it not been for his curiosity, it could have easily distracted Mitch.

Cameron sat slightly forward, then looked right at him. "That disk could very well be the key to finding the Fountain of Youth."

CHAPTER FOUR

To his credit, Mitch didn't laugh. But even his shades couldn't hide a raised eyebrow and a look of incredulity.

"The Fountain of Youth?"

She nodded.

"Ponce de León and eternal life, that Fountain of Youth?"

"Yes and no," Cameron answered, wishing she could look past the sunglasses to see how exactly Mitch was taking what she said. She'd explained her quest many times, to a variety of people, and gotten every response from eye rolls suggesting she was crazy to patronizing acceptance to genuine belief.

"Well, I need to hear more about this," he said, and not in a condescending way, "but first we should figure out where you're going. Where were you staying?"

"A no-name motel about a mile south of the causeway. But I'm suddenly not feeling too good about going back there."

"So let me get this straight," Mitch said. "You and your crew found this . . . whatever it is today?"

"A seventeenth-century cipher disk."

"A seventeenth-century cipher disk," he repeated. "And what, these guys in the powerboat came and tried to take it?"

She nodded again and explained how she had surfaced to find the *Eternal Sun* had been commandeered by Braves Hat and his gang, how she had made her escape, and how she'd been out of options when Mitch had happened by on his Jet Ski.

"No idea who they are?" Mitch asked.

"No."

"How well did you know your fellow crew?"

"Okay. We've worked together a week. They're locals I hired shortly before arriving." She tousled her hair. "They helped me escape. I don't think they were in on it."

Mitch nodded, not seeming convinced.

"I don't know what to think," Cameron said, leaning her head back. "My search has been pretty low-budget, mostly off the radar, and not many people care about the Fountain of Youth. They want gold doubloons and precious stones, not a promise of long life. Besides, most people think it's just a fable anyhow."

"But not you?"

"No."

He took a breath. "I tell you what. I can understand, given what's in the bag, why you aren't excited about going to the police and the publicity it could bring, and if the Coast Guard's going after the crew, I'm not sure it's urgent that you speak to them anyhow. And until we know more, I wouldn't advise going back to your hotel either." He looked her way. "I've got a suite at the Courtyard. You're welcome to hang out there, freshen up a little."

She looked at him. Normally, she would be hesitant to accept such an offer. But she had no other options. She didn't have a phone, didn't have a credit card or any cash, didn't even have a change of clothes. She needed a place to decompress, process what had just happened, and think. Assuming Mitch wasn't the kind of guy to take advantage of such a situation—and she didn't *think* he was from the little she knew of him—his offer was worth accepting.

"If you feel uncomfortable about it, I'll chill in the lobby and you can have the room to yourself."

"Mitch . . . I don't even have anything to wear."

"We can stop and pick up something."

"I don't have any money. I mean, I could probably use your phone to get into my bank account and wire some . . ."

"Don't worry about it. We'll figure that out later."

"Are you for real?"

"My mom always asks that too."

She exhaled a laugh. "Okay. Thank you."

"You're welcome."

"Um, I hate to ask, but do you mind if I make one more call?" she asked.

"Go for it."

She tapped in the number for Erik Diaz. A one-time boyfriend and partner/financier of her efforts to find the Fountain of Youth, Erik was now solely a financier. They had ended their romantic relationship for a variety of reasons, and now had a friendly if not occasionally strained relationship. Through it all, Erik still believed in Cameron's quest, and had the bankroll to make it happen. It was more complicated than that, of course, as was everything with Erik. But he, for his faults and their disagreements, was someone Cameron trusted, and that—combined with the fact that he was funding her current efforts—necessitated a phone call.

He didn't answer; instead the same voicemail message he'd had forever greeted her.

"Hey, it's Cameron," she said. "There's been a problem. I'm okay; I'm safe. I'll try calling you later."

She tapped the button to end the call, then extended the phone back to Mitch.

He didn't ask who she'd been calling, but instead signaled for a left turn. Cameron looked past him at the reflective glass front of Ron Jon Surf Shop. With locations across the country, this was the flagship store, and the largest, selling everything from clothes to swimwear to surfboards to souvenirs. She knew what the stores were like from having once spent a chaotic ten minutes trying to find a bathroom at the Fort Myers location.

Mitch turned onto a side street, then into the parking lot behind the massive store. It was painted a combination of pastel blue and varying shades of yellowish beige, resembling—at least to Cameron's eye—a giant sandcastle. Palms and manicured shrubs surrounded the exterior, enhancing the beach vibe. So did the salt air flowing through the open convertible.

Seeing no entrance from the back, Mitch varoomed through the parking lot, came out on the other side street, turned west, then made a U-turn to whip into a spot as close to the entrance as possible.

"Do you mind if we lock the duffel bag in the trunk?" Cameron asked.

"Not a problem."

They got out, her standing gingerly on the hot pavement. "I'm not sure they'll let me in like this," she said as Mitch closed the trunk on the duffel containing the disk.

"It's a beach store," he said. "If not, I'll buy you a pair of flip-flops and then you'll be good."

21

Ron Jon was massive, with a second level of merchandise ringing the first and glass panels letting in plenty of sunlight to add to the airy feel. The surfboard motif was obvious, from the surfboards used for décor to those depicted on shirts and shorts and hats. Cameron found a pair of flip-flops first and had Mitch quickly pay for them so she could wear them through the store. He rejoined her, she slipped them on, and they began browsing T-shirts.

"So is this what you do for a living?" Mitch asked. "Dive for buried treasure?"

Cameron looked around to see they were alone, then at him. He'd propped his shades on his hat, in front of the longhorn cow, and she could see his eyes. Brownish green, and not teasing or deriding as he asked the question. So she opened up.

"Yes and no. Unless you find a stash of gold, which I haven't, it isn't very lucrative. So my 'real job' is as a high school history teacher. The school year just finished, so I have a couple months to dive back into my passion, pun not intended."

He grinned as she selected a T-shirt off the rack. She held it in front of her and received a nod of approval. One item down.

"I've also worked every odd and side job imaginable. Waitress, desk clerk, research assistant, done some tutoring, cleaned houses for a while, delivered newspapers on the side for cash."

"Sounds hectic."

"It is."

"But worth it?"

"On days like today, yes."

She found a pair of shorts, a little too teenage girl for her taste, but they'd do in a pinch.

"What about you?" she asked.

Mitch flicked at a T-shirt on a hangar, the way guys did when traipsing around a store after a girl. "I'm currently unemployed."

Cameron stopped. "You drive a Porsche while staying in a suite on vacation, but you're unemployed?"

"Well, I made a lot of money when I was employed."

"Doing what?"

"Most recently, managing a private security firm."

She looked at him, eliciting a smirk.

"Age or appearance?" he asked.

"What?"

"I've seen that look a dozen times when I tell people what I do. They either think I'm too young to manage a firm or don't look the type."

"How old are you?"

"Pushing thirty-four. And I clean up nice," he said, taking off his cap to tousle his hair—and knocking off his sunglasses in the process.

"I bet you do," Cameron said to herself as he picked them up. She turned to look for underwear, since a change of clothes wouldn't do much if she was still chafing in a wet swimsuit. She didn't find anything, and settled for a new swimsuit that would at least be dry and serve a temporary purpose. She did not hold it up to get Mitch's approval.

He grabbed a tee of his own and they checked out. He flashed a credit card like it was an afterthought, and fifteen minutes after they'd entered the store, they exited into the bright Florida sun.

"I feel like this is on a loop, but thank you," Cameron said.

"You're welcome."

"I'll pay you back for everything, as soon as I can get to my money."

He waved her off.

This was surreal. First finding the cipher disk after years of searching, then having her excitement short-lived by the presence of "pirates" aboard the *Eternal Sun*, escaping, being rescued by a stranger on a Jet Ski, and now browsing for beachwear with her rescuer like it was any Saturday afternoon on vacation. As to the last part, if she wasn't careful, she would find Mitch's company enjoyable. It'd been a long time since she'd found any man's company enjoyable, and not because she was scarred by past breakups. She had simply been too busy pursuing the cipher disk and making a living on the side. Add to that, with her crew's status unknown and Braves Hat and gang possibly still after her, enjoying anything seemed frivolous.

They drove a few blocks south to the Courtyard by Marriott, a six-story building set back from the highway and with a parking lot shaded by multiple trees. That was good, Cameron figured, in case Charlie or whoever had been on the powerboat had seen her get into a black Porsche. It would be hard to spot it from the road.

Mitch's suite was on the top floor and featured an ocean view past another hotel or condo closer to the coast. The living room contained a sofa and chairs, work desk, mini bar, sliding glass doors leading to a balcony, and a separate bedroom on the left. Modern artwork on the walls and bright colors on the floors and furniture added to an airy, luxurious feel. Cameron's simple hotel room with 1980s-era décor and cheap furnishings was, by comparison, a dump.

"If you give me a moment to change, I'll head downstairs and give you some privacy," Mitch said.

"You don't have to do that," Cameron said.

"All right. Then I'm gonna hit the head, then it's all yours."

He ducked into the bedroom for just a second, emerging with a pair of khaki shorts, and then entered the bathroom. Cameron set the duffel bag on a small dresser beside the desk and withdrew the disk. She sat down on the nearest thing available, an ottoman, and balanced the disk on her lap.

Twelve inches in diameter, it appeared perfectly round. Almost imperceptible grooves divided it into pie slices. The grooves had worn and faded with time, and some were covered in a thin coat of sediment or patina. Even so, she identified thirty-two wedges in one quadrant, meaning one hundred twenty-eight all the way around. The outer inch of the cipher contained letters, in all caps. They repeated. A bunch of A's, less C's, some D's, a ton of E's. It continued all around the disk. Most letters of the alphabet were represented, but a few were missing. Then again, some of them weren't legible either.

The same was true of a second row of letters, inscribed inside the outer row, separated from it by a much deeper groove—a crack. The letters were smaller and not in any particular order. Inside them were four holes, maybe a quarter of an inch deep, spaced evenly around the circle.

"Leverage, so you can turn it?"

Cameron startled and looked up at Mitch. He'd shed the hat and his hair was a mess, something between frat boy bedhead and a hard worker at the end of the day. He carried some manufactured scent that he hadn't earlier. It was not unpleasant.

"Sorry," he said.

"No, it's fine. And it would make sense, being a cipher wheel, that it would spin."

"Find a letter on some ancient text, match it up on here, spin the wheel accordingly, and decipher a coded message?"

"Something like that."

"So why are there duplicates?"

"I don't know. Some ciphers have a secret key where every so many letters, you have to rotate the disk a predetermined number of spaces, making it harder for the wrong person—who didn't know the key—to intercept the message."

"Primitive encryption."

"Yeah."

"Shouldn't you be wearing lab gloves or something?" he asked.

"If three hundred years underwater haven't ruined it, my hands won't."

"Fair point."

"But I do need to clean it up a little."

"You have what you need for that? At your hotel, I mean?"

"No, but I could make what I need with some baking soda and lemon juice."

"There's a Winn-Dixie just up the road," he said with a smirk.

"Maybe later. Right now, I want to get out of this suit."

"Here, there's a safe in the closet," Mitch said. "I think it'll fit, and I'll let you pick the code. For your peace of mind."

"Thanks. Um, I feel bad, like I don't trust you."

"I get it. I'd do the same thing if I were you."

Cameron carried the disk over to the safe and placed it inside, then set the code while Mitch looked away. "You managed a security firm," she said when she was done. "That mean you can crack a safe like this?"

"Not with my bare hands," he said, grinning. "You hungry? I can order room service or something?"

"Yeah, a little, now that you mention it."

"I'll rustle something up," he said, then Cameron took the bag from Ron Jon and locked herself in the bathroom. She found herself thinking about Mitch as she showered, letting the hot needles of water wash the salt off her skin and massage tired muscles. He was thirty-three, good looking, well off, and vacationing solo having "retired" from his job? Then again, he hadn't said why he was unemployed. The cynical side of Cameron wondered if he'd been forced out for embezzling his own firm or sanctioned by the authorities for letting his employees go too far or maybe scandalized for taking advantage of a female employee he'd somehow convinced to shower in his hotel room. The rational side of Cameron said the late-night crime drama reruns were exaggerated and it was distinctly possible Mitch was a decent guy who happened to be in the right place at the right time. Even so, there was an air of mystery about him, one she admitted to herself being intrigued by.

She also replayed the day and the past week. Had there been any clue as to who Braves Hat and gang were? Had any of their faces looked familiar? Had she observed any peculiar or suspicious behavior from anyone around her? Had Sully, Marty, or Johnny given her any reason to think one of them was working against her? She couldn't think of anything, but, then again, it wasn't as if she'd been looking for anything off. As she'd told Mitch, most people didn't believe there was any truth to the Fountain of Youth legends, and, aside from its link to the fountain, the cipher disk didn't possess any intrinsic value—not compared to other more easily attainable treasures. Who these guys were and how they had found her was another mystery.

And this one was not so much intriguing as downright scary.

CHAPTER FIVE

Cameron dried off and dressed in her new clothes, then exited the bathroom to find Mitch out on the balcony. The TV over the desk was on, muted, showing golf. Cameron walked past it and slid open the door, joining Mitch on the balcony.

"Feel better?" he asked.

"Much." She leaned on the railing, the wind lifting her hair off her shoulders. "I just wish I knew what was next."

"I've been thinking about that."

"Yeah?"

"I think you should at least make a statement to the police. You can be selective in the details you give them, but it'll be good to be on record. Plus, maybe you can learn what they and the Coast Guard know."

Cameron sighed.

"But it's your choice. That's just the free advice." He nodded back at the small table between two chairs, on which was a tray containing a plate of fruit, a bowl of mixed nuts, and a metal carafe with two glasses. "Hungry?"

"Don't take this the wrong way, but I figured you more for a cheeseburger and fries sort of guy."

"I am," he said as he sat down. "But I took you for a fruit over grease sort of girl."

"Thank you, again."

They ate for a few moments, staring out at the Atlantic. Cameron looked for the *Eternal Sun*, but didn't spot it. If her navigation was right, and it rarely was, it should be about visible or maybe just behind the Emerald Seas Condominiums due east of the hotel.

"So tell me more about the Fountain of Youth," Mitch said between wedges of pineapple. "I thought it was all legend and myth. I didn't think people actually thought it was real."

"Most don't," Cameron said. "Most modern scholars and historians don't put any stock in the legend of Ponce de León searching for a fountain of perpetual youth. In fact, there was no mention of it back in the early fifteen hundreds when de León 'discovered' Florida. Those legends didn't come about until after his death, when several Spanish historians and a shipwreck survivor's memoirs noted that he'd been seeking the waters of Bimini to fight off aging or illness."

"Bimini? Like the Bahamas?"

She nodded. "Tradition holds that the Fountain of Youth is in Florida, but there are rumors and legends about numerous venues around the world, including the Bahamas. And there are a host of theories as to what the fountain actually is—a wellspring of rejuvenating water, a euphemism for treasure, or a transposing of the locals' word for vine—*vid*—with the word for life—*vida*—making the fountain of life actually the fountain vine, or the *cassytha filiformis*, a.k.a. the Bahamian love vine."

Mitch deposited a strawberry into his mouth, then sat up. "I'm hearing the words legend and myth and rumor a lot."

"Like I said, the traditions regarding Ponce de León didn't come around until after his death. There's no evidence that he was actually searching for the fountain when he came to Florida, or that he found anything. Which is why most modern historians regard it as nothing more than a myth, fodder for a Disney movie."

Mitch thought for a moment. "So where do the legends come from then?"

"Exactly."

He looked at her, waiting for an explanation. His ringing phone cut her off before she could say any more, and he dug it out of a pocket. "This is Owens."

Cameron took a bite of a strawberry.

"As a matter of fact, yes. One sec." He extended the phone to her. "For you."

"Me?" She put the phone to her ear. "Hello?"

"Cammy, is that you?" a familiar husky voice asked.

"Hi, Erik."

"Are you okay? You're safe?"

"Yeah, I'm fine."

"Oh, wow, that's a relief. I got your message, but it sounded harried at best."

"It was. I am."

"But you're safe?"

"I'm safe."

Erik was quiet a moment. Cameron looked at Mitch, who downed another strawberry, less the stem.

"I just heard from the captain of the *Eternal Sun*," Erik said.

"Sully. Is he okay?"

"Yeah. These pirates left a few minutes after your escape, he said. He and his boys are fine. Although the boat's radio was destroyed. They were worried about you. He said some guy on a Jet Ski picked you up?"

"Out of nowhere, Erik. He got me to safety, probably saved my life," she said, looking at Mitch. He doffed his cap with a wink, eliciting a smile from her.

"Where are you now?"

"At his hotel," she said hesitantly.

"Wow, he moves fast."

"It's not like that," she said. "I needed a place to lay low, and I didn't dare go back to my motel. In fact, I don't know where to go, Erik."

"I'll take care of that. And I'll square things with Sullivan and his crew."

"Thank you."

"He said you found the cipher?"

"I did. It's in good shape."

"And you have it now? You were able to get away with it?"

"I was."

"That's great, Cam. I don't believe it."

"It's been a hard day to believe."

Erik paused again. He did that a lot, which made talking to him on the phone annoying. But she had long stopped asking if he was still there. He always was.

"Cammy, I've got a villa on Tortoise Island, a little south of you. I'm pretty sure it's vacant as of this morning, but let me check. If so, you can crash there until we figure out what to do."

"Okay."

"I'll call you back in a few. You're sure you okay?"

"Do you want a distress word, Erik?"

"I'm sorry, Cam, I'm worried about you."

"Thanks, but I'm fine. I'll wait for your call."

"Okay. Give me fifteen minutes."

She said goodbye and ended the call.

"Boyfriend?" Mitch asked as he took the phone back from her.

"Ex. That obvious?"

"I've been talked to like that before, that's how I knew."

"Like that?"

"A little frustrated but with the frustration you have for someone you care about."

"He's also my primary financier," she explained. "It's complicated."

Mitch nodded

"He may have a place for me to stay. Then I'll be out of your hair."

"Too bad. This is way more exciting than anything I expected this weekend."

*   *   *

Cameron's ex-boyfriend called back about ten minutes later and confirmed that she could stay at his villa for the night. Since she had no ride (her hired crew and or Ubers had served as her transportation around town) and no money, Mitch offered to take her there, with a stop at the police station—her idea—first. She'd protested him driving her, but he'd insisted, and she'd given in.

The police station was on the southern side of Cocoa Beach, and not too far from Cameron's motel, which she pointed out as they drove. Mitch suggested they stop and pick up her things, but she was still nervous about being there or about someone watching the motel for her spotting his easily recognizable Porsche. So he proposed dropping her at the police station, then looping back to pick up her stuff. "If you don't mind a guy rifling through your belongings."

"At this point, I think we're past that."

She used his phone again to call the hotel and speak to a clerk, asking if she could "leave a key" for someone. She confirmed her identity and made the arrangement just as they reached the city hall building that also housed the Cocoa Beach Police Department. Mitch pulled the Porsche to the curb to let her out.

"Be careful," she said.

"I will."

He watched her until she was inside, then eased away from the curb. Five minutes later, he was parked in front of the Sunflower Inn, a three-story structure situated around a parking lot, swimming pool, and office building. It was, judging by the vehicles in the lot, at best a quarter full. The neon lights on the sign over the office boasted vacancy, cable TV, and cheap prices. Cameron had hinted several times to being on a tight budget, but he hadn't thought she meant this tight. Then again, he admired a woman—or a man, for that matter—who was dedicated to a cause at the expense of personal comfort.

Mitch parked and looked around, again not expecting to see anything suspicious and seeing exactly what he expected. He walked to the office, cooled by a rattling window air conditioner. Baseball highlights played out on a TV above the counter, which was manned by a middle-aged man with balding hair. Mitch explained why he was there, flashed some ID, and was given a keycard to room 213. The clerk also gave him a small travel bag, saying it had been dropped off for Cameron. Mitch peered inside and saw a tank top and shorts, some flip-flops, and a phone.

"Who dropped these off?"

"A man by the name of Sullivan. Said he was working for Miss Leigh."

"When was that?"

"Just a few minutes ago. Literally right after she called."

"Thanks."

He exited the office and walked past the pool, where a young boy and girl splashed in the shallow end while their mom spilled out of a swimsuit and read a paperback in a chaise lounge. Except for a twenty-something guy heading to his car, the grounds were quiet. So Mitch hurried up to Cameron's room and let himself in.

When he traveled, he generally took nothing out of his suitcase but a toiletries bag. Cameron had unpacked as if she was going to live at the Sunflower Inn, and she didn't travel lightly either. He quickly packed up her things, noting she had a lot of casual beachwear, half a dozen swimsuits, a few more formal items, and even a dress or two. She had pants, long-sleeved shirts, some rain gear, five kinds of shoes—which wasn't bad—standard jewelry and accessories, a laptop, and a couple of romance novels.

He made a final sweep of the room, then headed out with two suitcases and the travel bag. He liked what he knew of Cameron. Besides the obvious physical attractiveness, she had a sound head on her shoulders. That led him to believe there was a good reason she had dedicated her life to finding what most believed was nothing more than a myth, and he wanted to know more about that reason—and about her.

Stashing the suitcases in the trunk of his Porsche, Mitch headed back to the police station. It was late afternoon turning to evening, and the sun was low in the sky, casting the buildings and palm trees in a golden light. He tuned the radio to something lively, and considered the possibilities his next few days held. He hadn't come to Cocoa Beach "on the prowl" by any means, but if he was reading a few of Cameron's looks and comments properly, she held at least a mild interest in him too.

He arrived back at the police department a few minutes after six, and Cameron came out a short while later. She carried his duffel bag, with the cipher disk tucked inside. He'd let her take it with her, as if it was her bag, so she wouldn't have to let the disk out of her sight.

"How'd it go?" he asked, reaching over to open her door.

"Good," she said and got in. "They don't have much in the way of leads. Descriptions, a name, possibly a way to track down the powerboat, but that's about it."

"Well, I have some good news."

"Oh?"

"No bad guys staking out your hotel."

"That is good."

"And your guy Sullivan dropped off a bag with your phone and some clothes."

Her eyebrows went up. "Really?"

Mitch nodded.

"That's even better," she said as she buckled her seatbelt. "You know where we're going?"

"Erik texted directions." He tapped his head and pulled away from the curb. They had maybe a fifteen-minute drive to his villa on Tortoise Island.

"So," he asked as they cruised south on the A1A, "assume I'm a skeptic who doesn't believe in life-giving water. What makes you think it exists?"

Cameron turned to face him. "Are you a skeptic?"

"Let's say I'm not a believer."

"It's like you said earlier, where do all the legends come from? And they aren't alone. There are legends from around the world of places that provide healing or energy—Sedona, Arizona, the Dead Sea in Israel, Uluru in Australia. And why shouldn't there be? If you think about the massive size and scope of our universe, about all the intricacy, all the complexity and order . . . I can't believe this is all an accident, a product of time and chance. Someone or Something has to be behind it all, and why couldn't that Someone have put in Easter eggs for us to find?"

"Like power-ups in a video game?"

"I guess. I don't play video games," she said with a smile. "But if you can believe in some sort of intelligent design—and I think the evidence is increasingly in favor of it, not to mention plain logic—then why wouldn't you also believe that that design could include a spring or well of water that enhances and extends life?" She shrugged. "I don't necessarily think it keeps you from ever aging or makes you live to be a thousand years old, but might it boost your immune system, fight off diseases or slow down the aging process, just make you healthier and more vital?" She shrugged again. "Why not?"

Mitch looked over at her, seeing the passion in her eyes as well as hearing it in her voice. He didn't know Cameron well, but well enough to know she wasn't a flake, some flat-earther or moon-landing conspiracy theorist. And while he didn't necessarily agree with her assessment, it wasn't illogical. In fact, she made a pretty sound argument.

"Okay, let's say I buy that," Mitch said. "There *could* be a so-called Fountain of Youth. You said before there's no evidence it exists. So what makes you think it does?"

Cameron grinned. "No, I said there was no historical evidence Ponce de León was searching for it. But there is evidence that a man by the name of Diego Figueroa, a late seventeenth-century Spanish explorer, searched for and found the Fountain of Youth here in Florida."

"Really?"

"He returned to Spain, but left clues behind so others could find what he'd found. One of those clues is a carving in St. Augustine that, according to legend, needs to be deciphered."

"The disk you found."

Cameron nodded. "It's known as the Figueroa Cipher, and was thought to be lost forever until just recently when a hurricane unearthed evidence of a ship that was carrying one of Diego's sons, Enrique, from Cádiz to the Spanish colony of Florida."

"To find the Fountain of Youth."

"Right."

They had exited Cocoa Beach, and the thin island it was built on had narrowed to only about a hundred yards, the Atlantic on one side and the Intracoastal Waterway on the other. The terrain quickly widened again, making room for a small U.S. Air Force base, then more suburban sprawl. Shortly thereafter, Mitch turned down a narrow street lined by small, compact ranch houses, then south on another main drive, and finally onto a boulevard leading to Tortoise Island, a gated community spanning several islands and canals along the Intracoastal Waterway.

Following Cameron's ex's directions, they found their way to a large, Mediterranean-style house set back a hundred feet from the road at the end of a cobblestone driveway. Ten or twelve palms shaded the neatly cut grass, and hedgerows on either side of the lawn provided a measure of privacy. Mitch parked the Porsche in front of a triple-stall garage, and the duo got out.

"So, this is an upgrade over the Sunflower Inn," Cameron said, looking up at the two-story portico.

"I take it your ex-boyfriend does all right."

"Well, he doesn't drive a Porsche or anything," she said with a wink. Already holding Mitch's duffel, she reached for the travel bag, and used a code provided by Erik to have the front door open by the time Mitch arrived with her suitcases. The door opened to a wide vestibule with a sweeping staircase on one side and huge chandelier hanging from the ceiling. Mitch could see all the way down the main hall and through a dining room to a back patio and the sun reflecting off the water beyond it.

"Where would you like these?" he asked.

"Here's fine," she said.

"Are you sure?"

"I'm positive." She extricated the cipher disk from the duffel bag and handed it back. "Mitch, thank you so much. For everything."

"You're welcome."

"Give me a minute to sort through my stuff and I'll find my wallet and repay you for my clothes."

"Don't bother."

She tipped her head to the side.

"I'm serious, it's no big deal."

"Thank you."

Her smile was as sweet as sugar, and it prompted him to ask if he could ask her one more question.

"Yes," she said.

"Is Erik really your ex?"

Cameron's eyes narrowed. "Yeah."

"I mean, it is over between the two of you?"

They narrowed some more. "Yeah. Our relationship is business only."

"Then I have one more question."

She stuck her tongue into her jaw, holding back a smirk.

"Would you like to go out to dinner tonight?"

The smirk broke into another smile. "I would like that, on one condition."

"What's that?"

"You let me buy, as a way of saying thanks."

"I can deal with that."

"I want to clean up the disk, and then I'll let it sit for a while. Pick me up at . . . what time is it now?" She looked down at the watch she'd worn all day, some sort of dive watch, evidently. "Eight-thirty?"

"That works. What are you in the mood for?"

"Local seafood?"

"You got it. I'll see you at eight-thirty."

He turned and headed out to his car, looking back once to see Cameron smiling at him as she closed the large oak door behind him. He repositioned his hat with a smirk as he thought back to sitting on his Jet Ski, trying to plan his evening. He could never have imagined it turning out like this, but he was glad it had.

CHAPTER SIX

The sun had set, but the sky overhead was still light as Mitch cruised south on the A1A. After dropping Cameron at her ex-boyfriend's villa, he'd returned to his hotel and scanned the sports networks for a St. Louis Cardinals score (they'd lost 4-1 to Milwaukee). After making a reservation at a local seafood place, he'd showered and put on a crisp blue dress shirt and a pair of white chinos, and then watched the day fade over the ocean while pondering what Cameron would wear to dinner. He'd spotted several appealing options when packing her things earlier, and while she looked just fine in Ron Jon gear, there was no doubt she'd be stunning when dressed for an evening out.

The air was balmy, and Mitch had the windows and top down in the convertible as he passed through the checkpoint onto Tortoise Island. Imagine Dragons thumped through the stereo at the loudest allowable for a man now well in his thirties, and Mitch turned down the radio as he coasted into the villa's driveway. He parked and threw open his door, then removed the keys to alleviate a dinging sound. He stood and took a deep breath. The air was thick and salty, yet invigorating. He'd been almost everywhere in the U.S., but this was his first trip to Florida, and it wasn't disappointing.

He strolled to the front door, recessed under an archway, and rapped a brass knocker in the center of the oak door.

Somebody screamed.

Mitch tensed. Instinctively, he looked left and right and saw nothing amiss in the quiet neighborhood.

He knocked again, banging the side of his fist on the door.

This time he heard a muffled cry, several indistinguishable shouts and thuds, and then another cut-off scream. He hadn't been positive with the initial scream, but he was sure these latter noises had come from inside the house. He reached for the handle, found it receptive, and shoved open the door.

Years of training took over, and Mitch quickly surveyed the scene in front of him. A den to his left was dark, as was the hall at the top of the stairs on his right. The chandelier in the entry was dimmed but lit. The dining room at the end of the hall was equally dim. He started forward when a man appeared around the corner. He was dressed in black, and his eyes went wide when he saw Mitch. He reached for his back waistband, and Mitch didn't wait to confirm his suspicions, instead ducking into the dark den.

He heard another female exclamation, then a man. He uttered an indecipherable name, then a, "Let's go!"

Mitch peeked around the corner and saw the man in black disappear into the dining room. He stepped back into the hall, paused for a second, then hurried to the safety of a recessed doorway to a powder room. He paused again, listening, and heard running footsteps, radio static, and muffled voices.

He hurried forward again and peered around a corner into a kitchen. Empty. Unlit.

It was separated from the dining room by a counter, on the near end of which was a wall as long as the counter's width. Mitch used it for cover, then turned around it to look into the dining room.

A sliding glass door at the far end was open, leading out to the patio. He couldn't see the patio because the bank of windows lining the dining room reflected the light from a trio of lamps suspended from the ceiling over a long, glass table. At the end of it, Cameron sat in a chair, her arms behind her. She wore a lacy white sundress, her hair down in loose, wavy curls. Wide eyes narrowed when she recognized him.

"Mitch!"

"Cameron. Are you okay?"

"The disk! They came for the disk."

"Are they gone?"

"Everybody I saw."

Mitch reached her and placed a hand on her shoulder. Then he hurried to the patio door, crouching low as he looked into the darkness. There was just enough light in the western sky for him to make out the silhouettes of three or four people running out onto a dock at the end of the lawn, where a powerboat was moored with running lights on. Mitch knew he wouldn't catch them before they boarded the boat, which was already revved and ready to go. And shouting would do nothing but perhaps entice a volley of gunfire. So he turned back to Cameron.

She was bound with a zip tie that held her wrists behind the slats of the chair. She looked over her shoulder, shaking her head to get hair out of her face. "Did they get away?"

The whine of the boat's motor answered her question, and she lowered her head and swore under her breath. Mitch knelt down and retrieved a folding knife from his pocket. "Hold still," he said, and sliced the zip tie. Cameron pulled her arms forward, then spun off the chair.

"Hold on," Mitch said, holding out his hand.

"The disk," she said again. "Did they have it?"

"I didn't see."

"It was in the spare bedroom."

"Wait—"

She was already on the move, headed through the dining room and toward a dark hallway. Mitch seriously doubted any of the intruders had remained behind, but he'd have preferred to clear any rooms ahead of Cameron.

She flailed at a light in the hallway, then dashed through a door on the right. Mitch rounded the corner to see her stop in front of a writing desk in a large, plain bedroom. A dishtowel had been draped over the desk, but there was nothing on it. Cameron's eyes closed and she slumped back onto the edge of the bed, muttering another curse.

Mitch looked on either side of the desk, then on the slat-back chair in front of it, even though he was sure the cipher disk wasn't there. He turned to Cameron, expecting to see tears, either of sadness or anger. Neither was there.

"I cannot believe this," she said. "How did they find me?"

"Who besides Erik knew you were here?"

"Nobody."

Mitch sighed.

"No," she said, looking up. "Okay, I know what you're thinking. Why would Erik tell them where I was?"

"I'm not saying he did."

"I saw that look."

"You didn't tell them, I didn't tell them . . ."

"They could have followed us. Hacked his phone or something." She put her hands on her forehead. "I don't want to do this right now."

"Okay, okay." He sat down beside her. "We should let the police handle this anyhow. They committed burglary, unlawful imprisonment, probably a handful of other crimes. I know you don't want them involved because of the disk, but . . . they need to be."

Cameron sighed. "I know. But can you give me five minutes alone, first? I want to cry and it might be kind of messy."

"Take your time. I'm going to sweep the house and perimeter to make sure they're gone."

She nodded.

"Stay here, close the door. Just in case."

Cameron nodded, then offered a faint smile. "Thanks for rescuing me, again."

*   *   *

The Brevard County Sheriff's Office arrived by quarter to nine. By that time, Cameron had composed herself—without actually crying—and her anger was down to a back-burner simmer. She told the responding officers about the two men and woman who had broken into the house through the back door, surprised her in the kitchen while she was getting something to drink, and had tied her up to interrogate her while searching the house. She mentioned the disk, saying it was an archaeological discovery she had made that afternoon, but didn't divulge its significance. She had no idea who the trio was, but could indeed verify they were the same three she had seen aboard the *Eternal Sun* that afternoon—Braves Hat, Board Shorts, and Redhead.

The officers were thorough, and she filled in as many details as she could. This was her ex-boyfriend's villa and she had his permission to be here, which they said they would verify. Mitch was a friend she had met that day, which they found suspicious and which led to them questioning him for several minutes. Cameron recapped the earlier escape at sea and referred the officers to the Cocoa Beach Police Department or United States Coast Guard for more information.

After nearly an hour, which included taking descriptions of the trio as well as dusting the interior of the house for prints and searching the backyard for any evidence left behind (Mitch had not contaminated anything with his perimeter sweep, apparently), the officers left. Cameron collapsed in a dining room chair, and Mitch retrieved two bottles of water from the refrigerator.

"Nothing stronger?" she asked as he sat down adjacent to her.

"Not that I saw."

39

"Thanks," she said, and unscrewed the cap on her bottle. She took a long drink. "I should call Erik, before they do."

"Yeah."

"Have you seen my phone?"

"Uh, yes," he said, standing and fetching it off the counter.

"Thanks." She started to dial, then stopped. "You think they'll find it?"

"Probably not."

"Well, you don't beat around the bush at least."

Mitch shrugged. "Not for not trying, because I think they will follow through. But to them—nobody's life is in danger anymore, nobody's missing, nobody was hurt, and you yourself said the disk didn't have much intrinsic value—"

"I wanted to deflect any attention away from it."

"I get it, but I doubt they'll devote all their resources to finding it. And even if they did, it's not going to be easy."

She sighed again.

"Did you take any photos of it?" he asked.

"Yes, but they won't help."

"Why not?"

"Because there were ten or twelve letters on each row that were indecipherable from wear, sediment, whatnot. I did an initial cleaning and then was going to let it sit for a while, while we had dinner. I moved it to the spare bedroom so it wasn't sitting out in the open, just in case. I never thought somebody'd actually break in."

"I never asked," Mitch said, leaning forward. "They didn't hurt you, did they? You're okay?"

"I'm tougher than I look," she said with a wink.

He nodded.

"I should call Erik."

"Can I get you anything?"

"No," she said, reaching out and touching his arm. "You've done enough."

He sat back and finally reached for his water, and she called Erik. He didn't answer. "Come on," she mumbled, tapping the screen of her phone to disconnect the call, then immediately calling again.

"Hey, it's Erik. Leave me a message."

"Erik, it's Cameron again, and you need to call me, before the Brevard County Sheriff's Office calls you. You won't believe who showed up at your villa tonight. I'll be up. Call me."

She dropped her phone on the table and ran her hand slowly through her hair. "I am going to go change."

"Too bad," he said. "You look great in that dress." It wasn't creepy the way he said it, the way she'd been "complimented" before. She did, however, question his motives nonetheless.

"Are you just trying to make me feel better?"

"No, but if that's a side benefit, so be it."

"I'm too mad to feel better," she said as she stood up. "But I do appreciate the sentiment." She started for the hall, then stopped. "And it is too bad, because you do in fact clean up nice."

Why are you flirting right now? she asked herself as she stood there, smirking at a relative stranger. She was angry, depressed, more worried than she was admitting to herself, and just wanted to have a drink and go to bed, and yet she was flirting? But he *did* clean up nice, and the scent of his cologne was getting to her—in a good way.

He stood too. "I don't know about you, but I'm still hungry."

"I'm too mad to eat too." She put a hand on her stomach. "But I am hungry."

"What are your plans for tonight?"

She looked at him, wondering if he was about to get creepy.

"Hear me out," he said. "I don't think you should stay here, not since they know where you are."

"Where am I going to stay?" she asked, knowing what he was about to suggest and wondering if she was really tired enough to accept.

"My hotel. I can crash on the sofa, or if you want, I'll get you a room. We'll order a pizza or something and you don't have to worry about them coming back."

"Why would they come back?"

He shrugged. "They can't interpret the disk and want an expert? They want to silence loose ends? I don't know. But I'd feel better if you were somewhere safe."

"And you think that's your hotel?"

"Or any hotel. Just makes sense to stay in one place. And that way we can share a pizza."

41

She hesitated.

"And a bottle of something stronger."

She felt like hesitating some more, but she was too tired to be a prude. "You just clinched it."

"You change and get packed, and I'll book a room for you."

"Will you let me pay?"

"No. You're buying dinner, remember?"

"Well, now I owe you two dinners."

"I accept."

She gave him a long smile before turning down the hallway to her room.

CHAPTER SEVEN

It took Cameron longer than it should have to pack up her things in preparation for moving to her third residence of the day. She really should have been questioning why Mitch—a man she hadn't known six hours ago—was going out of his way to help her, chauffeuring her around and paying for her accommodations, not to mention saving her life repeatedly. But instead, she was busy fussing over what to wear. Normally, after a day like this, she'd have thrown on some sweats and called it good. Instead she found her best clean pair of jeans and changed shirts three times before settling on a soft-wash T-shirt with a Team USA logo stamped on it.

With a sliver of moon lightening the eastern sky, she and Mitch left Erik's villa a little after ten. Erik had still not called back, so she tried him again as they drove, then called a local pizza place and had them deliver a large Hawaiian to Mitch's suite. They beat it by five minutes.

"You said earlier not that many people care about the Fountain of Youth," Mitch said after the first bite of his third slice. They were back on the balcony of his sixth-floor suite, enjoying the balmy evening. "Do you have any idea who else might be after it—who these guys could be or who could have hired them?"

One of the sheriff's officers had asked Cameron a similar question, when his partner had been talking to Mitch. She gave him the same answer now she had given the officer then. "No. I mean, sure, I know other people who have something of an interest in the fountain, but nobody else I know is actively looking for it. I certainly don't know anyone who would go to these sorts of lengths to get it. I have no idea."

"What about your crew?"

"What about them?" she said, taking a bite of her pizza.

"Any chance they could have connections to somebody?"

"Yeah, me. I hired them."

"How'd you find them?"

"The Yellow Pages."

"Really?"

"Might as well have," she said with a shrug. "I didn't hire them because they had any connection to the Fountain of Youth or the *Descubridor*."

"The what?"

"The Spanish ship the Figueroa Cipher was on."

He nodded.

"I hired Sully and the boys because they were an available crew with a seaworthy boat and they'd work for what I was paying them."

"You mean what Erik was paying?"

She looked at him.

Mitch held out his hands.

"I've put every spare cent of mine into this search. I can't even remember the last time I satisfied a craving with a trip to Starbucks. But my meager funds won't get me anywhere, so that's why I have Erik."

"I didn't mean to insult you."

"No, but you meant something," she said, then took a bite and watched him squirm. Only he didn't.

"Yeah, I did. Because we keep coming back to Erik. He's bankrolling your search, he provided the place to stay—and was the only other person who knew where you were—and he's your ex-boyfriend."

"So? What's that got to do with anything?"

"I don't know, maybe nothing. But there is a reason he's an ex, right?"

"There is, and it's none of your business."

He held up a hand.

Cameron sighed and set down her pizza crust. "Look, I'm sorry, Mitch."

"It's okay."

"No, it's not. I'm just stressed." She sighed to prove it. "But I'm telling you, Erik wouldn't give me up like that. He's far from perfect, and there are numerous reasons he's my ex, but he wouldn't do this. Zero chance. And he wouldn't have to. We're not searching for a buried chest full of gold. This isn't a case of finders-keepers. The person who gets there first gets the same thing as the one who gets there last."

"Except for the fame, notoriety, prestige . . ."

"Well, that might tempt him," she said, "but he still wouldn't do this."

"Okay. If you say so."

"I do."

Mitch reached for another slice. "So recap your research for me. How'd you ever find this Figueroa Cipher and whatever this boat is?"

"The *Descubridor*. Spanish for *Discoverer*."

"Okay."

"It wasn't easy. I've spent years studying all the rumors and legends, especially about Ponce de León. And there is just nothing there. Nothing at all to suggest he actually searched for the Fountain of Youth."

"And yet numerous people wrote that he did?"

"Right."

"Why?"

"I don't know. But the important thing is that certain people believed the legends about Ponce de León."

"This Diego Figueroa guy?"

"Yes."

"How'd you find out about him?"

"I dug through genealogy records from St. Augustine, Tampa, the Keys, Puerto Rico, and Spain, and stumbled upon his name. From there, I did all sorts of research on Figueroa and learned about his voyage to Florida in 1698. That's how I found the carving in St. Augustine. I'm not the first to have found it, but nobody knew what it meant."

"What genealogy records?"

"Ponce de León's. Diego Figueroa is a sixth-generation descendent of Ponce de León. His full name is Diego Ponce de León de Figueroa."

Mitch paused mid-chew and sat up. He finished chewing and swallowed. "So Ponce's great-great-great-great-great grandson found the Fountain of Youth because he believed, mistakenly, that Ponce himself had found it?"

"One too many greats, but yeah, that's the theory."

"Okay, then what?"

Cameron's phone buzzed in her pocket, and she sat up straight. She licked a couple fingers, accepted a napkin from Mitch to finish the job, then retrieved her phone. It was Erik. She excused herself and stepped inside to take the call.

"Erik," she said by way of answering.

"Cammy, are you all right?" he asked with a curse. "I just got off with a detective from BCSO."

"I'm fine. But they got the disk."

45

"They took it?"

"Tied me to a chair while they searched the house."

"Oh my—Cam, are you hurt?"

"Erik, they didn't hurt me. I am fine. Just mad."

"How . . . Cammy, I'm sorry. I thought you'd be safe. I have no idea how they knew where you were, twice now."

"Yeah, well, I'm trying to figure that out too. Not that it matters anymore."

"Are you still at the villa?"

"No, I didn't feel safe there. I'm in a hotel." She looked down as her foot pawed the carpet. She didn't see the need to tell him she was staying in Mitch's hotel, on his dime, after agreeing to dinner with him. Erik wasn't jealous of her, but still.

"You're okay? Have enough money? Clothes?"

"Yeah, I picked up my stuff from my first motel."

"You're sure?"

Cameron sighed.

"Okay, I'm sorry, Cam. I just . . . I don't want anything to happen to you."

"I know, Erik."

"Look . . . I'm going to catch the first flight down. Can you get to St. Augustine tomorrow?"

"St. Augustine?"

"Yeah. I'll fly into Jacksonville and drive down there. You don't have a car, do you?"

"I'll manage, Erik."

"I'll book a flight and text you when I know when I'll be in."

"Okay. Not too early."

"Right. I'm glad you're okay, Cam."

"Yeah. I'll see you tomorrow."

"Sleep well."

"Right," she said, then hung up the phone with a laugh. She turned around and saw Mitch coming in through the sliding glass door.

"Everything okay with Erik?"

Cameron's shoulders slouched. "You wanna take a walk?"

"A walk? It's almost eleven o'clock."

"I know. And I should be dead tired after today, but I'm not; I'm restless. Besides, if I go alone, I'll probably get mugged the way this day is going."

"Yeah, I don't doubt that," he said with a grin. Then a shrug. "Yeah, let's go for a walk."

*   *   *

Mitch and Cameron walked high up on the beach, where the sand was soft and cool. Cameron's hair floated behind her in the breeze, as did the tails of a loose sweater she wore over her USA T-shirt. Mitch still wore the crisp dress shirt he'd donned for dinner, sleeves rolled up, and was not cool. Then again, this was Florida in June.

They'd crossed the parking lot of the condo east of the hotel, then taken one of numerous wooden walkways through the seagrass and dunes to the beach, setting out to the north. There were a few others out on the beach at this time of night, mostly folks with flashlights looking for crabs as they skittered across the sand, but Mitch and Cameron were essentially alone.

She explained what Erik had said about meeting in St. Augustine the next morning, giving no indication why there instead of meeting him in Jacksonville or him coming to Cocoa Beach. But Mitch didn't concern himself with that for now. He was doing his best to believe Cameron that her ex wasn't behind her troubles, but that meant coming up with an alternative. As they trudged along, he tried to think of one . . . and couldn't.

"You're quiet," Cameron said.

"So are you."

She raised an eyebrow at him.

"You were telling me about getting on Diego Figueroa's trail."

"Right," she said, and took a few steps before continuing. "Once I was on his trail, I made a second trip to Spain, spent a few weeks in Cádiz, another in Madrid, a weekend in Barcelona. I dug up everything there was on Figueroa— his ancestry on both sides, his life, his life's work. I read countless books, sorted through more legends and rumors—all the really fun stuff that never makes it into the movies. And what I found was an old—I hate to use the word, because I found it credible and substantiated it in several places—but an old legend that Diego Figueroa had found what he termed 'the secret of eternal life.'"

"That's somewhat vague, isn't it?" Mitch asked. "How do you know he didn't get religion or have some spiritual conversion?"

"Because there were three different sources—a journal from one of his great grandsons, a Spanish historian from the early 1700s, and a shipmate's 'memoirs'—all claiming that he had gone to Florida or the New World in search of a fountain or spring." She dragged a strand of windblown hair away from her face. "And couple that with an old shipping log from Cádiz that said Enrique Figueroa, Diego's son, set out for Florida in 1705 aboard the *Descubridor*, and it would suggest Diego didn't merely get converted by door-to-door missionaries."

"Okay, that seems credible enough, if your sources were solid."

"Believe me, they were."

"How does that get us to the cipher disk?"

"Diego's other son, Javier, died in 1745 from typhus. Before he did, he wrote a letter to his two sons, telling them that their uncle, Enrique, had been lost at sea while in possession of a disk that would lead to the discovery of '*agua eterna*.'"

"Eternal water."

She nodded. "Javier said in this letter that he never believed his father's claim, but he wanted his sons to know since he was dying. Furthermore, there's a rumor—and this is just a rumor—that King Philip V of Spain was approached by Diego in 1701 with an offer to help him find eternal life. But Diego had made himself something of a *persona non grata* with the Spanish throne."

"Why's that?"

"Various things. Mostly he disagreed with their centuries-old penchant for conquest and treasure. And there were rumors that he'd become friendly with some of the Native Americans in Florida, who were a serious thorn in the flesh of the Spanish."

"There really are a lot of rumors here."

"The further you go back in time, the less certainty you have—records fade away, texts become corrupted or disappear, eye-witness accounts become less reliable if credible at all. And we're talking centuries here, not millennia. Imagine trying to verify something from the Middle Ages or the Roman Empire or the time of the Pharaohs."

They walked for a while, then turned back toward their hotel.

"Okay," Mitch said, studying the sand in front of him. "What about the disk? Did Javier's letter say how it would lead to *agua eterna*?"

"No. That part's a guess. There's the carving in St. Augustine, but it doesn't give any clues as to the location. I was hoping that, with the disk, I'd be able to put two and two together and figure out where the fountain was, or figure out the next clue."

Mitch kicked at some sand. Something was bugging him, but he couldn't quite place it. He tried mentally retracing Cameron's trail from the rumors about Ponce de León, down to his descendent Diego Figueroa, to one of his sons being lost at sea aboard the *Descubridor* with the cipher disk. Something didn't add up, maybe? Or maybe it was simply that he'd never heard anything more about the Fountain of Youth than the Ponce de León rumors.

"What you thinking?" Cameron asked.

"Don't get me wrong, you've done a lot of work here."

"But you don't believe it?"

"It's not that. It's just . . . how does no one else know about this? How is this not in the history books or—at least some of it—common knowledge?"

"Because it goes nowhere. Nobody knows where the Fountain of Youth is. The secret died with Diego Figueroa. Plus, like I've said, very few people believe in the Fountain of Youth—at least not in a real, tangible way."

"How'd he die?"

"He was killed in the War of Spanish Succession."

"So much for eternal life."

"Well, I don't think it works against man-made forms of death. It's not an invisible shield against swords and arrows or bullets."

"I guess," Mitch said. "What about this carving in St. Augustine? What's the connection to Figueroa?"

"It has his name on it."

"That's a connection all right."

"Most people have no idea who he is, however. He was at odds with the Spanish government, rejected by King Philip V, and died a few years later. When Enrique's ship was lost, and with it the cipher disk . . ."

"Until a hurricane unearthed it?"

Cameron nodded. "Hurricane Matthew, in 2016."

"You said the carving doesn't give any hints where the fountain is?"

"Not in and of itself. It's been a dead end, which is why nobody's come close to finding the Fountain of Youth. There has to be a perfect storm of knowing about the carving, knowing Figueroa's history, knowing about the disk, and knowing—post hurricane—where the *Descubridor* lies. And," she added, "believing there's actually a literal Fountain of Youth to be found."

"So in theory, it shouldn't be hard to know who else is after it."

"In theory. But until about three o'clock this afternoon, I thought I was the only one."

"What about Erik?"

"I told you, I trust him."

"I didn't mean that he was behind this. But would he know of someone else who might be?"

"He didn't say anything when we talked, but I'll definitely ask him tomorrow."

"Speaking of tomorrow, you have a plan on how to get to St. Augustine?"

She looked up at him, the corners of her mouth raised. "No."

"You want a ride?"

"You headed to St. Augustine?"

"My itinerary's wide-open."

Cameron stopped. "Mitch, what are you doing in Cocoa Beach?"

"Whatever I want."

She tipped her head to the side.

"I mean it. I'm free as a bird, Cameron. I was literally sitting on my Jet Ski trying to figure out what was next when I saw you dive over the side of the boat. I like you, I'm intrigued by your search, I'm a little worried about your safety, and I hear St. Augustine is nice this time of year. That's it."

She stared at him for several seconds, slowing breaking into a half smile. "Erik texted me. Brunch is at ten, and St. Augustine is a hundred and twenty miles up the coast."

"Then we should get some sleep."

CHAPTER EIGHT

Cameron looked like the All-American girl on vacation when Mitch knocked on her door at seven-thirty the next morning. She wore a white cap-sleeved V-neck that bloused around her waist, clam diggers, and white canvas shoes. Her hair was slung over her shoulder in a loose ponytail, and her eyes sparkled belying the lack of sleep she had to have gotten, considering it had been close to midnight when they'd parted in this same spot the night before. She greeted him with a smile, and his *second* thought was that she looked like she belonged in a toothpaste commercial. His *first* thought, and the one that stayed with him, was that he was looking forward to the trip north with her.

They loaded their luggage into his Porsche, then picked up some pastries, coffee, and juice from the hotel breakfast area. By twenty to eight, they were on the road, headed first north through town, then crossing several bodies of water via causeway and cutting a few miles inland to Interstate 95. The morning had dawned clear and a little sticky, but since they would be facing away from the sun, Mitch had left the top down on the Porsche. It made talking difficult, so they both settled in for the ride, her cross-legged with her shoes off and him with an elbow stuck out the window and one hand on the wheel. A few times, when he remembered the goons who'd attacked Cameron aboard her dive boat and broken into Erik's villa, he glanced in the rearview mirror. But traffic on I-95's three northbound lanes was so sporadic on a Sunday morning that he realized he would have long ago spotted a tail— assuming he could identify one.

They passed through Titusville, Daytona Beach, and Palm Coast, and Mitch's stomach began to growl. He also got tired of the scenery. Florida was great on the beach. Inland it was nothing but a mess of never-ending, overgrown forest. So he powered up his window, then got Cameron's attention and motioned for her to do the same.

"What's up?" she asked as he turned down Matchbox Twenty on the radio.

"Tell me more about Erik."

She sat up a little straighter. "You mean Erik my business partner or Erik my ex?"

"There a difference?"

"No. But I'm wondering why you'd care about my ex."

"Because it impacts how you view him."

"You think I've got a blind spot?"

"No. It's my line of work again. I like to know all angles before I enter a situation."

"It's not a situation; it's brunch. And you're unemployed, remember?"

"Touché."

She grinned, then sat back. "Erik Diaz is a ven—"

"Wait, his last name's Diaz?"

She sighed.

"So if you'd have married him . . ."

"I would have been Cameron Diaz," she said with an eye roll. "But it never came close to that."

"I dated a girl named Dana in high school."

Cameron frowned.

"She would have been Dana Owens, in theory."

She frowned some more.

"Queen Latifah's birth name."

"And how in the world could you possibly know that?"

"She said something about it once. She was a daydreamer."

Cameron nodded. "Erik's a venture capitalist. He lives in Atlanta, spends half his life flying around the country. He's made a good living for himself, and seen more than a few long shots come through, which are two reasons he supports my research."

"What are the other reasons?"

"I told you, we're still on good terms. But the romance is over."

"I'm not jealous, Cameron."

"Your green eyes say otherwise."

"I just like to—"

"Know all the angles," she said with a sigh.

"No romance between you two. I got it."

"In fact, I'm pretty sure he's serious with somebody. I've heard him mention a Jessie several times."

"Not like a football-playing Jesse?"

"A what?"

"Never mind."

"You get enough sleep?" she asked.

"No, did you?"

"No," she said, settling back into her seat. A half mile later she said, "Erik lives a hundred miles an hour. I don't think he's ever used a sentence that's more than ten words. He walks around with a Bluetooth headset, always has another deal to make or close. It was part of the reason it didn't work with us. There were a lot of them, but I knew I'd always be second to his work. Anyhow, he can come across as brusque, as too busy, as if you're just another data point. But deep down, I know he cares about people. The exterior can be hard to crack."

Mitch nodded, surprised at how she was suddenly opening up.

She turned his way. "So if he makes you feel like a nobody, don't take it personal."

"Got it."

"He's not funny, but thinks he is. I humor him with at least a smile."

"Noted."

"And he's a terrible worrier. Not about weird stuff like satellites falling on us or getting sick all the time, but the way a guy who's over invested has to check the stock market twenty times a day."

"Or about you? I heard half of your conversations."

She exhaled. "I think he feels responsible, since he's funding my search."

"What's he get out of it?" Mitch asked.

"Besides incredibly long life?"

"Well, besides that."

"Nothing."

"Nobody does anything for nothing. Especially not fund what has to be at least a nominally expensive 'treasure hunt.'"

"Or chauffer a complete stranger around, buy her a hotel room, drive her across the state?

He turned slowly her way as another smile broke out. "Touché."

"Okay, Mr. Nebulous, your turn. Why aren't you still managing a security firm and why are you romping around Florida solo?"

"It's pretty simple, really. I made very good money, invested it wisely, and didn't need to keep working."

"You retired at thirty-three?"

"Not permanently. I'm sure I'll find something to do eventually to make spending money. But this isn't so much a vacation as an open-ended journey."

"To where?"

"Wherever."

She studied him for a moment.

"What?"

"What aren't you telling me?"

"An awful lot, but none of the biggies."

"Biggies?"

"I'm not on the run from the law, I'm not hiding from an ex or my family or expectations in my hometown, and I'm not disillusioned with life and looking to find myself. I'd just never been to Florida before."

"I think I believe you," she said. She looked out her window for a while, then looked back. "You're really just bumming in Florida until you decide not to?"

"Really."

"Hmm."

"Hmm what?"

"Then you are either a stroke of remarkable good luck . . ."

"Or?"

"Or the other shoe's going to fall and this is going to blow up in my face."

"No other shoe," Mitch said. "What you see is what you get. I promise."

"I think I believe you," she said again after a moment. She turned her eyes straight ahead. "There's one other thing you should know about Erik."

"What's that?"

"He's got a nose for business and a nose for people. He can sniff out a phony a mile away."

Mitch shrugged. "I'm not worried."

Cameron winked as she said, "I *think* I believe you."

*   *   *

St. Augustine was the oldest city in the United States, having been settled in 1565 and continuously inhabited ever since (although but barely a few times). Situated just inland along the Matanzas River, the city was home to a variety of attractions—from pristine beaches and parks to unique dining experiences to museums and historical sites. But what made St. Augustine famous was its Old Town and Historic District, featuring narrow cobblestone streets, Spanish Colonial architecture, numerous historical buildings dating back centuries, and the best shops, restaurants, and lodging—all in the shade of live oak trees and with views of the river.

Cameron had been there numerous times, and the quaint appeal of the city never lessened. Today, however, as they entered the city via Highway 1 (also known as Ponce de León Boulevard) and crossed the San Sebastian River on King Street, she was in business mode. Erik's other benefit, as she'd informed Mitch, was his list of contacts. She was hoping he had learned something from someone about who Braves Hat and his gang were, who they were working for, and how she might be able to get the Figueroa Cipher back. It was a long shot, she knew, but he'd come through before.

"You sure about this?" Mitch asked as they turned onto a narrow street leading into an older, residential section of the city. Spanish moss grew thick on trees that cloaked the street, blocking out much of the morning sun.

"Yeah, it's in an old house."

Erik had made reservations at Preserved, an upscale bistro that served Sunday brunch, starting at ten. And Cameron's watch ticked to 10:00 as they came to an all-way stop at the corner of Bridge and MLK Boulevard. On their left, a three-story blue and gray Victorian-style house was rimmed with an iron fence and surrounded by bright pink and red flowers. Signage was subtle, but Cameron recognized it from a previous visit, when she and Erik had been working and traveling together. Forever ago.

They parked in a lot behind the building and made their way to an outdoor hostess desk on a porch that wrapped around the building. When Cameron mentioned Erik's name, the hostess quickly took them to a small table on the east side, still in the shade. Erik was scanning a menu when they arrived, and he immediately dropped it and stood.

He wore a peach dress shirt, the sleeves rolled up to mid-arm and light blue pants to match a jacket draped over his chair. His hair was perfect, faded to a slight bouffant in the front, meticulously gelled as always. His cologne was strong and his breath smelled like peppermint as he rushed forward to embrace Cameron.

"I'm so glad you're all right, Cammy," he said, giving an extra squeeze before a quick peck on the cheek.

"Erik, this is Mitch Owens, my rescuer twice over. Mitch, Erik Diaz."

"A pleasure," Erik said, extending a hand. "Thank you so much."

"Same here," Mitch said. He clipped his sunglasses over the collar of a Kansas "Dust in the Wind" T-shirt and shook Erik's hand. If there was any alpha-male head-butting or jealous suspicion between them, Cameron didn't pick up on it.

"I'm sorry, Cameron didn't mention bringing a plus one, or I'd have asked for a larger table," Erik said.

"I didn't know he was coming until late last night—"

That drew a raised eyebrow from Erik

"—and it slipped my mind this morning," she said quickly.

"Not a problem," Mitch said, reaching for a chair from an empty table beside them. For a second, Cameron thought he was going to go all senior-higher and straddle the thing backwards, but he sat down like a gentleman.

As they scoured menus, ordered, and waited for food to arrive, Erik made Cameron recount everything that had taken place in the last twenty-four hours. When she was done, he took a sip of his mimosa and leaned forward.

"I made a bunch of calls this morning. Here's where we're at. Based on your description and Sullivan's description, the authorities think we're looking at a husband and wife team. Shay and Lora Hogan." He reached for a folder in the briefcase beside his chair, set it on his plate, and opened it. He extracted two photos, which he handed to Cameron. "They're copies."

Braves Hat and Redhead, only without the hat and with shorter hair.

"That's them," she said, turning the photos to Mitch.

"Couple of thugs for hire, from Boston originally. Work up and down the East Coast."

"He doesn't look like a Shay."

"Short for Seamus. Irish. Both of them."

"How'd you get these?" Mitch asked, taking the photos to study them.

"Friend of a friend works for the A.G." He looked back at Cameron. "Third guy they think is Dax Wilder." He produced another photo. Board Shorts.

"Same story, only he's originally from Memphis. And then they're guessing the fourth man is Kevin Stuart, a known criminal associate of Wilder from his days running confidence games in Charlotte. No photo."

"It doesn't matter. I couldn't see his face under the cap."

Mitch handed the three photos back to Erik. "Anything to tie them to the cipher disk or the Fountain of Youth?"

"No. They're hired guns. Literally."

"But the cops are looking for them, right?" Cameron asked.

"Yes and no."

"Why yes and no?"

"According to the friend of a friend," Erik said, looking at Mitch, then back at Cameron, "there's some outside pressure not to . . . over exert themselves on this one."

"What does that mean?"

"It means the Hogans have some friends in high places."

"They committed piracy on the high seas, a home invasion, grand theft," Mitch said. "It should take a presidential pardon to protect them."

"I'm just telling you what I know. There's an A.P.B. out for them, but it's not exactly urgent."

Cameron huffed.

"I'm sorry, Cammy."

"What about the disk?"

"What about it?"

"If the cops find the Hogans and Wilder and Stuart, what happens to the disk?"

Erik held out his hands. "It's evidence. After that . . ."

Their food arrived—steak and eggs for Mitch, smoked salmon benedict for Erik, and banana nut French toast for Cameron—but she'd lost her appetite. The guys were not slowed by bad news.

"So now what?" she asked after nibbling at her breakfast. She reached for her ice water and took a sip.

"We let the police handle it," Erik said.

"I mean about finding the Fountain of Youth," she said, aware that they had privacy in their corner of the porch.

"Yeah," Erik said, dabbing his mouth. He sat back. "I'm pulling the plug, Cam."

"What?"

He shook his head and reached for his mimosa. "This is too dangerous. You were nearly killed. Twice," he added, then took a gulp.

"They only tried to kill me once."

"Quite a distinction to note."

"Erik, we cannot quit now."

"Cammy, I don't want something to happen to you. We always talked about the dangers, the possibility of dangers." He shook his head. "Now they're realized, and worse than we imagined. These are bad people, and they're just the muscle. Whoever hired them, whoever is pulling strings, is not someone you want to mess with."

"Erik."

"Besides, without the cipher disk, you're at square one. Maybe not forever, but for now, I think it's time to draw back."

Cameron pursed her lips, knowing that when Erik made up his mind, it was made up. All her powers of persuasion had proven impotent to change his mind. She had always worked to prejudice him before he made a decision, and with moderate success at times. Now, it was too late.

Erik's decision irked her.

What irked her more was an underlying sense that he was right.

CHAPTER NINE

Erik picked up the check, and Mitch let him. Erik pumped his hand like they were old buddies, nipped Cameron on the cheek, told her he'd be in touch if he heard anything, and practically dashed off with a final swig of his mimosa.

"He always like that?" Mitch asked, smiling at a waitress who took his empty plate.

"Like what?"

"Insensitive."

"You noticed that, huh?"

"I try to mind my own business, and I certainly don't mean to insult your ex, but I got the feeling this was a business transaction to him. As long as you're unhurt and not a potential liability, all's good in his world."

"That's about the size of it."

"Was it always like that?"

"No, not at first."

"Well, for what it's worth, I'm sorry."

She waved a hand. "I'm used to him by now."

"I mean about your search."

"I'm not quitting," she said.

"You're not?"

"No. During your career comparison, I stewed a little and then decided that I've come this far and I'm not giving up."

He looked at her.

"Don't believe me?" she asked.

"I believe you. I just don't know what your options are."

"Neither do I," she said. "Drive me somewhere?"

He nodded and they got up. Out of the shade of the porch, and with what little breeze there was blocked by the trees in the neighborhood, the heat was almost stifling. Mitch couldn't wait to get moving in the convertible.

"I have a hunch," Cameron said as he turned out of the parking lot onto Bridge Street.

"Where am I going?"

"Um, back to the main drag."

He turned left at the all-way. "Your hunch?"

"The Hogan Gang. I think they're here."

"In St. Augustine?"

She nodded.

"Steal the disk to interpret the carving."

She nodded again. "Whoever's behind this has to know his or her stuff, meaning they know about the carving and Enrique's journey on the *Descubridor* and Javier's letter to his sons. There's no explicit directions to interpret a carving in St. Augustine with the cipher disk, but they kind of fit hand in glove. Plus, you commit a crime in Cocoa Beach, you probably don't want to hang around."

"Especially if you're Lora Hogan."

Cameron frowned.

"Unless the red hair was a wig, she'd stand out in a crowd."

"Lot of redheads in the world."

"Yeah, but that was bright red—almost ruby red. Not the typical orange-red you usually see."

"I didn't know you were an expert in hair color."

"Just on good-looking women."

"I see."

"Erik seems connected. He have any other friends of friends you can tap, maybe somebody with connections in St. Augustine?"

She raised her eyebrows. "He made it pretty clear he was out."

"He was, yeah."

"I don't know his connections, and certainly not well enough to contact them if I did." She sighed. "But that gives me an idea."

As Cameron reached for her phone, Mitch turned right onto King St, a.k.a. U.S. 1 Business. It led past the famed Ponce de León Hotel, once a luxury hotel built by Henry Flagler. Now the ornate, Spanish Renaissance-style structure was part of Flagler College, its grounds lined with lush green grass and palm trees. The architecture was the same across the street, at something called the Lightner Museum and a large building containing a hotel, restaurants, and shops.

Mitch turned back to Cameron, who appeared to be holding. Then she spoke. "Evan, it's Cameron Leigh. I'm in town and I could use your help. Can you give me a call when you get this? Thanks." She lowered her phone and gazed out her window.

"Who's Evan?"

"You're going to laugh."

"Okay."

"He's a guy I dated briefly."

"I didn't take you for a guy in every city kind of gal."

"I'm not. We literally went out like twice, and that was more work related than anything."

"What's he do?"

"He's a private investigator."

"In town?"

She nodded. "I was hoping he might have some connections that could pinpoint where the Hogans are."

"To what end?" Mitch asked.

"I don't know," she breathed in frustration. He let it go. "Turn at the light," she said.

They had reached the end of the road, literally. On their left, a small oval-shaped park was home to a statue of none other than the discoverer of Florida, Juan Ponce de León. Directly ahead, a narrow strip of land separated them from the Matanzas River as it flowed lazily toward its outlet about a mile away. When the light turned green, Mitch stopped taking in the sights and turned north on a four-lane road he quickly identified as the A1A.

The road paralleled the river, which was dotted with sailboats and sloops and small yachts, all anchored out in the river. When the road curved back inland, Cameron directed him to turn into a parking lot. A National Park Service sign by the entrance to the lot identified the old stone structure on a small hill beyond the parking lot as Castillo de San Marcos. Without asking any questions, Mitch found a parking spot, and they got out.

"You want to pop the trunk?" she asked.

He did, then stood and stretched. Nearer the river, and straight inland from its mouth, the breeze was a little stronger, but still didn't do much to cool what had to be pushing up against a ninety-degree day. Couples with little kids in tow or in strollers, singles with fanny packs and cameras around their necks, and a group of ten or twelve kids all in the same colored shirts were roaming the sidewalk leading up to the old structure or lining the river. Mitch craned his eyes and could see patina-covered cannon poking out of embrasures in the battlements atop the stone walls, over which flew a white flag with a red X.

The trunk closed, and he turned to see Cameron threading her ponytail through a bright orange cap with a white tiger paw emblazoned on the front.

"Clemson?" he asked.

"My alma mater."

He nodded.

"What?"

Mitch grinned. Normally, he found baseball caps on women to be a little, well, butch. But it worked for Cameron, as he suspected most apparel choices did.

"What?" she asked again.

"Just a little bright orange, that's all."

"What, instead of that faded clay-shingle roof orange you wear?"

"Burnt orange is iconic."

"Uh-huh."

He grinned again, then nodded at what he had determined was an old Spanish fort. "What are we doing here?"

"You'll see."

She led the way up the sidewalk, past a small sign announcing that Castillo de San Marcos, having been built between 1672 and 1695, had helped Spain hold Florida against English attacks before serving as a British stronghold during the American Revolution and then as a part of the U.S. coastal defense system. As to whether the fort was somehow connected to Diego Figueroa and the Fountain of Youth or he and Cameron were merely sightseeing, Mitch was unsure.

After paying the entrance fee, they crossed a drawbridge to a ravelin, a triangular fortification guarding the fort's entrance, and then another drawbridge over a deep moat. Void of water, the moat contained only grass. Beyond it, the walls of the fort rose approximately thirty feet to the top of the battlements where cannon still aimed out toward the water. Then they passed through a gated "sally port," inside of which was a bookstore and gift shop, and emerged into the courtyard of Castillo de San Marcos.

The grass in the center was roped off, but a stone-paved walkway led around the square courtyard. Doors and windows opened to guard rooms, storage rooms, officers' quarters, and a powder magazine, all built inside the walls and in many cases restored as miniature museums. To the right, a staircase led to the gun deck and the four bastions in the corners of the fort.

Cameron nudged Mitch, then nodded at the stairs. "Want to look around?"

He dipped his head. "This is your show."

She turned for the stairs and Mitch followed. Up on top of the gun deck, the breeze was stronger and the views of the river even better. Back to the south, Mitch could see the towers of the former Ponce de León Hotel, as well as several other historic St. Augustine buildings, all backed by a blue sky and the tufts of a few cumulous clouds beginning to form.

Mitch continued to follow Cameron as she walked leisurely along the wide, concrete deck. Facing the river, the battlements were only about a foot high, with wooden decks canted toward them spaced out every few dozen feet. Platforms for cannon, he realized. Cameron continued to the diamond-shaped bastion at the northeast corner of the fort, stopping beside a rounded tower projecting from the end of the bastion, like a sentinel watching over the mouth of the river. She stopped, and Mitch stood beside her, scanning the river, from the drawbridge east of downtown to the marshy inlet north of the fort.

"My dad loved seeing places like this," Cameron said.

Mitch noted she used the past tense. He took off his sunglasses and looked her way, waiting until she turned. "Is he why you have such an interest in digging through the past?"

"Everywhere we went, he would talk about the past. Civil War battles or the Underground Railroad or pre-Revolutionary War exploration. And he was a great storyteller. Anybody can give you the facts, but he made them come alive." She shrugged. "I guess, somewhere along the line, the passion rubbed off on me."

"Was he the one who put you onto the Fountain of Youth?"

"No. Not exactly," she added. "Dad was more of a war buff. That's why he would have loved seeing the fort."

Mitch said nothing.

"Mom, on the other hand," Cameron said with a soft laugh, "couldn't have cared less about what happened centuries before—who used to live here or there, whether or not a battle was fought on this or that piece of ground. She was more interested in modern stories, what people were feeling and dealing with, what was going on in their lives."

"So she would have been bored here."

"Well, she also loved art and architecture, so who knows."

Mitch again said nothing.

Cameron stuck her hands in her pockets and sighed. Then she turned and looked behind them. Mitch eyed her out the corner of his eye. "Looking for the Hogans?"

She whipped her head around. "What makes you say that?"

"I figure the reason we're ultimately here is to see this carving you keep talking about. So it makes sense before we do you'd want to get the bird's-eye view, see who's here. It also explains the hat."

"The hat?"

"Maybe keeps them from recognizing you."

"I'm wearing the hat because it's sunny and bright."

He nodded.

"But you're right on the rest. Wanna see it?"

"Yeah."

They circled the fort on the gun deck, then descended to the courtyard. "In 1702, the British laid siege to St. Augustine," Cameron said as they reached the bottom of the stairs. "About fifteen hundred residents of the city had to take refuge in the fort until the Spanish fleet arrived from Havana to rescue them. A few decades later, the Spanish renovated the interior of the fort, enlarging some of the rooms and shrinking the courtyard."

"You work summers here as a tour guide or something?"

She smirked at him. "Part of the reconfiguration included a new chapel, over there." She pointed at an arched doorway in the north wall. "But that was not the chapel in 1698 when Diego Figueroa visited the fort."

"Where was it then?"

"Here, in the south wall."

They had stopped in front of a dark doorway, adjacent to what Mitch guessed—based on the bars in the windows—had been the jail. The wall above the doorway was crumbling, but Mitch could see the faint remnant of an ornate cross carved into the stone. He removed his sunglasses again and followed Cameron inside, then waited for his eyes to adjust to the darkness.

The room was now configured as a bedroom, with period-accurate bed frames, a writing desk, a couple of chairs, and a dressing table. A plaque on the wall described the day-to-day life of an officer, while a life-size mannequin in an eighteenth-century Spanish soldier's uniform stood beside the desk. Mitch had visited several other Revolutionary War- or Civil War-era forts across the country, and this was standard.

"Over here," Cameron said, and he followed her to the wall beside the bed and a small end table. The wall was formed of hundreds of stones covered by plaster that had chipped and worn over the years, leaving the original stone in some places. One stone stood out among all the others. It was nearly twice the size of the next largest, several feet high as it stood on end. If it had ever been covered by plaster, every last bit had been removed. And whereas the rest of the stone used in construction of the fort was a type of sandstone known as *coquina*, this stone was a dark gray granite.

Then there was the carving. They were alone in the old chapel-turned-officers' quarters, and Cameron pulled out her cell phone and turned on a flashlight app. It revealed the clarity of letters after three centuries.

> *I found what men have lost lives and fortunes seeking.*
> *Je partage le secret avec ceux qui ont des yeux pour voir,*
> *afin qu'ils puissent jouir de la vie éternelle.*
> *-Diego Ponce de León de Figueroa, 1698*

Mitch turned to Cameron. "It's not in Spanish."

She shook her head.

"Diego was Spanish, right?"

She nodded.

"So why—"

She shrugged. "Nobody knows. Maybe because he wanted to throw off other Spanish-speaking people. Maybe because he was at odds with the Spanish government and wanted to taunt them. Maybe because he was flaunting his education."

"You happen to read French?"

"No, but I've had this translated. It says, '*I share the secret with those who have eyes to see, so that they may enjoy eternal life.*'"

Mitch repeated the words in his head. "Not very specific."

"No."

"It doesn't even refer to the Fountain of Youth."

"No."

He read it all again, carefully studying the French to see if any English or Spanish words jumped out at him, if the French could be some sort of a diversion. But nothing stood out, aside from the easily translatable words like *secret* and *éternelle.*

An older couple entered the room, and Mitch and Cameron immediately lost interest in the carving. They wandered around the room, looking at the furniture and reading another small plaque on the south wall until the couple left. Then they returned to the carving.

"What's this?" Mitch asked, pointing at more words in the *coquina* well above the granite slab.

"What's what?" She stepped in to look, then switched on the flashlight again. "It looks like . . . Latin?"

"'*madmodum statutum est homi bus semel*' missing patch '*hoc autem iudici,*'" Mitch read. These words hadn't aged nearly as well.

Cameron snapped several photos with her phone's camera, and stood up satisfied that she had an image that wasn't blurry.

"You see this before?"

"No, but there's a few other carvings in the stones. Names, dates. Most in Spanish, most not preserved well."

"Are they relevant to the search?"

"They don't seem to be. None in granite, none matching the style, and many of the dates are well after the Figueroa Carving. Copycats."

"Hmm." He looked back at the granite slab again. "Any ideas where this came from? Or why? What was Figueroa doing in the fort?"

"The scuttlebutt I found on that is that he was friendly with one of the commanders here and was invited to share his quarters while waiting for a ship to take him back to Spain."

"And he just carved his cryptic message into said commander's bedroom wall?"

"I guess. Only it wasn't his bedroom wall then, it was the chapel."

"See, that's the odd thing," Mitch said. "Why doesn't he come out and say Fountain of Youth? Or hint at it at least? He writes about finding eternal life on the wall of a chapel. How do we know he didn't just have a 'come to Jesus' moment?"

"I don't know much about coming to Jesus, but people don't typically lose lives and fortunes seeking him, do they?"

Mitch shrugged.

"And what about the disk? If this was some testimony about a spiritual conversion, why make a disk to interpret it?"

"A lot of questions."

"And not enough answers," she said.

Mitch ran a hand through his hair. "Okay," he said, "where do we go from here?"

Cameron shrugged. "I have no idea."

CHAPTER TEN

Where they went was to get ice cream cones at MAYDAY, followed by a walk along the narrow but modernized streets of St. Augustine's historic downtown. The temperature had hit ninety, and the ice cream was a refreshing treat. It was also a distraction from the fact that Cameron had no idea what to do next. Not unless she could track down the Figueroa Cipher.

On the way out of Castillo de San Marcos, they had stopped to chat with several park rangers and show them pictures of Seamus and Lora Hogan and Dax Wilder. Mitch had surreptitiously snapped pictures of Erik's photos, and Cameron hoped somebody could ID the thieves. It would prove her hunch correct, that they had come to St. Augustine with the disk and were working to decipher the carving in the old fortress. She wasn't sure how it would help them beyond that, but it didn't matter. Nobody recognized them.

"Oh, I plugged that Latin phrase into my phone," Cameron said as they walked. She then had to address a drip in her mint chocolate waffle cone.

"Yeah?"

"If you fill in a few missing words, it fits as a Bible verse from the book of Hebrews."

"Doesn't happen to mention water of life or something, does it?"

"No." She licked another drip, then dug out her phone with her free hand. "'*And as it is appointed unto men once to die, and after this the judgment.*'"

"That's encouraging," Mitch said, then took a big lick of his peanut butter and Oreo ice cream.

"I can't figure any connection to the Fountain of Youth, unless it's that the fountain would put off the death and judgement bit." She licked again. "Or that whoever etched this was countering the idea of a life-giving fountain. But like I said before, there's nothing to suggest any of the other engravings in that room are tied to the Figueroa Carving."

"Left, right, or straight?" Mitch asked at an intersection. They had been walking on a pedestrian-only street between old buildings turned into tourist shops. Cameron turned her head left and right. Neither direction appeared all that inviting, but the river was left, so she nodded that way and started walking.

She continued to work on her ice cream, trying to figure out how to ask Mitch what his plans were without being too forward. She was hoping he'd stick around, and not just as an expense account. She enjoyed his company and liked not being alone in her search, especially with the Hogans, Wilder, and Stuart out there. But she also knew that unless they were able to get their hands on the disk, her search was stuck in neutral.

They walked for a block on a one-way alley, then cut between buildings on a narrower cobblestone walkway, and found themselves at the four-lane highway beside the river. They crossed it and turned south, on a sidewalk beside the river. Cameron stole several glances at Mitch, wishing he'd take off those sunglasses so she could look into his eyes to get a glimpse at what he was thinking. Was he hanging around to protect her? To help find the Fountain of Youth? Because he enjoyed her company? Or because he had nothing else to do?

Her phone buzzed, and she nearly dropped the rest of her cone digging it out of her pocket. She sighed when she saw it was nothing more than a casual "how's it going" text from her older sister. She explained as much to Mitch as she returned the phone to her pocket. "I don't know what's up with Evan. It's a Sunday, and he can't be that busy."

"Missed calls happen."

"I texted him too, while you were chatting up that one park ranger."

"You mean the guy who wouldn't stop talking?"

She nodded.

"Let me ask you something," he said a few steps farther down the sidewalk. "Let's say he does call back, has nothing. Let's say the Hogans are gone? What next?"

"I don't know."

"I don't mean what's your next step in trying to recover the disk or locate the Fountain of Youth. I mean, what are you doing tomorrow?"

"Going home," she said. "Why? How do you mean that?"

"If you're going home, then that's it. But if you were going to stay here, pursue some other angle . . ." he shrugged. "I was going to ask if you want a partner."

She smiled at him, but only for an instant. "There is no other angle. Not right now."

He frowned.

She licked.

"Or, I thought maybe you'd want to blow off your frustration."

"Blow off my frustration?"

"Yeah. Get away, cruise down to the Keys or something."

"And you wanted to know if I wanted a partner for that?"

Mitch grinned. "Like I said, I have no other plans."

"Mm-hmm."

Her phone buzzed again. "I'm going to have to talk to her appar . . ." She glanced at the display and saw it wasn't her sister. "It's Evan," she said, then swiped to answer the call. "Cameron Leigh."

"Cameron," came a somewhat energetic voice, enunciating each syllable of her name. "Out of the blue."

"Hi, Evan."

"Sorry I missed your call," he said. Energetic but with a Southern drawl, one of the odder voices she'd ever heard. "I was in church, then lunch. I just got free. You're in town?"

"Yeah, just arrived this morning. My friend and I could use your help."

"What's going on?"

"Are you still a private investigator?"

"I am."

"And you're in town?"

"Yeah. Cameron, what's up?"

"Any chance we can meet somewhere?" she asked, looking at Mitch. "This is going to sound so stupid, but I'd rather not talk about it on the phone."

"Are you in trouble?" Evan asked.

"No. But I do need some help. Please, Evan?"

"Yeah, of course. Where are you?"

"Walking around. We can be anywhere."

"Okay," he said, then paused for a moment. "Meet me at the Great Cross, at two. You know where it is?"

"Yeah. Two o'clock, we'll be there. Thanks, Evan."

"You're welcome."

She lowered the phone and briefed Mitch on the other half of the conversation.

"Let's go," he said. "I just wish I hadn't left my cloak and dagger at home."

*   *   *

"The Shrine of Our Lady of La Leche," Mitch read as he turned into a parking lot just beyond a modern-looking structure that resembled a city library. "Our Lady of The Milk?"

Beside him, Cameron shrugged.

"You're not Catholic, are you?" he asked.

"No. Not really."

"Not really?"

"My grandma was Catholic. Mass every Sunday, confession. It never trickled down."

"She ever talk about a Lady of The Milk?"

"I don't think so."

"Is Evan a Catholic?"

"Not when I knew him."

Mitch nodded as he parked. There were only a few other cars in the lot, but it was now Sunday afternoon, so unless this was one of those all-day African-American churches he'd heard existed in the Deep South, the parking lot should be empty. He got out and checked the sky. It felt like a day where storms could build up, and although his trip to Florida had been dry so far, he'd heard afternoon storms were common. It didn't look foreboding anytime soon, so he left the top down.

Cameron had shed her hat and shaken her hair out of her ponytail, and he wasn't sure if that had to do with respect for the shrine or because of Evan. At any rate, he followed her on a path toward the shrine, and then down a sidewalk leading toward a small pond. A bridge traversed the pond, and directly in line with the bridge, maybe a hundred yards beyond it, was a tall, thin cross jutting into the blue sky. Cameron had read a paragraph about it on their walk back to the car, and supposedly it had been built to commemorate the four hundredth anniversary of the arrival of Christianity on the shores of

America. She hadn't read a history of the shrine or the old Mission Nombre de Dios on the grounds.

"So you must be pretty familiar with St. Augustine," Mitch said. "Know your way around, know who to contact."

"It's the base for any Fountain of Youth search, the lack of credence to the Ponce de León rumors notwithstanding. For the better part of two centuries, this was the hub on the east coast of Florida. It's where the history is."

"I suppose."

"In fact, there's even a Fountain of Youth Archaeological Park just north of here that has a small aquifer-fed spring that claims to be the Fountain of Youth." She shrugged. "It's a fun little place to visit, but that's about it."

"You're sure? You're not spending all this time and money looking for something somebody else already found?"

"They have found some remains of an ancient Spanish settlement, but there's no reason to believe it's anything more than Ponce de León's original landing site in 1513, if even that."

"You're the expert."

She looked at him.

"I mean it."

She nodded and led the way over the bridge, through a small copse of trees, and out onto a promontory at the end of which was the cross. Made of stainless steel plates, it took on a golden color in the afternoon sunlight as it towered 208 feet above the grassy promontory and a small bay in the Matanzas River.

"What's this guy look like?" Mitch asked.

"Average height, weight. Short blond hair. Pretty regular. Cute face."

"You say you dated him a couple times?"

"You covering all your angles again or are you jealous?" she asked, closing one eye to look at him.

"Depends on how cute the face."

The cross was anchored in a concrete pillar on a small, brick platform. As they took the trio of steps to the top, a man climbed up from the sidewalk on the other side. He wore a backward baseball cap over a crop of long, blond hair, a short-sleeve buttoned shirt, and a pair of cargo shorts. Flip-flops slapped against the brick as he approached.

"Cameron!" he said, breaking into a dimpled smile.

"Evan? Wow, you look different."

He removed the cap and ran a hand through his hair, holding it between his fingers for just a second. He returned the cap. "Well, it's been a few years. You look great," he said, and they exchanged a quick hug. She introduced her "friend" Mitch, and he shook hands with the private investigator.

"What brings you to St. Augustine?" Evan asked.

"Same thing as last time," she said.

"The Fountain of Youth?"

She nodded.

So did he, with a trace of disdain if Mitch read him right. Evan then held out his hands. "How can I help?"

They moved over to a railing that looked out at the river, and Cameron explained about the attack on the *Eternal Sun*, the break-in at Erik's villa, and their lack of clues as to where the disk was. She concluded with her hunch that the Hogan Gang had brought it to St. Augustine.

Evan shook his head. "What do you want me to do?"

"We have identities for three of them—maybe four. I was hoping you could . . . do what you do and see if any of them are in the area."

"Identities," he said, standing up from leaning on the railing. "What do you mean identities?"

"Names and faces." She nodded at Mitch, and he quickly accessed the photos on his phone. Evan took a brief glance at them before refocusing on Cameron.

"Are the police involved?"

"They're how we have the identities."

"You're working with them?"

"No. We heard it through the grapevine."

"Cameron, this sounds like a job for them. I don't know what I could do."

"You have contacts in town, don't you? Ears to the ground, word on the street? Night club bouncers and bartenders and desk clerks who might have seen them, C.I.s who know something about other criminals in the area?"

"I think you've been reading too many spy novels."

"I don't read spy novels," she said. "Come on, you have to have something?"

"Cameron . . ." He shook his head. "I don't like this. These guys sound dangerous." He looked at Mitch, then back to her. "Do you not trust the police?"

"We trust them," Mitch said. "But we're afraid they have bigger fish to fry than a stolen artifact."

"Not to mention what we really want is that artifact," Cameron said. "So we can continue the search. This is a huge breakthrough, Evan."

He sighed.

"Please."

"Look, I don't know a lot of bouncers and bartenders, and I don't have any criminal informants. But I can reach out to some people who might have heard a name or seen a face." He tipped his head to the side. "It's a big city though. I wouldn't get my hopes up."

"Hopes are all we have left," she said.

"I'll get on it first thing in the morning."

"In the morning?"

"I try not to work on Sundays," he said. "Or ask other people to."

"Since when?" Cameron asked.

"About eighteen months ago when I found Jesus. Or, I should say, he found me."

"I'm sorry, but what does that have to do with Sundays?"

Evan looked at both of them before answering. "I believe it's important to honor the Sabbath," he said. "To take time from work to rest and worship God."

"But you met us today?"

"As a personal favor."

"This work would be a personal favor," she said. "Evan, I don't want to force you to do something you don't believe in, but this is really important, and time-sensitive."

"The fountain's always been there, hasn't it?"

"Yes, but the Hogans haven't."

"We think they're working for someone else," Mitch said. "It could only be a matter of time before they figure out how to use the disk or pass it on to whoever hired them, and then it will be too late."

Evan still hesitated.

"What about people who have to work on Sunday?" Mitch asked.

"Please," Cameron said, placing a hand on Evan's arm.

He sighed. "Send me the names and photos and I'll make some calls."

"Thank you."

"But, Cameron, I am worried about you."

"Don't worry, I have Mitch," she said, looking at him. "He's already saved my life twice."

"The second time was debatable," Mitch said.

"It's not just that, Cameron. Look, I know you've always been driven and determined, but I don't want this quest to consume you. Cameron, you're never going to find fulfilment and satisfaction from a temporal source. The only place you'll ever be fulfilled is in Jesus."

Cameron nodded but said nothing.

"I'll make some calls and let you know if I find anything."

"Thank you."

"It was good to see you again, Cameron. Be careful."

"You too, Evan. I will be."

"Mitch," he said with another handshake.

"Evan."

He turned and walked back the way they had come, and Mitch and Cameron stood by the railing for a moment. "What do you make of that?" Cameron asked, looking out toward a high-rising causeway over the river.

"Of what specifically?"

"Not finding fulfillment or satisfaction in something 'temporal.'"

He shrugged. "I guess it depends. I knew guys whose work defined them. If they succeeded, they were fulfilled. If they failed, they weren't. I knew other guys who always seemed unsatisfied, always wanting more. Other people seem content with three squares and a place to lay their head at night."

"What about you?" she asked. "Are you fulfilled?"

"I guess. Whatever that means." He shrugged. "I worked hard but it was what I did, not who I was. Now I'm hanging out in Florida with you, eating PB and Oreo ice cream, the breeze on my skin and the salt air on my tongue. Yeah, I'm satisfied with life."

"I didn't take you for a poet."

He shrugged again. "What about you?"

"I don't know."

Mitch turned and leaned against the railing, peering up at the cross, its arms hardly visible from this angle and close proximity. It looked like a big pole. He turned back to Cameron. "So, you think he'll come through for you?"

"If he can."

"If his contacts work Sundays, you mean?"

She snickered.

"Sorry, I don't mean to pick on him. But I have to say, I have trouble seeing you with him."

"I wasn't really with him. We went out a few times. I don't think he was such a Ten Commandments stickler back then." She wrinkled her nose. "Isn't not working on Sunday one of the Ten Commandments?"

"I couldn't tell you."

"I didn't think anybody did that anymore. I thought that was kind of an Amish thing."

He shrugged. "I always had to work Sundays."

"I suppose, people need security twenty-four/seven."

He nodded.

"What'd you do before that, anyhow?"

"I played football."

She raised an eyebrow. "Like, pro football?"

Mitch nodded.

"Like NFL football?"

"Uh-huh."

She whacked his arm. "How come you didn't say anything?"

"It's not something I brag about."

"Why not?"

"Mostly because it sounds like bragging."

"Who did you play for?"

"Three years with the Raiders, one with the Bears, and a cup of coffee in the pre-season with the Patriots."

"You played with Tom Brady?"

"Put your tongue back in your mouth. He puts his pants on one leg at a time like everybody else."

"I don't believe it. What position did you play, linebacker? You look like a linebacker."

"H-back."

"What's that?"

"Fullback slash tight end slash wherever they wanted to stick me. Lot of special teams."

"I can't believe it."

He shrugged.

"So that explains being retired at thirty-three."

"Sort of. I was a seventh-round pick, and I knew right away I wouldn't make millions upon millions. So I didn't live like a millionaire. I saved most of it, invested well, and then found a gig with a good-paying security firm. I studied business at UT, saw an opportunity to form my own firm, and it took off."

"You are full of mystery."

"So now what?"

"I plan to at least stay the night in town. And since we can't do much of anything more until we hear back from Evan, I'd like to drop my stuff somewhere, find a hotel pool, and go for a swim."

"Yeah?"

"Helps me relax. And cool off," she said, squinting against the sun.

Mitch looked at Cameron for just a moment, picturing her in a swimsuit, and nodded. "Sounds like a plan to me."

CHAPTER ELEVEN

The pool at the Holiday Inn was nothing special, but it was long enough for Cameron to swim some laps. The exercise was good for her body and her brain, both of which were feeling the stress of the last twenty-four hours. The sky above was still mostly blue, but an occasional cloud cast the entire pool and surrounding deck in shadow. The rest of the time, the hotel itself shaded half the edge of the pool and the south side of the deck, where Mitch lounged on a lawn chair.

Cameron could feel his eyes on her as she swam. Not in the creepy way she'd been ogled before, but the same way she imagined she would appreciate his former H-back's physique if he were in the pool instead of hiding behind a magazine he'd picked up in the lobby.

She turned and stroked to the other end of the pool, replaying her conversation with Evan. He'd changed since she'd known him, and not just by growing out his hair. He'd been a fun-loving, devil-may-care sort of a guy, the reason she'd been drawn to him while he'd done some investigative work for her. Now he objected to working Sundays and was worried about whether or not she was fulfilled.

She turned again, this time swimming over to the edge of the pool, where a plastic bottle of water sat half empty. She took a swig, then hung her arms over the edge and looked at Mitch. "What are you reading, anyhow?" she asked.

"Not much," he said, putting down an issue of *Sports Illustrated*. He reached for a bottle of Coors.

"Did you ever win a championship when you played football?"

"National champs my freshman year at Texas."

"Really?"

"I was a second-string upback on the punt team, so I didn't play much. Didn't even travel to some road games, but I was part of the team and in uniform the night we beat USC in the Rose Bowl. Greatest night of my life." He took a second drink. "Why?"

"What about in the pros?"

He grinned. "I told you, I played for the Raiders and Bears."

"And the Patriots."

"I was cut after a couple of pre-season games. Never even made the playoffs in the NFL."

She nodded. "Was your career unfulfilling?"

He shook his head. "No. Would I have liked a Super Bowl ring, sure? But I was living my dream."

Cameron floated back away from the edge of the pool.

"You thinking about what Evan said?" Mitch asked.

"A little. And I feel like you just said. I don't think finding the Fountain of Youth or anything else I've looked for will make or break me. It would be like winning the Super Bowl. It's really important to me, but am I incomplete without it . . . ? No. The quest, the hunt—it fuels me. I'm living the dream too."

Mitch sat up. "I've never been the religious type. I guess if Jesus or faith or something brings Evan fulfillment, brings him something he's lacking, then good for him. But if you're happy without religion, if you're a decent person without it, then what's the point?"

Cameron ducked under the water, then lifted her head. She wrung out her hair. "What time is it?"

Mitch retrieved his phone from the table beside him. "Little after three-thirty."

"I'm going to swim a few more laps. Then how do you feel about an early dinner?"

"We did skip lunch."

She rolled over and began stroking toward the far end of the pool. *And what about after dinner?* she asked herself. How long could they draw out hanging around together? Sooner or later, they would have to call this quits and head their separate ways. That, or admit they weren't together for the purpose of finding the Fountain of Youth. And she wasn't quite sure she was ready for that.

79

And why not, Cameron? How long has it been since you even went on a date, much less were with someone?

She turned around.

Is the issue that you just met Mitch or that it's been so long you're not sure you're ready to entertain romantic possibilities? Then again, who said anything about romance?

"Cameron!"

She finished her stroke and stopped, turning toward Mitch's voice to her right. He held up her cell phone, which she'd left with a towel on a spare chair. She swam to the edge of the pool, and he met her there with the phone and a towel. She quickly wiped her face, then leaned on the towel on the edge of the pool and swiped her phone. "Cameron Leigh."

"Cameron, it's Evan."

She looked up at Mitch. "Did you find something?"

"Yeah, I did."

"Okay. Can I call you back in a few minutes? I want to get someplace where Mitch and I can both talk."

"Sure. I'll be right here."

"Thanks, Evan."

She ended the call and handed the phone back to Mitch, explaining her plan. He reached a hand to her and hoisted her up out of the pool. She stood dripping like a rain shower while he grabbed her another towel. She dried off briefly, then wrapped one towel around her waist and continued to blot her arms and hair with the other while she followed Mitch inside. In a few minutes, they were in the single room they'd reserved for the time being, with plans to get another if they ended up spending the night in St. Augustine. Cameron shivered against the air conditioning, and quickly dug through her suitcase to find a pair of sweats and a T-shirt to put on over her swimsuit. She looked at Mitch, who nodded as he dropped into a chair by the window. She dialed Evan's number, tapped to put it on speaker, then set the phone on the corner of the bed.

"Hey, Cameron."

"Hey, Evan, thanks for waiting. I'm here with Mitch."

"Hey, Mitch."

"Hey, Evan," he said with a wink at Cameron.

"What'd you find?" she asked.

80

"I have a friend who works for the visitors bureau, and in such a capacity, he has relationships with a lot of hotel and bed and breakfast owners. He owed me a favor, and so I asked him to circulate the photos you sent me to some of his more discreet contacts he has at hotels near the fort. I figured you were interested in the fort."

"We are."

"He got a hit."

Cameron and Mitch met each other's gaze.

"They didn't use the names you gave, but the clerk at the Casa Monica recognized two of the faces. According to her, they are part of a contingent of four staying in the Flagler Suite at the Casa Monica under the name Harrison Van Buren."

"You're sure it's them?"

"I spoke to the clerk myself. She identified the larger man and the woman with red hair."

"The Hogans," Cameron said.

"She said he gave an ID of Scott Holmes."

"Same initials," Mitch said.

"But the suite is under this Van Buren guy's name?" Cameron asked.

"Yes," Evan said.

"The Flagler Suite at the Casa Monica?"

"Right. Through tomorrow night."

"Did she say anything else?"

"I didn't ask much else."

"Thanks, Evan."

"Cameron, what are you going to do?"

"I don't know."

"You should contact the police. In fact, I should. If not, I'm withholding information."

"Do an old friend one more favor, please? I promise, I'll contact the police. Just please let me handle this. I have a better chance of getting the disk back I think if this comes from me."

He paused.

"Please."

"You promise you'll contact them? It would be borderline criminal not to."

"I promise."

"Okay."

"Thank you, Evan. I owe you one."

"No you don't. Just take care of yourself, Cameron. You too, Mitch."

"Will do, bud. Thanks."

"Goodbye, Evan," Cameron said, then ended the call.

Mitch slapped his thigh. "So that's that," he said. "We call the police."

Cameron winced. "Only thing is, I didn't say *when* I'd call them."

*   *   *

Mitch and Cameron sat in opposite sides of a booth at a Denny's inside a Days Inn, within walking distance of their hotel. It was a little after four-thirty, meaning a good six hours after brunch, and despite the ice cream earlier, Mitch was having no trouble attacking a stack of pancakes that were part of his All-American Slam. Cameron had ordered a salad, and done little more than pick at its contents. It was one thing to know where the "Hogan Gang" was hunkered down; it was quite another to know what to do about it.

"How are the first couple bites?" the waitress asked. She was plump and cheery, and with hardly any other diners, prone to hovering. But when Mitch assured her everything was delicious, she left them alone and they were able to talk freely.

"Okay, we have three problems as I see it," he said as he reached for more syrup.

Cameron looked up from a piece of grilled chicken she'd been toying with. "Which are?"

"First, we should be going to the cops. A crime was committed—several in fact—and they're already on the case. Plus, this is their specialty. It's not ours."

"Isn't this what you did for a living?"

He raised an eyebrow at her. "Not even close."

She sighed.

"Two, these guys are dangerous. Erik was right about that, and I don't want anything to happen to you either. Or to me for that matter," he said with a grin. She didn't return it.

He cut into his pancakes, dabbed them in syrup, and took a bite.

"What's three?"

"Three is the fact that even if we got rid of one and two, we have no idea how to get the disk back. We know next to nothing about these guys—how secure they are in the suite, how well they're armed, what they're willing to do for the disk. We'd be going in blind."

Cameron sighed, dropped her fork, and reached for her ice water.

"And that's not even mentioning the trouble we could get in."

"Trouble?"

"You're talking about committing a crime."

"You can't steal something from somebody if it isn't theirs," she countered.

"Depends on the D.A., but suppose I give you that one. We're still stuck on the other three."

"We're not stuck on two. I know this can be dangerous, but so is life. So is playing in the NFL. You could get paralyzed or get CTE. Or scuba diving— You know how many things can go wrong underwater? Life's dangerous. I'm willing to take a risk for something important. And you are too, or you wouldn't have darted into gunfire to save me yesterday."

"There's a difference between running into a burning building to save somebody and running into a burning building *with* somebody."

"To save something else."

"Without a plan for how to save it?"

"We'll figure that out."

"Still, why not call the cops?" he said before taking another bite.

"It's like you said before, this isn't priority one for them. Erik agreed. Plus, if they get involved and make a recovery, the press gets involved. And while they process the disk as evidence, the discovery of the *Descubridor* and the existence of the disk become public knowledge. And it's not like every treasure hunter in the country will descend upon us, but it will draw out the kooks and the amateur detectives who want to find the Fountain of Youth or a pot of gold at the end of a rainbow or whatever they dream up. And the other thing we have to consider is what Erik said about outside influence. What if the Hogans or this Van Buren guy—whoever he is—have a mole or have their hooks into the local police or the D.A. or somebody higher up the food chain? Not only might we not get the disk after all, but we might put ourselves in greater jeopardy. Right now, they think we're out of it."

She finally took a bite, and Mitch sat back with his water in hand as he considered her little speech. Truth be told, he'd been pondering some of those same points. While Cameron had showered after her swim, he'd called up a former colleague of his and asked him to look up Harrison Van Buren. Turned out there were thirty-seven of them in the U.S. alone, three who lived in Florida, and another eleven in the Southeast. None had, at least upon a quick and dirty search, any connection to the Hogans or their criminal associates or obvious ties to a search for the Fountain of Youth. The closest was a thirty-four-year-old man from Raleigh, North Carolina, who had written a book about the "golden age" of Caribbean piracy.

Mitch had also spoken to another contact from his days in the security world, a hacker who had been able to provide him with specs of the Casa Monica Resort & Spa, including the multi-story Flagler Suite. But specs were a long way from a retrieval mission, even if Cameron were able to persuade him to stage one.

"What do you think?" she asked, dabbing her mouth with a napkin.

"I think you make a good case."

A smile teased at the corner of her mouth.

He wiped it away. "Or as good of a case as can be made. But we still don't have a plan for how to get the disk."

"What are our options?"

He sighed.

"Please, Mitch. I know I'm asking a lot of a stranger, but you've got to understand, I've dedicated years of my life to this quest. If we can't figure out a way, if we have to call the police and let the chips fall where they may, okay. But if there is another way . . ."

The waitress returned, just checking in and refilling drinks. While she poured, Cameron continued to stare at Mitch demurely, not quite batting her eyelashes, but close. He was not the dumb jock who would jump off a building if a pretty girl asked him to, but neither was he totally impervious to the coaxing of a good-looking woman.

The waitress left, and Mitch leaned forward. "There are several ways we could go about it."

Cameron smiled.

"*Could* go about it."

"I'm listening."

"None of them are good."

"What are they?"

"Smash and grab. Knock on the door and kick it in when they open it. Likely as not gets one of us shot, or both."

"Okay, scratch that."

"There's the *Mission: Impossible* route, grappling hooks from the neighboring building, zipline down to their balcony, cut our way through the glass. Looks great in the movies, but not really practical."

"What else?"

"Old-school *Mission: Impossible*."

"Old-school?"

"The TV show."

"There was a TV show?"

"Way back in the day."

"How old are you again?"

"My grandpa loved it, was always watching reruns when I was at his house. It drew me in."

"That's cute."

"Whatever. Old-school IMF was less zipline and more disappearing ink and disguises, but I still don't see how that would work. Unless . . ."

"What?"

He hesitated, considering something.

"Come on, Mitch."

"I'm thinking."

She waited patiently for a few seconds, then started tapping her fork on her napkin.

"Okay, okay," Mitch said. "Look, I can think of three legit ways we could *maybe* make this happen."

"I'm listening."

"We get them to leave the room without the disk, then we sneak in and get it. We incapacitate them in the room somehow, then we go in and get it. Or, we get them to bring the disk out."

"How do we do that?"

"You said you worked a lot of jobs. Ever in the hospitality business?"

"I worked one summer as a clerk at a Hampton Inn."

"So you're familiar with check-in and check-out procedures, creating keycards, that sort of a thing?"

"In general, yeah. Why?"

"They know your face, but not mine—not likely, not with me wearing a cap and sunglasses. And I could shave," he said, rubbing his chin.

"That'd be a shame."

He looked at her, and she winked.

Mitch looked away, out at the pavement baking in the hot Florida sun. A little more than twenty-four hours ago, he'd been soaking up the sun while riding the waves—literally and figuratively, just hanging out without a care in the world. Now he was seriously contemplating a heist with a woman he'd just met. Speaking of that woman, her winks and grins and sideways glances were as disconcerting as they were appealing, similar to how the aspects of his rapidly forming plan waved red flags while simultaneously falling into place.

"Look," he said, "don't get your hopes up."

Her smile widened.

"I said don't get your hopes up. I still need to verify a couple things, and we're going to need some lucky breaks."

She nodded.

"And even then, it's kind of a long shot." He shook his head. "I can't believe I'm even considering this."

Her smile burst forth like sunlight after a thunderstorm.

"Quit smiling and finish your salad," he said, stabbing his fork into his pancakes. "We've got a lot of work to do."

CHAPTER TWELVE

Darkness had fallen over Florida's "First Coast," a little earlier than expected thanks to a bank of storm clouds that had rolled in. They'd blocked out the sunset and created a canopy of moisture that had, as of yet, remained overhead. Rumbles of thunder and an almost perceptible electricity in the air hinted that it wouldn't remain dry for long.

Speaking of electricity, Cameron's heart was practically tachycardic as she and Mitch entered the lobby of the Casa Monica Resort & Spa, just across the street from Flagler College on St. Augustine's main drag. The good news was the lobby was nearly empty, but for a clerk at the front desk and a couple people at the bar off to the right. The bad news was that the emptiness—along with the Moroccan-themed décor and Moorish arches and the soft, string music—created a sense of intrigue and suspense that did nothing to calm her nerves at what lay ahead.

If Mitch shared her anxiety at his hastily concocted plan, he didn't let on. He had shaved off his beard, leaving something between a goatee and a Fu Manchu. He wore blue jeans with a new pair of boots, and his slow, lanky pace was as much a result of adjusting to them as for effect. The white dress shirt was his own; the sport jacket he wore over it and the gold chain he wore under it had been purchased at a thrift store two minutes before closing. So had been the cowboy hat that was nearly big enough to function as an umbrella if the rain started falling.

Cameron clung to his arm as they walked, which was difficult in four-inch heels. They had been a bargain buy at a strip-mall shoe store, and luckily matched a mini skirt far shorter than anything Cameron would normally wear. A yellow off-the-shoulder blouse revealed plenty of her shoulders and neck, and her low, loose chignon made ample room for faux diamond earrings to dangle off her ears. She was the tacky, flirty, slightly ditzy blonde, a stereotype that was somewhat offensive to her but served a purpose, especially since the clerk behind the curved, marble-topped front desk turned out to be a young man—and thus not the clerk Evan had spoken to. Lucky break number one.

"Can I help you?" he asked, tearing his eyes away from Cameron's neckline to look at Mitch.

"Cade Barnett," Mitch boomed in a subtle but unmistakable Texas accent. "I've got a reservation in the Flagler Suite."

The clerk's eyes narrowed slightly. "The Flagler Suite, sir?"

"That's right. And should be a bottle of champagne on ice. We're celebrating," he said, turning down to Cameron with a wink.

She flashed a coquettish smile in return.

"I'm sorry, sir," the clerk said, "but that suite is occupied already."

"You must be mistaken."

"No, sir. I checked a group into that suite last night."

Mitch squinted at the man's nametag. "Nick, is it?"

"Yes, sir."

"Check your computer, please. I made this reservation months ago, and we have been looking forward to this night," he said. He gave Cameron a squeeze.

"Well, this is odd," Nick said as Mitch leaned in. "Oh dear. It appears we have a double booking."

"So you do see our reservation?"

"Yes, sir. One night in the Flagler Suite."

"There you go," Mitch said, tapping the edge of his wallet on the counter.

"But I'm sorry, Mr. Barnett. Like I said, that suite is already occupied. We'd be more than happy to put you in one of our other suites for the evening, complimentarily, of course."

"I appreciate that, but I'm afraid we must insist on the Flagler Suite. We have," he paused to look at Cameron, "history there."

She wiggled on his arm. She had no idea what she was doing.

"I'm sorry, sir, I really am."

"Can't you offer these other folks one of your other suites?"

"Well, they've already checked in."

Cameron slumped her shoulders. "Ca-ade," she whined.

"When did this other group make their reservation?" Mitch asked.

Nick consulted his computer screen. "Uh, just yesterday evening, in fact. I'm not sure—"

"Well, there you go," Mitch said again. "We've had ours booked for weeks. We should have priority."

Nick pursed his lips.

"I really don't mean to cause trouble," Mitch said. "If this were any other situation, I'd take another room and wave your complimentary offer. Things happen. But we flew in from Amarillo this afternoon, we're leaving on a two-week Caribbean cruise tomorrow, and we just had our hearts set on the Flagler Suite, for old times' sake."

"I understand, sir," Nick said. "Let me contact my manager."

"I appreciate that."

On cue, Cameron bounced on Mitch's arm, like an impatient toddler. He reached into his wallet and extracted a twenty-dollar bill. "Here, Sugar, why don't you go get yourself a drink. I'll take care of this."

Cameron snagged the bill between two fingers, reached up to peck his cheek, then turned and sashayed toward the bar. She looked over her shoulder once, ready to blow Mitch a kiss or send him her sultriest look if Nick was watching. He was not, however, his head studying his computer screens while tipped to the side to hold a phone on his shoulder. So she quickened her pace down the hallway to the ladies' room. Once inside, she peeked under the stall doors to confirm she was alone and let out a huge breath.

Mitch's buddy from his time as a security guy had come through for them. After downloading detailed floor plans of the Flagler Suite and the rest of the Casa Monica, he had hacked into the resort's reservation system to identify not only the reservation under Van Buren, but any other rooms and suites. Then he had created a second reservation for Mitch's alias, Cade Barnett, pre-dating it to six weeks ago. That had gotten them in the door, but they were a long way from home.

Cameron went to work. Practically kicking off her shoes, she swung her large, thrift-store purse off her shoulder and pulled from it a blue blazer that had survived with minimal wrinkles. It fit over her yellow top, and she had no trouble pulling a pair of matching slacks over her mini-skirt. She stepped back into the heels, did her best to straighten out a few wrinkles, and then removed the chignon and bound her hair in a tight, no frills ponytail. A pair of cheap cosmetic glasses completed the transformation. She wedged the purse into the trash bin, and less than five minutes after entering the restroom, emerged as her third personality of the day.

Now it was up to Mitch.

*   *   *

Mitch's freshman year in college, he and a couple of buddies had bought some cheap fake IDs and made a beer run at a local grocery store. He'd learned two things that night. One, there was a direct correlation between guys who couldn't hold their liquor and guys who couldn't keep their cool under pressure. Two, the secret to a good con was owning it. If you believed it, they'd believe it.

Oh, and three, don't buy ten-dollar fake IDs.

Mitch's phone buzzed, and he looked down to see a one-word message from Cameron:

Out

He returned his phone to his pocket and looked at Nick, who was furiously doing something on a keyboard while waiting for his manager. She arrived a minute later, and Mitch nearly did a double take. She wore a navy blue blazer over a yellow blouse, and her blond hair was fastened behind her head. She was older than Cameron, and the facial resemblance wasn't that strong, but at a quick glance—say from someone at the bar—Cameron could pass as her. Maybe it wouldn't matter, but if it did, this was another stroke of luck.

"Mr. Barnett," she said in a silky smooth voice, "I'm Rachelle, the manager. Let me start by apologizing for the inconvenience. I'm not sure how the system accepted duplicate bookings, but clearly it did. Believe me, I understand the frustration something like this can cause, but I'm sure you also understand the frustration to the current occupants of the Flagler Suite if we were to force them to switch suites. Is there anything we at Casa Monica Resort & Spa can do to make another suite accommodating for you? Complimentary spa vouchers, a free stay at any of our other properties?"

"Rachelle," he said, working up the Texan accent again, "I do appreciate the situation. And it's like I told Nick here, I wouldn't put up any sort of a stink about this, except that the Flagler Suite holds a special place in our hearts. I'm not a nostalgic man, so to speak, but my little lady is. I surprised her with a stay here on the drive from the airport, and it would break her heart to take it away now. And given that we did make our reservation first, I'm afraid I must insist as respectfully as possible that it be granted."

Rachelle nodded with a forced smile. "I understand. Naturally, it will take a little time for us to manage the transition."

"Of course." He stepped to the side and retrieved his phone again, then pretended to scroll through e-mails or texts or social media while eavesdropping on Rachelle's call to the occupants of the Flagler Suite. She explained the situation a couple of times, apologized profusely, comped their second night in the St. Francis Suite, and practically gave away ownership in the hotel as means of appeasement. She concluded by promising to send up a bellhop in a few minutes, once they had time to pack.

Mitch pecked out a one-line text to Cameron, but didn't press send yet. Instead, he caught Rachelle's attention with a nod. "I think I'll step out and get some air for a few minutes," he said.

"Give us about half an hour to turn over the suite," Rachelle said. "We can text you when it's ready."

"Appreciate it," he said, giving her his cell number. He then turned and headed for the front door, pressing send on his text as he did.

*   *   *

Cameron forced herself to breathe normally as she sat in a chair by a fountain at the far end of the lobby, obscured from view of the front desk by a trio of arches, high-backed furniture on the other side of the fountain, and the fountain itself. The bubbling water and soft background music drowned out even Mitch's booming Texan voice, so she was sure it would do the same for hers when the time came.

Her phone buzzed, and she glanced down at the message:

Call 1 minute

She counted out sixty seconds in her head, then pressed dial on the number already entered into her phone.

"Casa Monica Resort & Spa, this is Rachelle. How may I help you?"

After practically running down hallways, up stairs, through the pool area, and back down stairs to get into position, Cameron was still breathing heavily. Maybe that would help her disguise her voice. She did her very best to sound like a stone-faced redhead. "This is Lora Holmes in the Flagler Suite. There's no need to send a bellhop or prepare another suite. We'll be checking out."

"Are you sure, Mrs. Holmes?"

"Yes."

"Is there anything we can do to persuade you to stay in one of our other suites?"

"No, there's not. My husband will be down when we're through packing to check out."

"I understand. If there's anything we can do—"

"You've done enough," Cameron said, feeling rotten for her snippiness. She disconnected the call without another word, then texted Mitch:

call complete ur clear

She sat back and took more deep breaths. Maybe they should have gone for the *Mission: Impossible*-style zipline after all.

*   *   *

It was not yet raining, but had to be on the verge of doing so. The air was charged, and the thunder was almost constant. The fronds on palm trees across Cordova Street were oddly still. No breeze stirred the languid air. Growing up and living in Tornado Alley, Mitch was more than accustomed to storms, and anything short of a full-blown supercell didn't even give him pause. Especially tonight, when he had bigger things on his mind.

He turned and walked north, to King Street, and then walked east. He passed a side entrance to the resort and another leading to the James Coleman Gallery. A flash of lightning lit up the white exterior of the building, then a clap of thunder echoed off its walls. Mitch turned onto a cobblestone driveway that led under the resort to a valet station and then to the parking lot behind the building. As had been the case a short while ago, when he had dropped off the Porsche, a single valet manned the small marble-topped desk just off the entrance to the hotel. There was no one else in sight.

Mitch presented a claim slip to the valet, who reached for a walkie-talkie on the desk. He squawked it once, then gave the vehicle type and plate number. He was greeted with silence. He squawked it again. "Jimmy, you there?"

Nothing but dead air greeted him, and Mitch looked up casually.

The valet sighed and looked around. "Give me a minute, I'll go get it. Storm's probably messing with the signal."

Mitch nodded and smiled, and then waited until the valet had rounded the corner before deactivating the "homemade" UHF/VHF jamming app on his phone, a holdover from his previous line of work. He looked up as the doors to the hotel lobby opened and Cameron stepped out, looking not unlike Rachelle in her blue pantsuit.

"Clear?" she asked.

"Go for it."

She ducked behind the valet desk, and Mitch looked up at a security camera. He smiled.

"Okay, looks like I can scan a card from here," she said.

"Good. Always nice when Plan A works."

It took her less than a minute to make a pair of "skeleton keys" that would provide access to any room in the hotel, including the vacant—they knew from Mitch's buddy—Alcazar Meeting Room on the second floor. By the time the valet returned with the Porsche, Cameron was standing beside Mitch, their arms around each other, keycards pocketed.

"Ready?" Mitch asked.

"Yep."

Mitch provided the valet a ten-dollar tip, and he and Cameron got into the car. Intermittent raindrops pelted the windshield as he turned east on the one-way King Street, and intensified by the time he had rounded the block and parked facing east just before the entrance to the valet tunnel. He quickly removed his cowboy hat and jacket, and he and Cameron got out and hurried down the sidewalk and into the side entrance of the hotel. They walked past Café Cordova to the bank of elevators just off the lobby. He gave Cameron a wink as she opted for the stairs. Then he grabbed a rolling luggage cart and entered the elevator.

He forced himself to take deep, calming breaths as he checked his appearance in the mirror. It was all in the presentation, he reminded himself. *If you believe it, they'll believe it.*

He exited the elevator and rolled the cart to the entrance to the bi-level Flagler Suite. With one more deep breath, he rapped his knuckles on the door. When it opened, Mitch found himself looking at a marble statue—cold, white, but beautiful. The bright red hair stood in stark contrast to the face, as did green eyes that narrowed as they looked at him. "Yes?"

Mitch flashed a smile. "Ma'am, I'm Karl, the assistant manager here at Casa Monica. I wanted to apologize again for the inconvenience and personally offer my assistance."

"We can actually manage fine on our own."

"I'm afraid there's been a slight snag," he said.

Her entire body participated in a sigh. "What?"

"Given the unusual timing of this, uh, transition," he said with a forced smile, "we're a little short on our housekeeping staff. We can offer you a secure room in which to store your things while we have the St. Francis Suite finalized for you, and in the mean—Hello," he said as a man appeared behind the redhead. Seamus. "I was just telling your wife that we can store your luggage for you while your suite is finished, and in the meantime, we'd like to offer you a private waiting room and complimentary drinks, as an apology."

"Yeah, sure, whatever." He looked Mitch up and down. "You're the manager?"

"Karl," he said. "Assistant manager."

"Isn't this a little below your pay grade?" the man asked, looking at the luggage cart.

"Nothing's below my pay grade, sir."

Seamus nodded.

"Do you need any help?"

"No, we've got it." He reached for the cart and wheeled it into the suite. The redhead—Lora—closed the door and Mitch waited, hoping they weren't onto him. He hadn't noted suspicion or recognition in their eyes, but that wasn't a guarantee they hadn't figured out who he was.

Two minutes passed before the door opened again. This time it was a man matching the photo of Dax Wilder who backed the luggage cart out. Mitch did his best to ignore the suitcases and bags on it, wondering which of them contained the cipher disk. Instead, he motioned for Dax and presumably Kevin Stuart to follow him with the cart while the Hogans brought up the rear. He led them to an elevator and pushed the button for the second floor. He kept a smile plastered to his face and mixed repeated apologies with small talk as he led them to the Alcazar Meeting Room, which he unlocked with the skeleton keycard Cameron had made.

"Your luggage will be secure here until your suite is ready," he said. "Follow me, and I'll set you up with some drinks and snacks."

Utilizing a back staircase, he took them back toward the lobby but avoided the front desk by cutting through the Cobalt Lounge to a separate room with soft lighting, eclectic paintings adorning the walls, and a couple clusters of seating options. "Please, make yourselves comfortable," Mitch said.

"It shouldn't be too much longer. In the meantime, can I get you something to drink?"

*   *   *

Cameron navigated the hallways to the south stairwell and climbed to a landing halfway between the second and third floors. Ensuring that she was out of sight of anyone entering the stairwell from the second floor, she waited. The minutes dragged on, and she did her best to calculate how long it would take Mitch to get to the Flagler Suite, then come down to the Alcazar Meeting Room. She realized she had no idea because she had no idea if the Hogan Gang would be ready right away or not. But as the minutes ticked down, her brain envisioned all sorts of disaster scenarios. The fact that their plan was on track so far was borderline miraculous, so it was bound to come off the rails somewhere. To take her mind off the possibilities, she thought about the cipher disk and the reason she was doing all this. She hoped in the end it would be worth it.

She heard a door open and tensed. She heard footsteps, along with Mitch's voice—now void of any Texas accent—explaining something about a shortcut and apologizing for the rigmarole. She waited until she heard the footsteps fade and a door clang shut. Then she hurried down half a flight of stairs and exited onto the second floor. She saw no one as she walked briskly to the Alcazar Meeting Room and let herself in.

The luggage cart was sitting there, packed full, and she had to harness an urge to ransack its contents. Instead, she made a quick, methodical search of two suitcases, four duffel bags of various size, a garment bag, an unlocked suitcase, and a couple small traveling bags.

There was no disk.

She checked them all again. Nothing. A second briefcase was locked, but it was too small to contain the disk, she thought, and definitely too light.

So where was it?

CHAPTER THIRTEEN

Mitch paid cash for a Jack Daniels, a Grey Goose martini, a bee's knees, and some pitas and hummus. He was on his way back to the seating area with a tray—the bartender hadn't objected when Mitch had asked to carry everything to "his friends" himself—when his phone buzzed. He set the tray down and pulled out the phone.

"Hello?"

"Mitch? It's not here."

He kept his voice calm, knowing the Hogans were just around the corner. "How's that?"

"I searched the luggage twice. It's not here."

He took a breath. It had to be there. There was no way they had left it in the room. Could they have already passed it to Van Buren or a middleman? Had they left it in their vehicle? Was all this for naught?

He closed his eyes, picturing the group. No backpacks, no valises or briefcases. Lora Hogan. Had she been carrying a purse?

"Mitch?"

Yes. A big one. Big enough to hide a disk? It was close.

"Okay," he said, quickly forming a plan. "Go back to the bathroom," he whispered, turning his body away from the doorway to the seating area.

"What?"

"Make sure nobody's in there, and wait for Lora."

"Lora. Why? What if somebody is in there?"

"I'll follow her in."

"Why, what's going on?"

"No time to explain. Just get there pronto."

"Okay."

"I'll see you soon," he said a little louder. He ended the call and picked up the tray again. He'd never liked it when his quarterback called an audible, suddenly changing the play at the line of scrimmage. He preferred carrying out a well-formed plan as originally designed. But sometimes the defense showed blitz and the quarterback had to adjust.

He turned into the separate seating area. He handed out the drinks, then set the hummus and pitas on an ottoman between the four thieves. He withdrew the tray. "Is there anything else I can g—"

He had purposefully given Lora her drink first, then faced away from her to pass out the other drinks and set down the hummus, and as he withdrew the tray, he "accidentally" swung it into her drink. His accident hadn't been perfect, and didn't knock the drink out of her hand. But it did cause her to jerk her hand out of the way reflexively, in the process sloshing gin and lemon juice onto her bare knees and the bottom of Bermuda shorts.

Lora swore in frustration as she set her glass down.

"I am so sorry," Mitch said. "Oh my, I'm sorry. Here, here, there's a restroom just down the hall," he said, hoping talking quickly and starting toward the bathroom would lead her to follow him. "I'll show you."

She sighed in frustration, but grabbed her purse and stood. Mitch hadn't paid attention before, but as she lifted the purse, it appeared to be extra heavy. He'd known women who carried everything but the kitchen sink in their purses, but had never seen a woman's forearm strain as she lifted hers, and Lora's forearms were plenty toned.

"I'm really very sorry," he said over his shoulder, hoping Cameron had indeed double-timed it to the restroom. He walked slowly, and turned back again. "You can skip the TripAdvisor review," he said with a fake chuckle. Lora didn't seem amused.

At the entrance to the ladies' room, Mitch stepped out of the way. "I'm very sorry again," he said.

"Forget it," Lora said as she and her purse pushed through the door.

*   *   *

Cameron was out of breath as she ducked into the ladies' room for the second time that night. As had been the case fifteen minutes earlier, it was empty.

Okay, now what, Mitch? How are you getting Lora to come in here? And why?

She didn't have long to ponder. The door began to open, and she quickly turned toward the sink so Lora wouldn't recognize her. She had no idea what to do next, so she washed her hands. No sooner had she turned the water on than she sensed a person beside her. She kept her head down, taking a sideways glance at green Bermuda shorts and white legs.

"Ugh," Lora said, then reached for a paper towel. She stopped.

Cameron couldn't help but raise her head.

Lora turned toward her. Their eyes met in the mirror, and Lora's began to narrow. She opened her mouth, but before she could say anything, her eyes went wide. Then a muscular arm wrapped around her neck, jerking her back and off her feet. Her scream was caught in her throat, but Cameron had to keep from shrieking herself as her brain tried to keep pace with her eyes.

Mitch held Lora tightly, her chin in the crook of his elbow as he applied pressure. Lora kicked at his shins, and tried to elbow him in the stomach, but was no match for him physically. In seconds, she had gone limp. After several more seconds, Mitch released his hold and laid her down gently on the floor.

"Get against the door," he said. "Don't let anyone in."

Cameron moved on autopilot, turning her back against the door. Mitch had already slipped Lora's purse off her shoulder. Squatted down beside her, he opened it and tugged out a circular object wrapped in a bath towel. He peeked briefly and nodded.

"How do we get it out of here?" Cameron asked.

"Your purse. What'd you do with it?"

"In the trash can there."

"Get it out."

She did, and opened it so he could insert the disk and bath towel inside. It barely fit.

"Can you manage?" he asked.

"Yeah."

He turned and picked up Lora, dragging her to the nearest stall. He propped her up on the toilet and closed the door. Then he nodded at the bathroom door.

"Peek your head out. If it's clear, turn right and keep walking. I'll be right behind you."

Cameron nodded and did as he said. The hall was empty, and she turned toward the Costa Brava restaurant. She merely smiled as they passed a hostess, and shrugged the heavy purse higher on her shoulder. They emerged under a canopy to the sidewalk along Cordova Street, greeted by the hiss of steady rain on the pavement.

Mitch slipped out from behind her. "Let's go."

She followed behind him, trying to ignore the fear that Seamus, Dax, or Kevin—or the hotel staff—would give chase at any moment. She focused on speed walking in high heels on wet pavement while carrying a twenty-pound purse. A crack of thunder rattled the windows of the hotel and set off a car alarm as they turned the corner, but by now the Porsche was in sight. They jogged the last few steps, by which time Mitch had beeped the doors open. Cameron banged her purse on the frame of the car as she got in, and muttered a quiet curse as she reached for the door. She took a look behind her, getting rewarded with a blast of wind and rain. But she saw no pursuers.

Mitch fired up the engine, waiting for a single car to pass, and eased onto the street. He turned left at St George Street, then left again onto Cathedral Place. He turned right at the next intersection to avoid going back past the Casa Monica, and ended up circling Flagler College to get onto westbound King Street, which took them across the San Sebastian River. Cameron sighed with relief when yet another look over her shoulder revealed no one giving chase on the rain-slicked streets.

"I don't believe it," she said, exhaling. "We did it. That actually worked."

"I'm going to start calling you Cinnamon."

"What?"

"*Mission: Impossible*," he said, waving her off. They idled at a stoplight, the wipers on the Porsche struggling to keep up with the downpour.

Cameron looked behind her again, seeing headlights approaching. She told herself they were just headlights.

"They have no idea what we're driving," Mitch said.

"But they could figure it out."

The arrow turned green, and Mitch turned south on Ponce de León Boulevard, a.k.a. U.S. 1.

"They'll realize they've been had, that we stole the disk, and it looked like Lora saw you enough to know who you are. But they don't know who I am, what we're driving, or where we're going. Where are we going?"

"South," was all she said. They hadn't fine-tuned details beyond their immediate escape.

"They're not going to go to the cops, considering they're wanted by the cops, and they're not going to cause a scene at the hotel either, for the same reason. And even if they did, Damion's deleting the second reservation and scrubbing any security footage of us he can find. Best they'll have is descriptions of us."

"And the valet knows our faces, the license plate."

"True, but that doesn't do four people on the run much good. Which reminds me, you want to grab my jacket?"

She turned over her shoulder and retrieved his jacket from behind the seat. "What do you want?"

"The burn phone is in there."

Along with their many other preparations that afternoon and evening, they had purchased a cheap, prepaid cell phone for this specific reason. She handed it to him, and he dialed 9-1-1.

Cameron heard the dispatcher, and then Mitch said, "There are four people at the Casa Monica Resort & Spa who match the description of wanted criminals Seamus and Lora Hogan, Dax Wilder, and Kevin Stuart. They were last seen in the Cobalt Lounge."

He powered off the phone as he turned off U.S. 1 and onto State Road 207. Alternating between keeping one hand on the wheel or driving with his knees, he proceeded to disconnect the battery and remove the phone's SIM card.

"You want me to do that?" she asked.

"I got it."

"Animals are flying past the window two-by-two. I'd rather you keep your hands on the wheel."

He grinned at her, then handed her the phone components and put his hands at ten and two. He seemed perfectly calm, and Cameron allowed herself to breathe easily. She put the phone, battery, and SIM card into the jacket pocket and returned it to the backseat. Then she shrugged out of her wet blazer and undid her ponytail.

"What about the hotel?" she asked, raking her hands through her hair.

"What about it?"

"I feel bad using them the way we did."

He shrugged. "If they play it right, they can turn a little hassle and confusion into a real boon—helping arrest four wanted criminals."

"You don't think they'll press charges against us?"

"They don't know who we are. And even if they put the pieces together, they have no actual evidence."

"What about fingerprints?"

He shrugged again. "I touched the serving tray, some glasses, door handles. I guess if they make a federal case of it, get a real bulldog on it, sure, we might have to answer some questions. But they won't be able to prove anything criminal. And I still think when the cops show up and find the Hogans there, we'll be shoved to the back burner."

"I hope so."

"Relax, Cameron. We're home free."

She exhaled again. He'd assured her that evening that the plan would work, at least in theory. She'd believed him then, so now that it had gone without a hitch, she decided to keep believing him. Her attention shifted to the weight of the disk heavy on her legs. She eased it out of the purse and unwrapped the towel. "They cleaned it up," she said.

"Oh?"

She flipped on the car's dome light. "The patina's gone." She rotated the disk. "It's all legible. My goodness, it's like it's brand new."

"Net win. They saved you some work."

"I can't believe this. I thought it was gone for good." She analyzed it for a few minutes more, then shut off the dome light. "I can't wait to take a better look at this. Thank you, Mitch."

"I'll say this, meeting you has sure made for an exciting weekend."

*   *   *

A couple minutes later when they reached the interstate, Mitch confirmed the direction again with Cameron, and headed south on I-95. They drove in silence for a few miles, framed by nothing but trees on either side of the roadway. The rain had let up, so when he spotted a sign for a gas station, he asked about stopping to change out of their wet clothes (and the ones they had last been seen in, for what it was worth) and grab something to eat. Cameron agreed, and he exited the highway and turned into the parking lot of a Flying J Travel Center, complete with another Denny's and ample parking for vehicles, campers, and semis. A concrete oasis in the midst of the forest.

They parked in a corner of the lot and locked Cameron's purse in the trunk. They had packed up their luggage and checked out of the Holiday Inn in St. Augustine before starting their escapade, so they had all their luggage with them. He quickly changed shirts behind the trunk, and then offered to guard everything while Cameron took in a small bag with a change of clothes.

"You know, if this was a movie, I'd come out and you'd be gone."

He tossed her the keys.

She tossed them back. "I think you've earned my trust." With a smirk, she headed toward the travel center entrance.

Mitch took his cowboy hat, his jacket with the phone components still in the pocket, and her purse now without the disk, and stuffed them all in a nearby garbage can. Then he paced the parking lot, breathing in the post-rain air and mentally going over the last few hours. He wanted to make sure his assurances to Cameron that they were in the clear were backed by reality. And while there was no telling how the Hogans would respond, what the cops would do when they arrived on the scene, how thorough any investigators would be, or what pull the Hogans or Harrison Van Buren might have with the powers that be, he didn't envision a scenario where a statewide dragnet was issued for him and Cameron. They had covered their tracks.

She came back ten minutes later in blue jeans and a purple Clemson Tigers shirt, her hair in a fresh ponytail, and her bag slung over one shoulder. She carried a package of Oreos in one hand and balanced two coffee cups in the other. Mitch took the bag from her and put it in the trunk, then accepted a cup of coffee.

"I hope you take it black," she said.

"I generally don't take it at all. But it'll do." He looked down at the Oreos.

"I have a sweet tooth."

"Okay."

She stepped forward and gave him a slow kiss on the cheek, her free hand holding the back of his neck. "Thank you very much, Mitch. This means the world to me."

He smiled. "You gonna share those Oreos."

"Yes."

"Are they Double Stuf?"

"Of course."

"Consider me thanked. Let's go."

They walked around opposite sides of the Porsche. He stopped, leaning on the roof of the car. "So where are going, besides south."

"Ultimately, Tampa, if you're up for it."

"Why, what's in Tampa?"

She looked him straight in the eyes. "The other cipher disk."

CHAPTER FOURTEEN

Mitch sat in the driver's seat for several minutes without starting the car.

"Are you mad?" Cameron asked, biting her lip.

"I'm not sure yet."

"I'm sorry I didn't tell you, but I was keeping the circle tight. I didn't even tell Erik."

He slowly turned his head. "Why didn't you tell Erik?"

She exhaled. "Because I wasn't sure I trusted him."

"You told me you trusted Erik. We've been basing decisions on your trusting Erik."

"I do. I mean, I trust that he would never hurt me, that he wouldn't sell us out to the Hogans. But . . . I don't know how to say it." She shrugged. "I wanted an ace up my sleeve, to know something he didn't, as insurance. And I kind of wanted to surprise him, to show him I knew something he didn't—that I could do this on my own."

He looked out the window. For a minute. Then turned back. "Is that why you didn't tell me?"

"No. With you . . ." She sighed. "Mitch, I honestly didn't know how long we'd be together, how much to tell you or how much you'd want to know. I didn't even know you yesterday morning, and everything's been going a hundred miles an hour since, and . . . I'm sorry. But after everything you've done for me, after what you risked for someone you didn't know yesterday morning, you've proved that you're trustworthy."

Mitch studied her as rain began to fall again. She felt as if he could see into her soul, and hoped he saw pure intentions. He took a deep breath and looked away.

"I'm sorry," she said again. "If you want to drop me off somewhere and be done with me, I'll understand."

"Is that what you want?"

"No. It's not."

His granite expression broke. "It's not what I want either."

She smiled in relief as he started the car.

"Tell me about this other disk."

Cameron took a deep breath and tore open the package of Oreos. She handed him two, took a bite of one herself, and started explaining. "Everything I told you before was true. I just left out a few details."

"We'll save defining the word 'true' until later," Mitch said as he turned onto the highway leading back to the interstate. "Go on."

"Instead of making one disk, Diego Figueroa made two, and according to Javier's letter to his sons, they're both needed to find *agua eterna*."

"How so?"

"I don't know." She blew into the hole in the lid of her cup, then took a quick sip. "Half the message is in English and half in French, so maybe it has something to do with that. Or maybe it has to do with Diego having two sons. At any rate, when Enrique sailed aboard the *Descubridor*, he had both disks with him, not one."

"So why was one of them laying with the wreck off Cocoa Beach while the other one's in Tampa?"

"The *Descubridor* was sunk by pirates in 1705, at least according to legend."

They passed a semi, and Mitch kicked the wipers into high gear for a moment. Then he extended a hand. Cameron slapped a couple more Oreos into it. She took a drink of her cappuccino before continuing.

"I did some digging a few years back, back before Hurricane Matthew unearthed the *Descubridor*, hoping that I could identify the pirates and in so doing figure out where the ship lay. Through a series of old, half-disintegrated journals and letters and more legends and myths, I determined that the *Descubridor* was set upon by a pirate by the name of Benjamin Lovelace."

Mitch inhaled an Oreo and shifted lanes. He was keeping to the speed limit, according to a couple glances from Cameron. No need to draw any unnecessary attention.

"Lovelace was an English privateer who worked up and down both coasts of Florida. His ship was ultimately sunk and he was killed in a skirmish with the Spanish just south of the entrance to Tampa Bay."

"Time to dive the wreck of another ship?" Mitch asked.

"No. It's been thoroughly salvaged. More research, more reading, more dead ends ultimately led me to a small museum in Clearwater, west of Tampa. The owner's got a collection of pirate trinkets and pirate-related items, along with an assortment of objects recovered from sunken pirate ships."

"Including the disk?"

She nodded.

"Have you seen it?"

"No."

"Have you spoken to him recently?"

"No."

Mitch nodded.

"I knew where it was, and as far as I knew, no one else did. It didn't do me any good until I had the other disk that was sunk with the *Descubridor*, so it seemed safest and easiest to leave it where it was."

"How'd you know this Lovelace didn't take both disks?"

"I didn't for sure. But the curator only had the one, and there was no evidence pointing to a second disk in any of the research I did on Lovelace. If he hadn't taken it," she said, lifting her cup for another drink, "I figured the only place left was under the sea."

"Makes sense, I guess. Pirates attack a ship, plunder it, sink it. They could have easily missed something that went down with it."

"Apparently so."

Mitch grinned. "That could explain why the Hogans were hanging out at the Casa Monica in the first place."

"They couldn't solve the carving with just one disk."

He nodded.

"They don't have to worry about that anymore," she said, crunching into another Oreo.

They drove for about half an hour, with Cameron pulling up GPS on her phone to find the best route across the state to Tampa. It was pushing ten-thirty as they neared Daytona Beach, where I-4 branched off toward Orlando and Tampa. It was another two and a half to three hours from there, and with no particular need to be there anytime soon, they decided to call it a night.

They found a Holiday Inn Express just off the interstate, right down the street from the famed Daytona International Speedway. It had vacancies and parking set back from the road, so they paid for two rooms and checked in. Mitch helped Cameron carry her luggage to her room, and then she followed him back into the hallway.

"Mitch."

"Yeah?"

"I really am sorry about keeping things from you. I didn't mean to be dishonest."

"Forget it," he said.

She smiled. "Shoot to check out around eight? I could use a good night's sleep."

"I'll see you at eight."

"Thanks again, Mitch. I can't say it enough."

"You're welcome. I'll see you tomorrow."

He turned into his room, and she retreated to hers. She closed the door and stood against it for several minutes, thinking how close she had come to inviting him over under the auspices of unwinding or looking at the disk with her or maybe with a downturned chin and upturned eyes and an offer to repay him.

She took a deep breath, glad she hadn't said anything.

And a little disappointed too.

*   *   *

"How'd you sleep?" Mitch asked the next morning as he met Cameron outside her door. She wore the same purple Clemson shirt as the night before, but with a pair of khaki shorts. They were light enough to contrast nicely with her tanned skin. He didn't let his eyes linger.

"Once I got to sleep, great. It took a while. Thanks," she said as he took a bag off her shoulder.

"Your mind running about the events of the day?"

"More like wondering what the disk would reveal."

"I assume it's back to St. Augustine after Tampa?"

"Not necessarily. We know the words on the carving. In theory, we should be able to solve its riddle without being present."

"I suppose."

"How'd you sleep?" she asked.

"Terrible."

"Oh?"

"I'm pretty sure the Daytona 500's in February, so I have no idea why the airport was so busy last night."

"I thought I heard a jet this morning."

He yawned to prove his earlier point.

"Want me to drive?"

"I'll be all right, but thanks."

They checked out of their rooms and then drove a short distance to a Waffle House for breakfast. After they ordered, Cameron leaned forward. "Can I ask you something?"

"Sure."

"Are you sure you want to go to Tampa with me?"

"You trying to get out of it?"

"No, I'm not. Honest," she said, meeting his eyes.

"Okay."

"It's just . . . this may not be as easy as it seems." She looked both ways; they were alone. "We find the other disk, are able to borrow or buy or even see it, then we still have to figure out Diego's code. Maybe it's easy but maybe it's not. And then, that still doesn't guarantee finding the Fountain of Youth will be a snap. This could take a while."

"I'm in no rush to be anywhere. And frankly, I'm intrigued by all these artifacts and codes and such. I watched *Raiders of the Lost Ark* like a dozen times as a kid, never thinking I'd get to do something like it in real life."

"Nothing so adventurous, I hope."

"Now, if we end up having to spend hours and hours in a library doing mind-numbing research, I may lose interest. But for now, this is fun, and driving around the Sunshine State with good company beats hanging out on the beach by myself."

"Good," she said with a grin.

"It works both ways, too. If I become dead weight, let me know."

"I don't think I'll have to worry about that."

Their food came quickly, a cheesesteak omelet for him and a traditional waffle with a side of sausage for her. He plowed in with relish, but she seemed hesitant.

"Something wrong, honey?" the waitress asked, observing the same thing.

"No, it's fine," Cameron said. "My appetite just isn't what I thought."

The waitress nodded and left them again.

"You all right?" Mitch asked.

She looked at him and sighed. "There's something that's been on my mind, and I don't know how to ask it but just to ask."

"Okay."

"I'm out a business partner, and since you are interested—at least until it gets tedious," she said with a half smile.

"You're looking for financial backing?"

"Not so much that as a financial partner, an investor."

"And what's my return on investment?"

"Perpetual youth?" she said, raising her eyebrows.

He grinned as he took another bite.

"The truth is, I can't cut you in on a percentage of the treasure or a recovery fee because there is no treasure or fee. And there's not a limited supply of water so I can't offer you something you won't have access to anyhow, if you even believed in it."

"You know, if this doesn't work out, you might have a career in sales."

"Shut up," she said, reaching for her coffee. She took a drink. "I never intended to profit from the fountain. But there could be profits, could be fame or recognitions. And you're not just a guy who helped me along the way like Sully and the boys. You're a part of the team."

Mitch took and swallowed a bite of toast. "What are you looking for financially?"

"I'm not completely tapped. I have enough money to pay for some travel, modest accommodations and food, at least for a little while. It's if we have to hire another salvage crew or something like it that I'm in trouble."

"Well, how about this. I'd be eating and sleeping with or without you, so it's only fair to pick up my share. And it sounds like you'd be going to Tampa and pursuing this with or without me, and since you've got the cash for that, you pick up your share. Beyond that, we'll see what needs arise. If I'm still part of the team, I'm in for at least half. But we'll cross that bridge when we come to it."

"That's fair. I'm sorry, I know it's uncouth to ask for money, especially since we—"

"Cameron, don't worry about it. I get it. And if we're really on the precipice of finding whatever it is that has been believed for centuries to be the Fountain of Youth, then I don't want concerns about money to get in the way. We'll figure something out."

"Okay."

"Besides, this is too much fun to worry about money."

CHAPTER FIFTEEN

The interior of Florida was terribly boring. Trees, trees, and more trees. The sky was overcast and the air thick and stale, reminding Cameron what had finally soothed her to sleep the night before—more rain.

"You know, I've been thinking about something you said last night," Mitch said as they headed southwest on I-4.

"What's that?"

"How the Hogan Gang—I guess more likely the Van Buren Gang now—anyhow, how they couldn't decipher Diego's carving with just the one disk, and how they didn't have to worry about even that anymore."

"Yeah."

"They could have photographed it. You said the photos you had taken wouldn't help because it was corroded. But if they cleaned it up, they could know everything about it we know. Unless there's more to it than meets the eye, it'd be pretty easy to duplicate."

"But it's just one disk. They need both. Javier's letter was clear about that."

"I know, but the point is, they're halfway there, not back at square one."

"If they're out of jail."

"Right. Not so much them as Van Buren. I don't know who he is, but he's powerful and can surely hire more thugs to come after us."

The heat in the vehicle was dissipating.

"I don't mean to scare you," he said looking over. "Just saying we should be careful."

"What do you have in mind?"

"For one thing, I'm going to swing by the airport in Orlando and trade this car in for something a little less noticeable."

"That's a shame. First your beard, now the car," she said, reaching over and stroking the bottom of his chin, now void of any hair.

"Figured I'd start over," he said.

"Any other security measures?"

"I don't know that we'll need them. Knowing we went to Orlando won't lead them to Tampa."

"They'll expect us to be in St. Augustine."

Mitch shrugged. "Or getting out of Florida via the nearest, cheapest airport. And that's assuming they're tracking these things."

Cameron sighed. "This was more fun before the criminal element showed up."

"Sure, but without them, you'd never have met me."

Gradually, the pines and scrub were broken by suburban sprawl, a host of smaller communities connected to Orlando. By the time the skyline of downtown Orlando was visible ahead of them and traffic had slowed them to an inconsistent speed, the cloud cover had begun to break up, and the sun's rays intensified despite the Porsche's air conditioning's efforts.

They drove through downtown before Mitch followed Cameron's phone's directions to Orlando International Airport on the southeast edge of the city. It took forty-five minutes to fill up the Porsche with gas, return it, and rent a silver four-door Hyundai Elantra. Cameron also withdrew five hundred dollars in cash from an ATM, stuffing it in her suitcase to go with a hundred and change in her purse. By eleven o'clock, they were back on I-4, again headed southwest away from the various Disney resorts and the city's sprawl.

"You ever go to Disney?" Mitch asked.

Cameron looked down at the hem of her shorts. "No."

"That sounds sad."

"We didn't have a lot of time. Or money. We didn't travel very much when I was little."

Mitch nodded.

"I'm not really a theme park person anyhow. I'd rather go for a walk on deserted beach or in the backwoods or something."

"Rollercoasters?"

"I get a little queasy. Even airplanes can push my stomach to the limits."

"Aha."

"What about you?"

110

"Are you asking about my stomach, my entertainment proclivities, or whether I've ever been to Disney?"

"Any and all," she said. "This is boring," she added, gesturing at more trees along the road.

"I have an iron stomach," he said, "which I've inherited from a long line of Owens men. I'm good with walks on the beach or hikes in the woods or spending all day fishing in a small Texas lake. I'm also good with a big city and nightlife. But I'm sort of with you on theme parks, and I've never been to Disney World or Disney Land. I did go to Worlds of Fun in Kansas City when I was twelve."

"Wow, I feel like we've known each other for years now."

"If only."

The clouds had completely parted, leaving a bright blue sky by the time they reached Tampa. Just north of downtown, I-4 emptied into I-275, which looped through Tampa and St Petersburg across the bay. They followed I-275 briefly, but diverted onto Highway 60 instead of crossing the bay on the interstate. After skirting the airport, they rimmed the northern edge of Old Tampa Bay, and agreed to pause for lunch before crossing the water into St Petersburg and Clearwater.

Whiskey Joe's Bar & Grill was situated on a small beach just off the highway. Taking advantage of a gentle breeze off the bay, Cameron and Mitch ate on the patio, splitting orders of blackened mahi and grilled shrimp tacos. She did her best to relax and enjoy the meal and the environment—and the company—but it was hard with the anticipation and excitement of possibly seeing the second disk that afternoon. She had called en route to Tampa and gotten the museum's answering machine greeting. She hoped showing up unannounced wouldn't be a problem.

"What do you know about Lovelace?" Mitch asked, reaching for a chip with queso dip.

"Not very much," Cameron said. "He was born in Portsmouth, England, in 1677, joined the British navy when he was fifteen, was arrested for mutiny a few years later but escaped death or prison. By 1700, he was sailing with pirates and a couple years later he had his own crew."

"Not very much?" Mitch asked as he took another chip.

Cameron shrugged. "Somehow, he got back into the good graces of the English, at least enough to work for them as a privateer. He had about a five-year window of pillaging and plundering before his career and karma caught up with him in the form of the Spanish."

"And we're sure he and his crew hit the *Descubridor*?"

"Reasonably sure, yes." She let him mull on that for a moment while she took a bite of one of the grilled shrimp tacos, savoring the flavor of pico de gallo and fresh lime. She swallowed. "When you go back that far, three hundred years plus, you get a wide variety of records. Some are very detailed and accurate; some are little more than rumors."

Mitch took a gulp of his Corona.

"But," she said, reaching for her own bottle, "I'm confident enough to come here and see a guy I spoke to on the phone once for five minutes." She took a drink.

"Aren't you afraid somebody else has scooped you and found it in your absence?"

"The research I did that led me to Lovelace, to this museum, took a lot of work, a lot of connecting dots. Not to mention my trip to Spain to learn about the existence of the two disks in the first place, all to find something few people even believe exists."

"Fair enough."

"But yes, I'm terrified. Which is why I'm anxious to finish these tacos and get going."

"Then let's do it," Mitch said. "You gonna eat that?"

She slapped his hand away from last taco, then flashed him a smile as she tipped her bottle up again.

*   *   *

It took thirty minutes to drive fifteen miles across the bay and through Clearwater to a side street lined with aging commercial properties and void of almost any vegetation. Mitch pulled to the curb between a nail salon and a single-story brick-faced building that housed a barbershop, a consignment store, a Thai restaurant, and a pair of vacant office spaces. In the hundred feet between the salon and the brick building was an old ranch-style house with a wide front porch. Faded blue siding and scuffed white trim caused what was otherwise a quaint house to fit in well in the neighborhood.

Mitch got out, squinting against the midday sun reflecting off the pavement. He searched the sky for any sign of relief, but saw nothing but blue.

He turned his gaze to the front window of the house. Red letters with white trim had been painted on the window, spelling out "Morgan's Pirate Den." Smaller letters beneath them were illegible from the street thirty feet away. On the opposite side of the door from the window, a sign read "DLC Insurance" and pointed around the corner, where the porch presumably led to a side door.

"Not exactly the Louvre," he said as he rounded the front of the Elantra.

"That works in our favor," Cameron said. "The *Mona Lisa* hangs in the Louvre and everybody knows it."

He conceded her point with a bob of his head and followed her up the steps of the porch, then stopped suddenly when her shoulders sagged.

"What is it?" he asked.

Cameron's eyes pointed the way to smaller letters on the window. They revealed the museum's hours, 10-5 weekdays, and 11-4 on weekends. The exception was Monday, when it was closed.

"I've heard of restaurants being closed on Mondays, but never two-bit museums."

"It would explain why no one answered when I called."

"They didn't have the hours on their website?"

"They don't have a website," she said, turning her eyes toward him. "Or a Facebook page. I figured that was good. The fewer people who know about this place, the better." She walked over to the window and peered inside. It was dark, and other than a few knickknacks on display in the window, Mitch was unable to see what was inside the museum.

Cameron left him staring at the hours and walked to the end of the porch. She peeked around it, then walked to the other end, toward DLC Insurance. She disappeared and returned a few seconds later.

"Doesn't look like there's a residence in the back or anything. Insurance place looks closed too."

"The whole town close on Mondays?"

"Maybe," she said, looking around. Mitch did too. There were no other houses or even apartments in sight from which maybe an owner could see he had customers and decide to open shop. "What's another day?" Cameron breathed out as she walked back to Mitch.

"I've got time."

She looked down at her watch. "Two-thirty. How you want to kill an afternoon?"

Mitch squinted out at the sun again. "This area's known for its beaches, isn't it?"

"You don't have to ask me twice."

They spent a few minutes debating their options and decided to book hotel rooms on the beach, check in and stow their luggage, and then hit the sand. While Mitch found his way back to Highway 60, Cameron searched for deals on her smartphone. She found a good price on rooms at the Sandpearl Resort on Clearwater Beach, and an hour later they were padding across white sand in bare feet. They weren't alone. The beach was crowded for a weekday afternoon, and they wandered south a hundred yards, away from a public park and closer to Pier 60, a nightlife hotspot that jutted out into the Gulf of Mexico.

After traipsing through the sand and wading out into the water, they spent a few minutes actually swimming. Then Cameron went to catch some rays and read while Mitch decided to swim to the pier and back, about half a mile total. He was far from an expert swimmer, and didn't get a lot of chance to practice his stroke. As a result, he found himself tiring as he got closer to where Cameron had camped out. He thought about angling toward shore, but pushed himself on, rewarding himself with thoughts of a cold drink when he was finished.

Breathing heavily, he finally slogged to shore. After checking with Cameron, he walked up the beach to the Tate Island Grill, the beachside eatery on the Sandpearl property. He ordered a frozen rum drink and a piña colada and carried them back to the beach, where he collapsed into a chaise lounge next to Cameron. She slipped a bookmark into the novel she was reading and set it on the towel beside her chair. He handed the piña colada to her.

"Thank you." She took a sip and sighed. "Isn't this beautiful?"

He looked at Cameron, stretched out in a green- and white-striped two-piece and nodded. "Yes it is."

She whacked him in the arm and took another sip. Her aviator shades hid her eyes, but judging by the upturn in the corners of her mouth, Mitch guessed they were sparkling. He turned his head and took a gulp of his drink, and nearly blacked out from a freeze headache. When his head cleared a moment later, he examined the beauty Cameron had referenced, white sand as far as the eye could see in either direction and the glistening blue gulf.

"Between you and me," he said without looking her way, "I'm okay the museum was closed." Now he turned his head. "This beats an afternoon of deciphering hieroglyphics."

"There aren't any hieroglyphics."

"Do you know that? You haven't seen it, have you?"

"No. But it was described to me. He said nothing about hieroglyphics."

Mitch shrugged and took a smaller drink this time. The freeze came again, but it was manageable.

"I'm just hoping we're smart enough to figure out how the two of them work together," Cameron said.

"What if it's in French?"

She lowered her sunglasses and looked over them at him.

"What?"

"Pretty sure they use the same alphabet we do."

"I don't know," he said. "I didn't take French at Texas."

She took a big sip through her straw. "The thing that confuses me is all the letters repeating. But I guess they'd have to with that many. But why are they all in order? I don't know." She took a deep breath and a look out at the water. "This is nice, but I'm anxious to get studying and try to figure it out."

"Well, in the absence of that, how about dinner?"

"Is it that time already?"

"By the time we shower, get dressed, find a place . . . And, if you want to enjoy a sunset on the beach afterwards . . ."

She looked at him again, this time making no effort to hide the smile on her face. "Just let me finish my drink first."

"You got it," he said, and before thinking chugged some more of his drink and paid the consequences.

CHAPTER SIXTEEN

Cameron looked simply stunning in a sea-green knee-length sundress, her hair teased and falling over her shoulders. Mitch was glad he'd at least put on a collared shirt to go with his shorts.

They had finished their drinks on the beach, then showered and discussed dinner options. Cameron had expressed a desire for seafood, and Mitch had done the rest, finding a place in downtown St. Petersburg. He didn't tell Cameron where they were headed but asked her to trust him as they drove east. She had tuned the radio and sat back, her hand feeling the breeze out the Elantra's open window. A heart-shaped diamond necklace sparkled against her skin, but wasn't half as bright as the glow in her smile. Mitch hoped his after-dinner surprise would add to it.

Fresco's Waterfront Bistro provided views of the municipal marina, and they dined on the deck. The white hulls of dozens upon dozens of sailboats and pleasure cruisers glowed yellow and orange in the evening sunlight. With the air still warm and the soft breeze carrying the cawing of gulls and the lapping of water against the dock, it was the perfect ambiance for entrées of Maine lobster tail and jalapeno bacon tuna.

While they ate, Cameron told Mitch about her childhood growing up in the tidewater region of Virginia, the daughter of a wealthy aristocrat who'd fallen for the son of a Blue Ridge coalminer. She told happy stories with a smile, albeit seemingly forced at times. Mitch's history with women was equal parts surprising insights and laughable misreads, so he didn't dwell on the space between the lines. Instead, he reciprocated with some of the livelier adventures from his time in Austin at the University of Texas.

They ate leisurely and left room for dessert, but when Cameron asked about ordering off the Fresco's menu, Mitch said they'd grab dessert later. "We have a sunset to catch."

Her smile widened.

Mitch picked up the check over her "we agreed to go Dutch" protest, and they got back in the car. After passing downtown and the seemingly crooked home of Major League Baseball's Tampa Bay Rays, Tropicana Field, they headed south.

"Aren't we going to be a long way from the hotel?" Cameron asked.

"You in a rush to get to bed tonight?"

"No."

He nodded. When he cut over on the Pinellas Bayway, then followed it south over several bridges to a V-shaped island that formed the north end of the outlet of Tampa Bay, Cameron turned to him. "You're sure you've never been to Florida?"

"No, but I can read a map."

"Does that woo the ladies in Texas?"

"No, most of them can read maps."

"So can I."

"Good to know," he said as they entered Fort De Soto State Park. He turned right on a road that followed the point of the V and then headed north. The road was flanked all along the right by ground-level palms, and on the left by a mix of trees and grass-covered dunes that mostly blocked the view. It was nearing eight o'clock when they reached a large parking lot at the end of the road. A few dozen cars speckled the parking spaces, but the lot was mostly empty, and Mitch parked near a trailhead leading to the beach.

"Do you have a particular reason for picking this beach?" Cameron asked as she slid her seatbelt back.

"Well, I can't promise it's deserted, but it should have quite a few less people than Clearwater Beach. It was also voted one of the best beaches in the country. Figured it'd make a good place to watch a sunset."

Cameron's smile was radiant.

"Let's go," he said.

They set out for the beach and started north, staying in the dry sand just above where the water was lapping. The waves were small, slow, smooth. The low, golden sunlight was doing wonderful things with tendrils of Cameron's hair as they fluttered in the breeze. There were a few other stragglers and couples wandering the isolated beach that might as well have been a hundred miles from civilization.

"Can I ask you something?" Mitch said as they walked.

Cameron looked at him and nodded.

"It's personal, so if you don't feel comfortable answering, you don't have to."

She continued looking, waiting.

"Why the Fountain of Youth?" He shook his head. "There have to be tons of ancient mysteries to solve, treasures to find—gold or otherwise. Why this?"

She plodded on for several paces, looking down. When she lifted her head, she looked right at him again. "I heard the rumors as a little girl, about water that would grant perpetual youth to all who drank it, and I remember being fascinated by the concept. But I never put any stock in it, never believed in it any more than I believed in Santa Claus."

She took a few more steps, and this time looked out at the gulf. "My dad died when I was fifteen from an odd form of stomach cancer. Came out of nowhere. Nothing he did wrong or didn't do to take care of himself. Just one of those things."

"I'm sorry."

"Mom died eight years later. She had a heart attack at fifty-one. No warning signs. Just dropped over."

"Wow."

"You can say that again. I mentioned a sister the other day. There are two, one older, one younger. Combined they have four kids, and I can't stop thinking about what happens if they get stomach cancer or heart disease, and die suddenly. Or slowly. What if I have kids?" She looked at Mitch. "I know I can't avoid death. I don't believe there's any water that will give me eternal life. But of all the treasure legends or ancient mysteries to explore, the one that fascinated me as a child suddenly seemed more relevant."

She kicked at some sand and turned, stopping to stare out at the water. Mitch came around beside her.

"I did some initial research, mostly out of grief, and that's when I stumbled upon enough evidence to make me think maybe there really was a Fountain of Youth. And it's like I told you the other night, the concept of places or substances on earth that could augment or enhance life dramatically aren't that out there. What if there's a source of water that has a certain set of minerals or nutrients that could fight off cancer or heart disease, Alzheimer's or dementia, cure anxiety or ease mental disorders? What if it increased life expectancy by a couple of decades, made the so-called golden years actually golden, lessened those 'natural' causes of death? What if there's a cure for cancer?"

She looked at him again.

"I don't think it's crazy to believe such a thing could exist in our world—that it does exist. Now imagine I can find it, bring that water to my sisters, their husbands, my nieces and nephews, me . . . my children someday. Imagine not having to go through what we did when Mom and Dad died so young . . ."

Mitch sighed softly, looking out at the orange reflection of the sun glinting off the ripples of gray-blue water. Cameron slipped behind him and resumed walking. He waited a moment before following her.

"You think that's nuts?" she asked when he caught up.

"No."

"What do you think?"

"I think you're right, it does sound nice."

"But?"

He took a deep breath. "I'm not sure I buy into 'Easter eggs.' I don't know how so-called miracles happen or why people who visit certain places seem to get healed, but I'm not ready to chalk it up to magic or anything like that either." He shrugged. "I don't know. I've always been a meat and potatoes guy. Maybe you're right, and there is a mystical fountain of life. But, I'm afraid there's not."

She took a few more steps, head down again. "So why are you here, now?"

"It's gonna sound cheesy."

She stopped walking again.

"Because I believe in you. I don't think you're crazy. I don't think your research is crazy. I told you I'm intrigued by all this, by the mystery of it."

Cameron smiled again.

"And for the record, there are other people who don't think this is crazy either, to the point of risking serious jail time to get what you have."

She dug her foot into the sand again, sweeping sand around.

"I'm also intrigued by you," he said, and she raised her head. "I'm intrigued by your work, your passion, your determination. I want to know more about you, about what makes you tick. I know a little about Cameron the archeological adventurer; I want to know more about Cameron the woman. And if I have to chase around Florida with you to get some answers, so be it."

With a smile again threatening to come out, she reached for his hand and gently led him farther up the beach. The sun was low, just minutes from setting, and Mitch stopped. To their left, a small island rose up out of the surf. It was little more than a sandbar, a hook-shaped spit of land that extended away from their beach at an angle, white sand with a few tufts of seagrass. And it was abandoned.

"What?" Cameron asked.

He looked at a hundred-foot wide expanse of water between them and the small island. At low tide, the water was only a foot or eighteen inches at its deepest. Cameron picked up on his idea, and dropped her flip-flops in the sand. He tossed his shoes beside hers, and they waded out into the warm gulf water, still holding hands. The waves were almost nonexistent behind the barrier of sand, and the water only traced the bottom of Cameron's sundress.

They walked at the edge of the water, letting the waves wash over them and then back out to sea. When the sun kissed the surface of the gulf they stopped and turned to watch it. The entire sky was tainted by haze and had turned a bright yellow fading to orange fading to a reddish sun that slowly dipped beneath the horizon. They had stopped holding hands, and instead stood close together, so close that the breeze swirled the hem of her dress against his leg and lifted strands of her hair onto his shoulder.

The sun disappeared.

Cameron turned to face him. For several long seconds she just stared into his eyes, and then she reached up to trace his cheek with her hand. "Do you miss it?"

"The beard?" He shrugged. "It'll grow back."

"Good," she said, "although it does feel nicer this way." She slowly dropped her hand to his shoulder, and then down his arm. "Mitch."

"Yeah?"

"You know I've said thank you a hundred times."

"I lost count at eighty-five or ninety."

"And last night I gave you a kiss on the cheek, as a thank you."

"I remember."

"Well," she said, making eye contact with him, "this is not a thank you." She stretched up onto her toes and kissed him, slow and soft and a little salty and about as good as he'd ever been kissed before. She then took half a step back, still not taking her blue eyes off him.

"So what was that for?" he asked.

She winked and slid her hand down to his, grabbing it again. "Because I'm intrigued by you too." Then she pulled him back the way they had come.

*   *   *

Instead of getting back on the interstate, Cameron had suggested they drive along the beach. So after exiting Fort De Soto Park, Mitch turned west and eventually onto Gulf Boulevard, which ran north through St. Pete Beach, Treasure Island, Madeira Beach, Indian Shores, and ultimately to Clearwater Beach. It was bordered by hotels, condos, beach houses, and an array of restaurants and shops. The beach was never more than a block to the west, and the connected peninsulas and islands jutting into the Intracoastal Waterway were on the east. They drove with the windows down, breeze blowing across Mitch, flitting through Cameron's hair, and brushing over her hand as it dangled out the window. A mix of reggae and Caribbean and salsa music played on the radio, and Mitch chose to relax instead of get annoyed at the stop-and-start traffic on the boulevard.

He could still taste Cameron's lips, and as much as he had enjoyed their kiss, he enjoyed the lighthearted way she'd been behaving ever since even more. Gone were the stresses of searching for artifacts, interpreting clues, and dodging bad guys' bullets. Gone too was the sadness that had tinged her eyes when she'd told him about the death of her parents. In their place was the fun, carefree, uninhibited woman he'd suspected had been waiting to come out. Splashing him as they waded back through the channel to the "mainland," tuning the radio and singing along to Bob Marley's "One Love," and rubbing his relatively smooth cheek again while talking about the sacrifices in the line of duty.

"You've really got a thing for beards, huh?"

She shrugged. "Dad had a beard most of the time. I guess I find it comforting."

"Comforting."

"It's a sign of masculinity, of strength. I know you can be just as strong without a beard, but, I don't know. I like it."

"I thought liking masculinity was sort of passé."

She raised an eyebrow.

"You know, no woman needs a man, they're strong enough, we're lucky you let us be part of the reproduction process."

121

She raised another eyebrow.

"I need to stop listening to talk radio."

She reached over and cranked Jimmy Buffett a little higher.

About half an hour into their drive, she suggested dessert—in the form of pie. When efforts to find a suitable restaurant along Gulf Boulevard proved fruitless, they opted for a Winn-Dixie and bought individual slices of refrigerated Key lime pie. They took them back to their hotel, and out onto the patio around the pool. A few people were swimming, a few more were enjoying drinks or the distant sounds of a live band at Tate Island Grill. It was all background to the privacy of their small table, as was the gulf breeze that ruffled the leaves of palm trees around the patio.

"I have a confession to make," Cameron said as she eased her fork through her now soft pie.

"The Fountain of Youth is all a ruse to lure strange men into an exotic vacation with you?"

"No."

"Because that would be okay."

She felt under the table for his leg, and kicked it with the side of her foot.

"Your confession?"

"Earlier, you talked about how I wasn't crazy, and how other people thought that because they were willing to go to great lengths to find the fountain."

He nodded and took a bite. The pie was almost as delicious as Cameron's lips.

"There are people who think there's more than water to be found," she said, looking down at her pie.

"Like what?"

She shrugged. "The usual. Treasure of some sort. Gold, jewels, relics."

"Are you one of those people?"

"No. I've never found anything to substantiate the rumors. I've barely found the rumors. I think they stem from Diego being the descendant of a conquistador, the history of the Spanish government's lust for gold, an idea that the Native Americans who inhabited Florida centuries before the Spanish arrived must have known about it, drank from it, and naturally stashed anything of value by this magical fount."

Mitch nodded and took another bite.

"I figured you should know, the people we're up against may have more than a mystical fountain in mind."

Mitch swallowed. "Is Erik one of those people?"

Cameron rolled her head from side to side. "I don't think so. I think he wants to believe it, but I don't think he does."

"Well, it would explain why Van Buren's goons are so eager to find the fountain, and to find it first."

"I have this eerie feeling we haven't seen the last of them," Cameron said.

"I'd better grow that beard back."

She kicked him again.

They finished their pie and lingered for a while. The live band had packed up, and now canned music flowed through hidden speakers around the pool. When Cameron hid a second yawn, Mitch decided to call it a night.

The elevator was cool compared to the outside air, and so was the hall leading to their rooms. Cameron stopped by her door, holding her keycard.

"Morgan's opens at ten," Mitch said.

"Ten."

"Gives us time for a decent breakfast first. After sleeping in," he said as she fought off another yawn.

"Sorry."

"Last night catching up with you?"

"Must be it."

She flipped her card over in her hand.

Mitch reached for her hand. "Today was fun."

Cameron raised her eyes to his. "Yeah, it was."

He squeezed her hand, then leaned in for a quick kiss. Quick, because a long kiss might not have stopped, and Mitch wasn't sure either of them was quite ready for that. And because he'd long ago learned one of the secrets of life was to leave yourself wanting more, whether it was skiing in Aspen or a couple of beers with buddies or kissing a pretty girl.

"I'll see you in the morning," he said, then dropped her hand. She turned into her room, and he watched her go, watched the door close, before going to his room for the night.

CHAPTER SEVENTEEN

Cameron left the sliding glass door to her balcony ajar and fell asleep to the sound of the gulf waves rolling ashore. She slept soundly and woke early. After a quick peek from her balcony to see that another brilliant morning was dawning, she put on a pair of jogging shorts, a spandex top, and a pair of running shoes, and headed out to the beach. It was dead calm, pleasantly cool, and the beach was empty. She jogged north, to where the beach thinned and the hotels and condos were replaced with private homes, many of which featured their own path through the grass-covered dunes to the beach. What a life.

In addition to keeping her body toned, running gave Cameron a chance to think and process what was going on in her life. Of late, her concentration had been on finding the Figueroa Cipher and, in turn, the Fountain of Youth. But this morning, she kept thinking about the previous afternoon and evening with Mitch. Both had been perfect, from chilling on the beach to a delicious dinner on the bay to a romantic sunset kiss. Then a second in the hallway. Albeit short, little more than a good-night kiss, it had been initiated by Mitch, and had hinted at a restrained desire she found alluring.

Cameron ran until the houses stopped completely, and a thin strip of beach separated the gulf from a wild, nature area. It was beautiful in the morning light, and she spent a moment catching her breath before turning back toward the hotel, she guessed about two miles away.

On the return trip, her thoughts turned to the day's events. As much as she would enjoy another relaxed, romantic day with Mitch, they had come to the west coast of Florida on business. The possibility of seeing the second cipher disk, of being able to put the pieces together and solve the riddle of the Castillo de San Marcos Carving thrilled her. But she also was tempered, knowing searches like this were seldom as easy as they seemed.

Cameron was breathing hard when she returned to the Sandpearl, and after taking a few minutes to cool down, she returned to her room and showered. She put on a peach maxi sundress and twisted her hair into a loose braid. Then, with a touch of excitement, she texted Mitch. He was ready and waiting, so she stepped into a pair of slides, then grabbed a large straw sun hat, sunglasses, and her purse, and exited into the hallway.

Mitch was leaning against the wall opposite her door. He wore a pair of gray shorts and a plain white T-shirt. His sunglasses were clipped over the collar and the worn, faded Texas Longhorns hat he'd worn when he rescued her on his Jet Ski was tipped back on his head. He looked up from his phone, and his eyebrows went up.

"Good morning," he said.

"Morning. You didn't get all dressed up for me, did you?" she asked, with a smirk.

"I didn't know we were shooting a Royal Caribbean commercial."

She pinched her tongue in her teeth.

He winked. "It looks good on you."

"Thanks."

"I mean it. Just makes me want to sweep you off to the Caymans instead of a dive museum."

"You can buy me breakfast first."

"It's a deal."

They found a casual restaurant less than a block away and dined al fresco. They didn't discuss the previous night, but focused on the visit to Morgan's Pirate Den. Cameron was nervous, in small part because she feared the disk wouldn't be there for any number of reasons, and in larger part because she had yet to figure out a strategy for obtaining the disk. She'd taken for granted that when the time came, she'd find a way. Now that the time was almost at hand, she wasn't so sure.

"Well," Mitch said as he mopped up the last of the syrup on his plate with his final bite of pancake, "if you can come up with a southern accent to go with that outfit, I'd imagine you could just smile and ask for it."

"Well, I declare," she said in her best Scarlett O'Hara, "someone is laying it on rather thick."

"I take it back, let me do the talking."

She smacked him with the back of her hand.

"I figured you've heard all the regular compliments, so I was trying to be clever."

"I thought you were shooting for charming."

"Shooting for?"

She winked and sipped her orange juice.

They killed a little time after eating, then headed back across the causeway to Clearwater and to a faded blue building on a side street. It was five after ten when Mitch parked in front of Morgan's Pirate Den, the window of which featured a sign that read "Open."

"Ladies first," he said, and Cameron turned the knob and swung the door inward. A bell tinkled overhead, and an odd smell nearly stopped her in her tracks. She realized it was pipe smoke. Years and years of pipe smoke.

They were in a small room with linoleum floors and walls painted pastel pink. The walls were covered with nautical charts, pictures of replica pirate ships, and paintings depicting everything from a schooner flying the Jolly Roger to a gang of pirates lugging a chest through a forest of palms. The only break in the collection of frames was a large Union Jack hanging on the left wall and covering a doorway. In front of it, a small glass counter was littered with brochures, a requisite for all commercial buildings in tourist areas.

Mitch nudged Cameron's arm, and she followed his gaze to where a ten-foot-long plastic shark hung from the ceiling. It was frightening, not in its realness, but for its cheesiness. Blue skin, a clown-like wide mouth, and a tricorne pirate hat on its head. Cameron tried to buoy her quickly sinking spirits and fight off the fear that Morgan's would be all kitsch and little substance.

A doorway to the right opened to a brightly lit room, and Cameron started in that direction when a man emerged from a dark doorway straight ahead. He was young, decked in faded jean shorts and a green T-shirt with what looked like a U with horns. It vaguely resembled some or other sports team logo Cameron had once seen. He had short dark hair and skin so tanned it was brown.

"Hey," he said. "Wow, visitors before noon. Welcome to Morgan's Pirate Den. Admission's only five dollars per person."

Mitch dug into his wallet for a ten, which the man pocketed. A sign on the glass counter listed the price of admission, cash only, so Cameron knew he wasn't scamming them. Still, a cash register or a receipt would add a little credibility to the transaction.

The man pointed to his left, their right, into the well-lit room. "In here is the Caribbean Room, dedicated to the golden age of piracy. Through it on the right is our collection of weapons, and on the left our rare finds. And this is the gallery—various ships and maps, as you can see. If you have any questions, let me know. I'm Billy."

"Are you the owner?" Mitch asked.

"My dad, William. I'm a junior."

"We're actually looking for a particular object," Cameron said.

"Oh, what's that?"

"A cipher disk, believed to have come from the wreck of Benjamin Lovelace's ship."

"Ol' Bloodbeard, huh?"

"Bloodbeard?" Cameron asked.

"That was his nickname. We've got a whole wall dedicated to stuff he pillaged. This way."

Mitch gestured for Cameron to go first, so she followed Billy into the "Caribbean Room," a standard-sized living room full of display cases, shelves, and stands. They contained everything from chunks of wood with gold plaques fastened to them to old coins of various shape and metal to scraps of parchment and clothing. Model ships were suspended from the ceiling, with little notecards dangling from them to identify them. While less corny than the plastic shark in the entry, it felt more like a private collection of junk than a museum. But if it had the disk, Cameron didn't care.

Billy avoided the weapons room and led them into what Cameron deduced had been a kitchen. It had the same linoleum as the entry and offered views of the "backyard," through a wide window above a counter covered with little figurines, small fake trees, and a couple buildings that appeared lifted from a model train layout. Where the sink would have been, beneath the window, the counter was now recessed by a foot, with Plexiglas in the front to hold in "the ocean," some dark blue concoction that resembled water and enabled model pirate ships to square off in battle. They were replete with miniature figurines on deck, ripped sails, and cannon with wisps of cotton to emulate smoke. Tacky and weird, it was also well done.

"My step-brother's a geek in his spare time," Billy said. "This is the Bloodbeard wall," he said, pointing to their left. Aside from a doorway, the wall was black with a white skull and crossbones hand-painted on it. Billy pointed out several Spanish doubloons and pieces of eight, a goblet allegedly belonging to the Queen of France, various Aztec and Incan relics, fragments of letters, and splinters of wood from Lovelace's ship, the *Scourge of the Seas*. All were kept in plastic display cases mounted on the wall or, in a few cases, freestanding on the floor. Cameron listened with as much attention as possible, her eyes scanning the wall. She saw it as Billy stepped to the side.

"And this," he said, "is what I think you're looking for." He moved so Cameron and Mitch could approach a three-foot-high display case. Tilted on an angle on a maroon velvet background was a disk identical to the Figueroa Cipher. The bronze was shiny under a recessed light in the ceiling, but to Cameron's disappointment, was only half visible due to a green patina and grayish brown discoloring that covered half the disk's surface. It made reading all the letters (or using a photograph of the disk to interpret the carving) impossible. Even so, she could tell it contained different letters than the Figueroa Cipher.

"They're not in French," Mitch said from over her shoulder.

"Funny." She turned to Billy. "I understand your dad found this?"

"About ten years ago. He and my step-brother—Kenny—and I were diving the wreck of the *Scourge of the Seas*, which people have been doing for years, and he literally stumbles over the thing. He had no idea what it was, but that's the case with a lot of stuff around here."

"He didn't clean it up?" Mitch asked.

"He doesn't a lot of stuff. It looks more natural this way. With this—cipher disk or whatever you call it—you can see what it is, so why bother?"

"Is he here?" Cameron asked.

"Nah. He's out fishing. Every morning."

"Fishing fishing or diving for treasure?" Mitch asked.

"Fishing fishing. Marlin or mackerel, if he's lucky. Otherwise dinner."

"Any idea when he'll be back?" Cameron asked.

"One or two. Depends how the fishing is." Billy shrugged. "Same routine every day. Out at dawn to fish, come hang out here, and repeat."

"Does he have a cell or satellite phone—any way to get a hold of him?"

"Not really. Why?" Billy shook his head. "He doesn't know anything about it."

"I'd like to talk to him about buying it," Cameron said.

"Buying it? Nah, Dad won't sell it. He won't sell anything he's found." Billy shrugged. "I mean, you can talk to him when he gets back, but I wouldn't hold my breath."

Cameron exhaled in frustration. But she resolved not to give up until talking to William Morgan. Unfortunately, that would be at least several hours, so she exhaled again.

"He does have a ship-to-shore radio for emergencies," Billy said. "Maybe the Coast Guard or something could reach him."

"We can come back later," Cameron said. "One or two?"

"Generally, but it really depends on the day."

They thanked Billy, then browsed for a few more minutes. A little after ten-thirty, they exited into the sunlight. "Déjà vu much?" Cameron asked.

"Yesterday turned out okay."

"Yes it did."

"Hit the beach again?"

"Mmm, maybe later. Any chance I could persuade you to take me shopping?"

"Shopping?"

"I could use a few things, and I like to browse in new towns."

Mitch shrugged.

"You don't mind?"

"I actually don't mind shopping."

"You don't?"

"In my experience, it generally involves following good-looking women around while they try on things that make them more good-looking. It's not the hardest sell."

Cameron squinted at him.

"What?"

"Just wondering if you have an angle?"

"No angle," he said with a shake of his head.

"Then let's go."

"Lead the way, Contessa."

She whacked him with her hat and got into the car.

*   *   *

Other than another roll of deodorant and some toothpaste, Cameron bought nothing. Mitch found a clever (so he thought) T-shirt and tried to talk her into one, but she passed. They picked up lunch at a Mexican food truck by the water, and after eating, crossed back over the Intracoastal Waterway and strolled through the park and along the beach. The white sand was burning hot, but the gulf breeze was refreshing, and it was hard to switch out of vacation mode and back to business. But shortly after one, they brushed off the sand and drove back to Morgan's Pirate Den.

It was closed.

Cameron turned to Mitch. "Are we being played?"

"No. Why would they play us?"

"It feels like we're being played."

"The old man probably hooked a two-hundred-pound marlin and needed Billy to help gut it."

"There's a nice image."

"Seriously, why would they hold onto the disk for a decade, then when we come along, play hard to get?"

"Maybe somebody else got to them first."

"Who? This was your little secret."

She sighed. "You're right." She took a few steps down the porch and peeked around the corner.

"What, you want some home and auto coverage?"

"Maybe they know where Billy went."

"It's an insurance company, not the CIA."

Cameron made a shooing motion with her fingers. "You find him your own way." She strode along the porch to the side door to DLC Insurance. The door was locked, and she frowned as she turned to the window. Aside from standard lettering on the glass with the company name, it was blank. No posted hours. No "gone to lunch" sign. She pressed up close, using her hands to shade the side of her vision. She saw a standard receptionist desk in a small room, a potted plant, a bookshelf, a multi-function printer, a few filing cabinets, and a door leading deeper into the house. No people.

She was about to knock when a voice from behind her startled her. "You need insurance, I'd go elsewhere."

Cameron turned to see a young woman heave a white trash bag into a dumpster. Judging by her shirt and the leaking garbage, Cameron deduced she worked at the Thai restaurant in the brick building next door. The blue hair and pale white face belied that observation, but who was she to judge?

"Why's that?" Cameron asked.

"The lady who works there's a real stiff. Never so much as grunts hello."

"You see her a lot?"

"Comes in for lunch once or twice a week. Always to go, always in a hurry, always rude."

Cameron nodded. "She's not over there now, is she?"

"No. Keeps weird hours, it seems."

"What about the pirate museum? You know the owners?"

"The kids stop in sometimes, Billy and Kenny, I think. Weird hours too."

"They often close down midday?"

The blue-haired lady shrugged. "I dunno. I don't pay that much attention. I gotta get back."

"Thanks," Cameron said and returned to see Mitch leaning on the railing of the porch, looking at his phone. She leaned in. "What doin'?"

"Looking for a phone number."

"For what?"

"Here."

"Here?"

"I thought maybe the step-brother was minding the shop and got busy setting up his model pirate world."

"I have the number on my phone."

"I figured, but you were off playing Nancy Drew."

She lifted herself onto the railing and tipped her head back so her hat would keep the sun off her neck. "You try knocking?" she asked, swinging her crossed legs back and forth.

"Tried the knob."

"You want the number?"

"I would," he said, slipping his phone back into his pocket, "but I think our white whale just showed up."

Cameron turned a quick gaze to the far side of the street, where a man in a Hawaiian shirt and a pair of cutoffs got out of a pickup truck that was at least a decade old.

"White whale?" she asked, glancing back at Mitch.

"Ahab, his whale, *Moby Dick*."

"That doesn't make any sense."

"It worked up here," he said, aiming a finger at his head.

"Uh-huh."

She got off the railing as the man turned up the short walk to the steps leading to the front porch.

"Hallo," he called out. "Waitin' on me?"

131

"Are you William Morgan?" Cameron asked.

"Guilty as charged." He wiped his hand on his pants, which did nothing in the way of cleaning whatever was on it. Cameron shook hands anyhow.

William Morgan looked old enough to be Billy's grandpa. His skin was red as a lobster and had the same texture as leather. His chin and jaw were covered with several days' of gray stubble, the same color as a ponytail that hung onto his back. Morgan was big, with ape-like arms and a chest and belly that strained the buttons of his Hawaiian shirt. He was barefoot, and his cutoffs were torn in several places, revealing more of his upper leg than Cameron cared to see. There was nothing appealing about the man, save for his eyes, which twinkled with life and warmth as he shook both of their hands.

"Come on in," he said. "Excuse my appearance."

"Good day fishing?" Mitch asked.

"Never had a bad one."

"Catch anything?"

He waved a hand as he turned the knob. "Junk. What can I do for you folks? I get the feeling you're not just tourists wandering around."

"We stopped in earlier and talked to Billy," Cameron said. "We're interested in the cipher disk you found on the wreck of the *Scourge of the Seas*."

Morgan's eyes practically danced. "The Bloodbeard Cipher? Well, isn't that a coincidence?"

"Coincidence?"

"You're the second person to inquire about it in the last couple months."

CHAPTER EIGHTEEN

Cameron flicked her eyes to Mitch, then back to William Morgan. "Someone else knows about the cipher?" she asked.

He nodded and scratched his jaw. "Got a call a month, maybe two ago. Guy said he'd heard I had a collection of Bloodbeard memorabilia and wondered if I happened to have a cipher wheel. Told him I did, told him a little about it." Morgan scratched the other side of his jaw. "It was an unusual call, but I didn't think much of it until you two showed up and mentioned it."

"Do you know who the caller was?" Cameron asked.

"Didn't give his name. It was an out-of-state number's all I know. Four-oh-four, I think."

"That's Atlanta."

"Yeah?"

"I live in Atlanta. That's my area code."

"Well, that is a coincidence."

"You didn't hear anything else from this caller?" Mitch asked. "Didn't call back, show up here?"

Morgan shook his head. "Like I said, didn't think of it again till you all showed up. You want to see it?"

"Please," Cameron said. Morgan led them back through the Caribbean Room and into the former kitchen, now housing the model layout and the collection of Benjamin "Bloodbeard" Lovelace artifacts.

"Did the caller say what his interest was in the disk?" Mitch asked as Cameron studied the disk again.

"Nope. Just asked if it was here, had me describe it a little. Only talked for a minute or two."

She looked at the disk again, closer than last time. Several of the thin "pie slices" contained two letters; two N's had a tilde above them, suggesting they were Spanish; and half a dozen had no letter at all, but rather a short dash. It piqued her curiosity, but this was not the place for in-depth examination.

"How'd he get the name Bloodbeard, anyhow?" Mitch asked, his eyes roving to several of the other pieces on the wall. "He a redhead?"

"No. Black as the devil's eyes," Morgan said with raised eyebrows as he began the tale. "According to legend, it was shortly after Lovelace became captain of the *Scourge of the Seas*. He set upon a Spanish galleon off the west coast of Cuba. They put up great resistance, and a fierce battle ensued. Cannons were blasting the ships to bits, pistols cracking, sabers slicing. The cries of injured and dying men were almost as loud as the explosion of the guns."

Cameron winced as Morgan got wound up. "Lovelace had just boarded the Spanish galleon when a stray sword slash cut his chin. Blood gushing from his face, he charged on, dispatching several men on his way to the captain's quarters, where he skewered the captain and his wife. His crew ultimately took the ship, and Lovelace never once wavered, despite the flow of blood staining his beard. One surviving Spanish crewman said he resembled something from another world."

"I didn't think he left survivors," Cameron said.

"Normally he didn't, but he made an exception, supposedly because he'd seen such fear in the eyes of those he'd fought with that he thought letting them live to tell the tale would create more fear in other captains and crews than would his sinking the galleon and killing everyone aboard. Thus the legend of "Bloodbeard" was born, and a streak of scarred flesh through the middle of his black beard made him easily identifiable wherever he went."

"Interesting," Mitch said.

"That's funny, I never came across that in my research," Cameron said. "Although I didn't do that much." She shrugged. "Do you know anything about his attack of the *Descubridor* in 1705?"

"Sounds vaguely familiar," Morgan replied. "Where was that?"

"Off the Space Coast, near modern Cocoa Beach."

"Most of my work and knowledge has been in the Gulf of Mexico," he said. "That's where the *Scourge of the Seas* was found, which is why I even know of Bloodbeard."

"Do you know anything about the cipher?"

"A little. I know it's a cipher wheel," he said with a smile that revealed stained yellow teeth. Coffee or nicotine or both. "I had no idea what it was when I found it. I thought maybe it was some Mayan calendar or something, until I realized the letters were Latin. I spent a few minutes online to figure out it was a cipher wheel, but I couldn't make heads or tails of it." He shrugged. "But it looks good on the wall."

"It does that," Mitch said.

"What's your interest in it?"

Cameron saw no way out of telling him, and said, "We think the cipher is a key to finding the Fountain of Youth."

"The Fountain of Youth," Morgan said slowly. "And maybe the Lost City of Atlantis too?" He laughed. "Or the gold of ancient El Dorado?"

"I know it sounds like the plot to the next Indiana Jones movie, but I'm serious."

He stopped mid-laugh. "The Fountain of Youth? You truly believe it exists?"

"I do."

"A magic spring of water that grants all who drink eternal life?"

"Maybe not quite so dramatic as that, but yes."

Morgan looked to Mitch and then back to her. He shrugged. "Okay. I guess it makes me no difference what you believe. Would you like to hold it, take a closer look?"

"I would, thanks," Cameron said. "In fact, we'd like to buy it."

"Buy it?"

She nodded.

"I'm afraid it's not for sale."

"We haven't even mentioned a price."

"The price don't matter," he said. "This place isn't much, and half of what I've got is more tacky than historically relevant. But it's still mine. Every item in this museum is something I've found or salvaged myself, or been given to me by friends who've done the hard work. It's not for sale."

Cameron licked her lips and took a breath, trying to figure out inroads to at least draw Morgan into a negotiation. At the same time, she tried to calm the panic rising in her; without this cipher disk, they were sunk.

"Could we borrow it?" Mitch asked.

Morgan turned to him.

"I can respect not wanting to part with something you worked hard for, and the truth is, we can't offer a ton of money anyhow. But my friend here has been working for years to locate the Fountain of Youth. It may seem like a punchline, but I've seen her research, and she's not tilting at windmills. It would mean a lot to her, and to me, if we could borrow the disk, study it, see where it leads, and then return it to you. And we will compensate you for your troubles."

Morgan pursed his lips.

"We're not trying to scam you," Cameron said. "There's no treasure we're holding out on. In fact, when we find the Fountain of Youth, we intend to let anyone who wishes drink from it."

"I have no interest in fabled waters," Morgan said. "I don't even want your money. But how do I know you won't take the cipher and never come back?"

Mitch reached for his wallet. "Sign out front says cash only. You have any way to process a credit card, or an ATM?"

"Nail salon next door lets me run a card if need be."

"What about a copier?"

"They got a machine over there too. Why?"

"I'll give you five hundred bucks for two days. Today's Tuesday? If we're not back by close of business Thursday, you can run another two-fifty on the card. If we're not back by Friday and you haven't heard from us, charge it to the max and call the cops."

Morgan narrowed one eye.

"I can give you half a dozen references if you want to check up on me, run a credit check, anything like that."

Morgan waved a hand, then extended it. "Five hundred bucks for two days?"

Mitch nodded.

"You got a deal."

They shook, and Cameron bit her lip. "Um, we'll also need to clean it."

"Clean it?"

"Get the grit and grime off it so we can read all the letters."

"So long as you don't damage it, I don't mind."

"That's the last thing we want. We'll be very careful."

"I let on that I leave items in their original condition for authenticity's sake," he said with a wink, "but truth is, I just don't want to take the time to clean 'em up. I'd a whole lot rather be fishing." He scratched his jaw. "Tell you what, you clean it up so it shines, I'll give you an extra day for nothing."

Cameron beamed. "*You* got a deal."

*   *   *

Mitch inhaled deeply as he and Cameron stepped out of Nails by Nikki. While Morgan and a middle-aged Vietnamese woman had spent ten minutes trying to fix some unknown problem with the salon's multifunction printer-copier, he had fought off the acetone fumes while simultaneously trying to decipher the stares he was receiving from the other "nail technician," a Vietnamese girl of no more than eighteen or nineteen. She was either attracted to him, afraid of him, or was trying to figure out why a white male was in her shop—he couldn't tell which.

Morgan and the woman finally figured out the machine and copied his license and credit card, and Mitch questioned his decision to give the number to Morgan. He'd had his identity compromised twice already, so having to cancel a credit card would be a minor hassle by comparison, and worth the joy it brought to Cameron's face. The woman then processed a five-hundred-dollar charge on Mitch's card, his initial payment to Morgan. He had no idea how the payment was getting from her to him, nor why she had to write a small memo on the keypad to get the card to process, but the small receipt she handed him was genuine.

They returned to Morgan's Pirate Den, where the proprietor dug around in a closet to find a box and some packing air bags with which to secure the cipher disk. At quarter after two, they exited the museum and walked to the Elantra, Cameron with the boxed disk in her possession.

"Where to now?" Mitch asked after starting the car and powering down the windows.

"Um, a grocery store."

"Hungry?"

"I need some items to clean the disk," she said.

Mitch reached for his phone, called up Google Maps, and found the nearest grocery store, a Save A Lot on Missouri Avenue. They were there in five minutes, and since she had the disk on her lap, he offered to run in.

"We need baking soda, lemon juice, and distilled water," she said. "And a couple of toothbrushes."

"Toothbrushes?"

"Nothing fancy, just cheap, plain brushes."

"Got it. Anything else?"

"Something to pick with. Some of the calcifications looked pretty thick."

"Okay." He got out, then leaned in his open window. "You like Combos?"

"Combos?"

"Round, cheese-filled crackers."

"Oh, yeah, of course."

"Pizza pretzel?"

"Uh-huh."

"Hang tight."

Like any man, Mitch had a little trouble figuring out where which items were in a new grocery store. But he found the baking soda, lemon juice, toothbrushes, distilled water, and a bag of Combos in reasonably short order. His search for "something to pick with" took a little longer. Screwdrivers seemed a little crude for the task, and toothpicks too flimsy. He finally found some metal kebab skewers that he deemed would work, and then made one last venture before checking out. He returned to the car carrying two plastic bags.

"I was getting nervous," Cameron said from under her floppy hat. "Here," she said, taking the bags from him even though she had the disk on her lap. "Find everything?"

She was already searching through the bags, so he didn't bother to answer as he got into the car.

"What is this for?" she asked, holding up a bottle of cabernet sauvignon.

"Do we need a reason?"

She pulled her sunglasses down.

"Celebration," he said. "When we decipher the ciphers."

"Shouldn't it be champagne then?"

"This way we can drink it even if we don't solve the riddle."

She slipped it back into the bag as he started the car. "Hmm. Kebab skewers."

"A little unwieldy, but we could bend them."

"They should work. Thanks."

He turned out of the parking lot and headed toward the causeway back to Clearwater Beach.

"So I've been thinking," Cameron said, her hand out the window, feeling the breeze.

"Yeah?"

"About who called Morgan about the cipher."

138

"Yeah, I was wondering. I thought you had an exclusive on its existence."

"So did I. I mean, it's not like somebody else couldn't have figured out what I did, done the research I did, but who? And why would they call about the disk and not follow up on it?"

"Come up with any theories?"

"Well, for starters, I ruled out a coincidence, that someone was interested in the cipher for any other reason. It'd be one thing to have someone call about Bloodbeard memorabilia in general, but the only way anyone could know about the cipher is to know about Diego Figueroa and the Fountain of Youth legend."

"I don't know all you learned in Spain, but that would make sense."

"That means somebody else knows what I know, but do they know all I know? We assumed the Van Buren Gang knew only of the Figueroa Cipher, but is it possible they also know about this one?"

"If so, why haven't they come for it yet?"

"I don't know."

"Not just after taking the Figueroa Cipher from you, a month or two ago after the call?"

"I don't know," she repeated. "The alternative is that there's a third party pursuing the Fountain of Youth, and either they only know of this cipher somehow or they never showed up in Cocoa Beach or St. Augustine, and both of those scenarios seem a little far-fetched."

"Does anybody else know you're here?"

"No."

"And you haven't told anybody else about the second cipher?"

"No one. Ever."

"And Morgan has my name and ID, but not yours. Even so, we should keep our eyes open."

Cameron sighed. "I guess we'd better get to work. The sooner we figure this out, the farther we stay ahead of whoever else is in on the hunt."

CHAPTER NINETEEN

They returned to the Sandpearl Resort and met in Cameron's room—a suite, technically. Mitch's idea, so they'd have a place to work. Along with a separate sleeping area, it featured a kitchenette, dining table, and living room that opened to a balcony with a straight-on view of the coast. Leaving her hat, sunglasses, and purse on the table, Cameron walked to the bathroom and fetched a bath towel, which she laid on the square glass coffee table. She then retrieved the Figueroa Cipher from the in-room safe and laid it on the towel. Mitch placed the Bloodbeard Cipher next to it, and they both stood back and looked at the disks.

"I don't believe it," Cameron said.

"So how do we crack the code?" Mitch asked.

"First, we have to clean off the disk."

"You're the archaeologist."

"Hardly." She walked to the bag from the grocery store. "Do you want to see if there's a small mixing bowl?"

He dug through a few of the cupboards in the kitchenette and came up with a rather large cereal or ice cream bowl. "This work?"

"I suppose. And a spoon."

He brought them both to the dining table, and she measured out several spoonfuls of baking soda into the bowl. Then she poured lemon juice and began to stir. She added a few more drops of lemon juice, a dash more baking soda, and finally one last drop of lemon juice to form a yellowish paste.

"You're a regular Pioneer Woman," Mitch said.

"Who?"

"One of those cooking show ladies. Ree Something-or-Rather."

She shook her head.

"Never mind. Now what?"

In response, Cameron took the paste over to the coffee table. Nudging a throw pillow aside, she sat down and carefully spooned her paste onto the corroded areas of the Bloodbeard Cipher. She didn't have enough, and got up to make another batch.

"Should I start scrubbing?"

"No, we have to let it sit for a while."

"Got ya," Mitch said, and shifted positions on the couch to study the Figueroa Cipher. "You know exactly how we're supposed to make sense of these two?"

"No."

"Javier Figueroa's letter didn't mention what to do with the disks—how to interpret them?"

"No."

"Hmm."

She poured a little more lemon juice, stirred, and returned to the table. Mitch was spread-legged on the couch, so she knelt down on the other side of the table, which gave her a better angle to the uncovered portions of the disk. When all areas that had corroded or taken on a patina were covered with baking soda and lemon juice paste, she set the bowl aside.

"Now what?" Mitch asked. "How long does this need to sit?"

"At least half an hour," she said, standing. She put her hands on her hips and turned to look out the balcony window. She looked back at Mitch. "I'm going to go for a quick swim."

"A swim?"

"Just in the pool. Get a little exercise, let my mind unwind, and this has to sit anyhow. It'll do me some good to clear my head of it for a few minutes."

He nodded.

"Wanna come?"

"Hotel pool at three in the afternoon? There'll be a million people down there."

"It's that or watching lemon juice dry."

"Six of one, half dozen of another . . ."

"Come on," she said, extending her hand. She made a quick "come here" motion with her fingers, and put just enough pout into her face to persuade him. It was a look she'd given various men for various reasons hundreds of times in the past, and it seldom (except with Erik) failed. And it didn't now.

They quickly changed into swimwear and headed down to the pool. True to Mitch's fear, it was incredibly crowded, and any sort of actual swimming was out of the question. Still, on what had become a stiflingly hot afternoon, the water was cool and refreshing, and flirting with Mitch for a few minutes did indeed help take Cameron's mind off the two cipher disks sitting on the table in her suite. Ever since procuring the Bloodbeard Cipher from William Morgan—and even before that, in fact—she'd been subtly nagged by the fear that despite having all the clues at her fingertips, she wouldn't be able to crack the code. Then what?

After half an hour, they both quickly used the outdoor shower to rinse the chlorine and contaminants off them, then changed into comfortable tees and shorts. Then they reassembled in Cameron's suite. It was just after four o'clock, and she was already feeling hunger pains. She pushed them aside and got to work.

She started by rinsing off the lemon paste with distilled water, and then using one of the toothbrushes to scrape away the corrosion. She showed Mitch how to gently use the bristles—figuring he, being a man, would attack the disk as if to scratch even the engravings off it—and then turned her focus to some of the harder calcifications. With one of the kebab skewers, she picked away, a painstakingly slow process. They paused twice to rinse the disk again, and finally, concluded that all the letters were legible, if not good as new. They made short work of setting aside their tools, and sat side by side on the couch looking at the two disks.

"They are pretty much identical, aren't they?" Mitch said.

"Different letters, different sequence, but yeah."

"Any clues how to do this, at all?"

"Beyond the basic rules of a cipher disk, no. And that's where it can get tricky," she said, leaning back on the couch. "In theory, once you figure out where to turn the disk, which letters correspond with which, it's a matching game. But there could also be a sequence to it."

"A sequence?"

"For example, every five or ten letters, rotate the disk X spaces. Or skip every other space. Or alternate disks by letter." She sighed. "We could be in for a long night of work."

"Good thing I bought wine."

It drew a small smile from her.

"Okay," he said, slapping his thighs, "how do we want to get started? This is your gig, so you call the shots."

She sat up. "I didn't come across anything in my research that would provide us any sort of legend or clue—nothing overt anyhow. I suppose I could have missed some coded reference somewhere, but if that's the case, we're hosed without a return trip to Spain."

"Say when."

"Easy, Mac. I don't think we're quite ready for intercontinental travel."

"Fair enough. Let's assume you didn't miss anything. Let's assume Diego made these with the intention that anyone who applied themselves could figure it out. How do we start?"

"With the words on the carving."

"You remember them?"

"Verbatim," she said, looking briefly and finding a notepad and pen on the end table. She uncapped the pen and began to write, but Mitch stopped her. "What?" she asked.

"Paranoia and one too many detective TV shows, but you'll leave an imprint on the page underneath. Tear off the page and write on a hard surface."

She shrugged and did as he said, speaking the words aloud as she wrote. "I found what men have lost lives and fortunes seeking. *Je partage le secret avec ceux qui ont des yeux pour voir, afin qu'ils puissent jouir de la vie éternelle.* - Diego Ponce de León de Figueroa, 1698."

"Run the French past me again."

She spoke slowly as she wrote again. "I share the secret with those who have eyes to see, so that they may enjoy eternal life."

"You're sure on the French translation?"

"Positive. I ran it past several experts. It's not like the carving is classified or something."

He nodded. "Eyes to see . . ."

"What?"

"Just rethinking our 'anybody could solve it' assumption." Mitch read the words on the carving several times. "Why is it in French?"

"Why is it in English?"

"Does having 'eyes to see' mean being bilingual? And why would that be a qualification?"

Cameron shrugged.

"English and French. They and the Spanish were the big three of the day, right? At least when it comes to colonization?"

"The Dutch factored in, especially in the Caribbean, but yeah."

"Some sort of 'We are the World,' let's all come together vibe? The Spanish guy uses English and French?"

"Maybe."

"Why is he making it hard to find?"

Cameron looked at him.

"If you found eternal life, wouldn't you want to share it with everyone, not make them jump through a bunch of hoops to figure out the secret?"

"There was something about that in Javier's letter, about Diego having at one time claimed that a person should have to earn the right to eternal life."

"You'd think he'd have at least given his son a clue as to how to do it."

"Maybe he did, but Javier didn't believe him or excluded it from the letter for some reason."

They stared at the disks a while longer.

"You know it was 1698 when he made the carving?" Mitch asked.

Cameron nodded.

"How?"

"Because it says 1698 on the carving."

He lightly backhanded her knee.

"It's well documented that Figueroa arrived in Florida in early 1698, having originally sailed to the Caribbean the previous year. He left by July in hopes of making it back to Spain before winter. It was his only trip to the New World, so it had to have been then. Why?"

"Just thinking, if he left a code to deciphering the disks, maybe he gave us the wrong year."

"Not unless all the rest of recorded history is wrong."

He sighed. Then got up and paced.

"There are dashes," Cameron said.

He turned around.

"On the interior row of the Bloodbeard Cipher, there are dashes." She counted quietly. "Twenty of them. And . . . one, two, three, four, five, six, seven, eight empty spaces."

"So only one hundred letters?"

"I didn't count."

"Assuming there are 128 spaces per row like on the other disk."

"I didn't count," she said, and then quietly did so. "Yep, 128 wedges of the pie, times two rows, equals 256 spaces."

"But only 228 letters." Mitch shrugged. "He ran out of time?"

"They're not in a row. And they're all on the inside."

"The empty spaces?"

"And the dashes."

"And there's none on the first disk?"

"No. Two hundred fifty-six letters. Well, more actually, because there are a few spaces with two letters."

"On both disks?"

She turned her eyes to the Bloodbeard Cipher. "Yes."

"Which ones?"

"'CH' a few times, double L's, and that's it."

"Isn't that Spanish? Double L's for sure."

"It is," she said. "And 'CH' is a Spanish consonant. Plus you have the tilde N. See?"

"Are the rest of these letters all Spanish?" Mitch asked. "I mean, all in the Spanish alphabet?"

"They have the same alphabet we do, but for a few added letters."

He paced some more. "So we have a carving in English and French, and the decoding disks are in Spanish."

"Well, at least contain Spanish letters."

"Right. And 256 and 256 is 512."

"You a math major at Texas?"

"More like in the sixth grade," he said. "Subtract the twenty dashes and eight empties, and you have 484 letters. Or, rather, spaces with letters." He turned his head to the paper containing the message from the carving. "And we have no idea where to start or which letters to use and not use."

Cameron exhaled and sat back. Mitch plopped beside her. "You want a glass of wine?"

"Yes and no. I want to stay sharp."

"It's just wine, not 100 proof vodka."

"For your linebacker's body, maybe. I can only have a couple glasses before I start to feel a little buzz, and I don't want to work on this buzzed."

"Something to eat?"

"It's a little early. Let's keep thinking."

They did, for nearly an hour, tossing out all sorts of theories as they analyzed the disks and made observations. The outer rows of both disks contained 128 letters (or in a few cases, Spanish characters) arranged in alphabetical order. The inner rows contained 128 letters (in the case of the Figueroa Cipher) and one hundred letters, twenty dashes, and eight empty spaces (in the case of the Bloodbeard Cipher) in no particular order. They spun the outer rings of each disk, hoping to line the two rows of letters up in such a way that they revealed a key or clue. They considered mathematical ideas, that the dashes were minus signs, that perhaps Diego Figueroa had been telling them which letters to use and which not to. They calculated the number of letters on one disk compared to another, and even made a chart to notate how many times each letter appeared on each disk and in total. By six o'clock, they had concluded nothing, and Cameron's stomach was noticeably growling.

"What are you in the mood for?" Mitch asked.

"Pardon?"

"Dinner. I'm insisting we eat."

She sighed. "Yeah. I'm up for whatever."

"Chinese?"

"Sure."

"You find a place, and I'll go get it."

"Deal."

He returned to his room to change into pants with pockets and to get his wallet and keys, and Cameron used her phone to find a nearby Chinese take-out restaurant. The first place she found didn't allow for online ordering, so she picked a place just across the causeway back in Clearwater. Mitch said that was fine, and they placed an order. He headed out to pick up their food, and Cameron strolled onto the balcony to take in the late afternoon sun. It was brilliant as it shimmered on the surface of the gulf, and despite the whoops and hollers and beat of the music from the pool area down below, and the crowds in swimwear on the beach beyond, she pictured herself back in the late seventeenth century—not on the balcony of a resort hotel, but on a quest to find the Fountain of Youth for the first time. What must have gone through Diego Figueroa's head as he hiked and cut through the interior of Florida, following unknown directions? Or when he found the Fountain of Youth and tasted the first drops of its water? Or when he created such intricate clues for future generations to follow? She still wondered at his motivation. What had prompted his making it hard to find, requiring "eyes to see" instead of plainly stating where it was? Did deciphering the disks depend on the answer to that question?

Tired of thinking, Cameron headed back inside. She figured she had half an hour before Mitch returned with dinner, and decided to take a real shower and clean up nice. After all, if she and Mitch were going to spend the evening in close proximity . . .

*   *   *

Mitch missed the Porsche, and had to settle for lowered windows as he cruised across the Causeway in the Elantra, Bruce Springsteen's "Glory Days" pulsing through the radio. So what if it was his dad's era, the Boss sounded good. And Mitch felt good, despite the block he and Cameron were experiencing with interpreting the disks. It would come, in time. They just needed to work the problem a little longer.

Bruce was interrupted by Mitch's marimba ringtone. He punched the car's stereo quiet and picked up the phone. "This is Owens."

"Hey, Owens," Cameron said.

"Hey. What's up?"

"We forgot egg rolls. Can you pick up a couple?"

"Sure thing. Are you vacuuming?"

"I started the shower. I can still feel pool germs all over me."

"That's an appealing thought. Now I have to stop at the local Y on my way back."

"Just get a couple egg rolls, and some sweet and sour sauce."

"You got it."

"Thanks."

He ended the call and turned Bruce back on. The song ended shortly, but Mitch's vibe didn't. He had no idea where things with Cameron were going, let alone their quest to find the Fountain of Youth, but for right now, he didn't much care. Heck, he didn't know where his life was going post-Florida. He was just enjoying the ride, and an evening like this—golden sunshine on the palm fronds and sparkling on the surface of the Intracoastal Waterway—made the ride a pleasure. The figurative and literal ride.

Whatever station he had stumbled upon followed Springsteen with Bon Jovi, and when Mitch's phone rang again, he glanced at the display. It was not the number that had just called him, meaning not Cameron, and since he didn't recognize the number or the area code, he let it go. He wasn't interrupting "We Weren't Born to Follow" for a probable telemarketer.

Halfway through the guitar solo, his phone buzzed a third time. Mitch looked down and this time recognized Cameron's number. With a smirk playing at his mouth, he swiped to answer the call. "Want some wontons too?"

". . . veggie."

"What?"

"Turn down the radio. I can hardly hear you."

He adjusted it marginally.

"I said pork, not veggie. For the egg rolls."

"You have a cabbage preference?"

"Shut up."

"Seriously, I'm almost there, so is there anything else you want?"

"That's all. A couple of pork egg rolls."

"With sweet and sour sauce."

"Yes."

"You got it."

"I promise, no more calls."

"I'll see you in a bit."

He tossed the phone out of reach on the seat, cranked the closing to the song, and smiled.

CHAPTER TWENTY

The aromas were too much for Mitch, and in the elevator on the way up to Cameron's suite, he dug out an egg roll and began snacking. It was half gone when he knocked on the door to her suite, and when she opened the door, her eyes went to the half still in his hand. "That better not have been mine."

She had changed into a pink sleeveless top and denim shorts, and with her hair out of the braid and hanging loose over her bare shoulders, she looked simply beautiful. Add in the aroma of citrus wafting out the door and the twinkle in her eyes, and Mitch found himself momentarily distracted. "Uh, no. I got extra."

"You going to stand in the hall eating?"

He made a face as he passed through the door, letting it shut behind him. They spent a few minutes sorting out the food—Hunan beef and white rice for him, shrimp with mixed veggies and fried rice for her, and egg rolls for both—then sat down on the couch, making room on the coffee table or the end table for their food and glasses of wine. Mitch had never been an expert at pairing wine with this or that food, and didn't know if a bottle of cabernet sauvignon from Save A Lot went with takeout Chinese food, but didn't much care. It suited his palette just fine.

"No chopsticks?" Cameron asked, looking into the empty bag.

"Uh, didn't look. Figured there was silverware here."

She started to get up, but he stopped her and got them himself.

"Kind of inauthentic not having chopsticks," she said.

"I always thought eating with a pair of sticks was kind of akin to writing checks. We've come up with better ways."

"Better? Chinese people eat just fine with chopsticks."

"I'm Texan, not Chinese. These will work fine," he said, holding up two forks.

"Can I ask you a question?"

"Sure."

"Do Texans make a point of proving how Texan they are, or is it just you?"

She was starting to smirk, so Mitch responded with a wink. "It comes naturally by being a superior people."

"Aha."

"Sorry about the chopsticks. It honestly never occurred to me."

"It's fine." She took a sip of wine and set her glass back on the end table. "So I've been thinking."

"And . . . ?"

She had stabbed a piece of shrimp and spoke before ingesting it. "The letters on the outer rows are in alphabetical order, while the ones on the inside rows seem random."

"Right."

"And the ones on the inside aren't in any obvious order—they don't make up the words of the carving or something. So maybe what we need to do is work through in order on the outer row. For example, the Figueroa Cipher has nine A's on the outer row. Maybe the first time we find an A on the carving, we look to see the letter under or inside—if you will—the first A on the cipher. The second time we find an A, we look to see the letter under the second A. And so on and so on."

"Okay."

"Make sense?"

"In theory. But there's 128 different letters that could be under the first A, depending on how you turn the outer ring."

"I know," she said, spearing another shrimp with her fork.

"And which disk do you use? There aren't enough letters on the carving to utilize all the spaces on the two wheels, so somehow we have to eliminate two of them."

"Did you count the letters in the carving?"

"No." He inhaled a bite of beef. It was spicy, but not too spicy. Then he dug the paper with the carving's statement written on it out from under the edge of the towel beneath the disks. While they ate quietly, he counted characters.

"Well . . . ?" Cameron asked.

"I'm double-checking." He forked some more beef to his mouth. She took a drink of wine. He sat back. "There are 196 characters or spaces," he said. "If you exclude punctuation, which I did because there's no punctuation on the disk."

"Okay."

"But there is a dash, and there's a dash on the carving, before his name."

"One-ninety-six?"

He nodded.

"What about without spaces?"

He looked back at the sheet and counted again. "Thirty-seven spaces, so 159."

"Hmm."

"You got the pen and paper over there?"

She reached for it and handed it to him. He tore off the top sheet, nudged the disks and a box of rice aside to have room to write, and began doing math.

"What are you writing?" Cameron asked, leaning in, her hair brushing against his arm and her perfume filling his nose. He found himself wondering if she always put on perfume after showering, because otherwise, it didn't make much sense given that all they had planned was deciphering two ancient bronze disks.

"Mitch?"

"Sorry. We came up with a lot of numbers earlier," he said, referring to the pad where he had written 512, 502, 492, 484, 256, 128, 120, 108, and 100.

"I thought those were from your fortune cookie."

"Clever. That's every possible combination of total characters, characters per disk, characters minus dashes or spaces or whatever. No combination leads to 196, and especially not 159."

"What are you thinking?"

"That maybe there's some clue as to where to start, where to align the disks."

He did some more doodling and figuring while they ate, wondering if 1698 factored in somehow, despite Cameron's earlier doubts. Maybe combinations of numbers, or maybe the dash was a clue. That's how it worked on the convoluted "treasure hunt" TV shows and movies. The archaeologist type stumbled upon an obscure deduction that could only be reached by the show's writers knowing the answer ahead of time, and it solved the whole thing. But Mitch had no idea what the writer was thinking.

They finished eating, cleaned up, and—in Mitch's case—poured a second glass of wine. They studied the disks for another fifteen to twenty minutes before Cameron got up with a loud sigh and walked out onto the balcony. Mitch stared at the disks for another couple minutes, willing himself to be able to solve the riddle for her sake, but he couldn't. He drained his glass, set it on the dining table, and joined her on the deck.

The sun was now low in the sky, hovering just over the surface of the water. Like the previous night, it had turned the entire sky a brilliant orange and yellow gradient. The scene made him think of their walk on the beach, of their kiss, and it made him quickly lose interest in a three-hundred-year-old puzzle.

"Did math come naturally to you?" Cameron asked, looking at him.

He frowned at the question, then shrugged. "Sort of. Algebra and my brain didn't especially agree, but numbers have always been easy."

"Numbers and my brain didn't especially agree," she said. "I'd stare at math problems and it was like Greek until all the sudden it would click, and then it was easy. And there was always this tipping point, where I could feel the gears tumbling into place. Until they did, it was incredibly frustrating."

"Like now?"

She nodded.

"Waiting for the tipping point?"

"Yeah. There were times with math, like with this sort of thing, where it started to click, and then it was almost fun. Problem-solving, deducing, working out a solution." She sighed. "We're not there yet, and like when the numbers didn't click, I don't know how to get there." She slumped, leaning her elbows on the railing.

Mitch placed a hand on her back and rubbed up and down. She turned her head to look at him but said nothing. After a moment, she looked back at the gulf.

He withdrew his hand and leaned beside her. "I did save room for pie, if you want to call it a night and go grab a slice, or some ice cream, and come back fresh tomorrow."

"Maybe later. I want to push through this a little. I just needed a minute."

"Well, in that case, maybe we should hearken back to my school years."

She turned back his way.

"I told you algebra was rough, all this solving for X, and trains going opposite directions from New York and Chicago." He shook his head. "I made it through by trial and error. A bit tedious at times, but it beat repeating seventh grade."

"Trial and error?"

"We've got 128 possibilities per disk, right? Easiest way to eliminate some of them is to try them. Presumably, Diego didn't intend for someone to end with more random letters when they translated the carving. We should start seeing words, and if not, we try the next letter on the wheel."

"And if there's specific sequence to tell us when to rotate the rings?"

"Then there will be a lot of error."

She smiled. "Worth a try."

They returned inside, leaving the sliding doors slightly ajar. For a change, they switched seats on the couch, and stared at the disks. "Which should we start with?" Cameron asked.

"You counted the A's on the Figueroa Cipher, right?"

She nodded.

"How about on the Bloodbeard Cipher?"

"Um, four," she said.

"How many A's on the carving?"

She began counting, her lips moving with each number. "Ten," she finally said. "But only nine in the actual quote."

"Count the B's."

"There aren't any."

"Okay, the C's."

"Three on the disk and . . . four on the carving, but only three in the quote. The fourth is in Ponce." She looked at him excitedly. "When you counted total characters, did you count just the quote?"

"No."

She slid the paper between them, and they both counted.

"One-twenty-eight?" Mitch asked.

"One-twenty-eight. That must be it. And it makes sense too," she said with a slight shake of her head, "you wouldn't normally put any stock in the signature or name, so why would it be something to decipher?"

"It wouldn't."

Cameron's eyes were vivid as she turned from Mitch back to the disk. A minute later, she looked back up. "Four D's on the disk, four in the quote itself."

"I hate to burst your bubble, but what about the second disk?"

Her shoulders dropped. "I don't know. But we're three for three on letters. Let's start the trial and error and see where we get. Maybe it will come to us."

"I'm game."

"Hand me the pad and pen."

He did, and she tore off a new page.

"Where should we start?" she asked. "We've got 128 possibilities."

"Right where it is now."

"You think it hasn't been moved since Diego made it? We moved it ourselves."

"We've got no rhyme or reason, so we'd have as much chance as turning it the wrong way as the right way. Might as well start where we are."

"Okay." She inched forward. "First letter is I. First I on the disk is a W." Mitch wrote it down.

"Skip the space, second letter is F. First F on the disk is an L."

"W-L," Mitch said. "I don't know any words that start W-L."

"But we might need to be thinking in Spanish or French, not just English. Not that that changes anything in this case. Next letter?"

"Sure."

She rotated the outer ring of the Figueroa Cipher one space. "First I is now G. First F is S."

"This might go pretty quick," Mitch said.

"Unless we're dealing with initials or something. Shorthand for something."

"I'll keep writing whatever you say so we can come back later, but let's keep moving."

They continued the trial and error while the sun sank into the Gulf of Mexico. A few times, they made rudimentary progress, starting to spell a word or phrase, but always derailing before getting anywhere close to a message.

They took a break. Mitch checked in on the Cardinals. They were scuffling, having lost four of five. Cameron poured herself a half glass of wine. They resumed their work, finding little if any headway. She finally flopped back on the couch, her hair splaying over the fabric. "That's it. We're all the way around."

Mitch set down the pad and pen.

"We didn't even get close," she exhaled.

"We need the other disk," Mitch said.

"But how?"

He shrugged.

"Did we err in our deductions somehow?"

He shrugged again.

"I mean, if I didn't know better, I'd think this was all just random."

Mitch stood and walked to the sliding glass doors. The sounds from the pool area floated up on the breeze and through the open door. He turned back. "But it's not."

She looked at him.

"The quote contains exactly 128 characters. There's the same number of A's, of C's, of D's. I bet if you go down the line, it matches exactly."

"Meaning?"

"Meaning, we're on the right track. We're just not far enough down it."

"Do we do the same thing with the other disk?"

"How so?"

Cameron sat up and began counting. Mitch walked over and sat beside her. "What are you thinking?"

"Sshh."

He sat back and waited. A few minutes passed.

"Four A's, four B's, five C's on the outer ring of the Bloodbeard Cipher," she finally said. "There are four A's, four B's, and five C's on the inner ring of the Figueroa Cipher." She looked back down. "CH is four and four. Double L's are four and . . . two, three . . . four. That has to be it. Find the corresponding letter on the inner circle and then find that letter on the outer circle of the other disk and deduce the corresponding letter there."

"And that will be the true message?"

"That or we'll need more wine."

Mitch grabbed the pad and did some quick math. "Just over sixteen thousand possibilities."

Cameron's eyes went wide. "Sixteen thousand?"

"A hundred and twenty-eight times a hundred and twenty-eight."

"There has to be some way to narrow it down. We could be doing trial and error for the rest of the week."

"Well, we can cut it in half, at least initially."

"How so?"

"You work off the actual disk, and I'll start halfway around off our paper. We have two or three letters to work off."

"Worth a try."

155

"In an hour, one of us goes down to The Marketplace to get some ice cream."

"Deal."

Cameron started at the top of the Figuera Cipher disk, and Mitch started at the bottom, albeit using the letters they had written on the paper as a guide. They worked the first couple together, both to make sure they were on the same page and for pacing. The first letter on the carving was an I, and the first I on the outer circle of the Figueroa Cipher corresponded to a W on the inner ring as Cameron looked at the disk and to an O as Mitch looked at their writings on the paper. Then they looked to the Bloodbeard Cipher. The first W on the outer circle corresponded to an N on the inner circle, and the first O to a C. The second letter on the carving, an F, corresponded to an L and then a dash for Cameron and an S and an S for Mitch. They concluded N-dash and C-S were dead ends, and moved on, turning the outer ring of the Bloodbeard Cipher one space.

Cameron reported a space and a dash, which constituted crapping out, and Mitch got to space, E-T, space, A-I-R-A-N, space before they concluded, even with their limited understanding of French, that it was a dead end.

They spun the disk another space and continued. An hour passed and they made four trips around the Bloodbeard Cipher, one for each of the first four letters at the top and bottom of the Figueroa Cipher. *Et airan* was as close as they had come to anything, and Google confirmed that meant nothing in French or any other language.

After a couple minutes debating who should go get ice cream, they opted to both go, and fold in a five- or ten-minute walk out in the night air. They strolled through the pool area, which had quieted somewhat, and across the dunes to the beach.

"Are you going crazy yet?" Cameron asked as Mitch took several deep breaths of salty sea air. "Losing interest, ready to bail?"

"Yes . . . and no."

She smiled, then grabbed his hand. "I'm glad." After a minute, she leaned her head on his shoulder, and they watched the distant waves lap onshore, the ripples of water catching the light of a quarter moon behind them.

"You ready to get back to it?" Mitch asked.

"Yes and no."

He squeezed her hand, then released it, and they walked back to the hotel, stopping in The Marketplace for a pint of rocky road ice cream. Back in the suite, they passed it back and forth, each with their own spoon, while they made a fifth trip around the Bloodbeard Cipher. They got nowhere.

Cameron excused herself to the bathroom, taking her spoon to the sink. Concluding that meant she was done with ice cream, Mitch dug down to the bottom and spooned another bite into his mouth. He kept working, figuring he'd make a run to the bathroom when Cameron was done and she could catch up.

His first letter on the inner circle of the Figueroa Cipher was a D, which, when he transferred that to the Bloodbeard Cipher, corresponded to an L. F corresponded to I which corresponded to another L. No good, and he moved on. Next came N-A-R-A space, which sounded like a dud as well. He moved on.

Cameron emerged from the bathroom and spent a few minutes tidying up in the kitchenette.

"You quitting?" he asked.

"No, but thinking of making some coffee."

"There's more hooch over here," he said.

"Wine will put me to sleep. You want some?"

He shook his head.

"That's right, you don't drink coffee."

She set about brewing some, and he kept going. N-E-I-space was a dead end, and so was N-S. He turned the wheel again.

With the coffeepot hissing and spitting, Cameron came over, leaning on Mitch's shoulder. "What are you doing, skipping ahead?"

"Yeah. P-A-R-A-dash. Para's a word in Spanish, isn't it?"

"Yeah, it means 'for.' You have 'para'?"

"Double-check?"

She peered down at the paper and disk for a minute. "Yeah, that's right. Scoot over."

He did, and she sat down. The next letter after the dash was an E, and then a blank space.

"So what's a blank space mean?" Cameron asked.

"I would think a space, but that would mean we have a lot of long words if there are only eight spaces, and then we have to explain what the dashes are."

"Dashes could mean skip, say if his message didn't take a full 128 characters?"

"Or the other way around."

"Let's leave them for now, see where we get."

He agreed, and they continued. When they stopped a few minutes later, they had a total of P-A-R-A-dash-E-space-N-C-O-space-N-T-R-A-R-dash.

"If we get rid of the dashes, we have P-A-R-A-E and a space," Mitch said. "Is that a word?"

"Not that I know of."

"And N-C-O isn't."

"No."

"Okay, so flip the dashes and spaces. Then we have *'para encontrar.'*"

Cameron's eyes widened. "I recognize that." She practically flailed for her phone and called up a translator on the internet. "'*Encontrar*' is Spanish for 'find.' Or 'meet' or 'encounter' or a bunch of other words. Keep going."

The next few letters generated the word '*la*,' which meant *'the'* in Spanish. Halfway through the next word, Cameron grabbed Mitch's arm. He had F-U-E-N.

"Mitch . . ."

"T," he said.

"Mitch!"

"E. '*Fuente.*'"

"'Fountain,'" she said. "'*Fuente*' is 'fountain.'"

Before he knew it, she'd grabbed both of his cheeks and planted a kiss smack on his lips.

CHAPTER TWENTY-ONE

Mitch and Cameron looked at each other. Her eyes radiated intensity as she tipped her head ever so slightly to the side, then leaned in and kissed him again. Then a third time, slower and softer as her hands slid down and clasped loosely around his neck.

Mitch sat slightly back. Cameron pulled her legs onto the couch and leaned in closer. They kissed some more. At some point, he reached his hand behind her head, then the back of her neck.

Then she stopped. She backed a few inches away, her eyes still vivid. She backed a few inches farther. "I'm sorry," she said.

"You don't have to be sorry."

"No, I mean . . . because I really kinda want to keep working on the disks."

He grinned. And nodded.

She leaned in to peck him one more time, then turned and faced the coffee table again. Mitch too sat forward, and together they continued to work on deciphering the disk. The next phrase—"*de la Juventud*"—translated as "of Youth," leaving them with "*Para encontrar la Fuente de la Juventud*"—"To find the Fountain of Youth."

Any doubts that they were on the right track were erased as Cameron forgot about her coffee and Mitch forgot about kissing—for the time being. They paused and went over what they had found so far, confirming they had decoded it correctly. They kept working, fighting the urge to go fast and forcing themselves to double-check their work as they went. Cameron eventually retrieved her coffee, and Mitch finished off the bottle of wine.

"Something's wrong," Cameron said when Mitch returned from the bathroom.

"What?"

159

"'*Reunifica*' translates to 'reunify,' but the next letters are A-dash-space-I-S-I-M-space-I-dash-C-O-N-M-I-G-O." She looked up. "'*Conmigo*' is Spanish for 'with me,' but I have no idea what A-I-S-I-M-I means, regardless of where I put dashes or spaces."

Mitch came and looked over her shoulder. He concurred with her decryption. "I assume you've put it into the translator?"

"Nothing."

"Hmm."

"The letter A is separated by dashes, and it means 'to' in Spanish. But I have no idea what 'isimi' means."

"'*Reunifica a isimi conmigo*,'" he read. "'*Reunifica*' means 'reunify,' and '*conmigo*' means 'with me'?"

Cameron nodded.

"Could '*Isimi*' be a name?"

"I suppose."

"'Reunify Isimi with me'?"

Cameron shrugged.

"Reunify seems like a rarely used word."

"This is Google translating. Could mean reunite. It's a general meaning."

It was Mitch's turn to shrug. "I'd say keep going and maybe it will make sense."

"Why not?"

They worked for another half hour and change, by which time both of them were yawning. But as Cameron looked up the last few letters, and Mitch checked her work, they had a mostly concise message.

"'*Para encontrar la Fuente de la Juventud reunifica a Isimi*,'" she said, with a quick, uncertain glance at Mitch, "'*conmigo en el campanario de la Misión San Francisco de Sevilla*.'" She tapped her phone a few times. "Which according to Google, comes out as 'To find the Fountain of Youth reunify Isimi with me in the bell tower of Mission San Francisco of Seville.'"

"Not exactly 'X marks the spot.'"

"No, but it's new clues. Clues only we have," she said with a smile that belied the late hour. "I'm going to get my laptop."

Mitch yawned.

"You don't have to stay up if you don't want, but I don't think I can possibly sleep now."

"Are you kidding? We finally have something to go on."

She reached for her coffee mug. It was cold, and she got up to reheat it.

"We're sure of this translation?" Mitch asked.

"How do you mean?"

"Not the translation, but we deciphered this right you think?"

"Has to be."

"Then I'm going to scramble these, just in case."

She tapped some time into the microwave. "Go for it."

Mitch turned the outer rings of the two disks, then sat back and waited for Cameron to rejoin him with her coffee and laptop. When she sat down, he directed her to turn sideways on the couch, and while she searched on her computer, he massaged her shoulders, sure they had to be as stiff and tired as his were. He peered over her shoulder as she rechecked her Spanish-to-English translation on several sites. With a few insignificant variations, the translations all agreed. Next, she searched for "*Isimi*" and Spanish missions named San Francisco or located in Seville, but got nowhere.

Cameron let out a huge sigh and dropped her head back onto Mitch's shoulder. He leaned his head onto hers, fighting off another yawn. The next thing he knew, he awoke with a start. The room was dark, and Cameron was gone. A folded blanket and a pillow sat on the end of the couch.

Mitch stood, and a deep breath turned into another yawn. He looked around. The balcony was empty. Cameron's laptop sat on the kitchen counter, next to her coffee mug. The laptop was powered off, and the mug still had an inch of liquid in it. He turned his eyes to the bedroom door, and saw that it was slightly ajar. Through the crack, he could see Cameron had pulled back the covers and crashed, still in her clothes.

He watched her sleep for just a moment, then turned and found the notepad they had used all evening. There were two unused sheets, and he left a brief note telling Cameron he had opted for a bed instead of a couch, and to call him when she woke in the morning.

Then, with a rueful grin at what might have been, he returned to his room for the night. He took a few minutes to get some air on his balcony, then ran a toothbrush quickly over his teeth. It was already Wednesday morning by the time he finally pulled back his own covers and crawled into bed. The excitement of the evening and all the fresh air took their toll, and he was asleep in minutes.

*　　　　　*　　　　　*

Cameron awoke in the middle of the night with a sense that someone was moving in her bedroom. She lay perfectly still, letting her eyes adjust to the darkness. She spotted nothing.

Quietly, she eased out of bed and peeked out into the living room. The couch was empty, the bedding she'd placed at the end of the couch undisturbed. The disks were still on the coffee table, and Cameron realized she had been dreaming about a ninja-like intruder coming for the disks. In reality, the suite was quiet.

She fetched a glass of water and walked out onto the balcony. She had no idea what time it was, other than nowhere near morning. The moon was now low in the sky over the water, and beautiful. Everything was quiet, and the night air was cool. She leaned on the railing for a moment, thinking.

What now? How did she figure out what *Isimi* meant? How did she figure out where *Misión San Francisco de Sevilla* was located? Was another trip to Spain really in order? That made her think of Mitch. How long would their . . . whatever it was last? And where was it going? Was it a nice Florida fling, a pleasant accompaniment to her search for the Fountain of Youth? Was there any future for them together? It was way too early to be thinking like that, but sooner or later, they would have to make a decision. Was there even one to make? What did Mitch think?

She sighed and gulped some water. Maybe it hadn't been a dream of an intruder to wake her. Maybe it had been subconscious questions and anxieties.

She drained the glass of water and went back to her room. Remembering that she was still in her clothes, she quickly changed into sleepwear and slipped back under the sheets.

She awoke several hours later, groggily aware that it was morning. As much to wake up as for hygiene, she took a shower, then dressed in a royal blue tie-sleeve blouse and Bermuda shorts. She set some coffee brewing, then found her phone to call Mitch. That's when she saw a note on top of the disks. She smiled as she read it, then tapped his number. The phone rang four times before he answered with a sleepy, "Hey there."

"Hey. Did I wake you?"

"More or less."

"Sorry."

"Don't be. What's the plan?"

"I don't know. Check-out's at eleven. We really have no reason to stay another day."

"Where to?"

"I don't know. Want to grab some breakfast and think about it?"

"Yeah. Give me twenty minutes."

"Okay. Buzz me when you're ready."

"Where we going?"

"How about grab something from The Marketplace and hang out on the lawn?"

"Works for me. I'll see you in twenty."

He clicked off, and Cameron filled a cup of coffee and went out onto the balcony. She remembered the coolness of night, but it was long gone, replaced by a stagnant warmth that even permeated the shade of the balcony. The sky over the gulf was almost as gray as blue, hazy, and the air was thick and heavy. Maybe dining al fresco wasn't such a great idea.

Cameron sipped her coffee, also remembering the thoughts that had rattled around her brain in the middle of the night. Regarding her and Mitch, she decided to let things play out as long as possible. There was no need to ruin their time now by worrying about what could come next. She instead turned her attention to the translation from the carving. It was all there in front of them, if only she could figure out what or who *Isimi* was and where to look for *Misión San Francisco de Sevilla*. Her search the night before had been far from exhaustive, in part because she'd been distracted by Mitch's backrub, but she didn't think she was going to be able to Google this one.

She smiled as she remembered the words of one of her college professors. An old throwback, he'd often ranted against people who used Wikipedia as a source or settled for the easy answers Google could provide. Someone on campus had even made a spoof Twitter account of the professor, with daily "get off my lawn" sort of tweets making fun of his diatribes.

Cameron suddenly sat up. College professors.

She stood and, cup in hand, went inside and booted up her laptop. While at Clemson, she'd had a couple of classes with an avid historian whose specialty had been sixteenth- and seventeenth-century Spanish colonialism. She had tried reaching out to him a few years ago to see if he could shed some light on Diego Figueroa's search for the Fountain of Youth—or the Fountain of Youth in general—and had been told he had retired. She couldn't remember now if she had been unable to get further contact information for him or had given up, but she knew she hadn't seen or spoken to Dr. Gabriel Kessler since graduation. But if there was someone who might know something about a Spanish mission in the New World, it would be her old professor.

She logged on to Clemson's website to find a general contact number, and then began what she expected would be a somewhat tedious process of reaching someone who could provide contact info for a retired professor. She tapped through two automated menus and talked to one real person, and was on hold when Mitch knocked on her door. She turned the handle and let him in just as a female's voice came on the line, asking how she could be of help.

"Yes, I'm looking for contact information for a Dr. Gabriel Kessler," she said, smiling at Mitch. He wore khaki shorts and a black T-shirt featuring a football player with an eyepatch and crossed swords behind him. She knew enough of the NFL to recognize it as the Raiders' logo and, although it was a bit crude, it worked for Mitch. So did the stubble that had grown back on his jaw and the unstyled brownish-blond hair.

"He was a history professor several years ago and I believe he's retired now," Cameron continued. "I was a student of his, Cameron Leigh, and I'm looking to get a hold of him."

"Let me consult our personnel files," the woman said. "Kessler, you said?"

"That's right, Gabriel Kessler."

"Let me put you on hold for a few moments."

"Thank you. Morning," she said to Mitch.

"Morning. You look nice," he said, then dropped a quick kiss on her forehead.

"Thanks. So do you," she said, touching his jaw with her hand.

"Who you holding on?"

"I'll explain over breakfast."

"You all packed?"

"More or less. Except for these," she said, nodding at the disks. "Yes," she said quickly as the woman came back on the line.

"Dr. Gabriel Kessler currently resides on Sanibel Island, Florida," the woman said. "I have a phone number, e-mail, or mailing address."

"How about all three," Cameron said, looking around for a piece of paper. She found the last page on the notepad they'd been using the night before, quickly uncapped the pen, and told the woman she was ready. She then copied down the information and thanked her before hanging up.

"Want to take our stuff down to the car now or after breakfast?" Mitch asked.

"After."

"Okay. You ready?"

"I am."

They headed down to The Marketplace, just off the lobby, where they purchased pastries, fruit, coffee, and juice for a makeshift breakfast. They headed out to the terrace, which was quiet in the morning hours. A few sunbathers, swimmers, and readers were scattered around the pool area, but Cameron and Mitch had no trouble finding privacy.

"How'd you sleep?" Cameron asked as she peeled a banana.

"Okay once I straightened out the kink in my back."

"Sorry. I didn't know if I should wake you or let you sleep on the couch."

"It's fine," he said, taking a swig of bottled orange juice. "You?"

"Not great. I woke up in the middle of the night and couldn't get back to sleep. Too many thoughts about too many things going through my head. Including how to solve the rest of the riddle."

"*Isimi* and the mission in Seville?"

She nodded, swallowing a bite of banana. "It hit me this morning. I had a professor at Clemson who is an expert on Spanish colonialism. Or, I should say, was. Now he's retired in south Florida."

"Oh?"

"Sanibel Island, in fact."

"Road trip?"

"I'm going to call him after breakfast and see if he happens to have time to see us. I wouldn't mind a second opinion on our interpretation and translation, in addition to hoping he knows something about what *Isimi* might mean or what specific mission it's referring to."

"Were you and this professor close, or was he just another prof?"

"Close?"

"I don't mean anything hinky," Mitch said. "I mean, would he remember you compared to all his other students?"

"I had him for several classes, and I was there to learn, not to get necessary credits. He might."

"Worth a call at least."

They finished eating, by which time the heat and humidity were already growing oppressive. They quickly headed back inside to the coolness of the lobby and discussed plans. Mitch was packed and ready, but Cameron needed a few minutes yet. He said he'd go fill the car with gas while she packed up the disks and a few other things and called Dr. Kessler. They both took the elevator to their floor, then parted, he to get his luggage and head back down, and she to finish packing.

Cameron stepped out of the flip-flops she had hastily put on for breakfast and carried them into the bedroom. She tossed them toward her suitcase, then dug the sheet of paper with Dr. Kessler's phone number from her pocket, hoping nine-thirty wasn't too early to call a retired man living on Sanibel Island.

The phone purred four times, and Cameron was about to disconnect the call when a deep but soft and a little scratchy voice said, "Gabe Kessler."

"Dr. Kessler, it's Cameron Leigh. I was one of your students about a decade ago at Clemson."

"Cameron Leigh . . . Yes," he said, his voice rising an octave. "Yes, you wrote wonderful essays."

"Oh, thank you."

"You cared about what you wrote, believe me, a professor can tell. Well, this is a surprise. What can I do for you, Ms. Leigh?"

"I was actually hoping to pick your brain," she said. She had wandered through the living room and stood looking out the sliding glass doors at the gulf. "My friend and I have been working on a project and we could use your expertise."

"I'd be happy to help," Kessler said, and she could hear the warmth in his voice that had made him a respected professor and tempered any frustration she'd felt at his rigorous exams. "Any particular area of my so-called expertise you have in mind?"

"This is going to sound odd, but I'd rather talk in person if that's possible. My friend and I are in the Tampa area right now, and the woman I spoke with at Clemson said you live on Sanibel Island. If it's not an inconvenience, is there a private room in a library or a community center or somewhere like that we could meet and talk?"

"I can do better than that," Kessler said. "Why don't you stop by my house? I'm right on the beach, you can't beat the views, and that will assure us privacy."

"I don't want to impose."

166

"Not at all. Remember, I'm retired, Ms. Leigh. I have an abundance of time."

"Are you free this afternoon?"

"Any time. If I don't answer the door, come around back and you'll find me on the beach."

"You're sure I'm not imposing?"

"I'm positive. I look forward to seeing a former student again and offering any help I can."

"Thank you, Dr. Kessler."

She confirmed his address and said they should arrive sometime early afternoon. The excitement she'd felt the night before when deciphering the carving had returned. There was no guarantee Dr. Kessler knew anything about *Isimi* or *Misión San Francisco de Sevilla*, but she was confident nonetheless. After years of hard work, meticulous research, and setbacks of every kind, she was now on a roll. A hurricane unearthed the Figueroa Cipher. Mitch came to her rescue and agreed to work with her after Erik pulled his support. They recovered the Bloodbeard Cipher and figured out the carving based on the two disks. And now, after not thinking about Dr. Kessler for years, having him suddenly pop into her head that morning felt like fate, as if it was her destiny to find the Fountain of Youth.

CHAPTER TWENTY-TWO

After stowing his luggage in the trunk of the Elantra, Mitch drove a few blocks north to a Speedway gas station, where he filled up the tank. Despite the haze in the sky, enough sun filtered through that he was regretting his decision to wear black. He distracted himself by wondering what was next if Cameron's old professor wasn't available or willing to help. Surely she wouldn't give up, but he hoped they weren't destined for hours in a library turning musty pages.

His phone buzzed as he was getting back into the car. He expected it to be Cameron, but it wasn't. The number looked familiar, and he realized it was the number that had called him the previous afternoon, between Cameron's egg roll requests. Curiosity winning out, he swiped his thumb across the phone as he sat down. "This is Owens."

"Mr. Owens, I have some information for you," said a croaky female voice, tinged with just enough of a Hispanic accent to be noticeable.

"Oh yeah? What kind of information?"

"Information about your traveling companion."

Without turning his head, Mitch looked around to see if there were any obvious signs that he was being watched. He saw none.

"Who is this?"

"My name is Olivia."

"And who are you, Olivia?"

"An interested party."

"Interested in what?"

"The same thing as you," she said, as if it were obvious, and also with a trace of flirt in her tone. She sounded like she was trying to have a Hispanic accent, either because it would make her sound sexy—which it did—or because it would disguise her true identity. That wasn't a problem, since Mitch had no clue who she was, and his subconscious efforts to connect the name Olivia to anything that happened in the last week came up empty.

He sighed. "How about we cut the vagueness? Tell me what you're talking about or I hang up."

"That would be a mistake."

Mitch said nothing.

"Mr. Owens?"

"I'm waiting."

"Ms. Leigh is not who you think she is."

"Until you tell me who you are, I'm not inclined to care what you say about her."

"Where are you now? Perhaps we can meet."

"Not until you give me something more than ambiguous notions and mysterious warnings."

"Give me fifteen minutes. Where can I meet you?"

"Goodbye, Olivia," he said, then lowered the phone and ended the call. He half expected her to call right back, and sat thinking, his car still parked by the gas pump. Everything about Olivia and her call screamed that she was bluffing, that this was a crank call or a scam or a distraction of some kind. Everything but one thing—that she knew to call in the first place.

Still in his hand, his phone buzzed. He looked down to see a text from Cameron.

Heading down to lobby.

He quickly thumbed a reply and started the car. He drove back to the Sandpearl, thinking more about Olivia's call. Who? What? Why? And most of all, was there any credence to her alleged information? He decided not to think about it. He'd never given rumors and allegations the time of day, requiring proof before buying in. And he wasn't about to make an exception now—not until Olivia got back to him, which he had a funny feeling she would.

He parked on the brick driveway and headed inside, where Cameron was waiting in the lobby, looking pretty as a picture as she sipped an iced coffee, her luggage beside her. She'd added a pair of silver hoop earrings that hadn't been there at breakfast, along with matching bangles on her wrist. She smiled when she saw him and stepped forward.

"You got everything?" he asked.

"Yeah. This is the heavy one," she said with a wink, and he took the suitcase from beside her. "Everything okay?" she asked.

"Yeah, why?"

"You look like you saw a ghost."

"The spittin' image of Captain Bloodbeard," he said with gravel in his voice. "No ghost," he added with a smile, having resolved not to tell Cameron about Olivia's call. If he wasn't putting stock in her equivocations, there was no reason to scare Cameron by mentioning it.

"So where we headed?" he asked as he loaded her luggage into the trunk.

"Sanibel Island."

"You got ahold of your professor?"

She nodded. "He invited us to his house."

"You have directions?"

Cameron waved her phone back and forth.

"Then let's go."

Leaving the beach behind, they crossed the Intracoastal Waterway and headed due east, through Clearwater toward Highway 19, then I-275, and eventually I-75 south toward Fort Myers. He asked, and Cameron said they were not in a particular hurry. So he made a slight detour and swung into a Dunkin' to supplement his breakfast. He also had a second motivation. The call with Olivia still had him a little on edge, and he'd noticed a black SUV following them across the causeway and through Clearwater. That didn't necessarily mean much, since a lot of vehicles would be traveling east on Highway 60 all the way through town, but the extra turns gave him a chance to see if his paranoia had any basis in reality.

The SUV kept going on 60, and Mitch put it from his mind. Leaving Cameron in the car, he purchased a couple of long johns and reemerged into the torpid air with a resolution not to let Olivia's mysterious call ruin their day.

"You really should get a coffee to go with that," Cameron said as he got back in.

"If it tasted half as good as it smelled. Another one in the bag if you want it . . ."

"I'm good, thanks."

They got back on the highway and headed east to Highway 19. Traffic was heavy on the three-lane southbound road, and they rolled slowly past mile after mile of commercial buildings and apartment complexes and condominiums. They weren't far from I-275 when the mass of vehicles came to almost a complete stop. After several minutes of bumper-to-bumper, Mitch began to strum his fingers on the wheel in frustration.

"Maybe we can FedEx the Bloodbeard Cipher back to Morgan," he said. "I'm not really looking forward to driving all the way back through this again."

"Sorry, but I wanted Dr. Kessler to see it before we took it back."

"It's fine," he said, then leaned to the side to try to see around a box truck in front of him. No dice. "What are your plans for tonight?" he asked. "Assuming Dr. Kessler can't point us to such-and-such a spot."

She shrugged. "I don't know. Depends on what he does give us. If he has nothing, we'll have to reevaluate and figure out what's next—how much time and money we want to spend." She sighed. "We may have to step back and do some research, think, clear our heads."

Mitch nodded, inched forward a few yards. He took a chance. "Well, if we do need to take some time to clear our heads, what would you think of getting away for a couple days?"

She didn't immediately answer, but slowly licked her lips.

"No agenda, no strings attached. Just sun and sand, and no pressure to crack a code or figure out the next clue."

"What about seafood?"

"Sun, sand, and seafood."

"That sounds very nice."

Mitch didn't say it, but he found himself hoping Dr. Kessler was a dead end. That was if they ever got there. He found a slight opening in the left lane and veered over, and again craned his neck to see what was causing the delay. Cameron too sat up.

"This can't be part of the regular commute, can it?" she asked.

"Not at this time especially," Mitch said. "You want to get on your phone and see if you can find an alternate route?"

"You going to jump the barricade?"

"There's an exit just a little ways up ahead. I can get over if it goes somewhere."

She searched on her phone and found that the next exit would indeed get them, without too much hassle, over to the interstate. Mitch maneuvered through two lanes of traffic with only minor rudeness and just made the exit. A couple minutes later, he had merged into the steady but moving flow on four lanes of Interstate 275. Cameron pulled her legs under her on her seat and leaned forward to tune the radio. She settled on The Beach Boys with a raised eyebrow toward Mitch. They weren't his cup of tea, but appropriate for the occasion, so he shrugged.

As they neared downtown St. Petersburg and the Tampa Bay Rays' home, "The Trop," traffic again picked up, but they kept moving. Soon they were free and clear again. They passed the exit they had taken the other night, to Fort De Soto State Park, and crossed a pair of causeways on either side of a tollbooth. Up ahead on the left, the dual spires of the Sunshine Skyway Bridge took shape through the haze. Spanning over four miles and towering 430 feet over Lower Tampa Bay, the bridge was an icon in southern Florida, as well as a vital connector between the Pinellas Peninsula and the mainland.

The interstate had narrowed to two lanes, flanked on either side by a single row of palm trees. Their fronds hardly moved in the languid air, reminding Mitch how hot it was outside, which in turn caused him to reach for the air conditioning knob to tweak it slightly. His hand bumped Cameron's as she reached for the radio, and they shared the typical smile/chuckle that went with such occurrences. Just a little touch, but the feel of her skin on his led Mitch to think about the possibilities if Dr. Kessler didn't pan out and their plans turned toward a couple of days of R&R on a desolate beach . . .

Something drew his eye, and he looked directly in the rearview mirror. The light had caught the reflection of a silver Passat practically touching his rear bumper, and he mumbled a complaint.

"What?" Cameron asked, turning around in her seat to look.

"Just some guy riding my tail," Mitch said, accelerating slightly, taking advantage of the open lane in front of him.

"Whoa," Cameron said.

"What?"

"That guy—Mitch!"

He had turned her way, and in so doing missed the black SUV that had come roaring around the Passat and into the lane beside him. In a heartbeat, it had edged past him, then started to veer into his lane. Responding to Cameron's eyes, he turned his head and saw that he was being cut off. His first thought was to punch the brake pedal, but he remembered the close-following Passat, and instead wrenched the wheel to the right as the SUV swerved fully into his lane.

Cameron screamed as Mitch just avoided a light pole, in the process turning back into the SUV. The vehicles collided, causing a deafening scraping of metal. The next instant, they plowed through a chain-link fence and down a shallow, paved embankment toward an access road that ran along the interstate and, beyond it, the open waters of Tampa Bay.

CHAPTER TWENTY-THREE

Cameron's body tensed as the Elantra hurtled toward a short guardrail that she gave no chance of stopping them at sixty or seventy miles per hour. The car began to spin, and her first thought was that Mitch was turning toward the railing and water so as to hit it head on instead of flipping over the railing. Then she saw that the SUV that had run them off the road had peeled off to the left, spinning them right.

Mitch cranked the wheel left now, into the void, and Cameron's body would have been slammed into the door if not for the seatbelt holding her in place. Next thing she knew, she heard a loud bang, more screeching metal on metal, and then an explosive pop. The car fishtailed, all while slowing, and then an airbag smacked her in the face.

She didn't black out, she didn't think, but for a moment, she was in a daze. She heard Mitch calling her name. She could feel something dripping down her face, and, in fact, feel her entire body. No pain, other than across her chest and sternum from the force of the seatbelt. She could taste blood, and salt, and deduced the dripping on her face was blood from her nose and tears from watery eyes, both the results of the airbag's sudden deployment. And she heard sirens, and wondered how they had responded *so* quickly.

"Cameron," Mitch said again, more clearly, and pawed at the airbag. The white in front of her eyes vanished, replaced by the blinding glare of the sun. "Are you all right?" he asked.

"Yeah. Yeah."

"You're bleeding."

"The airbag . . . my nose," she said, feeling it with her finger. It didn't hurt, but there was a trickle of blood coming from her right nostril. Mitch fumbled around for something while she looked at the SUV a hundred feet ahead of them. It scrambled up the paved embankment, through the chain-link fence, and back onto the interstate.

"Here," Mitch said, thrusting a napkin at her.

She looked down. "There's chocolate frosting on this."

"Better than blood," he said. "Are you sure you're okay?"

"I'm fine. You?"

"Yeah."

The sirens stopped as an SUV with "Pinellas County Sheriff" stenciled on the side coasted to a stop beside the Elantra. The radio was still blasting, and the air finding its way around the deflated airbags was suddenly cold. Mitch turned off the car and opened his door just as the officer reached the car.

"Are you both all right?" he asked with a heavy southern accent.

"Yeah, I think so," Mitch said.

"Ma'am?"

Chocolate-covered napkin held to her nose, Cameron nodded.

The officer reached for a walkie-talkie at his shoulder. "Dispatch, I need a bus at this location, access road to the north fishing pier of the Skyway Bridge. Be advised of a black, full-size SUV fleeing the scene southbound over the bridge on I-275. Unknown plate, likely will have damage or scrapes on passenger side."

"It was a GMC," Mitch said. "I saw the logo."

"Update, the SUV is a GMC, unknown model," the officer said. Mitch had gotten out to stand beside him, and the officer now ducked into the car. "Ma'am, I'm Officer Purifoy. Paramedics are en route."

"I'm fine, Officer Purifoy, really. Thanks."

As proof, she lowered the napkin, which had drawn no new blood from her nose.

"Very well, but you'll still want to be checked out when they arrive."

She nodded, then reached for her door handle. The door opened only a fraction, and she realized it was tight against the guardrail, itself just feet from the waterline. Her heart began to pound again as it hit her how close they had come to going in. She closed her eyes and sat back, causing the seatbelt to slacken slightly. She reached down to unbuckle it. Sirens distracted her, and she looked up to see a law enforcement vehicle of an undetermined branch go sailing by on the interstate, doing at least ninety.

Free from the seatbelt, Cameron crawled across the center console of the Elantra and, with a hand from both Officer Purifoy and Mitch, stepped out of the vehicle. Her first step on pavement was wobbly, and Mitch reached a hand to steady her. She ignored the hand and crashed into him in a giant hug.

*   *   *

The paramedics came and checked out both Mitch and Cameron. Nothing was broken or sprained, and other than for some seatbelt- and airbag-related bruising, neither would suffer any ill-effects from the crash.

The Elantra was not so lucky. It had massive dents and scrapes on the driver's side from banging against the SUV, even worse marks on the passenger side from the collision with the guardrail, a blown rear tire, and serious front grill damage and shattered headlights. Mitch had already reached out to the rental company and his insurance agency, setting the wheels in motion to have the damages dealt with and to procure another vehicle for them.

Officer Purifoy had remained on site, joined by another car from the PCSO. Mitch and Cameron had both given detailed statements, including explaining why they believed this was not a random incident.

"You all think this is related to these disks?" Purifoy asked.

"Possibly," Cameron said.

"The SUV never stopped, did it?"

"No," Mitch said.

"I was coming out of the rest area and saw the end of your crash. Saw the SUV speed away, but I didn't see anything before that."

"They came out of nowhere," Mitch said. "Cut me off and forced me . . ."

"What is it?"

"There was a silver Passat right on my tail. I never saw what happened to it."

"You think this was a two-pronged attack?"

"I don't know. They might have been riding my tail because the SUV was riding theirs, or they might have been there to box me in so I couldn't slow down." He shrugged. "Or they might have been tailgating."

"Notice anything else about this Passat?"

"Silver. It happened pretty fast."

Purifoy nodded as he jotted down the information. "Could be they wanted these disks, ran you off the road and planned to grab them. And it could be that they saw me and decided to drive off."

"You sound suspicious," Cameron said.

"Well, it's just curious, that's all," the officer answered. "You all said you stayed up in Clearwater. That's, what, an hour's drive?"

"About?"

"So why now, why here?"

"I was a little nervous when we left this morning," Mitch said, "and kept an eye out for a tail. I thought I saw an SUV following me, but it peeled off when we stopped for donuts. Could be it was the same one, I really don't remember."

"And it took them until now to catch up with you?"

"Traffic was kind of messy, and we took a few alternate routes. I don't know, I'm theorizing."

Purifoy nodded. "Why were you all nervous this morning?"

Mitch thought about mentioning Olivia, since she had been on his mind ever since the crash. But he didn't know how her call would relate to being run off the road. Sure, he could be missing something, and Purifoy and the proper authorities were the experts at investigating such crimes, but he didn't see the connection and didn't want to worry Cameron further if there wasn't a connection to be seen. So instead, he explained about their exploits several days ago back in Cocoa Beach and St. Augustine, limiting the details of how they had gotten the disk back.

Purifoy wrote down all the names of the Van Buren Gang, then asked if there was anything else. There wasn't at the moment, but they exchanged numbers and promised to be in touch if they thought of anything else or if the authorities managed to track down the SUV. So far, they hadn't. Once everything had been worked out with a towing company and insurance, Officer Purifoy gave Mitch and Cameron a ride to a Hertz in downtown St. Petersburg, near the port and a small, commercial airport. There was a lot of paperwork to be taken care of, but they finally let the duo leave with the only available vehicle, an army green Nissan Rogue. A little after one, they were back on the road.

Both were starving, but agreed to get going. Cameron didn't say anything, but Mitch suspected she shared his apprehension about attempting to cross the Skyway Bridge again. Even though he knew a second attack was highly unlikely, he kept a wary eye out as they flowed south on I-275. Both were silent as they climbed nearly twenty stories over the bay, this time without incident, and both exhaled when they reached Manatee County's terra firma on the other side of the bridge. Feeling as if they had crossed a barrier and not just a bridge, they agreed to break for lunch, and stopped at a Wendy's outside Bradenton.

"You okay?" Mitch asked Cameron as they ate at an outdoor table. The orange tank top she'd changed into, since her blue blouse had been speckled with drops of blood, revealed a bruise on her right arm.

"I'm fine," she said. "I'm just thinking through Officer Purifoy's questions again. Who, and why?"

"We don't know what resources Van Buren and his gang have," Mitch said. "They could have tracked us down. You remember what Erik said, about them having connections."

She looked down.

"What, did I say something?"

"I called Erik this morning."

Mitch said nothing

"I felt like I owed him something," she said. "After we found the second disk, and after we deciphered it . . . He's been such a big part of this quest all along, and I thought he should know." She tugged aside a strand of hair blown into her face by a rare breeze. "But it's like I told you before, Erik would never do anything like this. He would never do anything to hurt me."

Mitch took a bite of his burger.

"Do you believe me?"

He swallowed and nodded. "Yes. If you say he's not behind this, then I take your word for it. You know him a lot better than I do, that's for sure."

"But . . . ?"

"But, it is awfully coincidental," he said, realizing as he did that it was also awfully coincidental that they had been attacked just after his call from Olivia, despite his rationale that the two events weren't connected.

"It is," she said, "but I didn't give him many details. I didn't say where we'd found the disk, or even that we still had it. And all I said is that we were in Clearwater, not even Clearwater Beach, and I didn't tell him our plans. How would anyone have known where we were?"

"We have been using credit cards, if somebody had the ability to trace them. Or maybe they tapped Erik's phone and pinged yours? I don't know."

"They who? Van Buren?"

Mitch shrugged.

"Morgan's other caller?"

He shrugged again.

"And I called like ten minutes before we left. How would someone have latched onto us that quickly?"

"I don't know. It's all speculation at this point. The who, the how . . ."

"The why," she said. "What's the point of running us off the road?"

"To take the disks."

"Highway robbery in broad daylight?"

He shrugged yet again.

"And what if they were damaged when we crashed or flipped or plunged into the water?" she asked.

"Well, nobody said it was a brilliant plan."

She exhaled. Mitch took another bite and then a slurp of his soda, followed by a look up into the hazy white sky. The horizon had taken on a very pale blue hue, and although the air was still and heavy, it also seemed charged with storm potential.

"You think we should go on?" Cameron asked.

Mitch looked at her.

"I can't figure out why," she said. "It's like we've said, this isn't some typical treasure where whoever finds it keeps it and everyone else is out of luck, or where someone would want to hoard it and keep it from being found. Why would someone go through all this to stop us?"

"I don't know," Mitch said. "You did say some people bought into the idea of an actual treasure. That could motivate somebody."

"Yeah, but I don't know who actually puts credence in that."

He shrugged. "Either way, I'm game if you are. I don't like the idea of quitting because someone's trying to scare us off."

"Me either."

"We'll just have to be careful, and I think we should avoid reaching out to anyone."

"Like Erik?"

He nodded. "Not because we don't trust him, but because we don't know who's involved in this or what capabilities they have. The closer we play this to the vest, the better."

She nodded.

"There is one other possibility," he said, sitting back, wadding up his burger wrapper.

"What's that?"

"You also called Dr. Kessler this morning."

"You think someone's monitoring his calls?"

Mitch hesitated.

"Or do you not trust Dr. Kessler?"

"Just considering all options. Is there any chance he might not be trustworthy?"

"No. I mean, think what that would mean. He has no idea we're looking for the fountain, that we've found either disk, and he's just waiting around for us to call so he can figure out where we are and dispatch someone to take disks from us that he doesn't know until then we have?"

"Well, it's more likely Van Buren determined Kessler would be a possible source and monitored his calls too."

"In which case Kessler is trustworthy, which he is. I have no reservations about him."

"Okay," Mitch said. "I don't mean to question everyone you know."

"It's okay," she said, taking a breath. "We're both stressed."

"We need that vacation I talked about," he said again.

"After we talk to Dr. Kessler. Speaking of which, I should call him and let him know we'll be later than expected."

They finished eating and, as they got back into the SUV, she left Kessler a voicemail saying only that they were running late. The drive south on I-75 was largely boring, the scenery a combination of woods and swampland mixed with the sprawl of Bradenton, Sarasota, and Port Charlotte. The interstate then bowed inland around Fort Myers, and not until they were on its southern outskirts did they cut west, toward the Gulf of Mexico. Mitch was content to let Cameron and her phone provide directions, largely because he was bumming around Florida with a pretty girl and didn't much care where or when they arrived. After a dozen miles of meandering through outlying communities, they passed through a tollbooth and onto the Sanibel Causeway, a three-mile stretch with three separate bridges over San Carlos Bay. The first of those spans was elevated seventy feet over the surface and provided views of Sanibel Island and, beyond it, the darkening indigo sky.

"When does hurricane season start?" Mitch asked.

"Officially, June first," Cameron answered with a sideways smile.

"I wonder if they ever have to evacuate the whole island," Mitch said, surveying its flat span. "The whole thing looks susceptible to storm surge."

"Beauty has a price."

He winked at her. "We still talking about Florida hurricanes?"

She only grinned in reply.

Once over the causeway, the main road continued across the breadth of Sanibel Island, which was shaped like a bow. With approximately ten miles of shoreline around the curve of the bow, the island was popular with tourists and snowbirds, and was known the world over for its collection of shells and sand dollars along the beach. Mitch and Cameron had yet to see the beach, driving through heavily wooded commercial and residential neighborhoods before cutting over to Gulf Drive. Cameron looked at her phone for a moment, then directed Mitch to turn right, more or less west. They continued for a mile before she told him to slow down. Trees and brushes on both sides of the road were thick, except where they were broken by buildings on the right and tunnel-like driveways on the left.

"Should be the next one—No, this one," she said, pointing to the left. Mitch hit the brakes, then turned left onto a gravel driveway that cut through a row of thick shrubs and then meandered through several dozen naturally staggered palm trees. The gravel gave way to smoothed fieldstone as the driveway widened to form a circle around a fountain depicting a trio of dolphins leaping beside and over each other. Left of the fountain was a three-stall garage, connected to the main house by a pergola covered with flowering vines.

Mitch circled the fountain and parked in front of a two-story house— three, counting a cupola in the center—that seemed to sprawl across the grounds. Creamy yellow paint matched with white trim and shutters and blue shingles gave it a beach feel that was augmented by more palms flanking it on either side. A two-story colonnade covered the front entrance and a dozen feet of sidewalk leading to it, supported by a pair of white Grecian columns.

"Looks like Clemson pays their history professors almost as well as their football coaches," Mitch said.

"Dr. Kessler mentioned old family money a couple of times," Cameron said, unbuckling her seatbelt. She didn't move to get out, however, taking a deep breath instead.

"You ready?"

"I'm nervous."

"About meeting your old prof?"

"About this possibly being the end of the line. What if he looks at the disk and our clues and is stumped?"

Mitch shrugged. "Cross that bridge when we come to it. But we've unearthed enough now that I don't think the line ends, regardless of what Dr. Kessler knows."

"You just saying that to cheer me up?"

"Did it work?"

"Yes. A little."

He smiled. "No. I meant it."

She bit down on her bottom lip, then returned the smile. "Let's go see what he has to say."

CHAPTER TWENTY-FOUR

Cameron winced as she got out of the SUV. The air on Sanibel Island was as heavy and stagnant as in Bradenton, and the house was blocking any breeze that might have existed. As she and Mitch walked to the front door, she bound her hair in a quick ponytail, then reached for his hand.

He lifted his eyes to her, then squeezed her hand as she smiled. They let go, and she rang the bell.

Nobody answered.

"Let's check out back," she said, remembering what Dr. Kessler had told her earlier. They backtracked to the pergola-covered walkway and to an intermittent stone path leading through palms in the lawn around the side of the house. Their fronds fluttered lazily in breeze that Cameron felt as they turned the corner. The path turned to a wide, multi-tiered patio. The upper section contained a barbecue grill and a table with an umbrella, accessible from the house by a pair of French doors. Down a short set of stairs, the lower level of the patio featured a kidney-shaped swimming pool and a hot tub. The entire patio was surrounded by a lawn worthy of a golf course fairway. It stretched a few dozen yards to where the dunes and seagrass were kept at bay by a wood-beam retaining wall. More palm trees provided shade—or would have on a sunny day. A hammock spanned two of them, and Cameron suddenly felt like wiling away a sleepy afternoon.

Instead, she nodded at the break in the retaining wall, where a plank pathway led through the seagrass and small bushes. "He said to check the beach if he wasn't here."

"After you."

She started down the path, the sand on the planks crunching under her shoes. After fifty feet, the planks formed a small wood footbridge that spanned the dunes. As she climbed the bridge, the beauty of Sanibel Island washed over her. Despite the oncoming storm—and the freshening breeze that whipped into her face every strand of hair not held by her ponytail indicated it was indeed coming—the white sand and shells of the beach practically glistened as far as she could see in either direction. The gulf was gray instead of azure, but the crashing waves were still mesmerizing. Cameron was quickly losing interest in talking about old disks and mysterious codes, and was more and more intrigued by the idea of a quick dip, then a cool drink and a bite to eat while hunkering down from a storm.

Then she saw Dr. Kessler. He was walking on the beach, approaching from the left, a fishing rod in one hand and the day's catch in the other. He wore a blue button-down shirt with the sleeves rolled to the elbow, cutoff khakis, and boat shoes. As he drew closer, Cameron could tell he'd aged, which was no surprise, but he didn't seem old. His head had been balding already when he'd taught at Clemson, and now was buzzed. The pepper had mostly gone out of a neatly trimmed salt-and-pepper beard, but it gave him a wizened look. His skin was deeply tanned, almost taking on a maroon color, but wasn't weathered or worn. Cameron only hoped retirement treated her so well one day.

"Dr. Kessler," she said, as he turned onto the plank path.

"Miss Leigh. Just as I remembered you."

"Please, call me Cameron."

"And you may call me Gabe, now that we're not in class." He stopped as he reached them.

"This is Mitch Owens, my friend and recent business partner," she said, hoping her description was acceptable to him.

"Dr. Kessler, a pleasure," Mitch said, extending a hand.

Kessler switched the fishing rod to the hand that held the fish and shook Mitch's hand. "Gabe to you as well. Titles mean very little here. You have any trouble finding the place?"

"None," Cameron said. "Thank you again for your invitation."

"My pleasure. Your trip down all right?"

"Aside from car trouble, yes."

"You don't say. Anything serious?"

"It's a long story."

"Well, in that case, I hope you'll stay for dinner," he said, hefting the fish. "Freshly caught redfish."

"That sounds delicious," Cameron said. "But we don't want to take up any more of your time than necessary."

He waved her off. "It's like I told you on the phone, I have nothing but time."

"Give you a hand?" Mitch asked, nodding at the fish as they started walking.

"Thank you," Kessler said.

"They running good today or is it always like this down here?"

"May's the best season, when the water's not quite as warm, but it was a temperate spring, so the fishing's still pretty good. You a fisherman?"

"I fish, but I wouldn't call myself a fisherman."

"I am the same way with golfing."

When they got back to the patio, they climbed to the second deck, and Kessler instructed Mitch to set the fish on a counter built into the patio wall, next to the grill. "If it's all the same with you, I should get these cleaned before the storm comes, and then we can get down to business."

"That's fine," Cameron said.

"Can I get you something to drink? I've got several varieties of lemonade, sun tea I brewed this morning before the clouds came in, I can brew some coffee . . . ?"

"Tea would be great," Cameron said.

"Sure," Mitch said.

"Make yourselves comfortable," Kessler said, nodding at several cushioned wicker chairs on the patio. He ducked inside. Mitch took a seat, but Cameron turned and looked out toward the gulf, visible from the slight elevation of the patio. Towering over the gradient of indigo turned to slate gray was the thin outline of a billowing cumulous cloud. Several of them, in fact. The impending storm brought with it a tinge of excitement. Or maybe it was the prospects of talking to her professor.

He returned with a tray containing three tall glasses of iced tea and a small bowl with lemon slices. He had donned an apron over his shorts and, after passing out the glasses, began the work of fileting half a dozen redfish.

"You need a hand?" Mitch asked.

"You know how?"

"Ish."

Kessler grinned. "Thanks, but you're a guest. I don't want you to get all dirty."

Cameron sat down. "So, how long have you been retired?" she asked.

"Just over three years."

"Keeping busy enough?" Mitch asked.

"No, and that's just the way I like it."

"You two should compare notes," Cameron said. "Mitch is retired too."

Kessler raised a bushy gray eyebrow in Mitch's direction.

"He's a former NFL running back," she said.

"Is that a fact?"

"I hung to a roster for a few years."

"The Raiders?" Kessler asked, eyeing his shirt.

"Initially. Bounced around toward the end."

"And then you retired?"

"Not directly, and not permanently. More of a sabbatical."

"*You* keeping busy enough?"

"Lately. You know that old Johnny Cash song, 'I've Been Everywhere'? Well, I've been to Cocoa Beach, St. Augustine, Daytona, Orlando, Tampa, Clearwater, Sanibel . . ."

"And thankfully no karaoke bars," Cameron said.

Mitch took the insult with a grin and a swig of tea.

Kessler had stopped working, instead eying the gulf with a thousand-yard stare.

"Something wrong?" Cameron asked.

"What? Oh, no." He resumed working. "I'm just trying to figure out how someone your age," he said with a quick flit of his eyes at Mitch, "knows Johnny Cash."

"Is he the one who always wore black?" Cameron asked.

Kessler nodded. "But in answer to your question, Mitch, I fish now and again, do some gardening, a lot of reading and studying."

"Ever get around to writing that book?" Cameron asked.

"Book?" Mitch asked.

"Inside joke," Cameron said. "Dr. Kessler would often tell us, after relating some fascinating historical tidbit, 'I should write a book.'"

"And I would too," the professor said, "only I can't narrow down a topic of interest, and I don't suppose a thousand pages of an old professor's stream of consciousness would sell very well."

Cameron smiled as she took a drink of her tea, then watched a gull overhead soaring into the onshore breeze.

"What drew you to Sanibel Island?" Mitch asked. "Besides the obvious."

"My sister and brother-in-law bought this house about a dozen years ago. He was very big in real estate in Columbia, and this was their vacation home. When my sister died five or six years ago, he was looking to unload it and wanted it to stay in the family. I've always been partial to the water, to the pace of life here, and it's a little quieter than the east coast of Florida. It made perfect sense. And cents."

"It does seem a million miles away from everything."

"Like I said, the pace of life is nice."

Kessler made short work of deboning the fish. He took the filets inside, then disposed of the scraps and quickly washed his hands at an outdoor sink. He dried them on a towel with an eye to the sky, then looked down at Cameron and Mitch. "Care to take a walk on the beach?"

"Is there time?" Cameron asked.

"I haven't heard any thunder, so we should be safe."

She looked at Mitch, who shrugged.

"Okay."

Kessler instructed them to leave their glasses on the table for now, and he led the way back across the dunes to the beach. They stayed up high, on harder packed sand. Below them, beneath the high-water line, the sand was speckled with shells and globs of seaweed. The waves were high, several feet, and practically thunderous themselves as they crashed onto the beach.

"So, not that I don't cherish a visit from a former student in and of itself, but what brings you down to see me?" Kessler asked as they walked along the beach. "You said something about picking my brain about a project?"

There were a handful of others on the beach, but no one close to them. So Cameron had no reservations about speaking freely. She briefly explained how over the years, she'd become interested in the Fountain of Youth legend and developed a belief that it was real, if not the object portrayed in lore. She recapped her research, her trips to Puerto Rico and Spain, and her conclusion that Diego Figueroa had created two cipher disks and a stone carving that would lead to the fountain. Kessler listened stoically as she spoke and they plodded westward and a little north along the curved beach.

"When Hurricane Matthew dredged up the wreck of the *Descubridor* a few years ago, it gave me hope," she said. "It took me several years, but just last week, I was finally able to dive the wreck and find the Figueroa Cipher. That's where I met Mitch."

Kessler looked at her, waiting for her to continue. She explained about the hijacking of the *Eternal Sun*, how she had grabbed the disk and run, bullets flying, and how Mitch had happened along on his Jet Ski to save the day. He doffed an imaginary cap on cue.

"My goodness, this is quite serious," Kessler said.

"She hasn't told you the half of it."

He looked from Mitch back to Cameron.

"That night, they broke into the house I was staying at and tied me up so they could ransack the house and take the disk. Mitch arrived to take me to dinner just in time to scare them off."

"You have impeccable timing, it would seem."

"He does," Cameron said, tucking loose strands of hair behind her ears.

Kessler stopped. "So these pirates have the disk now?"

"No. We stole it back from them."

"You stole it back?"

They resumed walking, and she regaled him with an account of their scheme to get the disk back from "the Hogan Gang" at the Casa Monica in St. Augustine. Even as she recounted their adventure, it felt like eons ago, not a mere three days.

Suddenly a clap of thunder reverberated across the beach. All three turned their heads to the southwest, where a remarkable shelf cloud had developed. The billowing white top made the sky appear as if it was on fire, while the dark bluish purple bottom was streaked with wisps of rain.

"I think we might want to turn back," Kessler said.

Cameron could practically feel the intensity in the air as they started back to the house. To their right, the cloud metastasized and the waves assaulted the beach with increased force. Echoes of thunder rumbled and growled and grew increasingly frequent, until they were almost constant. Several times, the clouds above the shelf cloud flickered a faint orange from lightning. The wind was relentless, and carried with it a salty mist. The trio walked quickly, and reached the planks leading through the dunes just as giant drops of water began to sprinkle down around them.

"Cut that one a little close," Kessler said with a grin as they returned to the patio. Cameron helped him with the glasses while Mitch announced he was going to get the disks out of the car, seeing as how he had a feeling it might be pouring for a while. Cameron followed Kessler in through the French doors, to a wood-floored dining room that was a couple of steps up from the kitchen.

She had expected the interior to be bright and airy, white cabinets and sleek furniture. Instead, it felt more like a hunting lodge. The cabinets were dark, the kitchen counter made of black and gray marble, and the appliances were stainless steel. Not what she expected, it was still cozy, especially with the oncoming storm.

Kessler flicked on some lights and invited Cameron to make herself at home. "There's a powder room just down the hall," he said, pointing toward the front of the house. "We might be more comfortable in here," he said, gesturing toward a room off the dining room. He hit another switch on the wall, turning on several lamps in a study that contained a bookshelf that spanned an entire wall, a computer desk, a small work table, and a short couch and two chairs in the corner, by windows that were suddenly peppered with raindrops. "Please, have a seat," he said, and she sat down by the window and watched the storm.

Mitch came in a moment later, his hair wet and the shoulders of his shirt a shade darker than the rest. He carried the duffel bag containing the two disks.

"Thank you," Cameron mouthed.

"Can I get either of you refills?"

"I'm good, thanks," Mitch said.

"No thanks."

Kessler nodded and sat down in the office chair by his desk, turning it to face Cameron and Mitch, who sat beside her on the couch.

"So, you stole back the disk and then what?"

Cameron picked up the narrative, raising her voice over the drumming of raindrops and the nearly incessant thunder. Several booms rattled the windows as lightning lit up a sky that was almost as dark as night. She explained how she'd heard of the Bloodbeard Cipher and how they had found it at Morgan's Pirate Den, arranged to borrow it from the owner, and spent the afternoon and evening trying to decipher the Castillo de San Marcos Carving in light of it.

"And that's where you come in, we hope," she said. "We think we deciphered it, but we'd appreciate a second opinion and some help understanding just what we deciphered. Given your extensive knowledge of Spanish colonial America, we figured you're the person to talk to."

"I'm happy to help any way I can. Shall we look at the disks?"

Mitch laid the two disks out side by side on the table, and Kessler brought over a portable desk lamp and a pair of reading glasses. His methods indicated these weren't the first artifacts he had pored over in his study. Cameron let him analyze the disks for several minutes, then fielded a few routine questions about where they were found and what she knew about their history—all stuff she had already shared with Mitch.

"And you've deciphered them?" Kessler asked. "Or, rather, deciphered this carving with them?"

"We think so. Do you have a pen and paper?"

Kessler grabbed both off the desk, and Cameron promptly wrote down the message on the Castillo de San Marcos Carving, half in English and half in French.

"'*I found what men have lost lives and fortunes seeking,*'" Kessler read. "'*Je partage le secret avec ceux qui ont des yeux pour voir, afin qu'ils puissent jouir de la vie éternelle. -Diego Ponce de León de Figueroa, 1698.*'" He looked up. "English and French?"

"He was a troublemaker," Mitch said.

An earsplitting crack of thunder shook the house, and Cameron expected the power to at least flicker. When it didn't, and when the echo began to die away, she demonstrated how they had interpreted the disk to arrive at their translation. Then she wrote it down, and Kessler again read it.

"'*Para encontrar la Fuente de la Juventud reunifica a Isimi conmigo en el campanario de la Misión San Francisco de Sevilla.*'" The professor sat back in his office chair and removed his reading glasses. "And here I thought it was nothing more than a legend." He turned his eyes back toward the disks. "'*La Fuente de la Juventud.*'"

"You think this is legit?" Mitch asked.

"I think Diego Ponce de León de Figueroa believed the Fountain of Youth was legit, and went through a great deal of work to convey that knowledge. And as far as I'm concerned," he said with another look at Cameron, "that's a significant leap beyond what anyone searching for it in modern times has ever found."

CHAPTER TWENTY-FIVE

The thunder gradually faded, but the rain continued to come down in torrents. Mitch helped himself to another glass of tea, then rejoined Cameron and Dr. Kessler in the study. He was going through each letter, verifying their work of the night before. Ultimately, and to a beaming smile from Cameron, he concluded they had accurately deciphered the carving.

"Unfortunately, that's where we've run into trouble," Cameron said.

"*Isimi*," Kessler said.

"Yes. That and the mission. We could find no evidence of a Mission San Francisco, either here or in Seville. We're hoping one or the other rings a bell with you."

"Hmm," he said, sitting back again. He looked at their Spanish translation, mumbling phrases in both Spanish and English. He'd done the same thing once already, and determined that they—or, more accurately, Google—had nailed that translation as well: "To find the Fountain of Youth reunify Isimi with me in the bell tower of Mission San Francisco of Seville."

"There were a network of Spanish missions across *La Florida* in the late sixteenth and seventeenth centuries," Kessler said, "but disease and conflict with the English and Native Americans largely brought about their demise. They stretched from St. Augustine across the panhandle along the *Camino Real*."

"Any named for a Saint Francisco or tied to the city of Seville?"

"Not from memory, but that doesn't mean no. However," he said, scratching the side of his jaw, "I don't believe many of them had bell towers— if any. Most were built several hundred years before the missions in California and the American southwest—the iconic adobe walls, clay shingles, a bell tower. These were made out of palmetto thatch, wattle and daub, or left entirely open."

"Any chance this search takes us beyond Florida?" Mitch asked. He looked between the professor and his protégé. "Did Diego travel elsewhere?"

"You mean like Baja California?" Cameron asked. "I don't think so."

"Or Seville, Spain?"

"Diego was from Cádiz," she answered, "which isn't far from Seville. Maybe fifty or sixty kilometers. But I don't see the connection to the Fountain of Youth."

Kessler stood and walked to the bookshelf that spanned the entire wall. He scanned the tomes for several seconds, then pulled one from an eye-level shelf. He set it on the table, then repeated the procedure until half a dozen books were stacked beside the disks. "There are one or two others, perhaps. I'll have to let my brain ruminate. But, we can check the indexes for any references to Seville or Francisco."

They divvied up the books and spent the next half hour scouring not only the indexes and tables of contents, but also skimming various sections. Kessler looked down at his watch, a silver Casio or Seiko. "The library has a very nice reference section, but unfortunately they closed at five today."

"Honest question, not being a smart-aleck here," Mitch said, "but how much information is there in dusty books in libraries that isn't on the internet somewhere?"

"Quite a lot," Kessler said. "Especially in the dusty books," he added with a twinkle in his blue-gray eyes. "Don't get me wrong, the internet is a wonderful place, but it's far from exhaustive."

"Do you think the Sanibel Island Library would be the best place to go?" Cameron asked. "Or would another library closer to, well . . . I don't know closer to what. We don't know where the mission was, so we don't know which library would be close to it."

"Like I said, the reference section at SPL is pretty good. I'd make it your starting point."

"Got a hotel recommendation?" Mitch asked.

"You're more than welcome to stay here," Kessler said. "I have several guest rooms that can easily be made up." He waved. "But we can discuss that later. I don't know about you, but my stomach is starting to growl."

Mitch began to pack up the disks, but Kessler motioned for him to stop. "We'll come back to them later. I have a theory on *Isimi*."

"You do?" Cameron asked as she too stood.

"If you'll bear with me, my brain needs to deliberate sometimes. Perhaps it is the age. I can feel it rattling around in here," he said, tapping the side of his head, "ever since I saw that word. A little idle work, like making dinner, might just jar it loose."

"How can we help?" Cameron asked.

"Can you make pasta?"

"I can."

Kessler led them back into the kitchen and began digging through various cupboards. Mitch peered out at the rain—now just a steady shower—until Cameron tapped his arm. "Would you mind terribly running out and grabbing my blue and white checked shirt? It's on the top of my smaller suitcase. I could use an extra layer."

Noticing the cool temperature in the house in the wake of the storm for the first time, Mitch nodded. He only got marginally wet this time, and when he returned with Cameron's button-down shirt, she was filling a pan with water while Kessler was melting butter in a large saucepan on the stove. Knowing the danger of too many cooks in the kitchen, Mitch straddled a stool by the counter and watched Cameron. She put the button-down over her tank top, buttoning it halfway and rolling up the sleeves. Her hair was still in a ponytail, albeit a slightly messy one with wisps everywhere. It worked for her, and Mitch smiled to himself as he visually followed her around the kitchen, first setting water to boil and then chopping up a red pepper and fresh basil leaves.

"So you two just met Saturday?" Kessler asked, and Mitch realized he'd been caught eyeing Cameron.

"That's right," she answered before Mitch could get words down to his tongue.

Kessler measured something red into a small bowl. Paprika, maybe? Mitch wasn't much of a cook.

"Are you also a—how did you describe it, Cameron—a history hunter, Mitch?"

"No, not really."

Kessler said nothing, leaving the implied question in the air. His eyes were innocent, as was his tone, but Mitch caught a subtle protectiveness for an old student, and didn't blame the professor. His and Cameron's was an odd relationship, jetting around Florida together after only knowing each other a few days.

"Mitch claims I'm intriguing," Cameron said, "but I think he's just sweet on me." She winked, and said it like a tease, but it was the closest either of them had come to vocalizing their feelings for one another. If practically making out the night before didn't count.

He grinned and raised his glass of tea. "Guilty."

Eventually, he got around to setting the table while Cameron boiled the pasta, Kessler pan-seared and then baked the fish filets, and they combined to toss a salad. When time allowed, Cameron divulged a few more details of her search for the Fountain of Youth that had led her to the *Descubridor*, which dovetailed into a discussion about the originations of Sanibel Island. According to Kessler, one theory held that Juan Ponce de León had named it in honor of Queen Isabella I of Castile.

"He was over to this side of Florida?" Mitch asked.

"Yes. On his first voyage, after coming ashore near Melbourne Beach, his fleet sailed around the tip of Florida and came ashore somewhere in the general vicinity of Charlotte Harbor, where they encountered members of the Calusa tribe near if not on Sanibel Island. He also returned to the area on his second voyage to Florida, eight years later."

"When did the first humans arrive on the island?" Cameron asked.

"Supposedly the Calusa, some twenty-five hundred years ago."

"Supposedly?" Mitch asked.

Kessler hesitated a few seconds before answering, and turned to Mitch as if pulled away from another thought. "The Calusa spread throughout southwest Florida, but when they arrived on the island and whether or not they were the first humans is uncertain."

Mitch nodded.

"Another theory is that renowned pirate José Gaspar—known as Gasparilla—named the island for his Spanish lover, Sanibel. However, many of these legends and tales are highly dubious."

"Familiar story," Mitch said.

"Oh?"

"He means the Fountain of Youth," Cameron said. "He's a skeptic."

"I have trouble believing there's a fountain of water that grants eternal life," Mitch said, "and even you admitted most of the legends and stories about Ponce de León were unsubstantiated."

"Yes, about him," she countered. "But not about Diego Figueroa, as the disks would prove."

"Eternal life," Kessler said. "Is that what you're seeking?"

"I don't know," she said, pausing from slicing a tomato for the salad. "I told Mitch, I don't think there's any fountain you can drink from and live forever, but maybe it could have some healing properties, be some sort of multi-vitamin super drug. Is that crazy?"

"No," Kessler said, and seemed to be about to say more when his oven timer went off. He checked on the fish and declared them done. He pointed out a bottle of Chardonnay in the rack under the counter, and Mitch uncorked it while Kessler and Cameron took their various dishes to the table. As a clock in a distant room could be heard chiming the seven o'clock hour, the trio sat down to a delicious dinner of blackened redfish, angel-hair pasta with accoutrements, and a tossed salad.

The rain had continued to fall, steadily if not heavily. Kessler had opened a kitchen window now that the wind was down, and the sizzling hiss of rain falling on the patio provided a cozy ambiance to their meal. The perfectly seasoned fish was flaky and tender, the lemon and cayenne seasonings complimented by the contrasting spice and sweetness in the pasta. After a long, stressful day, Mitch was glad to relax and savor the delicious and ample servings.

"*Isimi*," Kessler said midway through the meal, setting down his wineglass as if a sudden revelation had hit him.

Mitch and Cameron both looked up.

"I mentioned the Calusa tribe. They occupied this part of Florida until the early seventeenth century."

"Were they done in by the Spanish?" Cameron asked.

"No. They actually resisted Spanish conversion, as their priests and leaders in particular derived a great sense of authority from their religious beliefs, and they didn't want to surrender that. At times, their interactions with the Spanish were quite tenuous, especially early on. But it wasn't all conflict. They even had some congenial relationships with various Spanish explorers— to the point that the Spanish were somewhat wary of the effects of such a comingling."

"So what happened to them?" Mitch asked, still holding a morsel of fish on the end of his fork.

"A combination of disease and attacks by other tribes. The Calusa, and to a large degree their culture, were wiped out."

"How does this tie to *Isimi*?" Cameron asked.

"Although the Calusa language largely disappeared with the culture, there are a number of words that have survived, and a number of places in Florida that are believed to have originated with the Calusa. One of them, is the city of Kissimmee, in the center of the state."

"Isn't that by Orlando and Disney World?"

"In the general vicinity, yes," Kessler said, and took another sip of wine. "If memory serves, the name is somewhat of a distortion of *iś*, meaning water, and *mi*, meaning over there or long. Thus, *Iśimi* would mean 'long water' or 'the water over there.'"

Cameron's blue eyes widened. "You think that could be where the Fountain of Youth is, in modern-day Kissimmee? The water over there or the long water? A long river or lake?" Her countenance fell. "But the carving says to 'reunify *Iśimi* with me in the bell tower of Mission San Francisco of Seville.' How do you reunify a place with a person at another place?"

"Well, the city is named after the Kissimmee River, so there's merit to that idea. But there's also another possibility," he said, taking another sip of wine. "In addition to the belief that the city was named after the river which drew its name from the old Calusa words for long and water, is another theory that the city and river were named after a Calusa person."

"*Iśimi*," Mitch said.

"Yes. I'm afraid the details are a little fuzzy. I have a colleague who might be able to flesh them out further, but the gist of it is there was a Calusa princess named *Iśimi*, a chieftain's daughter, who was tall and beautiful."

"A tall drink of water?" Mitch said.

"What?" Cameron asked.

"Something my dad used to say. He called a tall person a tall drink of water."

Cameron gave Mitch a momentary odd look. Then she turned to Kessler. "Any idea when she lived?"

"I'm afraid not."

"Would this colleague know?"

"I'm sure he would. We can give him a call after dinner, if you'd like. He teaches at Loyola University in New Orleans, meaning he's an hour ahead of us, so it won't be too late."

"I would sure appreciate it," Cameron said.

Mitch looked at her with a wink. "With any luck, our next stop can be the Big Easy."

CHAPTER TWENTY-SIX

The rain had all but stopped by the time they were done eating, and even a few rays of sunshine had broken through. Cameron suggested, before they reached out to Dr. Kessler's colleague in New Orleans, that they take a brief walk to work off dinner. Mitch suggested she and Kessler go while he took care of the dishes, giving them a chance to catch up. She wondered if it wasn't a ploy to earn some brownie points, but concluded it worked. Draining the last swallow of her wine, she turned to her old professor. "Shall we?"

"Why not?"

The air was still heavy with moisture, but nothing was falling as Cameron and Kessler stepped off the patio and onto the sand. The wind had completely died, but mushrooming clouds to the south indicated that all was not calm in south Florida. More clouds to the west obscured most of the evening sun, but that which came through colored the tall clouds bright orange to contrast with their dark lavender backsides. They were worthy of a painting, as was the entire panorama.

"Thank you again for your hospitality," Cameron said as they crossed the bridge over the dunes.

"You're more than welcome. And speaking of that, you are truly welcome to stay the night. I've got several empty guest rooms, and it's a long drive back to Tampa."

"I'll have to talk to Mitch, but thank you."

They turned south when they reached the beach, toward the beautiful, towering clouds. Exposed to the open water, they now felt a gentle breeze. Cameron wondered if the clouds on the horizon were dark because the sun was behind them or because they bore more precipitation. Kessler, apparently concluded the latter, as he mused that additional rain might be in the forecast.

Cameron decided to change the subject. "So this colleague, from your time at Clemson?"

"Yes and no. He was teaching at USC at the time, and we met at several conferences, struck up a friendship, found our areas of expertise were often complementary. Fortunately, history professors don't share sports rivalries."

"His expertise wouldn't also happen to include Spanish missions, would it?"

"Not that I know of, but we can certainly ask."

The beach was deserted, except for some seagulls, and some fresh shells deposited by the stormy waves. They were still big and loud, and Cameron thought of Mitch's proposition, that they spend a few days relaxing on the beach. Something about watching the waves could be cathartic, maybe do as much good for the soul as Figueroa's Fountain of Youth.

"Can I ask you something, Cameron?"

"Of course."

Kessler took a few steps, as if to gather his thoughts. "What is it you're truly seeking?"

She looked at him. "What do you mean?"

"I'm not in any way questioning your research or your discoveries, both of which have every indication of being legit. But the Fountain of Youth is a somewhat ambiguous target, and not a target pursued by most historians or treasure hunters."

"So why am I trying to find it?"

He nodded.

She shrugged her shoulders. "I guess the same reasons anybody would want to find it, to live a longer, better life."

"Not eternal life?"

"That's kind of a pipe dream, isn't it?" she asked. "I mean, nobody lives forever."

"I don't know if I ever mentioned it to you, but I'm Jewish."

"With a name like Gabriel Kessler, I kind of figured as much."

He smiled. "For thousands of years, the Jewish people have held to the promises in the *Tanakh*, what you may know as the Old Testament of the Bible, that an *eternal* God whose words are *eternal* and whose love is *eternal* and whose kingdom was *eternal* would reign forever over His people, Israel. For generations past, and indeed amongst true followers of Judaism today, *eternal* and *forever* mean just that. The expectation was and is that Yawheh, or Jehovah, would provide eternal life."

"Is this tied to the Fountain of Youth?" she asked, allowing her confusion to play on her face.

"So to speak," Kessler said. "When you spoke of eternal life, you seemed to do so almost apologetically."

"It kind of seems like a fairy tale," Cameron said. "I've learned to expect a certain reaction."

"Most world religions include a belief in an afterlife—a heaven, paradise, Valhalla. We've become very materialistic and driven by the temporal here in America, but believing in eternal life isn't an outlandish concept."

"You said it yourself, though. An *after*life. Those world religions are talking about what happens after you die, not providing a means to avoid it, to live forever, right?"

Kessler nodded. "True. But like you said back in the kitchen, you didn't think the Fountain of Youth could make you live forever. That—an unending life on earth—is indeed a pipe dream."

Cameron stopped. She turned to face the professor while tucking loose hair behind her ear. "Dr. Kessler, are you trying to convert me to Judaism?"

He smiled. "No. But there is another fountain, a '*well of water springing up unto everlasting life.*'"

Cameron frowned, and Kessler nodded toward the house. They began walking back.

"The Jewish scriptures promised a coming Savior, a Redeemer and Deliverer who would be an everlasting King—known as the Messiah or Anointed One."

"You're talking about Jesus?"

"I am. The *Tanakh* or Old Testament is full of references to Jesus, but many Jews even to this day don't recognize Him as the promised Messiah."

"But you do?"

"I didn't for many years, until a friend of mine, a Jewish rabbi from Brooklyn, encouraged me to study the *Tanakh*—really study it. I thought he was calling me back to my roots in Judaism, which I had admittedly walked away from during my time in academia. But the more I studied the Hebrew Scriptures, the more I realized they all pointed to Jesus. So," he said with a shrug, "I began to study Him in the pages of the New Testament of the Bible, and the more I did, the more I found the New Testament fit with the Old Testament like hand and glove, all centering around Jesus."

Cameron studied her shoes as they plodded through the damp sand for several steps. "I can't remember the last time I was in a church," she finally said. "I think it was for one of my college roommate's weddings. So admittedly I don't know all the details, but didn't Jesus preach more about not sinning and helping the poor? About how to live a life of purpose and fulfillment?" she added, remembering her and Mitch's conversation with Evan at the Great Cross in St. Augustine.

"Those things are all part of it," Kessler said with a nod. "But the primary reason Jesus came was to provide eternal life. He said, '*I will give unto him that is athirst of the fountain of the water of life freely.*'"

Cameron nodded.

"And I'm sure you've heard John 3:16, that "'*God so loved the world, that he gave his only begotten Son, that whosoever believeth in him should not perish, but have everlasting life.*' Cameron, if you want to live forever, you're right, there is no physical fountain that provides it. But there is a provision." He took a few steps, then looked up. "There's an old hymn that says '*There is a fountain filled with blood drawn from Immanuel's*—that's Jesus—*veins; And sinners, plunged beneath that flood, lose all their guilty stains.*'"

They had reached the plank pathway leading back to the house. The sun was gone again, and the breeze had strengthened. Looking out over the gulf, it appeared as if they were in for a repeat performance.

"I don't want to discourage you from looking for the Fountain of Youth, whatever it turns out to be. And I don't want to twist your arm to try to convert you. But I would be remiss if I didn't tell you about Jesus. He's not a fairy tale, not a feel-good notion. The prophecies about Him and the evidence that supports His claims are rock solid. And He is the ultimate answer to life's ultimate question. If you'd like to talk more about it, I'd be happy to discuss it with you further."

Cameron nodded, not sure what to make of the unexpected turn in the conversation. She addressed more hair blown across her face. "You've given me something to think about," she said. "And I mean that; I'm not blowing you off."

Kessler nodded. "What do you say we go call Dr. LaSalle?"

"Your colleague?"

He nodded again and turned up the path toward the house.

*   *   *

After making quick work of the dishes, leaving most of them to dry instead of accidentally rearranging Kessler's kitchen in the process of putting them away, Mitch scoped out the refrigerator for any beer. Finding none, he poured another half glass of wine and adjourned to the patio. He studied the western sky for a few minutes and concluded they were in for more storms. It was already after eight o'clock, and he wondered how long Cameron intended to stay at her old prof's house.

He took a sip of wine and lowered his eyes to see them coming over the dunes. He wished in that moment he could enjoy Cameron's approach, her natural beauty, the breeze-blown "messy" hair, the smoothness with which she walked and carried herself. Instead, he found his thoughts drawn back to the northern approach to the Skyway Bridge, to the attempt on their life or, at the very least, a risky attempt to run them off the road and scare them or take the disks from them. He also kept hearing Olivia's slightly throaty, slightly Hispanic voice in his head, offering him "information about your traveling companion." Cameron hadn't given him any reason not to trust her, and he didn't distrust her. Even so, he couldn't shake Olivia's warning that Cameron wasn't who he thought she was. What did that mean? Who did Olivia think that Mitch thought Cameron was? He'd cast aside such thoughts half a dozen times that day, and truthfully didn't know what concerned him more, Olivia's vague warnings or the fact that he couldn't seem to shake them.

"Everything all right?" Kessler asked as he and Cameron climbed to the upper tier of the patio. "You look upset."

"Just been a long day," Mitch covered, lifting his glass again.

"I was just trying to persuade Cameron to spend the night. It's really no trouble, and it is a long drive back to Tampa, especially with weather moving in."

"You think so too?"

"The forecast this morning called for storms all through the night, and the sky is starting to look ominous once more."

Mitch turned to Cameron, asking her thoughts without speaking. They had left Tampa with no specific plans of where to go next—other than perhaps someplace where they could get away from it all. But there was no reason they couldn't postpone that a day.

She shrugged. "I'm okay with it if you are."

"Sure. Why not?"

"Great," Kessler said. "I think I might have a peach pie in the freezer. One of the local schools sells them every spring as a fundraiser."

"That seals the deal," Mitch said.

"We're going to call Gabe's colleague in New Orleans," Cameron said.

"I'll grab our bags from the car before the rain hits again."

"Thank you."

He handed her his glass, then walked around the house to the Rogue. He retrieved their luggage, locked the doors, and entered the house through the front door. Cameron met him there with a peck on the cheek as she took her suitcase from him. "There are two rooms at the top of the stairs," she said. "Gabe said we could pick."

He followed her up the stairs, and they placed their bags in a pair of large, simply decorated bedrooms, both beachy but not frilly. A full bathroom was between them, stocked with anything they would need, according to Cameron who parroted Kessler.

"Nicest B&B I've ever stayed in," Mitch said as they walked back downstairs.

"I didn't picture you for the bed and breakfast kind."

"Not my choice."

Kessler was waiting for them in the living room, which covered the front corner of the house. Large, plush furniture faced a fireplace, in which Kessler had just ignited a small fire. A panoramic oil painting of a cloud-dotted sunset at sea hung above the mantle. The fireplace was built into the corner, with a three-pane window facing the driveway and a pair of sliding doors opening to the walkway along the side of the house. Like the rest of the rooms downstairs, it reminded Mitch more of a rustic resort than a beachside getaway, but he wasn't complaining. He took a seat in a large armchair and studied a three-foot-long tuna mounted on the wall.

"You reel him in?" he asked, nodding at the mount.

Kessler nodded. "Last Memorial Day weekend."

"Impressive."

The professor waved as he stood. Then he retrieved a smartphone from his pocket and sat down opposite Mitch. That left the couch to Cameron, who shed her shoes and pulled her feet up under her. Kessler tapped the screen of his phone a few times, then placed it on a glass coffee table in the middle of the group. The phone purred twice, then clicked.

"Dr. LaSalle."

"Dwayne, it's Gabriel Kessler."

"Gabe, to what do I owe the pleasure?" His voice had the sound of a professor, clipped and with a hint of an accent. It wasn't British, but sounded something like it, the way the proper diction of an educated person could—at least in Mitch's experience.

"I'm here with a former student of mine who has some questions that may fall under your purview."

"Oh, how so?"

"Her research has crossed paths with the Calusa tribe, in particular with the word '*Iśimi*.' I mentioned the theory that the city of Kissimmee drew its name from the Calusa language, but—correct me if I'm wrong—was there not also a Calusa princess called *Iśimi*?"

"Legendarily, yes," LaSalle answered, his voice crisp despite coming through the phone.

"What can you tell us about her?"

"Not a great deal is known about the actual *Iśimi*. She was the daughter of the last-known chieftain of the Calusa tribe before they died out in the early eighteenth century. There are a number of rumors about her, everything from being a voluptuous goddess who stood nearly two meters tall to her being an actual goddess—some sort of supernatural being—to her marrying a European explorer."

"Which one?" Cameron asked.

"Dr. LaSalle, my former student, Cameron Leigh."

"A pleasure," he said.

"Likewise, and I'm sorry to blurt out. But do you know which explorer *Iśimi* supposedly married?"

"I do not, and I would stress it is only a rumor, and one that doesn't even agree on the man's nationality. Some say Spanish, some Portuguese, some English."

"More rumor," Cameron muttered toward Mitch.

"Like I said," LaSalle continued, "not much is known about the actual *Iśimi*."

"That's the second time you've used that phrase," Kessler said. "'The actual *Iśimi*.'"

"Yes. Not much of the Calusa culture has remained, which is why we don't know much about *Iśimi* or any other members of the tribe. In fact, we're not positive she ever did exist. But what is known of her, or thought to be known of her, is largely drawn from an old portrait, if you'll excuse the pun."

"A portrait?" Kessler asked.

"Yes. I've not seen it, but from what I understand, it depicts a rather storybook-like and beautiful woman."

"It still exists?"

"Yes. I couldn't tell you where off hand, but I could find out."

"We would appreciate it, Dwayne."

"Let me make a few calls. I'll get back to you."

"Dr. LaSalle?" Cameron said.

"Yes."

"When was this portrait painted, any idea?"

"I'm not sure, but I believe the legend of *Iśimi* came into being rather late in the history of the Calusa people. Presumably it was around that time, but I'm sure the right experts could tell you better."

"Do you know who painted it?" Kessler asked. "Not much of the Calusa art has survived, from what I understand."

"Correct. No, this portrait was actually done by one of the few Europeans to achieve a friendly status with the Calusa, a Spaniard by the name of Figueroa."

CHAPTER TWENTY-SEVEN

"Can you believe this?" Cameron asked Mitch. Kessler had gone to put the pie in the oven and brew a pot of coffee after their call with Dr. LaSalle.

"At this point, yes," Mitch said.

"I mean, there's no way this is some other Figueroa, is there?"

"Not likely."

Dr. LaSalle hadn't been sure if the Figueroa who had painted the portrait of *Iśimi* had been Diego or not, but the odds of it not being seemed long, to say the least. Dr. LaSalle also hadn't known anything about *Misión San Francisco de Sevilla*, but Cameron was happy with at least one lead. Presuming Kessler's colleague was able to track down the current location of the portrait of *Iśimi*.

"Forty to fifty minutes," Kessler announced upon his return. They used the time to review what they had learned and surmised, to see if perhaps they had missed anything obvious. Cameron knew how easy it was to overlook a clue, or to assume something that shouldn't be and create a false clue. But after rehashing her research, their discoveries, and the information provided by Dr. LaSalle, they arrived at the same conclusion: Diego Figueroa, during his six or so months in Florida, had not only found what he believed to be the Fountain of Youth, but had also befriended some of the Calusa tribe and, presumably, had fallen in love with one of them, a woman named *Iśimi*, leading him to paint her portrait and include it in his roadmap of clues.

"Does that all make sense?" she asked when they were finished.

"Admittedly, there is a fair amount of speculation and conjecture," Kessler said, cradling a mug of coffee. "But Figueroa wouldn't have been the first European to find favor with the Calusa. And if Dwayne's information is correct, that Figueroa painted the portrait entitled *Iśimi*, it supports that idea."

"Did the Calusa have any legend or local lore about a Fountain of Youth or anything like it?" Mitch asked.

Kessler finished a sip of coffee. "Not that I'm aware of."

"I'm just wondering why the tie in. Even if Figueroa fell in love with a local girl, why incorporate her into the search for the fountain?"

"Because it would further upset the Spanish," Cameron said. "He wasn't on the best of terms with them, and we already speculated that the reason he used English and French on the carving was to thumb his nose at his own government, so to speak. Maybe this was the same thing."

"More than that, perhaps," Kessler said. "If he wanted to keep the Fountain of Youth from being discovered by power- and wealth-hungry governments—which is how he likely viewed the Spanish crown—incorporating a Native American tribe into the search might make it so distasteful for them that they'd abandon the search . . . or at least direct it elsewhere."

"Or slaughter them all in an effort to find it," Cameron muttered.

"Well, I suppose that's also a possibility." He sat back. "How does the interpretation of the carving read again?"

"'To find the Fountain of Youth reunify Iśimi with me in the bell tower of Mission San Francisco of Seville.'"

He nodded. "It does have a romantic sort of tenor to it. 'Reunify Iśimi with me' practically invokes the idea of lost love."

"So what does he mean by 'with me'?" Mitch asked. "A self-portrait? Was he expecting to remain in Florida or return to this mission—wherever it is—to provide the answer?"

"We need to learn more about this woman," Cameron said. "Or find the painting."

A distant buzzer sounded, and Kessler got up to get the pie. Mitch added a couple logs to the fire, and when he turned around, Cameron motioned for him to come join her on the couch.

Kessler peeked his head back into the living room. "It needs a few more minutes. Would either of you care for ice cream?"

"Sure," Mitch nodded.

"Why not?" Cameron said. "I'm going to need to go for a run tomorrow. I slacked today."

"You had good reason."

She lay her head on Mitch's shoulder, listening to the steady drumming of more rain. A few rumbles of thunder mixed in, but nothing like earlier, and with far less wind. This was a peaceful summer thundershower, and had it not been for Kessler's promise of pie, Cameron would have liked nothing better than to snuggle close to Mitch and slowly fall asleep to the rhythm of the rain.

An enormous boom sounded in the distance, followed by a receding whirring sound.

Cameron sat up. "That wasn't thun—"

The lights went off.

Mitch stiffened. He stood and walked to the window.

"You see anything?" she asked.

"No."

She withdrew her phone from her pocket and turned on a flashlight app. "I'm going to see if Gabe needs help."

"Hold on," Mitch said.

"Why?"

"I didn't hear any thunder."

"It's been thundering all night."

"Yeah, but the power just went out now. Why?"

"You think this is something else?"

"After what happened this afternoon . . ."

He came and took her hand, and together they walked into the kitchen where Kessler had already lit a pair of candles and was continuing to dish out ice cream. "Big servings, I guess," he said.

"This ever happen before during a storm?" Mitch asked.

"What, the power going out?"

He nodded.

"Now and again, during real bad weather."

"This isn't that bad," Mitch said, looking out the window.

"Sounded like a transformer blowing. It happens."

Cameron looked to Mitch, who didn't seem convinced. Kessler caught on. "Why, you think something else is going on?"

"I don't know, maybe," Mitch said, exhaling.

Cameron sighed as well. "Our car trouble today . . . we were run off the road."

"What?"

"Just north of the Skyway Bridge, an SUV came out of nowhere and clearly forced us off the road."

"My goodness, I had no idea. You're both all right?"

"Few bumps and bruises is all," she said, raising her arm to show off the worst of them, "but the car got pretty messed up. We think they were after the disks, or trying to scare us."

"They who?"

"We're not sure. Our best guess is the people who took the disk from me back in Cocoa Beach."

"And from whom you took it back in St. Augustine?"

She nodded.

"How could they have found you here?"

"I don't know," Mitch said.

"We didn't talk to anyone after that," Cameron said. "And nobody knows we're here."

"That's not entirely true. You had to call the university to get Gabe's contact info. If someone else called them . . ."

"That seems like quite a long shot," Kessler said.

"It does," Mitch agreed. "But so did that SUV showing up out of nowhere."

"I'll make sure the doors are locked," the professor said. "And the alarm system is on a battery backup, so I'll activate it as well."

Mitch nodded as Kessler headed toward the front door. Then he moved to check the French doors off the dining room.

"Mitch," Cameron said. "You really think this is somebody out to get us? Blowing a transformer to take out an entire neighborhood?"

"I don't think it's that, but I'm not convinced it's not. But that's a good idea."

"What is?"

"There's a cupola on the house, a third floor."

"So?"

"So, we can see if this is a neighborhood wide thing or not."

More thunder rumbled, louder than before, and the wind seemed to be kicking up as well. It should have been comforting, the stronger storm reinforcing the idea that the power had gone out for natural reasons. But somehow, the elements' renewed vigor had the reverse effect on Cameron's psyche.

207

CHAPTER TWENTY-EIGHT

When Kessler returned, he guided Mitch to the cupola. He climbed to the third story of the house, which provided him a view up and down the coast. As far as he could see, everything was black. He headed back down, joining Cameron and the professor in the living room, where they still had the light of the fire. Although not totally convinced, he tried to reassure them that, in all likelihood, the storm was indeed the culprit.

"I had no idea the quest to find the Fountain of Youth would engender such violence," Kessler said, handing Mitch a plate with a slice of pie and a generous helping of vanilla ice cream. "Running you off the road, at interstate speeds—you could have been killed."

"I know," Cameron said. "Saturday they were shooting at us, and then Saturday night, at the villa. And if they had caught us Sunday night, who knows . . ."

Not to mention strange calls from mysterious women, Mitch thought.

"Are you sure this is worth it all?" Kessler asked.

"We've been asking ourselves the same question," Mitch said.

The professor cut a wedge of pie. "Cameron, remember what I said to you on the beach earlier, about Jesus being the answer to life's ultimate question?"

Mitch looked up from his pie.

Cameron nodded.

"That question isn't about finding fulfillment or being a good person. It's 'What happens when I die?' And I don't mean to scare you, but that's a question that is very relevant to all of us, whether we're being harassed by villains or not."

Mitch took a bite. He hadn't expected Kessler to get religious on them. And while he wasn't really up for a lecture, Kessler was their host and he was Cameron's former professor. So he listened and ate.

"You're talking about the afterlife again," she said.

"I am. You as much as said it before, no fountain of natural water can grant perpetual youth or life. Sooner or later, everyone—whether they drink from Figueroa's fountain or not—is going to die. I'm pushing seventy; believe me, I know," he said with a faint grin. "But that only highlights the question of what happens after you die."

"Can anyone really know?" she said. "Until it happens, I mean."

"Not experientially, no," he answered. "The Calusa, for example, believed that when a human died, their soul entered an animal. The Spanish—like Figueroa, most probably—believed in good works and adherence to religious laws. Many of my own people believe that as well."

"Doesn't that make it all moot?" she said. "Every religion believes something different, so how can anybody know the truth?"

"I also told you Jesus isn't a fairy tale, not a quaint hero of Sunday school stories. He was a real person, who walked and lived and taught, with more evidence to support His existence than there is to support George Washington's."

"Really?"

Kessler nodded. "His words and His actions are documented and verifiable, and have stood the test of time and logic. They are what one author terms as *Evidence That Demands a Verdict*."

"A verdict about what?"

"Jesus taught extensively about the afterlife—about heaven and hell. The rest of the Scriptures do as well. So the question you and I face is, do we believe what Jesus said about the ultimate question of what awaits us after death and what are we to do about it?"

Mitch finally spoke up. "No offense, Gabe, but isn't there evidence that other religious leaders lived and taught as well? I mean, you can't really go back and prove that Jesus walked on water or turned water into wine, can you? Aren't those claims of the Bible, the same as the Koran might make claims about Mohammed or whatever texts would about the Buddha?"

"You're right, those other leaders did live and die, and their words are verifiable in many cases as well. And you also make a good point that the Bible is just a compilation of words unless it can be verified."

"So can it?" Cameron asked.

"Indeed. If you take a look at the internal validation of the Bible, its sixty-six books form a remarkably coherent, consistent message. It takes some study to understand it, to grasp the nuances, but the cohesiveness is there. And many of the contradictions that people think they have found or like to point out actually have explanations that in fact support the Bible's authenticity."

"Like what?" Cameron asked.

Kessler swallowed a bite of ice cream. "For example, and it is a rather simple one, but Jesus stated that '*the Son of man*'—that's Him—would '*be three days and three nights in the heart of the earth*' after He died and before He rose again. But a close examination of Scripture suggests He was crucified and buried on a Friday—Good Friday—and clearly indicates He rose again on Sunday. Now, as we count days, that wouldn't make sense. However, the way Jewish people of that time counted days, the first day—or Friday—counted as one, Saturday as two, and Sunday as three. Furthermore, the Jewish day began at sundown, so Thursday night and Friday would be one day, Friday night and Saturday two, and Saturday night and Sunday three. Thus, by Sunday morning, three nights and three days would have occurred." He shrugged. "It's not perhaps the most extraordinary explanation, but it is an example, and there are many more, if you are willing to look for them."

Cameron nodded.

"Additionally, the reliability of the current biblical texts is remarkable, so vastly outpacing any other ancient manuscripts so as to leave no doubt that the Bible we have today is accurate to the original texts penned thousands of years ago. Archaeological discoveries are continually adding credence to the Bible, and never disproving it. I could go on and on, as I'm sure you know," he said with a smile at Cameron. "But I want to come back to something you said, Mitch. Muhammed and the Buddha did indeed live and die, just like Jesus. But the primary thing that separates Jesus from all the others, and that thus makes Him the go-to authority on the afterlife, is that He rose from the dead."

"Do you really believe that?" Mitch asked. "He rose from the dead?"

Kessler nodded.

"People don't rise from the dead."

"Precisely. And that's what makes it so extraordinary!" He set down his plate and leaned forward. "I get your hesitation, believe me. As a lifelong Jew, I was opposed to this preposterous notion that Jesus had risen from the dead. It was blasphemous. Until I looked into the evidence."

"The evidence?" Mitch asked.

"Yes. The Apostle Peter wrote that they did not follow '*cunningly devised fables*.' Peter and the other disciples, along with over five hundred people saw the resurrected Christ. Men who had nothing to gain, and everything—including their lives—to lose by making such claims, were adamant that Jesus had risen from the dead. They went to their deaths—violent deaths—after spending their lives telling anyone who would listen that He was alive. And this after cowering in fear after His crucifixion, after denying Him three times in Peter's case. These men were absolutely transformed."

"Aren't lots of people transformed by a variety of religious beliefs?" Cameron asked.

"To an extent, yes. But the disciples were not only transformed, but also maintained their transformation in the face of horrible persecutions—imprisonment, torture, death."

"Don't you see that with a variety of religions too?" Mitch asked. "Believing something is true to the point of dying for it doesn't make it true."

"Hang on to that thought for a second," Kessler said. He stood and stoked the fire. As he did, he said, "One of the best arguments in support of the resurrection is the question of who would die for a lie? Like you said, people will die for what they believe to be true, but they won't die for something they know to be a lie. One of the early claims in regard to the empty tomb was that the disciples had come and stolen the body, that the resurrection was a hoax perpetrated by Jesus' closest followers to keep up a ruse or carry on a legacy." He slowly walked over to the chair and sat back down. "But let me ask you something. Put yourselves in the disciples' shoes. Say for a moment that you had helped fake Jesus' resurrection, for whatever reason. Would you be willing to be ostracized, imprisoned, beaten, or killed for a known lie?"

Mitch looked down at his unfinished pie.

"So the disciples didn't fake a resurrection," Cameron said. "But does that prove it happened?"

"It's not just that they didn't fake it. You also have to ask what made them believe it so strongly? Again, we're not talking a go to church once a month and on Easter and Christmas sort of religious movement here. These men dedicated their lives to spreading their faith and willingly died for it. If they weren't firmly convinced that Jesus was alive, why would they do that?"

"I don't know."

"Paul wrote in First Corinthians, '*if Christ be not risen, then is our preaching vain, and your faith is also vain.*' All it took for anyone in the first century to quash this Christian faith was to produce the body of Jesus. But no one ever did. The tomb was empty, a tomb blocked by a large stone, sealed, and guarded by Roman soldiers, the first-century equivalent of United States Marines. The theories that timid, fearful disciples or a group of mourning women came and stole the body of Jesus are an insult to logic and reason."

Mitch sat back. All his life he'd held that religious beliefs were well and good, generally speaking, but required a little bit of a suspension of logic. Being swallowed by a whale or surviving a den of lions were fun stories, but not real. Same for a crucified man being raised from the dead. But here was a man in Kessler, who, by all accounts was not suspending logic or reason, and was convinced the stories were real and true. And he didn't back up his assertions with some mumbo-jumbo about a feeling or hearing a voice in the wind or something; he backed them with pretty strong evidentiary claims.

"I don't mean to preach at you," Kessler said, "especially without being asked. But whether directly or indirectly, we all have to answer the question, who is Jesus? And if you diligently research the Scriptures, you'll find they stand the scrutiny. I was privileged a year or two ago to meet an author by the name of J. Warner Wallace. He's a former homicide detective who wrote a book called *Cold Case Christianity*. He used his skills as a detective to analyze the four Gospels—Matthew, Mark, Luke, and John—questioning their first-century accounts about Jesus the way a detective might review a cold case in the absence of any living eyewitnesses. He didn't set out to prove the Gospels, mind you, but to disprove them, but was swayed by the evidence that the Bible is indeed true and trustworthy. And he notes in his book the difference between what is possible and what is reasonable."

"How so?" Cameron asked.

"Is it possible that tuna on the wall would jump out of the ocean, into my boat, and flop right into my cooler?" He smiled. "I've seen some strange things, so I suppose it's possible. But is that a reasonable explanation for how he got on my wall?" He let the rhetorical question hang in the air for a moment. "Similarly, is it possible that all the evidence for the Bible and the resurrection are coincidences or 'fake news'? Sure, it is possible, a long shot of long shots. But is it reasonable? If you give it thorough scrutiny, it really is not."

Neither Mitch nor Cameron spoke. The fire crackled and popped. The rain continued to pelt the side of the house. Thunder rolled in the distance.

"I apologize, I didn't mean to browbeat you," Kessler said. "I told Cameron earlier I'd be remiss if I didn't tell you about Jesus. He is the answer to life's ultimate question of what happens when we die. The Bible makes it clear that we have all sinned, we have wronged a holy God. We don't like to think of ourselves as sinners, and maybe compared to what we read in the paper or see on the news, we're not so bad. But if the standard is perfection—never a lie, never a harsh word, never acting in jealousy or anger, not lusting or coveting or taking God's name in vain—we fall woefully short of the standard. God's justice demands that we be punished for our sin—that we go to hell after we die. But God's love demonstrated on the cross when Jesus died in our place removes the penalty from us and provides for us to have eternal life in heaven."

He cleared his throat.

"I know that sounds like a fairy tale to many people today, but I again refer you to the evidence of Jesus and the Bible that support and authorize Him to speak on the subject and that would demand a verdict on our part: Do we believe what He says? And will we accept His death as taking away our just-deserved punishment?"

Mitch was silent.

"This is a lot to think about," Cameron said.

Kessler nodded. "I once was where you are now, unsure about it all, thinking the stories were just that. Then I studied the evidence, and it changed everything. I hope you'll think about it too."

"I will," Cameron said, and Mitch looked at her. She didn't seem to be saying it to appease Kessler, and it kind of irked him. Something told him if Cameron got religious, she'd turn into a weirdo and not be as fun. Then again, he had no reason to think that. He'd known a few "Christians" in his time, and some of them were indeed weirdos. But some weren't—like Kessler. And there were plenty of non-Christian weirdos too, as his time at the University of Texas had conclusively proven.

Plus, he couldn't help but think of how Kessler had presented his arguments. He'd relied on evidence and logic, two things that resonated with Mitch.

Kessler slapped his legs. "Well, it's getting late. I suspect Dwayne isn't calling us back tonight."

"It doesn't look like it," Cameron said.

"You two are welcome to stay up as long as you like, help yourselves to anything. But I do believe I am going to turn in and hope the power's on when I get up."

He stood. So did Cameron, and thus Mitch.

213

"Thank you for everything today," Cameron said.

"You're quite welcome."

"We really do appreciate it," Mitch said, shaking the professor's hand. Kessler smiled, then took their empty plates toward the kitchen. Mitch took the poker and began spreading out the logs in the fireplace, then stepped back. Kessler's footsteps sounded on the stairs.

"What do you think?" Cameron asked from beside Mitch.

He exhaled. "I don't know. I wasn't expecting that."

"He made some good points."

"You think so?"

"You don't?"

"I don't know. I've always been a little irritated when people try to convert me to their set of beliefs. I'm doing fine on my own."

"I hear a 'but' coming."

"I didn't feel like I was being urged to join a cause. You know, save the whales, end world hunger, find your meaning in Jesus. This seemed more like a . . . I hate to say it, a lawyer."

"Making a case?"

"Yeah."

Cameron nodded.

"And I've never thought he had much of a case, or people like him. I don't know, I'll have to think about it. But I'm too tired tonight."

"Me too."

He looked at the fire, which showed no signs of going out anytime soon.

"You not coming up?" she asked.

"I'm going to keep an eye on this for a little while."

She nodded.

"So what's on tap for tomorrow?"

"I don't know," she said. "Depends on when Dr. LaSalle calls back, what he has to say. I was going to play it by ear."

"Worked so far."

She reached up and gave him a quick peck on the cheek. "Night, Mitch."

"Night."

He watched her exit the room, then poked the fire some more before sitting down on the couch. He replayed the long day in his head, thinking about Cameron—her waiting for him in the Sandpearl Resort lobby, her with a bloody and chocolatey napkin held to her nose after the accident, her walking carefree across the dunes. He wanted to dwell on those images, but they kept getting pushed out by Olivia's intimations that Cameron wasn't who she seemed, the fear that had briefly but violently surged through him when their car had plummeted toward Tampa Bay, and by Dr. Kessler's arguments on behalf of Jesus.

The fire ultimately dwindled, to the point that Mitch was content to leave it behind. He wearily traipsed upstairs to his bed. His brain had had enough, and he drifted off to sleep in no time at all.

CHAPTER TWENTY-NINE

Cameron awoke to the whiny revving of some kind of motor. She smelled exhaust. She sat up and looked at the blinking red numbers on the bedside alarm clock. They showed 2:24, which didn't jive, because light was streaming in through the blinds. Wait. Blinking numbers. Meaning the power had been restored two hours and twenty-four minutes ago?

She stood, stretched, and dug around in her suitcase for the items necessary for a shower. She had expected to be achy and sore after the previous day's crash, but felt pretty good all things considered. The bathroom was empty, and Mitch's bedroom door was open with no sign of him. She took a quick shower, dressed in her last clean pair of shorts and a charcoal gray T-shirt, and passed on doing anything with her hair. Just after eight, according to her cell phone, she proceeded downstairs.

Kessler stood by a griddle covered in slices of French toast and sausage links. A pitcher of orange juice was gathering condensation on the counter beside it. The coffee pot was full of dark liquid and the aroma of the beans mixed with the cinnamon in the French toast and was intoxicating.

"Good morning," he said cheerily. He was decked in a pair of khaki shorts, the same boat shoes as the day before, and a light orange shirt similar in style to the one he'd worn the day before. It was neither Clemson orange nor that ugly Texas orange. It resembled sherbet more than anything.

"Morning," Cameron replied. "Is this standard breakfast fare for a retired professor?"

"Hardly, but I doubted the two of you wanted a bowl of Mueslix."

"Thank you."

"How'd you sleep?"

"Like a baby, apparently. I don't remember anything." She sat at the counter, where a couple of plate settings were laid out. "Where's Mitch?"

"Out cutting wood."

"Cutting wood?"

"Quite a few trees down in the neighborhood," Kessler answered. "Nothing major on the property, just some limbs. But he was up and rarin' to go; I couldn't refuse him, so I pointed him to my chainsaw and he's been at it ever since."

Chainsaw. That explained the whiny engine noise.

"You ready to eat?" he asked.

"I am." She held up a plate and he placed two slices of thick French toast on it, and two sausage links.

"Juice or coffee?"

"Juice, then coffee," she said, and he poured her a glass. "Thank you."

He passed her a jar of maple syrup, then placed the last few slices on the griddle and wiped his hands on a dishtowel. "I got a call from Dr. LaSalle this morning."

"Already?"

"He was on his way to an eight a.m. class."

"What'd he say?"

"He made several calls last night and one this morning, and confirmed that *Isimi* is indeed a rather well-known portrait among a certain segment of the art community. He also confirmed the painting is widely acknowledged to have been painted by a D. Figueroa in the very late stages of the seventeenth century or early eighteenth, which fits your timeline."

"It does," Cameron said, having swallowed the first bite of French toast. "This is delicious by the way."

"It's the almond extract."

"Was he able to get a line on where the painting is now?"

"Not yet."

Cameron's shoulders fell.

"He was however able to track where it had been. Originally given to the Calusa tribe, to the chieftain, in fact, it was believed to have been taken by them to Cuba when a large number of Calusa people were migrated there by the Spanish. It was lost for centuries, until emigrants fleeing Castro brought it with them when they left Cuba. It was briefly owned by a Miami banker in the early sixties, then auctioned off in 1968 for a mere pittance, according to Dwayne. That's as far as he's gotten, but he has some calls out."

"Well, that's progress, at least."

"Dwayne's a bloodhound when you set him upon a quest like this. If there's information to be had, he'll find it in time."

She nodded and reached for her juice. "Do you know, are the roads bad?"

"I haven't been out to see. Why?"

"Well, I'm thinking we should visit the library today. And then . . . I don't know, I guess until we hear from Dr. LaSalle."

"If he doesn't call back this morning, I'll give him your number so he can call you directly."

"Is something going on this afternoon?"

"I'm due in Naples by dinner time," he said. "When I moved down here, I made friends with a few of my fellow academics, and we have a yearly long weekend fishing trip."

"Sounds like fun."

"If the weather holds."

Cameron looked out the window, where the moist air glistened in the sunlight.

"They're predicting storms for later," Kessler added. "At any rate, I'll be out of contact for a while, but you and Mitch are welcome to stay here as long as necessary."

"We couldn't," Cameron said. "And I didn't mean to imply anything earlier. We'll be out of your hair as soon as we can."

"Nonsense. There's no rush at all."

Mitch entered the house at that moment, a few flakes of sawdust still clinging to his clothes. He announced that everything was clear and that he had stacked what wood he'd cut by another stack on the side of the house. Kessler thanked him profusely and offered him breakfast, but Mitch chose to shower first. He was gone only a few minutes, then rejoined them for a stack of French toast and sausage. Cameron had moved on to an after breakfast coffee, and while Mitch ate, they discussed plans for the morning.

"I should get the disk back to Morgan," Mitch said in a brief break between bites. "Unless you need help at the library."

"No, I should be fine. Although I'm not sure I'm up for a full day of research, and it'll take you, what, five or six hours to get there and back?"

"Roughly."

"I can run you over to the library later, if you'd like," Kessler said.

"I don't want to impose any further."

"It's not an imposition. I need to pick up a few things for my trip anyhow, so I might as well drive you there."

"Then I'll pick you up on the way back," Mitch said.

She lifted her mug. "I guess that works."

Mitch downed half a dozen slices of French toast and slugged a couple mugs of coffee, then prepared to hit the road. He packed up the Bloodbeard Cipher and took his luggage. Cameron asked if Kessler would mind terribly if she did a quick load of laundry before heading to the library, and he, of course, was okay with it. Then, saying he'd call her when he was on the way back, Mitch shook hands with Kessler and thanked him for everything, and took off.

"He's a nice guy," Kessler said as he poured himself a cup of coffee.

"He is, isn't he?"

"Are things serious between you two?"

"No, not yet." Cameron shrugged. "Sooner or later, this quest of ours will come to an end and then I'm not sure what happens."

"It's been a long time, but I was young and in love once," Kessler said with a smile. He leaned on the counter. "If I may, a piece of advice . . ."

"Of course."

"Make decisions with this as much as this," he said, tapping first his head, then his heart with his index finger. "It's easy to be blinded by what you feel, and I don't want to diminish the excitement of being in love—or whatever stage you may find yourself in. But it's important not to let the feelings determine your choices, when it comes to love or anything."

Cameron nodded, unsure of what to think about that. She wasn't opposed to making heady decisions, and yet, wasn't love a matter of the heart, not the head?

"Were you ever married, Gabe?"

"Once, briefly."

Cameron waited, sipped her coffee.

"We fell quite hard for each other, despite our career ambitions and personalities not being on par. We thought love would conquer all."

"It didn't?"

"No. I wanted to blame her, but the fault was equally if not more so mine. I was driven by my work, by my research. I wasn't committed to my wife, to my marriage, and we split after a few years."

"I'm sorry."

"So am I. But," he said, pouring himself some more coffee, "I found that God could use even that for good. It was in the wake of our breakup that I was encouraged to rediscover my Jewish roots, which, as I mentioned the other night, is what led me to faith in Jesus. I reached out to Sophia after that," he said with a shrug, "but she had no interest in trying to restore things."

"I've been thinking more about what you said yesterday and last night," Cameron said.

"Yes?"

"I don't know. The whole afterlife, heaven and hell—I have trouble reconciling those things."

"Reconciling them how?"

"I'm sorry, but they seem to me like Santa Claus or . . . I don't know. I know you said Jesus wasn't a fairy tale, but it just seems so hard to believe in a scientific world."

"And yet you believe in the Fountain of Youth," he said, not indelicately.

"That's different."

"How so?"

"There are plenty of examples of spots of unique energy or healing powers. And I don't believe the fountain is some mystical, supernatural place necessarily. I think it might be like those places, a spring or a well that contains restorative properties. That's a long way from souls living forever in the clouds."

Kessler took a drink. "If I recall right, you once referenced intelligent design in a paper of yours, didn't you?"

"Wow, you remember that?"

"It's a rather unusual belief to encounter in a public university these days."

Cameron shifted on her stool. "I can't look at the order and precision in the world—in the universe, really—or the intricate workings of cells and DNA and think that it all just happened by accident. Never minding that science is pretty conclusive that matter can't come from non-matter. There has to be a first cause of some sort."

"I would agree," Kessler said. "So the question is, who is that First Cause? What is the Intelligence that designed the universe?"

"Isn't that the same question as last night, with a dozen answers by a dozen different religions?"

"Yes, and none of them can be put in a test tube and proven. It takes a measure of faith to believe the God of the Bible is the First Cause or to believe that Allah is the First Cause or to believe that the universe created itself. But as I mentioned last night, the Bible has unrivaled credibility and authority, and it tells us that '*by him were all things created, that are in heaven, and that are in earth, visible and invisible, whether they be thrones, or dominions, or principalities, or powers: all things were created by him, and for him*' and that '*without him was not made any thing that was made.*'"

Cameron nodded, amazed at Kessler's ability to recall Bible verses. Then again, knowing him as her former professor, it wasn't that amazing.

"But if you postulate a God, and really when you say intelligent design, that's what you mean—regardless of how you identify that God—but if you postulate a God who is the First Cause, is it that much of a leap in belief to also postulate a soul and eternity?"

Cameron narrowed her eyes. "I don't know."

"I've given you more to think about," Kessler said with a twinkle in his eye. "Many people would have you believe that faith is the opposite of logic and reason, or that science and the Bible don't match. But nothing could be further from the truth. Christianity is a thinking man or woman's religion in that it welcomes analysis and scrutiny. It is faith, certainly, but so is any worldview ultimately; there is no absolute proof that one or the other is true. But contrary to what many would say, faith in Jesus is supported by logic and reason."

Cameron was silent, not sure what to make of Kessler's assertions. He made sense, and yet it wasn't something she was ready to accept as proven fact. Nor was she ready to change her worldview, to have everything she'd thought and believed overturned so easily. On the other hand, if what Kessler said was true, it really shouldn't be ignored.

He began to clean up in the kitchen, and she offered her help. He refused and so, after switching her laundry from the washer to the dryer, she decided to take a walk on the beach. The air was still heavy and wet, as if a marine layer covered the coastline. Yet, the sun was shining and the sky overhead was a mix of blue with a few low, puffy clouds. And it was warm.

Cameron walked north, below the waterline, letting the warm gulf waves wash around her ankles and calves. The sensation of the water and the damp, mucky sand beneath her feet occupied her senses' attention, letting her mind wander.

What did she do with all that Kessler had said? She'd never given Jesus much of a thought, any more than she'd given any other religious figure much thought. She respected various religious beliefs, even found some comfort in some of them, but wasn't ready to embrace them as her own. She'd always thought whatever worked for others was great for them, but she was doing fine. Yet Kessler's words about logic and reason and evidence kept ringing in her ears, kept drawing her toward a decision. Was it true or not?

Part of her didn't like that, didn't like the impetus to accept or reject a rather narrow position. If Kessler was right, if the Bible was right, if Jesus' teachings on heaven and hell were right, what did that say of anyone who didn't buy in? What about all the good people out there who found meaning elsewhere? What about her sisters and her late parents? What about Mitch, a salt-of-the-earth guy?

Thinking of Mitch reminded Cameron of something else Kessler had said, about making relationship decisions with her head not her heart. Her heart was all in, at least theoretically. Under the right circumstances, she could see herself falling for Mitch. But logic and reason said this wouldn't work out. He lived in Texas; she lived in Atlanta. He was living life, having a good time; she was passionate about her work and research. More than that, they'd only known each other a week. What did they really have going for them but a shared cause that couldn't last indefinitely and basic physical attraction?

She tromped a little farther along, suddenly missing Mitch, wishing he was there to help her make sense of everything. But would he be thinking with his head or his heart when it came to her?

She stopped and stood in the shallow water, watching the waves rolling toward her. She slowly lifted her eyes. *God, if you're up there, if you're real like Dr. Kessler says, can you give me some clarity? Can you show me?*

She lowered her eyes and watched the waves again. The last time she'd prayed, or anything close to it, had been after her dad's cancer diagnosis. That hadn't done any good, and she almost felt foolish now for trying it.

She turned and started back toward Kessler's house. By the time she got back, dried off, and packed up the rest of her things, her laundry would be done and it would be time to go. She was excited about doing research, about a chance to take her mind off everything else and dive back into what had been driving her for so long.

CHAPTER THIRTY

Mitch was surprised by how messy Sanibel Island was. He only saw a couple major trees or limbs down, but small branches and boughs were everywhere, not to mention millions of leaves and a variety of small, windblown items. He had to navigate around several cleanup crews, but eventually made it to the causeway leading back to the mainland. It looked unaffected by the previous evening's storms, which must have been why they called them barrier islands.

A good night's sleep had helped clear his head, and last night's conversation with Dr. Kessler seemed like a fading memory. Not that he really minded, and he very much liked the professor and could see why Cameron still regarded him so highly. But Mitch wasn't ready to "get religion." It didn't fit him, wasn't something he needed in his life. In fact, as he buzzed north on I-75, he realized he didn't need much of anything. Except an excuse to stay in Cameron's life once they found the Fountain of Youth, assuming they ever did.

The clouds broke around Port Charlotte, and the thermometer in the Nissan said the temperature was pushing ninety. Maybe when he got back and picked up Cameron from the library, he could convince her to slip into a skimpy little bikini and go for a dip, whether in Kessler's pool, a hotel pool, or the Gulf of Mexico.

That thought stuck with him for a while, and he almost missed the exit onto I-275. He glanced at the clock, saw it was just after eleven, and felt good about the time he was making. At this rate, he could be back on Sanibel Island by late afternoon, the perfect time for a swim.

He smiled. Maybe he didn't even need an excuse to stay in Cameron's life. Maybe he could cowboy up and tell her how he felt about her, which he realized wasn't any sort of a mystery to him anymore. It had only been a week, but a week spent constantly in one another's company, and it confirmed to him that everything he knew about Cameron, he liked. Maybe it was finally time to get serious about a girl . . .

The twin spires of the Skyway Bridge suddenly appeared on the horizon, and the sight of them felt like a knife in the chest. Mitch had never been one to get nervous or anxious, besides a few butterflies before a big game. Nor was he superstitious, and he didn't avoid the few things that gave him a scare—he faced them head on. And yet, something about the bridge terrified him to his core.

He gripped the wheel a little tighter, resisting an urge to tap the brakes and disengage the cruise control. He could feel his heart beating faster as the Rogue climbed to the top of the bridge. He didn't dare look down, and he didn't even have a fear of heights. But he couldn't stop thinking about the low concrete barriers and whether or not they'd really stop an SUV doing almost seventy miles per hour. He was suddenly conscious of every other vehicle, though none posed a threat. The shoulder looked so narrow, and what of the drop? And what then?

Practically sweating, Mitch made it down to the other side and back onto dry land. He exhaled and shook his head at the absurdity of it all, apparently triggered by their close call the day before. The following causeways gave him no trouble, and he chalked it up to one of those crazy things. Soon he was zipping through downtown, paying attention to traffic and exit numbers, and all thoughts of the Skyway Bridge were behind him.

William Morgan had either taken the day off fishing or caught his quota early, because he was manning his own museum when Mitch arrived just before noon. The old proprietor gave Mitch back the copy of his credit card and driver's license, and Mitch, given the great difficulty it had taken to make the copy at the nail salon next door, had no doubts that Morgan hadn't bothered to make another to scam him. They shook hands, and Mitch headed back to the Rogue.

Despite his big breakfast, he was hungry, and spent a few minutes on his phone looking for nearby restaurants. Thoughts of Cameron in swimwear aside, he wasn't terribly eager to spend another three hours in the car right away, and skipped over several fast food options. He had just settled on a fifties-era diner near downtown Clearwater when his phone buzzed. The number froze him.

It was Olivia.

He spent several long seconds debating before finally swiping the screen. "Pat's Pizza, what can we get you?"

"Very cute, Mitch," came the same croaky voice, tinged with a Hispanic accent. She called him Mitch, not Mr. Owens as the first time. Even her tone felt a little more playful.

"What do you want?"

"The same thing as before, a fifteen-minute meeting."

"Afraid I don't have fifteen minutes. I'm almost to Orlando and I'm tight for a one-thirty fli—"

"No you're not. You're in Clearwater."

His eyes widened. There was no point in denying it, so he asked, "What, did you track my phone?"

"I'm guessing you haven't eaten yet, so let me buy you lunch while we talk."

"You're still not telling me why, Olivia. And I don't like all the subterfuge."

"I'm sorry, and I know you don't trust me. But just give me a few minutes. You need to know the truth about Cameron Leigh before it's too late."

"What truth?"

"I'll tell you when we meet."

"Tell me now."

"I can't do that."

"Why not?"

"Because you won't believe me."

"But if you can look me in the eyes you'll what, Vulcan mind meld me?"

"I'll show you the evidence."

Mitch was very close to hanging up, but something in Olivia's plea kept him from doing so. She didn't seem desperate so much as urgent. Maybe that was a matter of semantics, but her tone made it sound as if the urgency was for his benefit more than hers. Then again, that's what con artists did. Still, he did have to eat, and what better way to shut her up than to confront her and her evidence and get it over with?

"You pick the place," she said.

"Fine," he said. "Addison's, on Myrtle Avenue."

"I know it. Give me about fifteen minutes."

"This had better not be a scam," he said.

"I assure you it's not."

He ended the call and dropped his head. He still didn't believe Olivia, that there were any skeletons to be found in Cameron's closet. And yet, this was an easy bluff to call. So what was Olivia's angle? And how had she found him and known to call him right when she had?

He sighed and started the engine. One way to find out.

*   *   *

The Sanibel Public Library was tucked away in a grove of trees on the leeward side of Sanibel Island. Kessler drove Cameron in his Chevy Silverado pickup truck. He had offered that she could leave her luggage at his place and swing by with Mitch to get it when she was done. But they'd concluded that would be after he departed for Naples, so she'd taken everything with her, including the Figueroa Cipher.

"I have a question for you," she said as they drove.

He nodded for her to ask it.

"Aren't the claims of Christianity kind of exclusive? If everything you've said is true, it doesn't leave much room for any other beliefs or worldviews."

"They're very exclusive. Jesus said '*I am the way, the truth, and the life: no man cometh unto the Father, but by me.*' That is, no one gets to heaven apart from Jesus—not by some other religion, not by being good enough or better than the next person, but only by trusting in Jesus."

"Isn't that kind of harsh?"

"That's one way to look at it," Kessler answered. "But it all comes back to what is true. If Jesus is right, and no one gets to heaven but by Him, what is more harsh, to tell people there is only one way and require them to adhere to a specific and narrow set of beliefs, or to let them believe whatever they want, promote an idea of inclusivity, to their own peril?"

Cameron thought about that. It didn't sit well with her, with how she—and so many people in the world—looked at things. But if Kessler was right about what was true, then he had a point.

He turned into the library parking lot and coasted to a stop in front of the entrance. "I have something for you," he said.

"For me?"

He reached into the pocket of his shirt and withdrew a small book. "This is a copy of the Gospel of John. It was written from a perspective of proving that Jesus was and is who He claimed to be. It will answer many of your questions, I suspect, and raise quite a few more. But I hope it will encourage you to keep thinking about this."

"Thank you," she said, somewhat genuinely. Kessler had claimed he didn't mean to preach or browbeat her, and he certainly hadn't. Yet she couldn't help but feel as if she was a project of his, so to speak.

"I welcome any questions you might have. Give me a call, or better yet, stop in for some catch of the day."

She smiled.

"And please, keep me up to date on your search. I am more than a little curious."

"I will, Gabe. Thanks for the lift, and for everything, again."

"You're quite welcome."

She leaned across the seat to give her old professor a quick hug, then tucked his gift into a pocket of her travel bag. With a final smile, she hopped out of the truck, collected her luggage, and headed into the library. She would read the Gospel of John as a favor to Kessler, eventually. But for now, her focus was back where it belonged, on finding the Fountain of Youth.

CHAPTER THIRTY-ONE

Addison's Diner was just like a thousand others across the country, right down to the Formica serving counter and tables, red vinyl booths and barstools, and oldies music a little too loud in the background. Mitch had arrived in ten minutes and took a booth at one end, his back to a wall so he could see everybody. The place was busy but not crowded, and while he waited and pretended to study a laminated menu, he ran his eyes over each of the patrons. Nobody looked out of place, looked suspicious, looked like they were doing the same thing he was. Olivia had not, as best he could tell, sent a recon team.

A waitress stopped by the table, dressed as if she were headed out to a sock hop after her shift, and Mitch ordered a burger, fries, and a chocolate malt. When in Rome. Then he sat back and waited for Olivia. He had a view of the street and several parking spaces on either side of it. The Everly Brothers gave way to Little Richard on the jukebox. The waitress brought his malt in a tall, frosted glass with extra in a stainless steel tumbler. He checked his watch, noting it had been twenty minutes since he'd ended the call. If his burger and fries came before Olivia, he would ask for a to-go box and block any more of her calls.

A short woman in a bright red dress walked by on the sidewalk. Her hair was dark, her skin brown, and she could have easily been Hispanic. But she kept walking. Mitch took a sip of his malt through a wide straw, necessary given the malt's creamy thickness. Delicious.

He looked up and saw Olivia. Somehow he knew it was her, even as she stood in the doorway, looking right then left. She was tall, with wavy jet black hair and skin the color of caramel. She wore a knee-length patterned skirt, browns and oranges and reds, and a sleeveless orange top. She looked like a personal banker or a lawyer, maybe an insurance agent. Her eyes were dark, with plenty of mascara, and they settled on Mitch, bringing a thin, crooked smile to pouty lips. Businesswoman or perfume model.

She strode his way in stiletto heels, a medium-sized purse over one shoulder. "Hello, Mitch," she said in the voice the same as on the phone. He nodded at the opposite side of the booth, and she slid into it. "Thank you for taking time to see me."

"Before you make your pitch, I want to know who you are."

"That is fair. Do you mind if I order first?" she asked, holding up her menu. "I am famished."

"Go for it," he said, and took another sip of his malt. He'd ordered right away intentionally, so that he'd be free when she arrived and would have time to analyze her. She scanned the menu, and he scanned her, noting up close that she was even more beautiful than he'd originally thought. And she was doing nothing to hide it, from salon-worthy hair, copious makeup, and a low-cut blouse that challenged any standards of professionalism. How much of her dress and her playful tone were meant to disarm or persuade him? And of what?

The waitress came and took Olivia's order of a house salad, and she sat back with a freshly delivered glass of ice water and sipped it through a straw. Mitch waited.

She set the glass down and leaned on the table. "My name is Olivia de la Cruz, and I work for a very large, very powerful company that has great interest in finding the Fountain of Youth. We know about you and your relationship with Cameron Leigh, and about her years' of efforts to find it."

"What kind of company?"

"A pharmaceutical company. The third-largest in the U.S. We manufacture a wide variety of medicinal drugs and supplements, in addition to boasting one of the finest research and development departments in the country."

"This company have a name?"

"It does," she said with a smile.

"But you're not going to tell me."

"Would it matter?"

"It would when I try to verify that you're really Olivia de la Cruz and really work for said company and that you're not some femme fatale."

Olivia grinned and reached into her purse. She withdrew a business card, which she slid across the table to Mitch. It showed her picture, her name, and the standard contact information, all under ALLCAPS text reading HALL PARKER COOK. A business card could easily be faked, but authenticating at least the existence of the company and her position within it shouldn't be too hard.

"What do you do for Hall Parker Cook?" Mitch asked.

"I am a VP of Operations."

"That's ambiguous enough."

"It is supposed to be," she said. "My job is ambiguous."

He sighed. "Okay, I'll bite. You've got fifteen minutes."

"Cameron Leigh is not who you think she is."

"Who do I think she is?"

"A high-school teacher from Atlanta who spends her summers and vacations hunting for the Fountain of Youth."

"That's quite the profile you've compiled."

"I do only have fifteen minutes."

He slurped his malt.

"As I am sure you know, she attended Clemson University from 2008 to 2012. Did she mention anything to you about her time there?"

"Yes," he said, not willing to give Olivia any information she didn't already have, such as knowledge of Dr. Kessler.

"Did she mention this man?" Olivia asked, suddenly lifting a folder from her purse and opening it on the table. On top of a stack of several sheets of paper was a mugshot of a man, identified as H. Sorenson.

"Who is he?"

"A forger and con artist named Hunter Sorenson. He was in her class at Clemson, and after graduation, went on to a life of crime, most notably within the art and history communities. He has falsified a number of documents and discoveries and tainted just as many real breakthroughs."

"What a jerk," Mitch said lifelessly. "So? What's the graduating class any given year at Clemson, a couple thousand? I'm guessing Hunter Sorenson isn't the only one to run afoul of the law."

"If she did not tell you about him, I am guessing she did not tell you that she dated him junior year."

"And, what, they conspired over pillow talk to one day fake the discovery of the Fountain of Youth?"

"Your words, not mine."

Mitch sighed and sat back. "Krista McCleod."

"Pardon?"

"Hottest girl in my high school. I took her to my senior prom, and afterwards we made out in the back of my Camaro."

Olivia stared at him.

"I saw a couple years ago she was busted for operating a meth lab in her boyfriend's basement." He extended both wrists. "Wanna cuff me?"

He withdrew his hands as the waitress brought his burger and fries and a salad for Olivia. "Anything else I can get you?" she asked.

"No, thanks," Mitch said, and Olivia smiled at her.

The waitress left, and Olivia flipped over the photo of Sorenson, revealing a sheet of paper with writing too small for Mitch to read. Her well-manicured hand never left the folder. "What about this man?" she asked, flipping over the sheet to reveal a second photograph, this one a head and shoulders shot of a man turned only partway toward the camera. He was sitting down, on a bench, in what looked like a bus station or airport terminal. "Do you know him?"

Mitch nodded, recognizing the man from a few harried minutes at the Casa Monica in St. Augustine. "His name's Kevin Stuart."

"Where did you hear that?"

The answer was Erik Diaz, but he wasn't about to tell her that. Not that it mattered—she probably knew the answer already. Instead, he said, "Who is he?"

"His real name is Charles Calvin. Did Cameron ever mention his name?"

"Should she have?"

"Did she speak about her time in Cairo in 2015?"

"Is this Twenty Questions or something?"

Olivia sighed, and Mitch sat back to take a bite of his burger. It was excellent, but his mind wasn't on taste at the moment.

"In 2015," Olivia said, ignoring her salad, "Cameron spent several weeks in Cairo looking for lost Egyptian artifacts. While there, she was repeatedly seen in the company of Charles Calvin—dining together, visiting a mosque together, sightseeing at the Cairo Tower together."

"What are you, the Ghost of Boyfriends Past? And why were you following Cameron in Cairo in 2015?"

"We weren't following anyone. But the CIA was monitoring Calvin, who was at the time suspected of consorting with several members of the Muslim Brotherhood."

"What?"

"Their suspicions proved unfounded, but because of their surveillance, they observed him conducting what they termed 'reconnaissance' at the Egyptian Museum. They notified the Egyptian authorities, who failed to take the warning seriously, and on July 3 the museum was broken into and several sacred relics were stolen."

Mitch ground on a French fry. "Are you trying to tell me that Cameron was complicit in a museum robbery with a man who may or may not be tied to terrorists?"

Olivia flipped over the photo and slid the next sheet toward Mitch.

"What is this?"

"A phone log, showing nearly twenty-five calls and texts between Charles Calvin and Cameron Leigh between the time they met in Cairo in 2015 up until the most recent, just four weeks ago."

"Do you have the phone calls? Have the texts?"

"No."

"How do you have any of this?"

"I told you, we're very powerful."

He gestured at the folder. "You got tax returns in there too? Junior-high diary entries?"

Olivia stabbed a wedge of tomato from her salad and deposited it in her mouth.

Mitch took a bite of his burger, buying him time to think. Why had Erik said Calvin's name was Stuart? Was his intel wrong? Was Olivia's? Was one of them lying to him? And what of the link between Calvin and Cameron? As much as he hated to admit it, it was suspicious, at the least.

Olivia turned over the sheet and showed him another photo, this one of Erik Diaz.

"What about him?" Mitch asked.

"Are you aware of his relationship with Cameron?"

"I am."

"Are you aware of the romantic aspect of it?"

"Yes. He's her ex."

Olivia smirked.

"What?"

"Did you know that she's been in contact with him the last few days?"

"Yeah. She called him yesterday morning."

"Not just yesterday morning." She flipped over the photo. "She called Monday afternoon, and also texted him Tuesday afternoon."

Mitch flipped a fry down onto his plate. "Cut the show and tell, Olivia. Just say what you're trying to say."

"Fine." She closed the folder. "Cameron Leigh is still close with Erik Diaz, her 'former' boyfriend. She has a history with a known criminal and person of interest in the art community in Hunter Sorenson. And she has a five-year history with Charles Calvin, a suspect in the Egyptian Museum robbery and one of the men who, allegedly, tried to take the Figueroa Cipher disk from her. Like I said, she's not who you think she is."

"Do you have any evidence of any of this?"

"Evidence? I've just shone you the evidence."

"No, you've showed me that Cameron dated a guy a decade ago who turned out to be a criminal, met a guy while working in Cairo and has kept in touch—without any indication that she knew or knows anything about who he really is—and that she's still close with a former boyfriend and current business partner. Not exactly the Watergate tapes."

"To be fair, I'm not implying that she was involved in the museum robbery, but she is clearly connected with Calvin, and it calls into question everything she's told you about what happened aboard the *Eternal Sun* last Saturday."

"Does it? She never saw the fourth man. We never saw Calvin or Stuart's photo. Isn't it possible he was leveraging a perfectly innocent, professional relationship to learn what she knew?"

"I suppose, it's possible. But is it reasonable? Given her connection to Sorenson, the fact that she's still working with Diaz, and given this." She opened the folder and flipped pages to reveal one final black and white photograph, this one of Cameron. She looked much younger, and her hair was dark and messy. She wore no makeup, and dark circles under her eyes made her look like a raccoon. It was not flattering. Nor was the letter board she was holding, dated October 5, 2013, in Atlanta, Georgia. A mugshot.

"What's this for?"

"Petty theft. She stole a letter from a resident of a retirement home in Collier Hills."

"A letter?"

"From a Confederate colonel, allegedly detailing the location of a shipment of stolen U.S. currency. I've done a small amount of research, and from what I can find, this lost stash of currency is widely sought by treasure hunters and history buffs."

"And she took this from a retired guy in Collier Hills?"

Olivia nodded. "The case never went to trial. They settled out of court, and it was expunged from her record. But it still happened."

Mitch blew out a breath. "Why are you telling me all this?"

"So you would know the truth."

"To what end?"

"I mentioned before that my company has an interest in the Fountain of Youth. We would like your help in locating it."

"My help?"

Olivia nodded, and finally began stirring the dressing into her salad.

"You've clearly done your research," he said. "Meaning you know that seven days ago I knew as much about the Fountain of Youth as I do the Holy Grail as I do the Hope Diamond. Why would you want my help?"

"Because of your connection to Leigh."

"You want me to be a mole?"

Olivia nodded.

"Forget it."

She said nothing.

"You've made a nice case that Cameron's not an angel, but I kind of like a woman with a dark side. I'm not going to betray her so you can win some prestige or pad your stock price by announcing that Hall Parker Cook discovered the long-lost Fountain of Youth."

"You're certain?"

"I'm certain, and your fifteen minutes are up."

"One more counter offer," she said.

"This should be good," he said, reaching for his burger. It really was far too tasty to waste.

Olivia dabbed her mouth with a napkin, even though it wasn't necessary. "You work for us as an undercover operative—"

"You mean a mole," he garbled through a mouthful of burger and bun.

"Call it what you like. You work for us, provide us whatever information Leigh has so we can find the Fountain of Youth, and we *don't* publicize what I've shown you now, effectively ruining her quest if not her career."

Mitch stopped chewing. He gulped down the bite. "Blackmail."

"Call it what you like," she said again.

"I think the FBI actually coined the term. You're crazy."

She shrugged.

Mitch thought very seriously about throwing his malt in her face, but that wouldn't do any good. The steely look in her eyes told him she would indeed carry out her threat.

"Help us, Mitch. Cameron can still 'find' the fountain, still get the fame and notoriety, but we'll be there to do our thing. It's not like she could possess the fountain herself. Or," she said, poking her salad and stabbing several leaves of lettuce, "you can remain loyal to a woman who's suspect at best and see where that gets you when we expose her."

She smiled at him, sweet and salty at the same time, and then crunched down on the lettuce like an alligator clamping down on a helpless deer.

CHAPTER THIRTY-TWO

The recently remodeled Sanibel Island Library was a researcher's dream, from its vast print and electronic resources to its comfortable tables and chairs to a friendly and helpful staff that allowed an outsider—before Cameron even dropped Dr. Kessler's name—to make use of a vacant private study room. After gathering a number of reference materials, she threw herself into her work.

She focused her search on *Misión San Francisco de Sevilla*, not wanting to spend time looking for information on *Iśimi* that Dr. LaSalle may very well provide. For the better part of an hour, she consulted various books for any reference to the mission. She also read a number of pages about Spanish missions in Florida, taking advantage of a lifelong ability to quickly consume words and text. Much of what she found repeated or complemented facts she and Mitch had learned the night before from Kessler's library. The rest, while fascinating, didn't aid in her quest.

She took a break to use the restroom and find a snack at a vending machine, then returned to her work. She conducted a search for San Francisco or Saint Francisco. Weeding out references to the fourth-largest city in California and St. Francis of Assisi, she was left with next to nothing. Munching on miniature chocolate chip cookies, she turned her attention to the Spanish city of Seville. She spent thirty minutes in a trio of books, covering the history of the Andalusian city, but found no connection to the Fountain of Youth, Diego Figueroa, or anything in the New World.

She reached into the bag of cookies and found it empty. Needing to stretch, she stood and took the foil bag to the nearest garbage can. When she turned back to the table, her phone display was lit and it was vibrating on the table. The number was not familiar, but she picked it up and swiped it anyhow.

"Hello?"

"Is this Cameron Leigh?"

The voice was familiar, somewhat austere.

"Dr. LaSalle?"

"Yes. Gabriel Kessler called and gave me your number."

They had forgotten, amidst their talks and on the drive to the library, to do so. With Kessler headed to Naples and a fishing trip that would leave him out of touch, she was glad he'd remembered.

"Yes, he mentioned that," she said. "Did you find something?"

"In fact I did. A former student of mine, as it were, is an art critic here in New Orleans, and I reached out to her. She in turn contacted a colleague of hers, who I understand reached out to yet another colleague. All that to say, I just heard back from my former student, Mackenzie. She said *Iśimi* is currently possessed by a gallery in Miami." He paused for a moment. "Primero."

"Primero in Miami," Cameron repeated, fumbling around her assortment of open books for a pen and a sheet of paper. She found both and scribbled down the name. "Thank you so much, Dr. LaSalle."

"You're quite welcome. I didn't get any more details, other than what I've told you, but I'm sure you can reach out to the gallery with any further questions."

"I will. Thank you again."

"My pleasure. Good day."

Cameron put her phone down. She thought about calling Mitch with the good news, but decided to merely text him instead. Then, since she still had hours before he arrived, she packed up her current stack of books and set out in search of more. They had a line on *Iśimi*, but it wouldn't do any good if they couldn't also identify *Misión San Francisco de Sevilla*.

*   *   *

Mitch looked up at a wispy cloud that may or may not have been the remnants of a contrail. If everything Olivia said was true, how much damage would it do to Cameron if it came out? There was nothing actionable regarding her relationships with Sorenson or Calvin, and the theft of a Confederate colonel's letter had been settled and expunged. Legally, he didn't think she was touchable.

Her reputation, however, was another matter. Not only would exposing her remove any credibility she had in the world of "history hunters," but it could very well cause her to lose her job. There was also the issue of the conclusion of her search. Would Cameron's efforts to find the Fountain of Youth be derailed? Would she be discredited if she did find it?

And were these even the right questions? Did he believe Olivia and her evidence? More than that, did he believe her conclusions—that Cameron had lied to him about everything? Could it all—finding her in the waters off Cocoa Beach, rescuing her from Erik's villa, their IMF-esque job in St. Augustine— have been staged? It didn't make sense. Not only could Cameron not have known he'd be hanging around on his Jet Ski to come to her aide, but she also didn't have a motive for involving him. Unless she could determine people's locations and eating habits like Olivia had.

And yet, if Olivia's evidence was legit, the only other explanation he could think of was that Cameron had been duped by Calvin. Or Erik. Or both. And that still left her vulnerable to being exposed for all the same reasons, not to mention gutted when she found out she had been betrayed.

Mitch paced back toward the entrance to Addison's. Maybe he could play this out, pump Olivia for more info—say, what she knew about Erik, Calvin/Stuart, and the rest of the Van Buren Gang. He could also protect Cameron, at least until he knew more and—he reluctantly admitted to himself—until he decided what he believed about her.

Olivia was halfway through her salad when he returned to the table. He'd left under the auspices of going to the bathroom, not caring if she believed him or not. She looked up with a sultry grin as he sat back down.

"*If* I go along with your plan, how do I know you won't still expose Cameron?" he asked.

"You have my word."

He huffed.

"And I haven't lied to you yet."

Mitch stuck his tongue in his cheek.

"So what do you say?" she asked, fiddling with the straw in her water.

"I don't know," he said, reaching for his phone. "I need to do a little research first."

He intended to make her squirm by slowly researching Hall Parker Cook and Olivia's identity online. Their website looked legit. They were a major manufacturer of a variety of pharmaceuticals, based out of Raleigh, North Carolina, with offices in Atlanta, Jacksonville, and Houston. A quick survey of their website identified Olivia de la Cruz as a VP of Operations, and the picture on the site matched the beautiful woman across from him. For an extra measure of security, he sent a quick e-mail to the address on the website and the business card.

He sat back. "Show me your phone."

"What?"

"Let me see the e-mail I just sent."

Olivia pursed her lips, concealing a smirk, and reached into her purse. She came out with her phone, swiped and tapped it a few times, and turned it so Mitch could see the e-mail he had just sent. "Satisfied?"

"Not hardly," he said as his phone buzzed. He looked down to see a text from Cameron.

Heard from LaSalle. He has a line on Isimi,
at a gallery named Primero in Miami!
See you soon!

He smiled to himself at her excitement at seeing him, and decided that unless Olivia could produce far stronger evidence of Cameron's wrongdoing, he would give her the benefit of the doubt. Oddly enough, that sensation also buoyed his desire to protect her, which meant he had to go along with Olivia. He couldn't take the chance that she was bluffing or wouldn't go public or that it wouldn't hurt Cameron if she did.

He couldn't take *that* chance, but Cameron's text had given him an idea, and he decided to take another chance. Exhaling, he sat back. "It won't do any good to have me as a mole."

"Why's that?"

"Because I can tell you everything right now."

Olivia's eyebrows went up.

"We solved the riddle of the Castillo de San Marcos Carving. That's why I'm in town, to return the cipher disk we borrowed because we don't need it anymore."

Olivia cut to the chase. "What does the carving say?"

"Run it through the ciphers Figueroa set up, do the necessary translation, and it says, more or less, 'To find the Fountain of Youth, find Iśimi, and she will reveal all.'"

"Who is *Iśimi?*"

"A Calusa Indian princess. Or," he said, reaching for a fry, "more specifically in this case, a portrait of her painted by Diego Figueroa."

Olivia's dark eyes studied him carefully. "How do I know you're telling the truth?"

Mitch laughed. "Well, I could give you the Dewey decimal numbers for the dozen books we thumbed through, numbers for former colleagues Cameron's touched base with, walk you through every step of mind-numbing research. Or . . . I can tell you where to find *Iśimi*, which you should be able to corroborate without too much trouble, and that will prove this isn't some clever story I made up off the cuff."

Her eyes narrowed.

Mitch reached for his malt. It was a huge risk, divulging his and Cameron's latest lead, telling Olivia what they had discovered. But his alternatives were go back and be a mole, which he couldn't see himself doing, or call Olivia's bluff and hope she didn't expose Cameron. And this woman didn't look like a bluffer.

On the other hand, if she bought that they had reached the end of the line, she could go find the portrait of *Iśimi* and follow whatever clues it contained. Much like the Van Buren Gang with only one cipher, she and her cronies at Hall Parker Cook would be stuck without the knowledge of Mission San Francisco of Seville and the need to reunify *Iśimi* with Figueroa in its bell tower. And that would leave him and Cameron free to continue the search, one step ahead of Olivia.

Olivia mulled for a bite, then a rinse of water. She locked her eyes on Mitch's again. "Where is this portrait?"

"At a gallery in Miami."

"Which gallery?"

"First you provide me with some assurance that you won't expose Cameron."

"Like what?"

"I don't know. You've had an answer for everything so far, so I figure you're good for another."

"I don't suppose you'll take my word."

"The word of people who promise not to carry out their blackmail is usually about as reliable as a ten-day forecast."

Olivia furrowed her chin. Even that was attractive.

"All right," she said. She picked her phone off the booth and handed it to Mitch. "Will that satisfy you?"

"Not especially."

"Until I verify your evidence and have a chance to check it out, you can hold onto my phone—make sure I don't send any secret communications."

"I thought your plan was to send me back to Cameron."

"That's when I needed a mole. Now that I know everything there is to know, you're coming with me."

"Why?"

"Because I don't trust you any more than you trust me." She leaned forward. "So we'll go to Miami. You can filter any calls or texts or e-mails I get or send, which ensures Cameron's dirty little secrets stay just that, and I keep my leverage in case you're double-crossing me."

Not much of a bluffer, and pretty good at calling them out too.

"Cameron's expecting me back this afternoon," Mitch said. "If I don't show up, she'll know something's wrong."

"Give me your phone."

"What?"

"I'll text her a photo of us and say you ran off with a dusky Latina woman."

"Funny."

"Seriously, give me your phone."

"No."

She raised an eyebrow. "You have mine, to make sure I walk the line. Only fair I make sure you don't try to tip her off." She extended her palm and motioned for the phone with her fingers.

"So what, I just ghost her, leave her stranded?"

"She's resourceful. Besides, I'm sure a girl like her is used to being ghosted."

Mitch glared at her.

"If it makes you feel better, I'll text her that your mom is sick and you had to fly back to Texas to be with her."

"Except my mom lives in Minneapolis."

Olivia smirked. "No she doesn't."

Mitch quickly thumbed on his phone, working to delete Cameron's most recent text.

"Come on, Mitch."

"Hold your horses," he said, finishing the task. Then he sighed and handed over his phone.

Olivia examined it for a moment. Then her smirk widened. "What do you say we get out of here? We can still make Miami in time for a late dinner."

CHAPTER THIRTY-THREE

Cameron pounded the books until two, when she couldn't take any more. She thought for a while she'd stumbled onto a lead in the form of a Spanish explorer named Francisco Cavilla, who had been something of a contemporary of Diego Figueroa. But his only link to Florida seemed to be in the Keys, and even that was nebulous. He'd spent most of his time in the West Indies and the coast of modern-day Mexico, and there was nothing to link him to any missions or the Fountain of Youth. Nor was there any evidence that the man, born in Madrid, had any connection to Seville. It was a dead end.

She checked her phone and saw she had a text from Mitch, which meant he was on his way back. That brought a smile to her face, until she opened the text.

afraid I have 2 go home mom in hospital
and needs me ill call u when i can –m

She read the message several times, her emotions ranging from sadness to anger to fear. She felt terrible for Mitch, but the sadness was more related to the sudden end to their adventure. That led to anger when she thought that he couldn't even call her to tell her. That led to further scrutiny of the text, which didn't sound like Mitch. Using "texty" shorthand wasn't his style, and the lack of punctuation and grammar could have been because he was in a hurry or was rattled, or could have been a sign. Was this his way of telling her that he was in trouble? Had the Van Buren Gang gotten to him somehow?

She drafted several replies, but didn't send any of them. The "*ill call u when i can*" part seemed to suggest she shouldn't contact him. Was he just too busy arranging travel or worrying about his mom? Or was he trying to protect her?

She absentmindedly returned her books and reference materials, then headed outside, to a small ground-level patio. Even in the shade, the heat was oppressive, and the breeze either absent or blocked by the building and surrounding trees. Leaning against a support column, she read the message again, then typed a quick response.

I'm sorry. Let me know more when you can.

She agonized, then pressed send. Then she paced. What to do now? Her only contact on Sanibel Island—and her only means of transportation—was on his way to Naples. She had no car, a few hundred bucks, and no way to get to Miami to pursue *Išimi* and the Fountain of Youth further.

Maybe she should give up—at least for now. Go home, recoup, do some more research on *Misión San Francisco de Sevilla*, wait to hear more from Mitch, and reevaluate then. Or maybe she should find a motel with a pool, spend the night, and see what developed.

She paced a little more. Then she called the one person who had always been there in dicey situations.

"This is Erik."

"Erik, it's me."

"Cameron? Where are you?"

"It's a long story."

"What's going on? You don't sound good."

"I ran into some trouble, and . . . I don't know what to do."

"What's going on?" he repeated. "Are you still in Clearwater?"

"No," she said, hesitant to say where, given Mitch's earlier warnings.

For once, Erik didn't talk, waiting.

"Mitch had to go home," she said. "His mom's sick or something, I think, and so I'm stuck here and we have a clue, but I don't know how to follow it, or if I should, or what's going on with Mitch. And . . . Erik, I don't know what to do."

"Cammy, can I call you back in five?"

"What?"

"I've got a minor problem here at work. Five minutes, I'll call you right back."

"Yeah, sure."

"Five minutes."

His phone clicked, and she lowered hers. She resisted the urge to heave it into the marsh, and to explode emotionally. Typical Erik, always devoted to work first and foremost. Then the anger turned inward. What did she expect him to do, anyhow? What could anyone do?

Okay, Cameron, no more pity party. You make your own luck, so you've got to figure this out. On to Miami solo, or take a step back?

She paced some more. She could really use a deserted beach right about now, or an Olympic-sized pool, someplace to burn some stress and think. Taking a step back made sense, given recent developments and her cash-flow issues. But she was close, closer than she'd ever been, and she didn't want to lose momentum. She also didn't want to give her pursuers a chance to catch up and learn what she'd learned. Van Buren's people had cleaned the Figueroa Cipher, and thus could have photographed it. How long until they found the Bloodbeard Cipher, if they hadn't already? Then how long until they deciphered the carving and used their version of Drs. Kessler and LaSalle to find *Iśimi* and *Misión San Francisco de Sevilla*? All it would take was one source she didn't have, and they'd be ahead of her. She had to keep going.

Her phone vibrated. She looked down, hoping it would be Mitch. It was Erik.

"Wow, only three and a half minutes," she sniped.

"I'm sorry, Cam."

She said nothing.

"I'm sorry, but I'm clear now. What's going on?"

She took a deep breath, blew it out, and then recapped some of the basics—they had deciphered the carving, which he already knew, and had talked to "an expert" who put them onto the next clue, in Miami. She didn't reveal Kessler's name, or the name *Iśimi*—not yet, at least.

"But I'm low on funds again, and now with Mitch gone . . ."

"When did he leave?"

"He had to return the other disk to Clearwater, and he texted me a half hour ago or so. He's heading back to Austin."

"He texted you?"

"Yeah."

"That's cold."

You should know.

"Cam, where are you?"

"What difference does it make?"

"Because I'll come to you."

"What?"

"I shouldn't have dropped things so quickly the other day, and I feel bad. I want to help, I really do. And you're making progress, which to be honest, is more than I expected. I thought this disk would lead to months of research, more globe-trotting . . . Anyhow, I'm sorry about that."

"Thank you."

"I'm in Atlanta right now, but I can catch a flight to wherever you are."

"You'd do that?"

"It sounds like you need a friend . . . and his wallet," he said, and Cameron could picture the sly grin on his face. It drew one of her own.

"I'm on Sanibel Island."

"Sanibel? A little R&R?"

"No, tracking an expert. But he's gone now, and Mitch is gone, and I'm stuck here."

Erik took a breath, then another. "Can you get to the airport? Catch an Uber or a taxi or something?"

"The airport?"

"Southwest Florida International, in Fort Myers."

"I suppose. But I thou—"

"I'll be on the next flight and meet you there."

"Okay. I'll get there," she said. "Thank you, Erik."

"Don't worry, Cammy. Everything's going to be okay."

"I'm not sure I believe that, but I appreciate it anyhow."

"I'll text you when I have a flight. When you get to the airport, find us a good steakhouse for dinner."

"Okay. Thanks, Erik."

"See you soon."

She ended the call and leaned back against the same column. She wanted to cry, for a variety of reasons. Instead, she headed back into the library to reclaim her luggage from the front desk, locate the airport, and call an Uber. She wasn't sure if she believed Erik, but her hope was buoyed by the possibilities. Even so, it didn't override the sadness, anger, and fear regarding Mitch. She remembered her morning prayer on the beach, and sent another quick, it-can't-hurt message skyward, asking that everything would turn out all right.

*   *   *

"You got a text back," Olivia said as Mitch got back into the driver's seat of the Nissan Rogue, having just topped off the gas tank.

"From Cameron?"

She tipped the phone so he could read it.

I'm sorry. Let me know more when you can.

"You know, if there's a hell, I think you're headed there," he said.

"You can keep pretending you're mad at me if you want—"

"Pretending. You think this is an act?"

"Yes, because I think the person you're really mad at is Cameron, for not being who you thought. Or maybe at yourself for not seeing through it."

Mitch cranked the ignition to start the SUV. They had left the restaurant in his vehicle, with Olivia explaining that hers was "being taken care of." Mitch had then turned off her phone, pocketing the battery and SIM card. He had taken the most circuitous route possible, hoping to lose a tail, before getting on the interstate. Olivia had said nothing, keeping a bemused smile on her face. It had stayed there as they crossed the Skyway Bridge again, with Mitch making a concentrated effort not to show the tingle of fear that ran up his spine.

He had stopped for gas at the same exit he and Cameron had taken the day before, which prepared them for the three and a half-hour journey south and east to Miami. The exit made him think of Cameron, which made him question his decision to go along with Olivia. What if he had just ignored her call again? What if he had played his cards differently, calling her bluff or pretending to be a mole and rejoining Cameron on Sanibel Island? Was this the right move, what was best for Cameron? What would she do without him, without a vehicle?

And the biggest question of all, what did he make of Olivia's allegations? He wanted to talk to Cameron, to hear the truth from her. But Olivia hadn't allowed him that option, and now he had no way of reaching out to her. Well, that wasn't entirely true. But before he tried something covert, he needed to know his enemy a little better.

"Something on your mind?" Olivia asked as they merged back onto I-75.

"I want to know how you found me, how you knew where I was."

"Surely someone with your background should know how it's done."

"I know how it can be done. I want to know how it was done."

Olivia looked away out her window, then slowly turned back to him. "Have you paid your insurance premiums?"

He frowned, wondering what sort of code that was. And then it hit him. Olivia de la Cruz. DLC Insurance, in the other half of the building housing Morgan's Pirate Den.

"It's cute," she said, "the way the light bulb goes on."

He didn't take the bait this time. "You knew about the cipher disk?"

"For several months," she said.

"So why not twist Morgan's arm to get it."

"Because we didn't know what to do next. Leigh's been on this for years, and we knew she was onto the wreck of Enrique Figueroa's ship. We figured it was only a matter of time before she came for the other disk, meaning she'd have the necessary clues to find the Fountain of Youth, and then we could—"

"Pounce."

She dipped her chin in concession.

"How did you know she was onto the wreck? Sounds like you already have a mole."

"Not a mole, but we have our ways."

"So your incredibly large and powerful pharmaceutical company is just lazy, is that it?"

"You know how it is, you bring in a specialist for certain tasks—a punt, short yardage plays. Besides, we prefer to keep a low profile in this matter."

"So you saw us come the other day, then what?"

"We followed you back to your hotel, then set up surveillance. When it looked like you were headed out yesterday morning, we concluded you'd made a breakthrough. That's why I called."

"And today?"

"We had a tracking device on your Elantra, so the new wheels threw us. I decided to give you some leash, not pressure you. Then when you brought the disk back, well . . ."

"You were sitting there in the office?"

"It's how I knew where you were."

He exhaled. "Okay, who's the we?"

"Hall Parker Cook—"

"I mean this isn't a one-girl operation."

"I have a few field-reps in the Tampa area I was able to dispatch for a couple days. Now it's just me and you."

"You sure that's wise?"

Her eyes twinkled. "What, you're going to pull over and dump my body in the Everglades?"

"No, but you keep pushing my buttons . . ."

Olivia extended a finger and pushed on his bicep. Then she tipped her head back and laughed.

They rolled on for a few miles.

"Tell me about Hall Parker Cook," Mitch said.

"You found the website earlier."

"Yeah, but I must have missed the 'why we're deviously searching for the Fountain of Youth' page."

"I am not the one who's been devious."

"Oh? And how is the insurance side business? Racking up the clients?"

For once, Olivia didn't have an answer.

"You've got me over the barrel," he said. "What's your interest in some fabled spring? Doesn't the whole idea conflict with science and technology?"

"Depends where the fable came from. Did some simpleton hundreds of years ago associate drinking from a certain river with his sudden but explainable recovery from a common illness? If so, there's not much to this. But history is full of discoveries of various chemicals and minerals that have enabled us to develop vaccines and medications, that we're using to fight disease and sustain life. What if the Fountain of Youth is a spring of water that contains such nutrients?"

Olivia came alive as she spoke, and Mitch realized her goals were not that far from Cameron's—assuming she was being honest with him.

"So that's Hall Parker Cook's plan, harvest whatever they can out of the water to boost profits?"

"And help people. Check out our website. HPC is an incredibly environmentally conscious corporation, and our charitable work is second to none. Yes, we're a for-profit business, but not at the expense of others. Someone is going to find this water and use it for the benefit of society—or for something worse. We'd just prefer to be that someone and have the profits that ensue go to Hall Parker Cook instead of someone else."

"So the allure of gold and jewels and riches beyond belief have nothing to do with it?"

Olivia frowned.

"Don't tell me you haven't heard the rumors about Figueroa stashing some treasure by the fountain."

"I've heard rumors," she said, "but nothing coherent, and certainly nothing credible. Our interest in the fountain is solely for the fountain."

He was quiet for another minute, trying to decide if he believed her. At least this once, he did.

"So why not call Cameron up and make her an offer?"

"We did, over a year ago. She turned us down."

"What was the offer?"

"A partnership. Our money, her expertise. She'd get the credit, we'd get the water. No tricks."

Mitch focused on the horizon.

"And as I'm sure she's told you, we're not the only people who want to find it. But we are the only ones whose motives are pure and whose actions upon finding it will be as well."

He said nothing.

"We're not the bad guys, Mitch. I know this is a shock to you, and I know my methods may not agree with you, but I'm not the bad guy either."

He said nothing.

After a few minutes, she asked, "How about some music?" She reached for the radio and tuned in a jazz station. She settled back into her seat. "You like jazz?"

He said nothing.

CHAPTER THIRTY-FOUR

The Southwest Florida International Airport was twenty-some miles and nearly an hour's ride (meaning quite an Uber fare) from Sanibel Island. Compared to Hartsfield-Jackson in Atlanta, it was a cracker box, especially since Cameron couldn't pass through security to the concourses. Erik had texted during her ride, saying that his flight was due to arrive a few minutes before six. That left her several hours to kill in the terminal. So she found a seat near a palm tree and with a view out the window.

She thought about Mitch, who had not called or texted anything further. She tried to remember if he'd said anything about his mom and what this sudden ailment might be. She analyzed the text again and again, looking for nuance and hidden meaning—was he ghosting her? No, that didn't fit. He could have done that a dozen times more conveniently. Was he under duress and sending her some sort of warning? If so, she couldn't interpret it. Was this really how things between them would end, after so much potential?

To take her mind off it, she thought about Erik. For all his negative qualities, and there were enough to have driven a wedge between them romantically, she was grateful to have him in her life—to have him available to lean on. But how much could she lean? His comment about needing a friend and a wallet suggested he was willing to fund some of her search, but how much and for how long? Could all the evidence she'd found be enough to convince him that it was worth reinstating full funding? If so, while she would miss having Mitch around, there wasn't any reason she couldn't resume the search semi-solo, as she had previously. *If so.* A little eyelash batting might be in order.

She sighed, tired of thinking. She got up, toting her luggage with her to avoid getting airport security in a dither. She bought a coffee and scone at Starbucks, which counted as lunch. Then she returned to her same seat and

250

stared out the window. The sky had clouded up, suggesting more storms were on the way. That seemed somehow fitting, given the way this day had transpired.

She sipped her latte and flipped through a few pages of a newspaper left on a seat at the end of the row. She skimmed through some social media sites on her phone, catching up on a few friends' lives. She thought about texting Cindy or Chelsea, her sisters, but didn't have anything to tell them that wasn't depressing.

With a sigh, she got up and tossed the napkin and bag from her scone in the garbage, then stopped to look out the window. Contrary to last night's storm that had slowly engulfed the coast, this pending storm looked more typical of south Florida. Plenty of blue sky was still visible, but towering cumulous clouds identified popup thunderstorms racing inland.

Cameron returned to her seat, and with nothing else to do, dug out the small book Dr. Kessler had given her when dropping her off at the library. The Gospel of John. She had never read the Bible before, other than for a verse here or there somehow tied to a school paper or research project. She had no idea what to expect, other than maybe a woman on a donkey and no room in the inn. But she was thrown for a loop with the very first words.

In the beginning was the Word, and the Word was with God, and the Word was God.

That was rather cosmic. And what was "the Word"?

He was with God in the beginning. Through him all things were made; without him nothing was made that has been made. In him was life, and that life was the light of all mankind. The light shines in the darkness, and the darkness has not overcome it.

She kept reading, mostly out of boredom, but also feeling she owed something to Dr. Kessler. A man named John was introduced, presumably the author. Then a section about testifying to light, rejection by the world, being children of God. It was very confusing, and she was about to give up.

The Word became flesh and made his dwelling among us. We have seen his glory, the glory of the one and only Son, who came from the Father, full of grace and truth.

Cameron lowered the Bible and looked up. The Word became flesh? What in the world . . . ?

She looked around, checked her watch. It was four-thirty, and she figured she might as well keep reading.

There was no traditional Christmas story, shepherds and wise men and all that, but instead the John guy denied that he was anybody important, then saw Jesus and called him *"the Lamb of God, who takes away the sin of the world,"* which was the first Bible-sounding thing Cameron had read. Jesus called some disciples, then went to a wedding and turned water into wine, a neat little trick, she thought. Then he talked to a man named Nicodemus, more confusing stuff about wind blowing and being born of the spirit and snakes in the desert. Cameron was sure it all made sense if you talked the religious language, but to her, it wasn't doing much. But she pushed on, through the famous John 3:16 that Kessler had quoted the night before, and into chapter four. She paused, flipped to the end, and saw the book had twenty-one chapters. She'd give it five before quitting and writing her sisters after all.

> *Now he had to go through Samaria. So he came to a town in Samaria called Sychar, near the plot of ground Jacob had given to his son Joseph. Jacob's well was there, and Jesus, tired as he was from the journey, sat down by the well. It was about noon.*
>
> *When a Samaritan woman came to draw water, Jesus said to her, "Will you give me a drink?" (His disciples had gone into the town to buy food.)*
>
> *The Samaritan woman said to him, "You are a Jew and I am a Samaritan woman. How can you ask me for a drink?" (For Jews do not associate with Samaritans.)*
>
> *Jesus answered her, "If you knew the gift of God and who it is that asks you for a drink, you would have asked him and he would have given you living water."*
>
> *"Sir," the woman said, "you have nothing to draw with and the well is deep. Where can you get this living water? Are you greater than our father Jacob, who gave us the well and drank from it himself, as did also his sons and his livestock?"*
>
> *Jesus answered, "Everyone who drinks this water will be thirsty again, but whoever drinks the water I give them will never*

thirst. Indeed, the water I give them will become in them a spring of water welling up to eternal life."

The words jumped out at Cameron, and not just because they sounded familiar from her talks with Kessler. Jesus' conversation with the woman seemed to mirror her conversation with her old professor—one of them looking for natural water, and one talking metaphorically. And while the concept of believing in Jesus, becoming religious, seemed so foreign to Cameron, she also remembered Kessler's words about belief in the supernatural not being a big leap for someone who believed in intelligent design. Or a fountain with healing properties, properties that didn't spawn themselves. She decided to keep reading.

Jesus persuaded the woman, along with many in her town. He healed people and walked on water, if the Bible was to be believed. She hadn't done Kessler's research, hadn't backed it up, but everything she knew about the man told her he wouldn't fabricate something and he wouldn't buy it without kicking the tires, so to speak.

Jesus used more metaphors, comparing himself to bread and suggesting people eat his flesh and drink his blood. That had to be a metaphor, didn't it? Although Cameron knew a girl from college who actually believed when she participated in Holy Communion at her church, a wafer dipped in wine was transformed into the actual body and blood of Jesus. That was a bridge too far for Cameron.

She read on, slowing down when she got deep into chapter seven.

On the last and greatest day of the festival, Jesus stood and said in a loud voice, "Let anyone who is thirsty come to me and drink. Whoever believes in me, as Scripture has said, rivers of living water will flow from within them." By this he meant the Spirit, whom those who believed in him were later to receive. Up to that time the Spirit had not been given, since Jesus had not yet been glorified.

On hearing his words, some of the people said, "Surely this man is the Prophet."

Others said, "He is the Messiah."

Still others asked, "How can the Messiah come from Galilee? Does not Scripture say that the Messiah will come from

David's descendants and from Bethlehem, the town where David lived?" Thus the people were divided because of Jesus.

A clap of thunder caused Cameron to lift her head from the Bible, and she saw that the sky outside the terminal window had grown dark and was streaked heavily with rain. As if initiated by the thunderclap, rain began to fall and pelt against the windows. She watched it for several seconds, rethinking what she had just read. What did it mean that rivers of living water would flow from whoever believed in Jesus? And what did it mean to receive a Spirit? What Spirit? Why hadn't the Spirit been given yet? She scanned the last few verses of the chapter, about people arguing over whether Jesus was the Prophet, the Messiah, or neither. Cameron felt like the people, *"divided because of Jesus."* She didn't know what to think, but had grown weary of sitting. She closed the small Gospel of John and returned it to the pocket of her travel bag, then stood up to check the boards to see if the weather had impacted Erik's arrival time.

*   *   *

Mitch and Olivia made the turn east on I-275 in Naples just in front of an oncoming thunderstorm, but soon were racing east at seventy-five miles per hour through the Everglades on a stretch of highway known as Alligator Alley. They had hardly spoken over the last ninety minutes. Mitch had been thinking of Cameron, trying to piece together what he knew of her and what Olivia had alleged about her, what that meant, what he should have done and should be doing about it now. He also missed her, missed the thought of being with her right now and going forward.

Olivia chair-danced to the radio.

Alligator Alley was a four-lane highway through a swamp—endlessly straight with nothing to see but a canal here and there, and a few intersections with smaller roads bisecting the endless, flat terrain. The sun was shining again, but bubbling clouds revealed the location of storms north and east of them. It would only be a matter of time.

"Where is the painting?" Olivia asked out of the blue.

"What?"

"You said the painting was in a gallery in Miami. Which gallery?"

254

"Did I say that?" he asked with fake innocence.

Olivia smiled. "You don't want to play games with me."

"I don't want to do anything with you, in fact."

"Anything?" she asked, tilting her head.

"What? Are you serious right now?"

She winked and leaned back in her seat. "You can tell me when we get to Miami."

They drove without talking until suddenly subdivisions popped up out of the swampland. Olivia had ceased gyrating to jazz music or quasi-flirting and had stared straight ahead or looked out her window the entire way, not saying so much as a word. Mitch didn't even try to guess her feelings or motivations.

"You ever been to Miami?" she finally asked, sitting up a little straighter as several intersections brought an increase in traffic.

Mitch looked at her.

"I'm not making small talk," she said. "We're going to need a place to stay, and I'm wondering if you know the area."

"Are you testing me, or is there actually a hole in your research?"

She didn't answer.

"I've never been to Miami."

Olivia nodded, waited a few seconds. "About this gallery . . . Miami proper, or the Greater Miami area?"

"I don't know."

"It really is time to stop being cute."

"All I know is it's in Miami. I didn't Google Maps it."

"What's the name?"

He hesitated.

"Come on, Mitch. I've kept up my end of the deal by not exposing your girlfriend."

"And what's to stop you the moment I tell you?"

"You still have my phone."

"And you couldn't possibly find another phone, couldn't use your hotel phone, to make a call?"

"I guess you'll just have to keep me company to make sure."

Mitch exhaled, thought very briefly about swerving into a canal, and then said, "Primero."

She looked at him for a second, then nodded. "Can I have my phone?"

"Nope."

"Aren't we a little past this?"

He didn't answer.

"At some point, we're going to have to trust each other."

He didn't answer.

"Besides, if I was as malicious as you seem to think, I could have told one of my colleagues to release the information by such and such a time if they didn't hear back from me. Face it, if I want to expose her, I can. But I don't, and I won't, if you cooperate."

"Really?"

"Really."

"No, I mean you're sure the way you want to earn my trust is by playing the 'I can destroy you at any minute if I want' card?"

She exhaled. "Well, can I use the internet on your phone then?"

"Knock yourself out."

She retrieved his phone from her purse and opened a browser. He took a few peeks to make sure she wasn't up to anything surreptitious, but spent most of his focus on traffic. After several minutes, she announced that Primero was a little north of downtown, right on the bay, and was apparently very exclusive. She turned her attention to a place to stay, announcing that through Hall Parker Cook's various connections and partnerships, they were able to get discount rooms at a number of hotels worldwide.

"I can see why you people want to live forever," Mitch said. "You've got the world by the collar."

Olivia only smiled. Mitch continued east, now on I-595, toward Fort Lauderdale. There were four lanes, hundreds of signs, and thousands of cars. A typical afternoon, he figured.

"We're booked at the Fountainbleau Miami Beach," Olivia announced.

"Marvelous."

"Just stay on this and then head south when you get to I-95."

He did, through mile after mile of city. Aside from the abundance of palm trees and billboards advertising everything from Disney World to Everglades fan-boat tours, there wasn't much to differentiate Greater Miami from any other huge city. The only recognizable landmark was Hard Rock Stadium, home of the Miami Dolphins. The 'Fins had visited Soldier Field Mitch's one season with the Bears, the closest he had come to Florida during his NFL career.

A few miles north of downtown, I-195 branched off toward the east. Mitch guided them through a brief but heavy rain shower and across the causeway to the barrier island that was home to the communities of Miami Beach and South Beach. A few minutes later, once again bathed in sunshine, they arrived at the famed Fountainbleau, a sweeping arc-shaped hotel on the beach. Built in the 1950s and remodeled some fifty years later, the hotel had seen everyone from Sinatra to James Bond to real-life gangsters, and was a Florida landmark.

After dropping the Nissan with the valet at the main entrance, Mitch followed Olivia through the lobby, through glass-enclosed walkways overlooking the Fontainbleau's pool area, and up to one of the top floors in the Sorrento Tower. Their suite had views of both the Atlantic Ocean and the entire Fountainbleau grounds, including the main building and pools, along with a wraparound balcony, full kitchen, an in-room bar, and a private bedroom. One private bedroom.

"Nice digs," Mitch said as Olivia tipped the bellboy. "Where's my room?"

"I figured for security reasons, we ought to share a suite."

Mitch nodded. "Good idea."

She flashed him a leering smile.

He lifted his duffel bag and brushed past her, into the bedroom. Figuring their circumstances mitigated any need for chivalry, he tossed the duffel onto the bed and said, "You can have the sofa."

"We can settle sleeping arrangements later," Olivia said, undaunted. "Right now, I think we should get something to eat and plan our strategy."

"What strategy? Go to the gallery, look at the painting to figure out where the fountain is, then shake hands and call it a partnership."

"Primero is incredibly exclusive," she said. "From what I read online, access is by invitation only on a real who-you-know basis. This is not going to be easy."

CHAPTER THIRTY-FIVE

The rain was gone and the sun was shining brightly on wet runways and aprons by the time Erik's plane touched down at Southwest Florida International. It was another thirty minutes before he emerged from the concourse and waved to get Cameron's attention. She hurried over and embraced him in a tight hug, fighting off tears she couldn't explain.

"Cammy, Cammy, it's okay," he said as she stood back. He brushed hair off her cheek. "I'm here, it's okay."

"Thank you for coming, Erik. I just . . . I don't—"

"It's okay," he said again. "Let's get your bags before TSA has a hernia."

"Did you check a bag?"

"Just this," he said, shrugging his shoulders under the weight of a backpack. Cameron had never figured out how he—or any man—traveled so light. They picked up her luggage from where she'd left it a moment ago and headed for the Hertz desk across the street from the terminal, where they picked up a Mazda6. Fifty minutes after Erik's plane touched down, they took to the rain-slicked streets in search of dinner. Erik had done the work he assigned Cameron and had found a steakhouse not far from the airport. They arrived just before the next rain shower moved in, and were assigned a cozy booth by the window. After ordering, Erik leaned his elbows on the table. "Okay, Cammy, tell me what's going on. Spare no detail."

Over the next half hour, including salads and the start of their entrées, she recounted all of her and Mitch's work—from their efforts to take back the Figueroa Cipher from the Hogan Gang in St. Augustine to bartering with Morgan for the Bloodbeard Cipher and interpreting the Castillo de San Marcos Carving, then from being run off the road at the Skyway Bridge to their conversations with Dr. Kessler to her call from Dr. LaSalle that afternoon.

"He said the *Iśimi* painting is at a gallery in Miami—Primero."

"At a gallery?" Erik asked.

"The provenance is somewhat sketchy—originally possessed by the Calusa Indians, lost in Cuba for a while, sold at auction, and somehow ended up in Primero."

"But this Dr. LaSalle is sure it's there?"

"He seemed perfectly confident in his source."

"And it's just a painting of some Native American woman?"

Cameron shrugged. "I guess. I don't know the specifics."

"So how does that lead to the Fountain of Youth?"

She sipped her tea. "I don't know. We also need to find *Misión San Francisco de Sevilla*, and I've run into nothing but dead ends on that front."

"We'll figure it out, Cam."

"We?"

Erik nodded. "I always figured deciphering the carving was fifty-fifty at best. But you did that. There is another clue. There's light at the end of the tunnel. And I'm not going to leave you to do this alone."

She looked down.

Erik placed a hand on her arm. "This guy, Mitch, he means something to you?"

She slowly raised her eyes and nodded. "Yeah. At least, I think he might, in time. If there's time."

"What'd his text say again?"

She retrieved her phone and scrolled to the text, then showed it to him.

"He's a lousy grammarian."

"Erik."

He shrugged. "Maybe the stress of it all got to him. Maybe he'll call later and explain everything."

"I texted him about the gallery hours ago, and nothing."

Another shrug. "I don't know, Cam, but give him time. Don't write him off yet."

She smiled. "Thanks, Erik."

"Miami. What's that, a few hours?"

"At least."

"I suppose we could get a flight." He reached for his phone, and alternated eating and scrolling for several minutes. "There's a nine-fifteen," he said, checking his watch. "Otherwise nothing till morning. But it won't do much good to get there this late anyhow. Grab a hotel, drive there in the morning? I doubt the gallery opens before noon."

"Might as well."

They finished eating and checked into adjoining rooms at a nearby SpringHill Suites. After swapping her shorts for a pair of jeans, Cameron joined Erik in his room, and they did some research. They started with a basic internet search of Primero. It had no website, but from other sites, they were able to determine Primero was an elite, posh gallery located in a Miami high-rise right on the bay. It was not open to the public, and details of its collections were incredibly limited. So too was information about the identities of its owners or curators. Both Erik and Cameron had some sources in the art community who might be able to give them some more info and a possible line on the gallery's owners, but they decided to wait until morning before reaching out.

"Something on your mind?" Erik asked, and Cameron realized she'd been staring off into space.

"A million things."

He put his arm on the back of the couch, so he could massage her shoulders. "Come on, Cam, something's got you."

She turned her eyes from the distant wall to Erik, his face etched with sincerity she had rarely seen before. "Can I ask you something?"

"Of course. Anything."

"Do you believe in eternal life?"

He frowned as he gave a half laugh. "What do you mean?"

"I mean the Fountain of Youth, eternal life, the afterlife? I don't know, it's been on my mind a lot, and . . . I know you've never been all in on this like I have, but . . ."

"Are you asking if I'm here now because I believe in the fountain or because I believe in you?"

"Why are you here now?"

"For you."

She looked into his dark brown eyes, searching for authenticity. She wasn't quite sure if it was there, same as always.

"As for what the fountain is, or what it does, I don't know. Maybe it's just really good water. Maybe it has properties that make it conducive to long life. We'll find out when we find it, and I want you to find it."

He removed his hand from her back and grabbed a glass of water.

"What about eternal life?"

"What about it?" he asked with the same frown.

"Do you think there is such a thing, an afterlife?"

"I don't know. Where's this coming from?"

"Like I said, I've been thinking a lot lately."

He placed a hand on her knee. "Cameron, I don't know about eternal life. I'll worry about that later. Right now, I'm all about this life, and living it to the fullest. And tonight, right now, that means helping you in any way I can."

Cameron smiled.

"I still care about you, Cam. I know we didn't work out as a couple, and that's okay. But I do still care about you."

"I care about you too, Erik. And thank you, again."

He patted her knee, then withdrew his hand. He stood, drained his glass, set it on an end table, and said, "Now tell me more about this mission supposedly in Seville."

*   *   *

Olivia—or, more accurately, Hall Parker Cook Pharmaceuticals—was picking up the tab, so Mitch ordered a boneless rib eye and a half lobster tail from the somewhat pricey menu at Stripsteak, located just off the Fountainbleau's lobby. Both were worth the money. After dinner, they grabbed drinks at the Bleau Bar, then strolled past the pools and cabanas to the Boardwalk, an elevated wooden walkway lined with palm trees. To their left, the Atlantic Ocean shimmered in the moonlight. He'd put on a collared shirt and a pair of pants to satisfy the steakhouse's dress code, and she'd changed into an ankle-length flowing sundress that was just as alluring as her skirt and blouse. With the music from the poolscape on their right and the soft swish of waves on their left, with the balmy post-rain air on their skin, they could have been any of dozens of couples enjoying a romantic evening, had his mind not been on another woman across the state. And had hers not been on business.

"I did some more checking on your phone," she said, drawing an eyebrow raise from him, "and Primero is beyond exclusive. It's totally private."

"Well, that's a shame. I guess we'll have to call this off. You want me to drop you somewhere?"

She smirked. He took a swig of his after-dinner Coors.

"We're going to have to figure out an alternate way to get in."

"Alternate. As in rappel from the roof or what?"

"A little less Ninja than that," she said.

"You have a plan?"

"Maybe. Primero is private, but it is a gallery. It's not just a private collection."

"Meaning they do let people in, they're just selective."

"Very selective," she said with a nod, then a sip of her island breeze.

"So how do we get selected?"

"Well, if I could have my phone back, I'd reach out to some of my colleagues at Hall Parker Cook."

"Oh, a lot of pharmaceutical reps double as bigwigs in the art community?"

"I told you, we're the third-largest pharmaceutical company in the country. We have a lot of connections, beyond hotel discounts."

"Like what?"

"Like very wealthy officers and board members and shareholders, some of whom certainly run in the right circles or know people who run in the right circles to garner us an invite. Of course, we won't know until I make some calls."

"When we get back to the room so I can verify who you're calling."

"Then what are we waiting for?"

At the next opportunity, they exited the Boardwalk and headed back to their suite atop the Sorrento Tower. They went out onto the balcony, where the ocean waves and music from the pools was a muted backdrop. Mitch produced Olivia's cell phone, battery, and SIM card and placed them on a table between their chairs, letting her reassemble them.

"You want to quiz me on any code words or anything?" she asked.

"You want me to promise I won't throw you off the balcony?"

She powered on her phone, then made a series of calls to various people, most of whom didn't answer. She left voicemails with few details for them, and didn't provide those who answered with much more information. The best they got was a Hall Parker Cook board member from Fort Lauderdale who had "a possible line" and would call back in the morning.

When she was done, Mitch reached out for her phone. He took it apart and gave her the battery, so she would know he couldn't make any calls with it, then asked for the battery from his phone.

"This really is ridiculous," she said.

"Your idea."

"You know," she said, leaning on the table, "this evening could be a lot more fun if we gave each other our word, trusted each other's word, and decided to work together. After all, this is Miami . . ."

"Said the spider to the fly." He drained the last of his Coors. "Pass. And it's been a long day, I'm beat."

She nodded. "Give me a few minutes in the bathroom, and the bed is all yours."

"You can have the bed," he said. "I'll take the sofa."

She narrowed her eyes. "Why's that?"

"Because it's the only way I can guarantee you won't leave in the middle of the night."

Olivia stood. "You really should trust me, Mitch."

He said nothing.

"But it's your loss." She turned, and with a swish of her dress behind her, went inside.

*   *   *

Cameron lay in bed, unable to sleep. Her mind was spinning, occupied by one thing until another overpowered it and took its place, until another took its place, until the original came back and started it over.

What was going on with Mitch? Was there really a family emergency? If so, why had he been so abrupt and cold? Was it an excuse to get away, to "ghost" her? She couldn't believe that, but neither could she believe things were so bad with his mom that he couldn't spare a text or two in response. Not if what she thought was going on between them really was.

What about Erik? As glad as she was that he was back, there was something that seemed a little off in him coming to her rescue after cutting her off a few days ago. Had her discoveries really persuaded him that she was on the right track and closing in on the Fountain of Youth? Was he feeling guilty? Or, despite what he'd said earlier, did he still have some romantic feelings for her? The only reason she wondered is because she wasn't one-hundred percent sure she didn't have any lingering romantic feelings for him.

What about Isimi and Primero? Could she and Erik come up with a way to get into the exclusive gallery and see the portrait? Would they be able to figure out what Figueroa's clue was? Would it matter if they didn't get a line on

Misión San Francisco de Sevilla? And if they weren't able to find the mission, did that mean the end of her search for the Fountain of Youth?

Speaking of fountains, did she believe what she'd read in the Gospel of John about Jesus and eternal life? Was she ready to believe in an actual afterlife, a real heaven or hell? And did she believe Jesus was "the ultimate answer to life's ultimate question" as Dr. Kessler had said? And if so, what did that mean for, well, everything?

As the clock ticked past midnight and into Friday, Cameron gave up on sleep. She rummaged through her luggage for a clean swimsuit, put it on, then donned her shirt and shorts overtop it. Stepping into a pair of flip-flops, she headed down to the ground level and out onto the patio. It was completely empty, as expected, and private thanks to a row of palms and a hedge separating it from the parking lot. She slipped off her flip-flops, shed her shorts and shirt, and waded down into the pool. The water was warm and invigorating, and, even though the pool was small, she began swimming laps, letting the rhythmic movement and exercise calm her mind.

After a dozen laps, she turned on her back and floated with her eyes closed. She focused on the sensation of the water on most of her skin, and the warm night air on the rest of it. She had fallen asleep in a pool once before, and when she felt herself almost to the point of nodding off, decided it might be time to get out and head back to her room. She kicked a few times, and extended a hand to feel the edge of the pool. Then she finally opened her eyes and hauled herself out. She stood dripping on the concrete for a moment, then turned to the chair where she'd left her towel.

"Here you go."

She startled and nearly screamed as she looked up at a tall man in a light blue dress shirt, slacks, and loafers. His dark head was bald, offset by a jet-black goatee around a smiling mouth. He held a towel in his left hand, which was extended to Cameron.

"Th-thank y-you," she said.

"Kind of late for a swim, isn't it?"

"I g-guess," she said, blotting her hair, wondering where he had come from and what he was doing. And if anyone would hear her scream if he tried something.

"Well, to each his own—or her own," he added with a wide grin. "I just stepped out for some fresh air. You have a good night." He turned to leave, then spoke one final word that chilled her to the bone. "Cameron."

CHAPTER THIRTY-SIX

Mitch sat on the balcony looking out at the ocean. More rain had moved in, obscuring the moon and creating a soft hiss as it fell over the grounds of the Fountainbleau. It was the sort of thing that should have been soothing, that should have helped Mitch sleep. But he'd given up on that a while ago, at first because he couldn't get comfortable on the short sofa in the living room and then because he couldn't stop thinking.

He couldn't help wondering yet again if he should have handled Olivia differently—never taking her call or never meeting with her, ignoring her threats about Cameron, not trying to outwit her with the lie that *Iśimi* was the end of the line for finding the Fountain of Youth. Now that he'd come this far, he had no options but to see it through. But what happened when Olivia deduced that he'd been lying, that there was still more to figure out? Depending on what the painting looked like (and on how quickly he could think of something), he might be able to sell Olivia on some idea that would send her on a wild goose chase. But that didn't seem like a real strong possibility at the moment.

Maybe it wasn't too late. He could always back out of the deal, let Olivia do her worst, and go back to Cameron. Two things stopped him. One, he wanted to wait and see what she learned about Primero from her colleagues because, if he did go back to Cameron, it would be nice to have an "in" at the gallery. Two, maybe it was repetition, but Olivia's insistence that she wasn't the bad guy and was doing him a favor—along with her evidence—had watered the seed of doubt in his head to the point that he couldn't help wonder if Cameron wasn't who she said after all. His heart told him that wasn't his true, but his head wasn't so sure. Which to believe?

Speaking of his head, it was driving him nuts too. Every time he closed his eyes, he saw himself driving across the Skyway Bridge, only it was swaying back and forth and the suspension cables were snapping left and right, and if he didn't open his eyes, the car he was driving would plummet through a sudden gap in the pavement down toward a dark, roiling, churning, bottomless sea. If that wasn't bad enough, he kept hearing Cameron's voice in his head, over and over, quoting the English translation of the Latin verse inscribed above the Castillo de San Marcos Carving: *And as it is appointed unto men once to die, and after this the judgment.*

Mitch had never feared death or judgment. He'd never really thought about either one. Nor had he thought about sin and hell the way Kessler had talked about them the night before, and his inclination was to brush them off as the religious fervor of a zealot. He'd encountered them at UT, the kids who had Bible studies at lunch or Sunday night prayer meetings. Or long-haired private eyes who told him he needed purpose and fulfillment. But Kessler seemed different; Kessler hadn't made an emotional plea. He'd made an evidentiary one. And while Mitch had yet to verify Kessler's evidence, he had this sneaking suspicion the old professor wasn't blowing smoke. If it was true, didn't that require a guy like Mitch, who placed so much credence in evidence and facts, to do something about it?

What scared him most was that the same logic—evidence being key—that made him think Kessler was telling the truth was what gave him pause about Cameron. He still wanted to hear her side of the story, but wasn't sure what that side could or would be. It was no wonder he couldn't sleep.

The sliding glass door whooshed open, and Mitch turned to see Olivia standing there holding a tumbler with half an inch of bourbon in it. She wore a long, black Georgia Bulldogs T-shirt that covered all but an inch of a pair of shorts. With her hair pulled back and no makeup, she was merely good-looking instead of stunning.

"What are you doing out here?" she asked.

"Same thing as you, apparently. Not sleeping."

"It's raining."

"Thanks for the weather report."

She took a sip and padded over to a chair beside him, just able to stay out of the rain thanks to the overhang of the balcony on the floor above. She sat down. "Can we stop the hostility, please? I didn't have to come to you, you know."

"So this is out of the goodness of your heart? I could have sworn you said it was about finding the Fountain of Youth for dear old Hall Parker Cook. Remember twisting my arm to make me your mole?"

Olivia exhaled. "I did strong-arm you at first, and I'm sorry. But I didn't think I could persuade you to help otherwise."

"Not sure that's a justification."

She set her glass on the table. "Mitch, I meant what I said about Cameron. She's not who she says she is. Her affiliations with shady characters, her methods—expunged or not—they're dubious at best. And if she does get desperate and start crossing lines, I don't want to see anyone else tangled up with her."

Mitch was about to utter another smart-aleck remark, but she kept going before he could.

"But I wasn't sure I could convince you without a hook, without making you a captive audience, so to speak. So I provided a stick and a carrot. I know that seemed sneaky and underhanded and like twisting your arm, but the end does justify the means, I'm convinced of it."

Mitch was silent, thinking. That was a plausible explanation, certainly. Or another ploy. And speaking of ploys . . .

"What about all the winks and touches and flirting with me?"

"Would you believe I find you attractive?"

"Yeah, but that isn't it. It feels like you're trying to seduce me into compliance."

With a twinkle in her eye, Olivia slowly reached a finger to tap the side of her nose.

Mitch shook his head and looked out at the dark ocean. "Any other tactics I should know about? You slip some drugs in my drink earlier?"

"I swear, nothing else. And I am done."

"Done?"

"I've made my plea. So here," she said, reaching into a pocket somewhere under her shirt. She handed Mitch his phone. "I'm going back to bed, alone," she said, taking the final swig of her drink. "No more efforts to seduce you, no more strong-arm tactics. If you don't believe me, believe what I've said, believe what I've shown you, then you're free to call Cameron and explain everything. You're free to leave. I'll go to Primero by myself, assuming I can find a way in." She stood, the tumbler dangling from her fingertips.

"Goodnight, Mitch." She placed her other hand on his shoulder as she passed. "You should get some sleep."

He nodded as she entered the suite. The door closed behind her, and all he could hear was the rain. And his granddad's voice, one of those pieces of advice that stuck with a guy: "Never make a decision after midnight." So with a sigh, Mitch stood, went inside, did his best to prostrate himself on the sofa, and waited for sleep to overtake him.

*   *   *

Cameron stood there shivering, only in part from the air on her wet skin. Who was the man? How had he known her name? How had he known she would be swimming at twelve-thirty in the morning? How long had he been watching her? And what in the world had been the point of speaking to her at all? Was it a subtle form of intimidation? Was there some chance he was just an overly-friendly (bordering on creepy) hotel employee who knew guests incredibly well?

She finished drying off and stepped into her flip-flops, not bothering to dress but scooping her shirt and shorts off the chair. She practically froze in the elevator and hallway, and once she was safely locked in her room, put on several layers of clothes and crawled under the covers. Her mind and heart were racing again, and she continued to stare at the green letters on her bedside clock. The last she remembered seeing them, they read 2:07.

She awoke stressed, all the concerns of the night before still heavy on her mind, and now with the additional burden of the man she'd seen at the pool. As she showered and dressed, she tried to think of solutions, then debated whether or not to tell Erik about the man. Might as well, she concluded; she'd told him everything else.

When she was ready, she called him and they arranged to head down to the hotel's breakfast area. "How'd you sleep?" he asked when they met in the hallway.

"Not well. In fact," she said, suddenly realizing that the man she'd seen at the pool was likely a guest at the hotel, "what would you think of heading out right away and grabbing something on the road?"

Erik frowned. "I suppose. Any reason?"

"I'll tell you on the way."

"Are you sure?"

268

Cameron nodded.

"Okay, sure."

They backtracked to get their luggage and headed down to the car. Cameron kept an eye out for the man she'd seen the night before, but didn't spot him. She had no idea if she could identify a tail, but they made it to the interstate clear, as far as she could tell. At the next interchange, they exited, and, with a nod of approval from her, Erik turned into a Chick-fil-A. "Now, you want to tell me what this is about?" he said as they idled in line in the drive-thru.

"I couldn't get to sleep last night, so I went for a swim," she said. "When I got out of the pool, there was a man there holding my towel."

Erik frowned as he inched ahead.

"He said something about it being late for a swim, and then said he was just out to get air. And then he left after saying my name."

"Your name?"

Cameron nodded.

The car in front of them advanced, so Erik did too, lowering his window. A cheery voice greeted them, and he turned to Cameron. "What do you want?"

"I don't know. A chicken sandwich."

"Two chicken biscuits, two orders of hash browns, two coffees. Cream and sugar?" he asked Cameron.

"Whatever."

"Black," he said, then pulled forward after being given a total. "What'd this guy look like?"

"He was a big guy, but not real big. He looked like . . . a former football player," she said, thinking of Mitch. "African-American, bald, a smile like a crocodile."

"When was this?"

"I went down a little after midnight, so say twelve-thirty."

Erik stroked his jaw.

"I don't know what the point would be. He didn't threaten me or anything."

"Did it feel like a threat?"

"Yes and no. Erik, this is so weird. I mean, I never ran into anything like this until a week ago."

"When you met Mitch."

She looked at him. "Meaning?"

"Nothing."

"No, you meant something."

He exhaled. "Cam, I don't mean to trash the guy, and I'm not saying it's the case, but . . . isn't it possible . . ."

"Isn't what possible? Spit it out, Erik."

"You said it, everything started going haywire a week ago when you met him."

"He saved me when things had gone haywire. He didn't cause it."

"Perhaps not."

"Perhaps?"

"Cammy, I don't want to fight. It's just a little odd the way he showed up, got so close to you so quickly, and then disappeared. Maybe . . . maybe, Van Buren staged a smash and grab aboard the *Eternal Sun* but also had a backup plan."

"That doesn't make any sense," Cameron said.

Erik shrugged and pulled up to the window.

"No sense," she said as much for her own good as to him. It didn't make any sense. Why would he have helped her steal the Figueroa Cipher back? Why would someone have run them off the road? No, it didn't make sense. Did it?

"Here," Erik said, handing her a coffee.

She took it without a word, as well as a sandwich and hash browns. To his credit, Erik didn't push the issue, and the delicious chicken biscuit and hot coffee took the edge off Cameron's frustration with him.

Unfortunately, they couldn't dull the niggling little voice that said Erik's theory wasn't entirely without merit. She wished Mitch was there to answer the accusations, and his absence only gave them louder voice.

*   *   *

Olivia had lied. She wasn't done. She had moved from strong-arm and seduction tactics to psychological ones. The problem was, like so many psychological ploys, this one resonated. Her "Kum ba yah" moment the night before hadn't included a withdraw of the threat to expose Cameron, and, even if it had, it didn't negate her evidence against Cameron. Mitch wanted to look at the evidence closely, not on Olivia's terms. Then he wanted to talk to Cameron and give her a chance to explain. But before he did that, he wanted a peace offering of sorts—access to Primero to see *Iśimi*. And he had to admit, Olivia and her various contacts had a better chance of gaining access than Cameron did.

So after grabbing enough sleep to satisfy his granddad's advice not to make a decision after midnight, Mitch decided to at least give Olivia the rest of the day. He hated leaving Cameron in the dark, but figured it prudent not to contact her further until he had a better grip on the situation. He could always smooth things over, he figured.

Olivia emerged from the bedroom a little before seven-thirty. She had showered and dressed in bright blue clam-diggers and a loose, white, boat-neck blouse. Her hair was pinned up behind her head, and she was fastening the second of a pair of teardrop earrings as she entered the living room. "You're still here."

"I'm here. And you're acclimating to Miami Beach," he said, eyeing her outfit.

"It suits me."

"I'm going to shower," he said, then reached into his pocket for her phone. He held it up, then set it on the table.

Olivia eyed it, then him. "Does this mean we're working together?"

"For now."

"Fair enough."

He nodded and headed for the bathroom. The warm needles of water in the shower stimulated sore muscles but did little to calm the storm raging in his head. A night's sleep had done nothing to provide answers to his questions, and he wished he could go back in time a couple days before they had all been asked, sweep Cameron away to a romantic, isolated beach, and forget the Fountain of Youth, alleged indiscretions, death and judgment, and enticing pharmaceutical company spies. But it didn't work that way.

Olivia was sitting at the counter, a cup of coffee in one hand and her phone in the other, when Mitch came out of the bathroom. "What's the plan for today?" he asked.

"It depends," she said. "I have half a dozen more calls and texts out in addition to last night, plus a few follow-ups. And I think I may have our opening."

"What's that?"

"I have it from one source, and I'm working to confirm, that the owners of Primero are hosting a gala tonight."

"A gala?"

"That's right. The gallery doesn't have typical hours, and is by invitation or personal request only, but once a month or so, they open it up to a very select group of who's who. And tonight just happens to be the night."

"But we're not on the who's who, are we?"

"That's where Hall Parker Cook connections could come in. And why it depends on who gets back to me and what strings they can pull."

"So in the meantime we have some time to kill?"

She nodded after taking a sip of coffee. "What'd you have in mind?"

"First, breakfast. I'm starved."

"We can do that."

"And then I want to look over everything you have on Cameron."

Olivia said nothing.

"I want to make sure you've dotted your I's and crossed your T's. I want to see it for myself."

She nodded. "Okay."

"And then I want you to lay out in specific detail how you think this plays out."

"How this plays out?"

"When you find the fountain. What does Hall Parker Cook do, how do they get the rights to the property, what's the process for—for lack of better word—harvesting it? And how do Cameron and I fit into that?"

"Assuming your surveillance of the evidence comes out in her favor."

"We're not exactly talking about murder, here. I'm willing to overlook some indiscretions for the right woman."

"And you think she's the right woman?" Olivia asked, smirking and swinging the leg balanced on the knee of the other.

"Hypothetically."

The smirk slowly faded. "We can do all that. What do you say I call room service for some breakfast and we get to work?"

CHAPTER THIRTY-SEVEN

The Everglades were beautiful. Mile after mile after mile of swampland broken only occasionally by a canal, a crossroad, or a rare outpost could be seen by some as boring or ugly. But there was something in the simplicity that Cameron found appealing, and even calming. Then again, perhaps that was because she was in the climate-controlled Chevy and not out in the steamy, muggy swamp itself, subject to mosquitoes and alligators and snakes.

Erik hadn't said much in the last forty-five minutes, since speculating as to Mitch's possible involvement with Van Buren. Cameron had analyzed it every way she could, and while she had to admit that several events of the last week or comments made by Mitch were coincidental at best and suspicious at worst, the preponderance of evidence suggested Mitch was trustworthy. Or, at least, it had until yesterday morning.

"Cammy, I'm sorry if I upset you."

"It's fine, Erik."

"Really?"

"Really. Forget it."

His demeanor changed. "So, I made some calls this morning."

She turned, waiting for him to continue.

"Nothing yet. You?"

"I didn't even make calls yet. Sorry."

"It's okay. We'll have time when we get there."

She sat back. They had decided last night to drive to Miami in the morning, even before knowing anything more about the gallery and possible means for gaining entry to see *Iśimi*. For one thing, there was nothing more to be done in Fort Myers or on Sanibel Island, and a change of scenery could do them some good. But the primary motive had been to be ready the moment they gained access to Primero, especially given Cameron's encounter with the man at the pool the night before. They were sure they weren't the only ones looking for the portrait.

With an apology and an excuse of needing to dispense of the morning's coffee, Erik pulled into a rest area carved out of the swamp. While he headed inside to use the restroom, Cameron stretched her legs on the sidewalk. Mid-morning, the heat was already oppressive, but clouds resembling huge plumes of smoke foreshadowed afternoon storms that would bring some relief.

Cameron made a lap around the rest center and was just in time to see Erik emerge, his cell phone to his ear. He didn't see her, pacing instead the other direction before stopping and lowering the phone. He turned around, spotted her, and quickened his step.

"Cammy, great news."

"What?"

"Inside. This heat is miserable."

Back in the car with the A/C cranked, Erik announced, "I heard back from Jaren, and he told me there's an opening at Primero tonight."

"An opening?"

"Some sort of hoity-toity party. South Florida's top artists, critics, celebrities, wealthy elite."

Cameron's brief enthusiasm quickly faded. "That doesn't do us any good."

"Oh, but it does," he said, pausing to merge back onto traffic on I-75. "You remember when I told you about my cousin dating Miss Miami?"

"Yeah."

"I just called him, to see if there's any way she could get us access."

"A small-time supermodel is going to get her boyfriend's cousin access to a 'hoity-toity' party at a high-end gallery?"

"First of all, there's no such thing as a small-time supermodel. Second, he's sent me pictures, Cam, and . . ." he raised his eyebrows even over his sunglasses. "But I'm telling you, she's crazy about my cousin—and you've seen him, Cammy. If it's doable, I think we're in."

"When's the party?"

He turned his head. "Tonight."

"Tonight? How in the world—Tonight?"

Erik grinned. "We're going to have to buy you a dress."

*   *   *

Over a breakfast of ham, eggs, breakfast potatoes, and orange juice, Mitch analyzed Olivia's evidence against Cameron. She remained vague as to where and how she had procured the evidence, but she hadn't fabricated it.

College transcripts proved Cameron had shared several classes with Hunter Sorenson at Clemson University, and cell phone logs suggested they either had shared a relationship or been serious study buddies. And Sorenson's criminal record thereafter—including his sketchy dealings in the art world—was indisputable.

Cameron's time in Cairo in 2015 was well documented by airplane manifests, hotel receipts, and security footage from several locations around town, which, along with CIA photographs, connected her to Charles Calvin, whom Erik had identified as Kevin Stuart, the fourth member of the Hogan Gang. Calvin, while never charged with anything, had been suspected by the CIA as well as several foreign agencies and governments of robbing the Cairo Museum and consorting with terrorists, according to a variety of heavily redacted reports. And more cell phone logs showed that Cameron had maintained a relationship with Calvin until just recently. What they didn't show was whether she knew his alias, Kevin Stuart. Or if that really was an alias or the construct of Erik Diaz.

Speaking of Erik, Cameron had made calls and texts to him that she hadn't told Mitch about. But then again, she wasn't obligated to report every call or conversation, and, once again, logs didn't indicate if the calls were of a personal or professional nature, nor what was discussed.

Then there was the mugshot of C. Leigh from October 5, 2013, when Cameron had apparently been an unkempt brunette. She had graduated in 2012, which would have made her twenty-two or twenty-three. That didn't excuse her committing petty theft, but she wouldn't be the only young adult to make a stupid mistake. Mitch had certainly done things at that age he'd rather not have disclosed. But it did seem to contrast with the Cameron he knew now, suggesting maybe there was more to her past than she had let on.

All in all, Mitch concluded the evidence was solid; Olivia hadn't mislead him. There was nothing to tie Cameron to any of Sorenson's crimes or Calvin's alleged crimes, nor to prove she knew the fourth member of the Hogan Gang was her old friend. But it could still, especially with the addition of the theft charge—expunged or not—taint her reputation and ruin her credibility with those in the art and history world. What was more, it gave

Mitch legitimate cause to question Cameron. Had she merely kept certain unflattering but irrelevant facts from him, same as he hadn't told her about the time in college he'd gotten drunk and "written" his name on the side of the library? Or was the Calvin-Stuart connection something she'd known about, making her connection with him—and thus Van Buren—nefarious, changing the entire narrative of her quest to find the Fountain of Youth? And did stealing a letter from a Civil War buff show she was willing to do anything— like lie and steal—to get what she wanted?

He was still mulling that and still mulling the best way to play things, to get her side of the story and determine if she was one of the good guys or one of the bad guys, when Olivia came in off the patio. She shook her phone back and forth. "We're in."

"In?"

"Assuming you can play the role of my bodyguard, we've got an invite to the Primero gala."

"Bodyguard for what?"

"I'm a diva."

"I know, but what's our cover?"

"You are cute," she said. "We're still working on the specifics, but one of our board members was able to . . . 'reassign' an invite to a legend Hall Parker Cook's working on."

"Hall Parker Cook? You're telling me a pharmaceutical company has a backstopping division?"

"What do you say we get out of here, take a drive?"

Mitch raised an eyebrow.

"Do a drive-by of Primero, get the lay of the land."

"If you'll give me some answers."

"Answers to what?"

"I want the fine print about Hall Parker Cook, their interest in the Fountain of Youth and plans for it, and just how many resources you have at your fingertips."

"You drive?"

"Sure."

They headed downstairs, picked up the Nissan Rogue, and soon were making the slow drive south on the A1A, past art deco stores and shops, restaurants and clubs, and hotels. Then they crossed Biscayne Bay to the mainland via a causeway running parallel to a large island housing the Port of

Miami and cruise ship docks. While Mitch drove, Olivia bored him with enough details to convince him that Hall Parker Cook was indeed one of the premier pharmaceutical companies in the nation or she was a nerd with a detailed imagination. Then she outlined their plan.

"Like I told you, if the Fountain of Youth is real to whatever degree, someone is going to capitalize on it," she said.

"So it might as well be you?"

"Yes. Someone else might not be as responsible as Hall Parker Cook. Furthermore, someone else might not be willing to share the credit for the discovery with someone else."

"Cameron?"

"Or you."

"I'm not in this for the credit."

"Then why are you?"

"Originally, for Cameron."

Olivia turned her head. "And now?"

Mitch didn't answer.

"You asked earlier how it works, if we find the fountain."

Mitch waited.

"It depends."

"On?"

"Where the fountain is—public land or private. Either way, we'll seek permission or rights to the source, and there will have to be a lot of testing both before and after to verify what's in the water, why it's special."

"You mean if it's not supernatural?"

"Right," she said with a smile. "Then, if all goes well, a mountain of paperwork—permits, licenses, red tape wrapped in red tape."

"And how does Cameron get credit?"

"That depends too."

"On what?"

"How cooperative she is. And whether you decide if she's worth crediting."

Mitch was silent.

"You'll want to get in the right lane," she said as they crossed a final span. Skyscrapers towered over the teal water in both directions, but more prominently to the south. Behind them, the sky was filling with clouds, either the typical late-morning/early-afternoon buildup or harbingers of more storms.

Mitch hoped for the latter, to break the heat and humidity that had quickly ruined a pleasant early morning.

They exited the freeway and took the first right. After several blocks, Olivia pointed to a fifteen-story glass building on the left, on the corner. They made a lap around the building, which was bordered by a park, another skyscraper, an empty lot with realty signs on it, and a five-story condominium. The building was a square, with sleek projections on the north and south sides, and covered in glass panels that, in addition to catching the bay and sky's reflection, were tinged blue. Palms around the sidewalks and several water features in front of the lobby cemented the Floridian feel.

"Primero is on the ninth and tenth floors, south side," Olivia said.

"You got any schematics, any idea where the painting is?"

"Efforting schematics, but nothing more detailed than that. Why?"

"Just like to know what I'm getting into. We done?"

"Sure."

He accelerated. "Now what? Gala's not until late, I'm guessing."

"Nine, but we can be fashionably late."

"How do you wanna kill the afternoon?"

"You'll need some new threads, and what girl can't use a new dress?"

"South Beach?" Mitch asked.

"South Beach."

CHAPTER THIRTY-EIGHT

Miami's skyline at night was impressive, but after the glitz and glamor of South Beach, it was just another cityscape. Mitch and Olivia crossed Biscayne Bay in a newly rented BMW Z4, which she claimed better fit their persona as a diva and her bodyguard. Apparently a limo was beyond the pull of Hall Parker Cook. A new suit for Mitch and a pageant-worthy gown for Olivia had also been put on the pharmaceutical company's tab, and Mitch was starting to understand the high price of prescription drugs.

On any other day, this would have been fun, especially given how stunning Olivia looked in a black halter-top dress. But he couldn't stop thinking about Cameron, wondering how she would explain the "charges" against her and what that explanation would mean to him. More than that, he couldn't figure out what to do when he and Olivia saw *Iśimi*. Could he convince her that this was the end of the line, that there was nothing more to the Castillo de San Marcos Carving, that the portrait identified the location of the Fountain of Youth? And where would that leave him?

"Lot on your mind?" Olivia asked.

"Why?"

"You've got a strange look on your face."

"Been one of those days, again."

"I thought it was a good day."

He looked at her. "I know you and I aren't enemies anymore," he said, gesturing back and forth between them with his finger, "but this isn't a night at the Miami party scene for me."

"And it is for me?"

"I don't know."

"I'm all business, Mitch, trust me."

"We'll see."

They followed their route from that afternoon and arrived at the Primero office tower a little after nine. The sun had long set, and distant rumbles of thunder announced the arrival of another batch of storms. It had been storming for two days now, and that seemed just about right.

"Don't you want valet parking?" Olivia asked as Mitch turned into the driveway leading to the parking garage. She pointed at a small circle in front of the main entrance where a valet station was manned by a duo in blue vests.

"No."

"Hall Parker Cook will pick up the tab. And a diva like 'Bianca' would use valet parking."

"A bodyguard like me would want a more discreet exit strategy."

"Exit strategy? For what?"

"Contingencies."

"Okay then."

Mitch found a parking spot in the garage, then came around to get Olivia's door. "You ever done this before?" Olivia asked.

"Open doors or attend a fancy gala?"

"Be a bodyguard. You worked for a security company for several years, right?"

"Yeah."

She stood aside as he closed her door.

"A couple of times," he said.

"So you know how to act the role?"

"Uh-huh." He buttoned his jacket. "Ready?"

Her stilettos clicking on the concrete and echoing through the garage, Olivia led the way toward the elevators. She turned over her shoulder. "You're not going to ask about me?"

"Being a diva? No, I figure you have that down."

"Ha, ha."

"Olivia, I'm confident you can play whatever role you need."

"Bianca," she said. "We're officially under cover now."

"Yes, ma'am."

*　　　　　*　　　　　*

The lobby of the office tower was magnificent, from the imported Carrera marble floor to the blown glass sculptures hanging from the ceiling thirty feet above. A mezzanine level ringed the lobby, accessible by a pair of staircases on either side of a reception desk in the center. A dozen businesses—a jeweler, a women's fashion retailer, a legal firm, a couple restaurants and upscale bars, and an insurance company among them—were accessible from the mezzanine level, while beneath it, water walls fed into fountains that lined the lobby except where hallways branched left and right, just in front of a bank of elevators. Tropical but classical music softly played in the background.

A young man with a Bluetooth earpiece sat at the reception desk, and he told Cameron and Erik Primero was on the ninth floor and directed them to the elevators. They arrived at the same time as another couple, both older, both good-looking, both dressed immaculately. They rode together to the ninth floor, where Erik demurely let the other couple go first. As he moved to step out of the elevator, Cameron touched his arm. He looked up.

"Thank you," she said. "You didn't have to do all this, and I really appreciate it."

"Of course, Cam."

"I meant to ask you on the way over, did you make any headway determining who the owners of the gallery are?"

"No. I'm still not sure who they are—not all of them. Sounds like a cooperative. Kind of weird."

Cameron nodded. She had been hoping to get a chance to talk to the owners about *Iśimi*, possibly even bartering with them to borrow it as she and Mitch had with William Morgan. That, she knew, was a long shot, but getting more information about the painting and how they had come by it—anything that could provide an additional clue to the location of the Fountain of Youth—in theory wasn't. Who knew, maybe something in the painting's history could link to *Misión San Francisco de Sevilla* or explain how reunifying *Iśimi* and Diego Figueroa was supposed to take place.

"Well, thank you," she said again, then leaned in to peck him on the cheek. "Shall we?"

He nodded, and they stepped forward. A main hallway bisected the building. A gold placard on the wall identified the location of several businesses down the hall on the north side of the building, while large, frosted double doors directly ahead of them were labeled with the Primero logo. A man in a tuxedo stood outside it, and nodded with a firm expression as they approached.

"Erik Diaz and Cameron Leigh," Erik said.

The man consulted a tablet for a moment, then said. "Welcome to Primero."

Cameron exhaled. Miss Miami had come through—or, rather, Erik's cousin had. Cameron wasn't quite sure on the details, and hadn't had much chance to ask Erik, who'd spent most of the afternoon on the phone—a combination of business deals and confirming plans for the evening and what may or may not have been a call to a special someone. But the important thing was their names were on the list.

The man in the tuxedo opened the door and waved them through, where a man and a woman—both in tuxes—proceeded to search and frisk them with electromagnetic wands like TSA agents used at the airport. They were in a narrow corridor, with another set of frosted glass doors at the end of it. Exclusive indeed.

"You're all set, ma'am," the female "guard" said, handing Cameron her purse. It was new—as were her dress, shoes, and accompanying jewelry. All had been put on Erik's tab, as had an afternoon at their South Beach hotel's spa, getting a mani-pedi, facial, and fancy hairstyle for the evening. It was almost as if Erik had been trying to occupy her while he took care of business, but she wasn't complaining.

"Thank you," Cameron said, stepping to the side until Erik joined her.

"Ready?" he asked.

This time she nodded, and they opened the second set of doors leading into a two-story room with balconies on the right and left, and above. Directly ahead, glass windows and a pair of doors reflected back the light of several graceful chandeliers. Surprisingly, there was no art in the room, just several dozen people all dressed to the nines. Waiters and waitresses in tuxedos circulated with trays of champagne and hors d'oeuvres. The music of a stringed quartet emanated from speakers hidden somewhere among numerous potted plants and small trees. The air had a fragrance, something Cameron couldn't identify, probably a manufactured scent all for ambiance.

"How do you want to play this?" Erik asked.

"Play this?"

"I mean, do you want to split up and cover more ground or stay together?"

Cameron shrugged. "I'm not in a hurry."

He pulled a brochure from a small stand. It provided a basic map of the gallery, including names of rooms, but didn't specify what the various exhibits contained. So they started a process of trial and error. *Iśimi* was not in the room containing the gallery's rotating collection, nor in one dedicated to local artists. Under any other circumstances, Cameron would have thoroughly enjoyed the art. Even now, with everything she had gone through and everything that was at stake, she still was enthralled by it.

They circled back into the main foyer, and Erik broke off to announce he was going to get some champagne for them. Cameron looked around, people watching. There were plenty of patrons dressed like her and Erik, in the same formalwear one might wear to the opera or the symphony. Then there were those pushing the limits of fashion, resembling a toned-down version of Capitol citizens from *The Hunger Games*. On the other end of the spectrum were those who had managed something more casual—denim in some cases, a couple of T-shirts under blazers, or simple dresses or a shirt and tie with no jacket.

Erik returned without champagne and grabbed Cameron by the elbow. "We've got trouble."

"What?"

He began guiding her toward a parlor off the side of the foyer.

"Erik, what's going on?"

"Harrison Van Buren is here."

*   *   *

Mitch hadn't exactly lied to Olivia; he had done some "protective detail" work while in the security business, but nothing as glitzy as guarding a pop star or whatever Olivia was pretending to be. That said, he could play the role pretty well. Follow "Bianca" around with a disinterested frown on his face, look at everyone with suspicion, and intervene if anyone got too close to her. It provided the perfect cover for him to scan the artwork for *Iśimi*, and to try to figure out a way to ditch Olivia once they found the portrait. It wouldn't be as easy as he had hoped, given the apparent long reach of her and Hall Parker Cook's tentacles.

Olivia led the way into a room housing tiny, sundry pieces of art, an assortment of "period pieces," and sculptures of marble and wood and stone. Mitch had no idea what most of the sculptures were supposed to be, if anything. They were as eclectic as the clothing on guests. Mitch had seen it all when it came to women's attire, so nothing there threw him, but when he saw a biological male in a suitcoat and Capri pants, he knew he was out of his element.

Back in the main lobby, Mitch grabbed a couple crab puffs off a waiter's tray, drawing an eyebrow raise from Olivia.

"What, a bodyguard can't eat?"

"You should keep your focus on me, in theory."

"You should have people recognize you, in theory."

"Not my crowd," she said with a smirk.

They continued through several other exhibit rooms, one of which was full of paintings, but all landscapes. No portraits, much less one named *Išimi*. They peeked briefly into the Sensory Room, dedicated to experiencing art via the five senses, and Mitch quickly stepped back, pulling Olivia's arm.

"What is it?"

"We should—"

"Mitch?"

"You ever see *The Bodyguard* with Kevin Costner and Whitney Houston?"

"I think so," she said with a shake of her head. "Why?"

"Because I may need to get fresh with you."

"What?"

"There's a couple people here who shouldn't see my face."

Olivia went from confused to serious. "Who?"

"Redhead at your three o'clock," he said, taking a glance in the glass behind Olivia to see Lora Hogan, making what looked like a final glance at the Sensory Room before exiting to where he and Olivia were standing. "Behind me's a guy with a chiseled face and frosted tips."

"Who are they?" Olivia asked.

"Part of the group who forcibly took the Figueroa Cipher from Cameron, and from whom we took it back." He looked at the glass behind Olivia and realized it was a sliding door. "Turn around."

"What?"

"Turn around," he said again, reaching around her for the handle. She figured it out and beat him to it, sliding open the door and leading the way out onto the balcony. Steady rain was falling, but a balcony on the tenth floor hung over part of the ninth floor's balcony, providing them a dry place to stand. Or walk. Mitch motioned for Olivia to keep moving, away from the door and window panes the Hogans could look through.

"Now what?" Olivia asked.

"Now you tell me how Van Buren knew to send his goons here," he said, grabbing her arm and turning her around.

"What?"

"How'd they know?"

"I don't know. Why would I call them?"

He didn't answer.

"Seriously," she said, shaking her arm free, "why would I call them?"

"I don't know, but the only other person who knows is Cameron."

"Are you sure?"

He again didn't answer.

"Maybe she called her ex, or her old friend Calvin."

He sighed, looking through the rain at the Miami skyline.

"Or maybe whoever told her squealed," Olivia said. "Who knows how big the circle is. Either way, it doesn't change our plan, does it?"

"No."

"Then let's get back in there."

He sighed one more time. "You're right."

"See?"

"The sooner we find this painting, the sooner you and I can part ways."

*   *   *

Cameron and Erik were the only people in the parlor, and he led the way to a small couch in the corner. After looking around for a moment as if to get his bearings, he sat down. Cameron put a hand on his shoulder. "Are you okay?"

"What is he doing here?"

"You're sure it was him? I didn't see—"

"It was him." He shook his head. "I don't get it. Why is he here?"

"Isn't it obvious?"

He raised his head.

"He's trying to find the Fountain of Youth."

"Of course," Erik said. "I mean, how did he know? How did he know the painting was here, about the gala? How did he get in?"

"The same way he's known everything."

He looked at her.

285

She shrugged. "I don't know, Erik, but they seem to be one step ahead of me all the time. Who knows, maybe they tapped one of our phones or something."

"How . . . ?"

"I don't know."

He ran his hand through his hair, an unusual gesture because it messed up his perfect hairstyle. "Cammy, we uh . . ." He looked at her again. "We have to steal it."

"What?"

"We need to steal the painting."

CHAPTER THIRTY-NINE

Cameron sat down beside Erik. "What do you mean steal the painting?"

"We have to keep Van Buren from getting his hands on *Iśimi*. That has to be why he's here, to steal it himself. We need to get it first."

"Are you serious?"

"Think about it, Cam. If Van Buren gets the painting, all he'll need is to find the mission, and he'll have the fountain, and then . . ."

"Erik, this is crazy. We can't steal—we can't steal the painting," she finished in a hushed voice.

"We'll give it back when this is done. We can even say we did it to protect the painting from Van Buren, who won't treat it as carefully."

"How do you know what he'll do? You don't even know that he's here to steal it."

"What else would his plans be?"

"I don't know. The same thing we're doing?"

"We can't take that chance."

"Erik."

He shook his head. "It's the only way, Cammy."

"No. And how, Erik? How would we ever do it?"

"I don't know, but we'll figure it out."

"No."

"Cam, it's—"

"No." She stood. "No, Erik. This is absurd."

He stood too. "Wasn't taking the cipher from the Hogans at the Casa Monica absurd too?"

"That was different. It wasn't on display in a gallery. And they had stolen it from me. No."

"Cammy," he said, reaching a hand for her.

She eluded his grasp. "I'm sorry, Erik, but it's not happening." She gave one last shake of her head, then headed back into the main foyer.

* * *

"Come on, Mitch, I thought we were friends now."

He looked back at Olivia as they headed for another pair of sliding glass doors. "That might be a little strong."

She took hold of his arm. "Tell me you didn't have some fun."

He turned his head toward her alluring eyes and the sultry grin, but said nothing.

"What's your plan, anyhow, when this is done? Fly back to Texas and forget everything?"

"I don't know yet."

"You could always tag along," she said as he opened the door for her. She stepped through, then reached and grabbed his hand. "Help me follow *Iśimi* to the Fountain of Youth."

He looked down at her, at eyes that almost seemed to be pleading. For just a second, he was tempted, until he realized her statement indicated she wasn't forcing him to come along, that once they found the painting, he would be free.

Holding his hand with hers, she reached her other hand and gently clasped his elbow. "What do you say?"

A woman shrieked, and Mitch lifted his eyes from Olivia's to see the woman she had just run into. He stopped physically and mentally. It was Cameron, like he had never seen her before. Dressed in a long, flowing, garnet-colored gown, her hair up in a loose twist, and ornamented with sparkling silver jewelry, she looked like a princess. A confused princess.

Cameron's blue eyes went wide. "Mitch?"

"Cameron."

"What are—" Her eyes settled on Olivia, on her hand in Mitch's, on the lack of space between them. She was becoming an angry princess.

"It's not wh—"

"What I think?" She shook her head. "I take it your mom's feeling better."

"Cameron, let me ex—"

She raised a hand. "Forget it. Goodbye, Mitch."

"Cameron!"

She kept going, and Olivia's hand stopped him from following her. He dropped it with a huff and looked back at her. "You think you could snuggle any closer to me?"

"What?"

"I've got to go talk to her."

Olivia grabbed his hand again. "*We've* got a job to do, and if you want to do it without alerting Redhead and Frosty, we better get moving."

Mitch bit off a curse as Cameron disappeared through a crowd by the doorway.

*   *   *

Cameron made it to the women's room before breaking down. She lowered herself onto a settee and, grateful for the emptiness of the room, let herself cry. She'd actually held together quite well, given everything that had gone on. But realizing Mitch had lied to her, had not gone to see a sick mother but was consorting with some other woman, put her over the edge. It was bad enough that Cameron thought there might be something special between her and Mitch and now he had clearly moved on, but that he was *here*, looking for the Fountain of Youth without her. It was too much.

Everything, in fact, was too much. The weight of the search itself, coming so close only to be stumped and stymied, the attempts on her and Mitch's life, playing spy and being coerced by Erik to steal the painting. Not to mention everything Dr. Kessler had said about Jesus and the things Cameron had read in John. She'd finished the book that afternoon between shopping and the spa. There was so much in it she didn't understand, and at the same time, so much that rang true at her very core. One phrase in particular had stuck with her. John had written that Jesus had "*performed many other signs*" that weren't included in the book, but that the ones that were written had been so "*that you may believe that Jesus is the Messiah, the Son of God, and that by believing you may have life in his name.*"

Could it be that simple? Could eternal life—not some ethereal concept, but an actual, satisfying, fulfilling existence in the afterlife—be achievable simply by believing in who Jesus was and what He had done? She remembered what she'd told Mitch, about Javier writing that Diego Figueroa believed a person ought to have to earn eternal life. And she'd always thought being religious involved performing good works, trying to appease God or meet a certain standard. But in John she'd read the words of Jesus saying the work God required was "*to believe in the one he has sent.*"

Could it—eternal life, the answer to life's ultimate question—*really* be that simple?

The lights blinked and then went black.

Cameron stood, wiping tears with the back of one hand and placing the other on the wall for balance in a room that was suddenly inky black but for the faint red glow of an exit sign above the door. The bathroom was well soundproofed, but she could hear the vague buzz of murmuring and exclamations from outside. She wondered, could this somehow be Erik? No, he didn't even have a plan yet? Did he?

Her eyes were acclimating, and she started for the door to see what was going on. She had just reached it when the lights flickered twice, then came back on and stayed on. She paused. They had been out at most fifteen seconds, which couldn't be long enough for anyone to do anything, could it? One way to find out, she reasoned. Find *Iśimi.*

*   *   *

Mitch and Olivia had climbed to the mezzanine level when the power went out. When it came back on, Olivia grabbed his arm. "What do you think that was?"

"Not the storm," Mitch said, leaning over the railing and searching the foyer for the Hogans.

"We could be on a generator?"

"Back to full power? And I don't hear a generator. It'd have to be massive to run this place."

"And it couldn't be that somebody was using it to boost the painting. A fifteen-second power outage isn't long enough for somebody to grab a painting, stash it, disappear . . ."

"No, but it was long enough for a test."

"A test of what?"

"If it were me," he said, looking around for the sake of privacy, "and I was going to try to boost a piece, I'd need to arrange a distraction. But a place like this, the first sign of a distraction—"

"Like a power outage?"

He nodded. "—is going to draw everyone's attention, alert security. So you set off a dummy distraction, where nothing happens, and it maybe dulls alertness and makes people think the next one is a false alarm too."

"You think there could be another outage?"

"Could be."

"We'd better get moving."

Mitch stayed where he was.

"What is it?"

"There's another benefit to a false alarm," he said, reaching into his pocket. "It can give an observer a clue as to how security will react, how the crowd will respond, who might panic, etcetera."

"Frosty and the Redhead?"

Mitch nodded, scanning the map of the gallery.

"What are you looking for?"

"Where there would be a security station or server hub or something. He tapped an unidentified room on the map, then turned his eyes across the mezzanine to an unmarked door. "There."

"There's nobody around it," she said, following his gaze.

"No, and I don't see the Hogans, either. Or any signs of security personnel moving around."

"Lot of cameras. Place seems pretty high-tech. Why run a bunch of goons in bulging sport jackets around to scare the guests when you can do it electronically?"

"We should get moving, Mitch."

"Yeah." He tipped the map toward her. "They know my face, not yours, but we don't know where they are, either. You go this way, I'll go this way. Text me if you spot it."

"Okay."

"You find anything, call me," he said.

"I will."

He shrugged, pocketed the map, and followed the mezzanine around to a series of rooms on the other side of the gallery. He made it only to the top of the other staircase before spotting Erik Diaz climbing them. He didn't seem to spot Mitch and turned toward the hallway leading to more exhibit rooms. Mitch reached for his arm. "Erik, what are you doing here?"

He turned. "Mitch? Uh, hi."

"Are you with Cameron?"

"Yeah, sort of. I thought . . . I thought you were gone, back to Texas."

"It's complicated."

"Sure. Look, Mitch—"

"Can you tell Cameron I need to talk to her, for just a few minutes?"

"I'm not sure she's up for it."

"Yeah, she was pretty upset when I bumped into her. But please, it's important."

"I can't make any promises. Look, I've got to get going."

"Is something going on?"

"I've got to make a couple phone calls, and I'm late. Business, you know?"

"What about Cameron?"

"I'll try to talk to her, okay?" Erik said, patting Mitch's arm in an effort to close the conversation.

"I mean, where is she?"

"I think she went to powder her nose."

"Shay and Lora Hogan are here," Mitch said. "I don't know what their game is, but she shouldn't be alone."

"The Hogans? They're here?"

"Saw them downstairs."

"I saw Van Buren. I guess it makes sense."

"Does Cameron know?"

Erik nodded.

"What about Wilder or Stuart?"

"No, uh, no, I haven't seen them."

A hunch hit Mitch. "You know anything about Stuart having an alias—Charles Calvin?"

"No. I don't even know anything about Stuart except what I told you at brunch the other day. Who's Calvin?"

"I'm not sure."

Erik bit his tongue. "Look, I don't know where you've been or what's been going on, but I'm afraid Van Buren's here to steal the painting. I want to beat him to it."

Mitch looked around. They were still alone. "You want to steal it?"

"It's our only hope to keep Van Buren and his people from finding the fountain."

"Is Cameron on board with this idea?"

"I tried, but it's no use." He huffed. "I should have known better. That woman wouldn't steal a pen from a hotel room."

"She was the one who proposed taking the disk back from the Hogans."

"That was rightfully hers. But pilfering something from somebody else. Never."

Mitch frowned.

"What?"

"She must have told you."

"Told me what?"

Mitch hesitated.

"Come on, told me what?"

"How long have you known Cameron?"

"Since hortly after she graduated college. Why?"

"She never told you about the time she got arrested?"

"Arrested? Cameron? For what?"

"She took a letter from some guy, something about a Confederate colonel or general knowing where to find a bunch of U.S. currency. It was expunged but—"

"When?"

"October, 2013, I think."

Erik shook his head. "We started dating like a month after that. You must have your wires crossed. Cameron was never arrested."

"I saw the mugshot, Erik."

"The mugshot?"

"Yeah. She was a brunette then."

"Cameron was never a brunette," he said with a frown. "Wait, October of 2013? You sure it wasn't Chelsea?"

Mitch narrowed his eyes and stared at the wall, trying to picture the mug shot again. He exhaled. It had said "C. Leigh," not "Cameron Leigh." It could have been Chelsea, if the resemblance was close.

"Chelsea got busted for a DUI in 2013," Erik said. "She was a sophomore, made a dumb mistake, a one-time thing, and Cameron let her have it, from what I hear. And she had dark hair when I first met Cam."

"The DUI, you remember where it was?"

"Suburb of Atlanta. She was at Georgia Tech."

Mitch blew out a sigh. "You know anything about Cameron's relationship with a Hunter Sorenson?"

"What?"

"Never mind."

"No, she dated him in college. Why do you ask?"

"Has she had any contact with him since, do you know?"

Erik shook his head. "She mentioned something about seeing he'd been arrested. Said she was glad she'd dumped him when she did. Said he'd struck her as a little sketchy so she broke things off pretty quick. Made joint homework assignments awkward. Why?"

"Something's not right here."

"With Cameron?"

"No, with someone else. Please, I've got to talk to her. Ask her to give me five minutes when you see her?"

"Yeah, sure." Erik looked around, then lowered his voice. "Look, as much as I love reliving Cameron's life with you, Mitch, I need to get moving. You gonna help me with this?"

"Have you found it?"

"Not yet. That's why I'm in a hurry."

Mitch's phone buzzed. He scanned it, saw it was a text from Olivia. He looked up at Erik. "Sorry, man. That's a little drastic for me. But you get your hands on it, you and I never had this conversation."

Erik nodded and turned, and Mitch read the text from Olivia. She'd found the painting.

*   *   *

Iśimi was beautiful.

After leaving the bathroom, Cameron had searched for Erik in the foyer, then given up and resumed her search for the painting. It was not in any of the rooms on the lower level, so she took the stairs to the second floor and checked out a room featuring "cultural pieces." It took only a few seconds for her to spot the thirty-six-inch by twenty-four-inch portrait hanging between some kind of tribal staff piece and a feathered headdress. There was no one looking at it, and Cameron did her best not to make an obvious beeline to the painting.

Framed in ornate, gold-plated wood, the portrait depicted a woman with dark, flowing hair. She was clothed in a cascading waterfall in the general shape of a dress. The waterfall disappeared into a mist at the bottom of the painting. The mist was transparent, revealing the woman's bare feet as she walked toward a rising or setting sun on the right edge of the painting. She looked over her shoulder as she walked, and one arm extended through the falling water, the fingers outstretched but slightly curled, perhaps reaching, perhaps beckoning. A gold nameplate beneath the portrait identified it as *Iśimi* and listed the artist as D. Figueroa.

The painting was incredibly detailed, from the features of the woman's face to the proportion in her fingers and toes, and from the foliage on trees in the background to the waterfall's mist that appeared photographically real. Despite being over three centuries old, the painting was in immaculate condition, the colors as vivid as if it had been painted yesterday.

After a minute, Cameron forced herself to analyze the painting from a codebreaker's perspective. She remembered the words translated from the carving, "reunify Iśimi with me . . ." Was there some code that would be deciphered once this painting was in the bell tower of *Misión San Francisco de Sevilla*? Was there something in the painting that could be interpreted to provide a clue? And what could it be?

Realizing she was in a public place, and that public included bad guys who wanted the painting, Cameron opened her purse to withdraw her camera. Before she could, she sensed a presence beside her.

"Remarkable, isn't it?"

Cameron looked to see the woman who had been hanging on Mitch's arm downstairs. She was exotically beautiful, with smoky eyes that seemed to smolder as she looked at Cameron, a smirk tugging at the corners of her mouth. Maybe she always looked that way, or maybe she was doing her best to get under Cameron's skin. It was working.

"Who are you?" Cameron asked.

"A friend."

"Of whose?"

"Mitch," she said with extra enunciation.

"Good luck with that," Cameron said, turning literally on her heel and walking away.

*　　　　　*　　　　　*

295

Mitch found Olivia standing in front of a woman wearing a waterfall. At first glance, there was something of a resemblance—both dark haired, beautiful, darker skinned. Was there any chance . . . ?

"Beautiful, isn't she?" Olivia asked.

"Not what I was expecting, that's for sure."

"The compliment every woman wants to hear."

"Yeah, well, she can't hear over the din of the waterfall," he said, reaching for his phone. Looking around to make sure a couple suits weren't about to come snatch it, he snapped several quick shots, then pocketed his phone.

"What are those for?"

"Insurance."

"Insurance?"

"I just had an interesting conversation."

"Oh?"

"Seen enough?" he asked, reaching for her elbow.

"I don't know. This doesn't exactly put a pushpin on a map."

Firmly but without force, he grabbed her elbow and guided her away from the painting.

"What's going on?"

"I don't know. But I led you to *Iśimi*, which is the end of the line, so let's shake hands and bid each other well."

"The search isn't over."

"No, but our partnership is."

This time she grabbed his arm, stopping him as they exited back into the hallway. "What's going on?"

"Nothing. This was always the plan."

"Mitch, what happened? I thought we'd made nice—a couple of times."

He opened his mouth, but before he could speak, the power went out again.

CHAPTER FORTY

Cameron had stalked off into the adjacent room, this one a collection dedicated to photography. She didn't pay much attention to what was on the walls, because she kept thinking about the confrontation with Mitch's girlfriend and things she wished she had said to her—or to him earlier. Finally, after several good minutes of pouting, she remembered that the woman showing up had distracted her from taking a picture of *Iśimi* as she had intended. So, after taking a moment to work up her courage at possibly encountering the woman again and determining she didn't care what the woman thought, Cameron turned and walked back into the cultural collection room.

The woman was gone, and no one stood in front of the painting. There were two men chatting by an exhibit a little ways away from the painting, and several other couples or groups in the room. But no one by *Iśimi*. So Cameron withdrew her camera from her purse and approached it, only to have the room go completely dark.

Immediately the patrons began murmuring, shouting, even shrieking in alarm. Cameron looked around, expecting to see the glow of an exit sign, as she had in the bathroom, but there was none. She couldn't recall if there had been any in the individual rooms—she assumed there had to be, legally. But maybe this time, whatever had knocked out the power had knocked out the auxiliary or backup generators as well.

A blue glow slowly permeated the room as people activated their smartphones. A sliding glass door had opened, and Cameron could hear the sound of the rain. Then a few flashlight apps began panning around the room. Someone coughed. Then another. Cameron felt a tickle in her throat, and then noticed the bluish light in the room had become tinged with haze.

She turned and used the faint light to find her way to the hallway. She succumbed to a cough, and put her hand over her nose and mouth. Several others had the same idea, and formed a bottleneck by the exit. The hallway too was dark, and full of people, most of whom were moving toward the foyer. The air was clearer, void of smoke, and Cameron was relieved to break into the open space of the balcony over the main hall, even if she still couldn't see beyond what cell phones were able to reveal.

The entire gallery was dark, and the clamor was getting louder, with dozens upon dozens of people asking what was going on, shouting theories, calling for friends or loved ones, or announcing results of phone searches for news as to what was happening. Somebody mentioned that the downtown skyline was lit, that the outage appeared local. An authoritative voice asked for everyone to remain calm. Cameron would have managed had a hand not grabbed her elbow at that moment.

She stifled the shriek halfway through.

"Sshh," Erik hissed.

"Erik, where have you been?"

"Looking for our portrait."

"I found it, back in there," she said, gesturing toward the hallway, where smoke had wafted toward the ceiling.

"In there?"

She nodded, and Erik dropped her arm and practically pushed her aside. She followed as he charged down the hallway against a throng of people. Cameron managed to stay close behind him, and they reached the entrance to the Cultural Room just as a loud hum sounded and the lights flickered a few times and came back on.

Many of the patrons applauded and cheered, and the murmuring took on a cheery tone. Cameron ignored it, following Erik into the smoky room. The haze was already starting to settle, and any odor was quickly subsiding. Cameron came alongside Erik and they both stopped in front of *Iśimi*.

Or, rather, the vacant hooks on the wall where she had hung moments earlier.

"They stole it," Erik said. "I don't believe it, they stole the painting."

*   *   *

"What do you think the odds are the power just keeps flickering?" Olivia asked. She and Mitch stood near the landing of one of the spiral stairways leading down to the first floor of the gallery.

"About the same as you being on the level."

"Excuse me?"

"I talked to Cameron's ex."

"Diaz?"

"He told me Cameron's never been arrested. But her sister, also C. Leigh, was nicked with a DUI in Atlanta in October, 2013. You lied to me."

"I didn't. The info I was given must have—"

He put up a hand. "I don't what to hear it. I don't know what's going on here, and I don't much care anymore. I've come, I've seen, and I'm leaving."

"Mitch."

"Threaten all you want, but it won't matter," he said, turning.

Olivia grabbed his arm. "I was going to say, I don't think they'll let you leave." Her eyes went from his to the far staircase, where a man in a blue blazer and a patch identifying him as security had ascended to their level. Another was climbing the staircase by them, and they stepped back to let him pass. The two guards met up for a minute, then headed down the hallway toward *Isimi's* room.

"Doesn't look like they intend to stop me."

"No, but once they get in there and figure out what happened they will."

Mitch grabbed her arm and steered her farther away from anyone. "What are you talking about?"

"Think about it. The power goes out, twice, and now security is running toward where *Isimi* is."

He looked into her eyes, searching for more—such as knowledge that the painting had been stolen, not just a hunch. He saw nothing.

"Doesn't change anything," he said, retrieving his phone. He took a minute to send himself an e-mail with the photos he'd taken of the portrait. He then deleted them from his phone, and held it up to Olivia. "I've got what I need, so whatever happens next isn't my problem."

From down below, in the main hall, a voice called for silence. Mitch and Olivia approached the railing and looked down to see a man in a maroon tuxedo with his hands raised. He was flanked by a duo in blazers that matched those worn by the security guards who had just climbed the stairs. He called for silence again, and when he finally had a semblance of it, lowered his arms.

"Everyone, let me apologize for the inconvenience. We are investigating the cause right now, but believe it has been—"

One of the men in blazers beside him had put his finger to his ear, and now lowered it and leaned in to speak to the man in the maroon tuxedo. He said something back, then addressed the room again. "I've just received word that one of our displays has been stolen. We will be implementing inspection protocols. Please be patient."

"See what I mean," Olivia said.

"Are you involved in this?"

"What? No."

"Olivia."

"Mitch, I swear. I'm working with you."

"Not anymore," he said.

"Where are you going?"

"To find Cameron."

*   *   *

"I don't believe it," Cameron said. "It was just here. How . . ."

"Just here when? How long ago?" Erik asked.

"I don't know. Maybe a minute before you found me. There was smoke and . . ."

"Did you see Van Buren?"

"No. Just . . ."

"Just what?"

She sighed. "Mitch is here, with some woman. She was there."

"Mitch . . ."

"What?" Cameron asked.

"Didn't you say something about him working security?"

"I don't know. He does, but—"

Erik pushed past her and toward the door. Cameron followed as he stepped outside onto the balcony. A light rain was falling, which didn't stop Erik from hurrying over to the balcony railing. Rain notwithstanding, Cameron followed.

"Look at this," Erik said, nodding at a rope fastened to the railing. Cameron approached the railing and peered over the edge. She saw the rope dangling into the darkness, but nothing else. She lifted the rope, shook it, looking down to see how far the rope went. At least several stories, but she couldn't tell how many. It felt heavy enough to go to the ground, but could someone have really rappelled ten stories with a framed painting in hand? She'd seen on TV how thieves would cut the painting out of the frame to make it easier to transport. But in that case, where was the frame?

"Erik, what—"

He was gone.

"Erik?" she said more loudly, squinting into the rain to scan the balcony and the entrance to the Cultural Room. He was nowhere to be seen, but two men in blue blazers were. They exited onto the balcony one at a time, then flanked her.

"Ma'am, please step away from the railing."

"There's a rope here," she said. "I think someone used it to escape."

"Ma'am, away from the railing."

She took a few steps, and the man on her left took hold of her arm.

"What are you doing?"

The man on her right lifted his wrist in front of his mouth, just like on TV. "We have a suspect in custody."

"What?" Cameron asked. "A suspect. I'm not—"

"Ma'am, please come quietly with us."

"I'm not going anywhere with you. Unhand me."

"Don't make a scene. We've already contacted the authorities, and I'm sure they'll have some questions for you."

"For me? No, you've got this all wrong."

"You were seen in the vicinity of a missing display shortly before the power outage, no one can account for you in the aftermath, and now you're here by the likely escape route."

"No one could account for me? I was just with someone, and how could you have possibly asked that many people?"

The one on the right seemed to soften. "Look, the authorities will be here any minute and they will want to question you. No one is leaving the gallery right now, so please, let's find a place where you and they can have a chat and clear this all up."

Cameron wanted to protest further, but ultimately consented with a sigh. "I guess I don't have a choice."

They took her in through the cultural room entrance, which had been emptied. Then they marched her down the hall, which fortunately was mostly empty as well. It was bad enough being blamed for *Iśimi's* theft, but now being perp-walked? And what if Mitch saw her?

The guard not holding her elbow swiped a keycard to open a door off a stub hallway, and they ushered her into a lounge with several chic but not terribly comfortable looking pieces of furniture, glass end and coffee tables, and small baskets with bottled water and snacks. The guard released her elbow and nodded at a chair against the near wall. "Please have a seat," he said.

She thought about resisting out of spite, but saw no benefit in doing so. She sat down with another sigh that turned into a growl. Where had Erik gone? Had someone ratted her out, or was it just dumb luck that the security guards had shown up at the exact wrong moment? Who was Mitch's "girlfriend" and how was she involved? For that matter, how was Mitch involved? What had become of Van Buren? His presence here couldn't be a coincidence. And who had the painting?

And more importantly, as one of the guards remained in the room with her, hovering, how was she going to get out of this?

CHAPTER FORTY-ONE

Before Mitch could reach the exit, a duo of Miami PD detectives and a cadre of police officers had arrived and secured the premises. He was herded, along with the rest of the patrons, into various rooms for processing and questioning. As chaotic as a gallery full of party guests in formalwear being treated like 'bangers at a drug bust was, Mitch's head was even worse. As he waited his turn to explain who he was to the cops—and he'd overheard somebody mention FBI—he tried to figure out what to make of Cameron and Olivia's allegations and evidence, how they could be faked, what it would mean if they weren't, how trustworthy Erik was, whether Olivia had any credibility, and how much he should divulge when questioned. One good thing about the authorities being there was, if they were worth their salt, they should be conducting some sort of check on the patrons, and thus should identify the Hogans and their criminal history. Assuming Harrison Van Buren didn't have pull with these authorities or that the Hogans weren't already gone. Say, with the painting. Chaotic didn't begin to describe it.

The hours—plural!—ticked by, until it was well into Saturday morning. His nerves at their breaking point, Mitch was finally ushered into the gallery's kitchen, one of several rooms where a Detective Garcia and a Special Agent Jimenez were questioning patrons. They looked as worn and weary as Mitch felt, and he hoped he could skate by with a quick see-no-evil, hear-no-evil explanation. But without any idea if Olivia had already been questioned and if she had or hadn't stuck to their cover story, he realized anything other than the truth could end up making him look guilty. So he told the truth.

A redacted version of it.

He left Cameron's name out of it and said he was working for a woman named Olivia de la Cruz who had come to the gallery to view *Iśimi*, believing it contained clues that would lead to the Fountain of Youth. She had employed him to provide security and insisted on concocting an alias so as to deduce the clues in anonymity. He said it with an appropriate level of boredom and skepticism, painting her as the wealthy elitist hunting a lark while he merely did the grunt work and followed orders.

It was sort of the truth.

"What brings you to Florida, Mr. Owens?" Special Agent Jimenez asked. He was in his thirties, whiter than Mitch despite the Hispanic surname, and either was working on an ulcer or had consumed bad take-out before coming to the gallery, based on the way he popped antacids. That was more of a shtick for a detective, Mitch thought, but whatevs.

"Vacation," Mitch said. "I'm semi-retired, enjoying life, and thought the Sunshine State would be the place to do it."

"So how did you end up working for Ms. de la Cruz?" Detective Garcia asked. He was a decade older than Jimenez, had a trace of an accent, and talked with a resigned lilt. They'd been doing a nice job, intentionally or not, of tag-teaming their questions, and had apparently put aside any jurisdictional clashes.

"By coincidence," Mitch said. "We met on the beach, started talking, talked some more over drinks and dinner. Eventually, we got around to careers, and one thing led to another . . ." He let a smirk fade. "Why, she tell you it was something else?"

"Why would she have done that?" Garcia asked with a glance at Jimenez.

"Because looking for the Fountain of Youth comes off as pretty crazy to most people. She seems kind of embarrassed by it. Frankly, I would be too."

"We haven't spoken to her yet," Jimenez said. He looked at Garcia. "Send a text to Nick and your partner, tell them to keep an eye out for a de la Cruz or a . . . what was her alias?"

"Bianca," Mitch said with an appropriate eye roll and a pretty good job, he thought, of hiding his relief that his cover wasn't blown.

The duo asked a series of questions about where Mitch had been before, during, and after the blackouts and whether he had seen anything or anyone suspicious. He told the truth again, with slightly less redaction. Then, when they had wrapped up, he asked if they had a suspect.

"Not as of yet, why?" Garcia asked.

"Ms. de la Cruz suspected she was not the only party here at the gallery with an interest in *Iśimi* for its clues to the Fountain of Youth. She mentioned seeing a man and woman here who had been chasing it as well and who had, according to her, a criminal history. Said their names were Shay or Shane or something like that and Lora Hogan."

It was a risk, throwing out their names, because any research Jimenez or Garcia did into the Hogans and their recent past could also turn up Mitch's involvement in the Casa Monica heist. He was hoping they didn't dig that deep, or that he was long gone by then.

"Could you describe them?"

"He was a standard stiff, frosted hair. She was a flaming redhead, tallish. Had on a navy gown."

"Thanks, Mr. Owens," Garcia said. "We appreciate your cooperation."

Mitch stood and was escorted out of the kitchen by an officer. The gallery crowd had dwindled, and Mitch scanned the main foyer where most of the rest of the patrons had gathered, but saw no signs of Cameron. After ducking into the men's room for a minute, he showed an officer at the door a signed business card from Jimenez, which served as pass to get him out of the gallery.

He took a deep breath as he exited into the main hall and checked his watch. 1:19 a.m. He trudged toward the elevators, debating calling Cameron and trying to explain or waiting till morning. He had the same debate with booking a flight back to Austin. This was not how things were supposed to play out.

As he waited for the elevator to come back to the ninth floor, he swiped at his phone, seeing he had a missed call from Olivia. No voicemail. He didn't return it. He thumbed to his contacts, about to try Cameron even at this hour, when a soft ding announced the arrival of the elevator, then the doors behind him parted. An officer stepped out with a nod, and Mitch took his place in the elevator. He changed his mind about a phone call, opting instead for a text.

> *Cameron, I'm sorry. Please give me a*
> *Chance to explain face to face. I'm still*
> *in town. I'll wait for your call or text.*

"Hold the elevator."

Without thinking, Mitch jabbed the door open button with his thumb. He looked up as Erik Diaz darted onto the elevator. His eyes were bloodshot and rimmed with dark circles, his undone tie hung from his collar, and his breath smelled of vodka. When the door closed, Mitch turned his way. "Wasn't you, was it?"

Erik only shook his head.

"Where's Cameron?"

"I don't . . . I don't know, Mitch." He shook his head again. "I'm in trouble."

"What's going on?"

"Van Buren."

"What about him?"

"He has Jessie."

"Who's Jessie?"

"My girlfriend. I thought I could . . . Now . . ."

Mitch leaned forward to press the stop button, and the elevator halted. He turned to Erik "Take a breath and tell me what's going on."

"Harrison Van Buren grabbed Jessie a week ago, said if I didn't do what he said, he'd kill her. I know Van Buren, and he's not bluffing."

Mitch's eyes narrowed. "What did he want you to do?"

"Tell him everything I knew about the fountain and make sure you didn't find it."

"Or Cameron?"

He nodded.

"Did you send those guys after her on the boat?"

"No."

"Erik?"

"I swear. I still care about Cameron, as a friend. I wouldn't hurt her."

"But you knew?"

"I didn't."

"What about at your villa?"

"I told them the disk would be there, but they promised they wouldn't hurt her."

Mitch clinched his teeth.

"Mitch, you gotta believe me."

"I don't gotta do nothing."

"They were going to kill Jessie."

"What about in Tampa, on the bridge?"

"When you guys took the disk back from them, they put a tap on my phone. When Cameron called, they got a trace and knew you were there. Somehow they found you on the road. I didn't know."

"And they sent you here tonight?"

"No. Cameron reached out to me the other day, mentioned *Iśimi* was here, and I thought I had my chance. If I could see the painting before them, get a step ahead of them, I could barter for Jessie. When I saw Van Buren here, I knew he was onto the painting too, so I had to steal it. He beat me to it, and now . . ."

Mitch felt bad for Erik, but it wasn't his fight. And, if he had it figured right, and if there was any chance of Van Buren letting Jessie go, he would now, since Erik was of no use to him. Once sober, Erik should be able to figure that out for himself.

"Where's Cameron?" Mitch asked.

"I don't know. I looked everywhere."

"When was the last you saw her?"

"We found a rope off the balcony, in the room *Iśimi* was in, right after the blackout. I figured it meant the painting was gone, so I tried to get out of the gallery and find a trace of whoever took her. But the cops showed up and detained me."

"Where would she go?"

"I don't know."

"Where are you staying?"

"The Colonial, on South Beach."

Mitch pressed the button again, and the elevator resumed moving.

"I'm sorry, Mitch. I really am."

"Yeah."

"If you find Cameron, tell her, will you?"

"Tell her yourself," Mitch said. "I'll have my own apologies to make."

*   *   *

It was two-thirty in the morning before the authorities finally let Cameron go. She had been questioned by Miami PD, the FBI, a second FBI team, and finally the owner of Primero. She had convinced them that she had nothing to do with *Iśimi's* disappearance, that she was merely in the wrong place at the wrong time. Well, convinced might have been a little strong. They had taken her phone number and promised to be in touch if they had any questions, and urged her to reach out to them if she remembered anything else.

She stepped off the elevator, her heels in one hand and her purse in the other. The building atrium was vacant and dark, lit only by recessed lights under the mezzanine. The waterfalls had turned off, and the soft background music had ceased. The mood was eerie, and Cameron wasted no time striding for the exit, despite her sore feet and general fatigue.

The rain had abated, leaving the streets and sidewalk glistening. A gentle breeze stirred an otherwise still, muggy night. Cameron looked around, judged the neighborhood to be as safe as possible at the hour, especially given the speckling of police cars up and down the block. She leaned against a brick planter, dropped her heels with a clack, and retrieved her phone from her purse. Its display showed a dwindling battery, but she had enough for several calls at least.

The first went to Erik. He didn't pick up. She hadn't seen him or heard from him since he'd left her holding the rope—literally. She thought about calling Mitch, having read his text during a rare break in the interrogation. But she was still too mad, and didn't know what he could possibly say to make things right. Besides, it was the middle of the night, and he was likely sleeping, possibly with the sultry brunette who'd been clinging to his arm earlier.

So she called an Uber. Given the time and her location, she was told it would be close to a half hour wait. She sighed, accepted, and then hibernated her phone to save what battery was left.

It was actually thirty-five minutes before her driver arrived, by which time two police officers and the FBI agent who had questioned her first had offered her a ride. She didn't suspect ulterior motives, but declined nonetheless. Her Uber driver was polite and professional, and either a night owl or on drugs. He delivered her to her and Erik's hotel on South Beach safely, so she didn't care which.

Exhausted, she took the elevator up to the fourth floor. She still carried her heels and trudged barefoot to Erik's room. She guessed it was somewhere between three-thirty and four, but didn't care, banging on his door with her fist. He didn't answer. She didn't know whether to be mad or worried, and didn't have the energy for either.

Her room was right next door, and she let herself in, tossed her purse on the dresser and heels on the floor, and collapsed onto the bed without changing out of her dress or undoing her hair. Her body had shut down, but her mind hadn't. She found herself staring at the ceiling, replaying the day, Mitch's betrayal, the interrogation, and *Iśimi*. What was the clue Diego Figueroa had left in the painting of a woman wearing a waterfall? Was the water-like dress symbolic of the Fountain of Youth? Was she? What of the setting sun? What of her beckoning hand?

The numbers on the clock blinked 4:28, and Cameron realized she wasn't going to sleep. She got up and walked to the window, looking out at the tranquil Atlantic. It was inky black, with only the faintest hint of lightening on the horizon. With nothing better to do, Cameron decided to take a walk on the beach.

Grabbing just her keycard, she took the elevator down to the lobby and exited out onto the beach. The pre-dawn air was refreshing, and Cameron inhaled deeply as she crossed the dunes and began walking south. To her right, the neon and bright lights of the hotels and clubs were still aglow, but the hubbub and activity was minimal, at least by the noise. What few sounds crossed the dunes were quickly drowned out by the soothing, sibilant washing of waves on the sand.

Cameron plodded slowly, absentmindedly fiddling with the keycard in her hand and staring at the waves. Water made her think about the Fountain of Youth, about her years' long search for it, about the events of the last week. She'd thought finding the *Descubridor* had put her on the verge of her own discovery, then thought interpreting the Castillo de San Marcos stone with the two cipher disks had done it, then locating *Iśimi*. One clue led to another, and to another, and to another. Equally bad, she was alone again, not trusting Mitch and unable to rely on Erik.

So what? She'd found her way solo so far, persuading Erik to financially support her and convincing Mitch to help her when Erik backed out. She could do it again, or find another way to raise support, or . . . something.

Cameron stopped. Who was she kidding? It was one thing to conduct her own investigation and pursue an academic search. But with Van Buren and the Hogans involved and willing to steal clues and resort to violence, how long would it be until she got into serious trouble—trouble she couldn't get out of? She'd already been attacked multiple times, and if not for Mitch, might not be alive.

Dr. Kessler's words came back to her, about how everyone was going to die, and the ultimate question was what happened after death. Suddenly it was too much, and she dropped down into the sand, never mind that she was sitting on a three-hundred-dollar dress. She hung her head, then raised it to look at the faint orange gradient above the horizon and the glow beginning to spread over the ocean.

Water also brought to mind a verse she had read in the Gospel of John:

Everyone who drinks this water will be thirsty again, but whoever drinks the water I give them will never thirst. Indeed, the water I give them will become in them a spring of water welling up to eternal life. Jesus had also said, *"Let anyone who is thirsty come to me and drink. Whoever believes in me, as Scripture has said, rivers of living water will flow from within them."*

She had only read through the small book from Dr. Kessler once, but verses kept coming back to her. She'd found them running in her head throughout the day and night, and now again.

I am the way and the truth and the life. No one comes to the Father except through me.

For my Father's will is that everyone who looks to the Son and believes in him shall have eternal life . . .

I have come that they may have life, and have it to the full.

I have told you these things, so that in me you may have peace. In this world you will have trouble. But take heart! I have overcome the world.

Cameron didn't know how Jesus' overcoming the world might help with her current mess, but she didn't care. In that moment, she realized more than finding a physical fountain that may extend and improve life on earth, what she needed ultimately was a guaranty of eternal life, of having the penalty for her sin removed by the death of Jesus on the cross. She also realized that while she had never bought into the idea of the Bible being authoritative or of Jesus having answers to life's questions, it wasn't something she couldn't buy into.

"God, I don't really know how to do this, or what to say." She looked around, realizing that she was talking out loud. It was okay; there was no one else on the beach as far as the eye could see. "But I want the life you offer— eternal life. I believe it's true, that Jesus is the way and the truth and the life. I don't want to pay for my sins when I die; I want the—this sounds weird," she said, a smile on her face as she looked up. "I want the blood of Jesus to cover them. Is that okay, God, that I said it's weird? But I still want it. I want life to the full and to overcome the world, whatever that means."

She stopped talking and took several deep breaths. She closed her eyes and repeated the verse from John 4 in her head.

> . . . *whoever drinks the water I give them will never thirst. Indeed, the water I give them will become in them a spring of water welling up to eternal life.*

As she opened her eyes, she felt a smile cross her face. She'd done it; she'd found the Fountain of Life.

CHAPTER FORTY-TWO

Traffic on the A1A was light at three-thirty a.m. as Mitch left the Fountainbleau in the Nissan Rogue. The BMW he and Olivia had rented earlier had been gone from the garage beneath the office tower, so he'd taken—after a long wait—a taxi back to the Fountainbleau. Finding Olivia and her stuff gone, he'd quickly packed up and checked out. Now, he was faced with decisions. A sign along the road indicated I-95 and the airport were both to the right, across the bay. He could be on a plane that would have him back in Texas in time for a late breakfast. Or he could run the interstate back to Cocoa Beach, forget the last week, and resume his vacation.

Instead, he searched for a reasonable hotel with vacancies. The first he found and tried was booked solid, but a Marriott property a block east of the main drag had a room. He checked in, dropped his stuff, and treated himself to a long, hot shower. Though tired, he wasn't sleepy, so he dressed and then checked his phone.

Cameron had not called or texted back. So he got back in the Rogue and drove to The Colonial Hotel where Erik said she had been staying. He spent a few minutes finding a parking place, then debated whether or not to call her room. If she was sleeping, he didn't want to wake her, but he felt he had to talk to her. He couldn't leave Florida without resolving things. Or at least trying to.

The lobby of the hotel was quiet, which was expected given the hour. Before doing anything drastic, like rousing Cameron from sleep and further alienating himself from her, he decided on a different tack. He approached the front desk and waited a few minutes for a clerk to return from somewhere.

"Can I help you, sir?" he asked without a trace of sleepiness.

"I'm looking for a friend of mine who's staying here," Mitch answered. "I'm wondering if you could tell me if you saw her return tonight?"

"I'm afraid that our guest's comings and goings are their own business, sir. Especially given the hour."

"I can appreciate that, but it's important I find her. You don't have to give me her room number, but if I could just leave a message for her."

"I'm sorry—"

"If she's not here, I need to look for her somewhere else. Please," Mitch said, finding a picture of Cameron on his phone. He'd snapped it Sunday, at the beach, when she wasn't paying attention, a casual shot to use as her avatar in his contacts. "She likely would have been dressed up in an evening gown," he said. "Garnet red, hair up."

The clerk looked at the phone, and his eyebrows went up. "As a matter of fact, she exited out onto the beach," he said, pointing to sliding glass doors leading out.

"When?"

"Maybe fifteen minutes ago."

"Did you see which way she went?"

"I did not."

"Thanks," Mitch said. He pocketed his phone and headed out the doors, taking a sandy path through brush-covered dunes. The ocean was black in front of him, broken only by the foam of crashing waves. He stopped on the packed sand of the beach, looking left and right. He saw not a soul. Left, the beach stretched forever, whereas to the right it ran for at most a mile before ending in the South Pointe Pier. He doubted Cameron had walked even a mile, but only because it would be quicker to sweep the beach to the right, he turned south.

He'd been running ideas through his head of what to say and how to say it. Explaining "the other woman" was easy in this case, because there was nothing between him and Olivia. But as to why he'd abandoned Cameron, why he'd said nothing, why he'd taken Olivia's word—that was going to be a bit harder. First he had to find her.

The beach really was deserted, still ninety minutes before sunrise. At one point, a jogger passed him, but Mitch was otherwise alone. Gradually, the sky above grew lighter shades of black until it was dark blue. The water was still dark as ever, the waves pounding a steady rhythm. A shape took form up ahead, a person sitting on the beach. As Mitch drew closer, he realized it was Cameron, still in her dress, her hair still styled. Her gaze was to the southeast, where the sky was just light enough to reveal tufts of clouds, the remnants of the previous evening's storm.

Mitch approached slowly. He stopped several feet from her, hands in his pockets. She still had not noticed him.

"Hey, Cameron."

Maybe she had, because she didn't startle. Instead, she slowly turned her head to look at him. She said nothing, just directed her eyes back out to sea.

"I'm sorry," he said. "I know that doesn't begin to cut it, but I hope it gets my foot in the door. Because I can explain. Not everything. Some of it needs an apology. But there's more to it than you know."

She looked up at him, then down at the sand beside her. He considered that an invitation, and sat down, resting his arms on his knees.

"When I was a freshman in high school," Cameron said, her eyes again on the ocean, "there was this guy named Matt Richardson, a sophomore, and we did all the dorky, flirty things high school kids do. He finally asked me out, saying he had to wait until he got his driver's license so he could take me to dinner." She fidgeted with the hem of her dress for a second. "I spent a week looking forward to that Friday night, and he called fifteen minutes before he was supposed to pick me up to say he'd failed his driving test and we'd have to reschedule." She swallowed. "Fifteen-year-old Cameron managed to hold it together until the next day, when I was walking home from a friend's house and saw him drive by in his dad's car. Alone. That was the worst any boy had ever made me feel," she said, turning his way. "Until tonight."

"Cameron . . ."

"I will listen to your explanation, and your apology, but don't think either one can undo the hurt you caused."

He looked down. For several minutes, he said nothing, just listening to the waves. He sensed her looking at him and raised his head, meeting her eyes in the gloom. "I don't know where to start," he said.

She said nothing.

"Wednesday morning," he finally managed, "as we were leaving Clearwater, I got a phone call. She said her name was Olivia, said you weren't who you said you were, asked to meet with me. She wouldn't give me anything further, so I ended the call and forgot about it. Then yesterday, as I was leaving Morgan's after dropping off the disk, she called again. Said she had evidence, convinced me to have lunch."

Cameron licked her lips.

"She painted a picture that tied you to some shady characters, including Charles Calvin, who she claimed is Kevin Stuart."

Cameron's eyes widened. "What?"

"She said you'd been in communication with him recently, and had call logs and cell records to back it up. She kept claiming you weren't who you said you were."

"And you believed her?"

"I didn't know what to believe, Cameron."

"Did you ever think of talking to me about it before taking her word for everything?"

"It wasn't just her word. I told you, she had call logs."

"That prove nothing illicit."

"No, but given Calvin's alleged crimes and behavior, they would look bad. And she also had a mugshot, I thought of you—said you'd stolen a Confederate colonel's letter from some guy in some suburb of Atlanta."

Cameron shook her head.

"I didn't find out until talking to Erik tonight that it was Chelsea."

She said nothing.

Mitch exhaled. "Olivia said if I didn't help her, she'd expose you to the world. Expose your ties to Calvin-slash-Stuart. And if the things she said were true—even if you hadn't done anything wrong—it could have meant the end of your work and research, according to her."

Cameron shook her head again.

"She wanted me to be a mole, to come back and work with you. I tried to convince her that it wasn't worth it, that *Išimi* was the end of the line. I thought she'd let it go at that, then I could come back to pick you up, and you and I could go back to how things were."

"With you thinking I'm in cahoots with the Hogans?"

"I didn't think you were in cahoots with them. I . . . I didn't know . . ."

Cameron looked away, the pre-dawn breeze blowing loose strands of hair into her face. Mitch watched, waited. She finally turned back to him. "Calvin and I were colleagues. We worked together briefly, struck up something of a friendship, but that was it. Nothing romantic, no conspiring to commit crimes. I heard the allegations too, but the Calvin I knew wouldn't do those things, and my understanding is he was never charged."

"Have you kept in touch with him?"

"Now and again. We knew each other's interests, so we'd share a text or call if we learned or heard anything. Same as I do with dozens of people, and I don't condone or know what they do or don't do. But I have never—*never!*—willingly helped any of them do anything illegal. And I had no idea Calvin was or is Stuart."

"I believe you."

She exhaled and turned away again.

"I do, Cameron. Did I have doubts? Yeah, I did."

She looked back his way.

"But I wasn't convinced against you either. I didn't know what to think, and if it had just been some woman's claims and evidence, I would have come right back to Sanibel Island and talked to you face to face to hear your side. But Olivia insisted—and I believed her—that if I had done that, she'd have gone public with her evidence. And true or not, it could have been quite condemning."

"Are you trying to say you did this for me?"

"Yes, sort of." He sighed. "Cameron, I didn't know what to do. And I'm sure I played this wrong. I'm sorry for that. And I hurt you, and I'm extremely sorry for that. I don't know what I could have or should have done differently, but that doesn't matter now. What can I do now, in the present, to earn your forgiveness?"

Cameron smiled. It was a sweet smile, a contented smile, and Mitch smiled too, thinking she had forgiven him already, that he was going to get off easy.

Then she shook her head and said softly, "Nothing."

CHAPTER FORTY-THREE

The look on Mitch's face was a mixture of shock and sadness, and Cameron placed a hand on his arm. "It's not like that," she said. "But I've come to realize, forgiveness isn't earned." She withdrew her hand. "I've been thinking a lot about what Dr. Kessler said, about Jesus, about eternal life. He gave me a small book—the Gospel of John—and I read it cover to cover. And the more I read, the more I thought, the more I realized everything Kessler said was true, that what John wrote was true, that what Jesus said was true. True in the sense of being accurate and real but also true in the sense of being exactly what I need. I prayed and asked God to give me eternal life, Mitch, to forgive me. And so it only seems right that I forgive you too."

She wasn't sure how he'd handle the news, given his doubts and uncertainty about what Kessler had said. But she felt like it was her first test, whether this was real or not. Would she sweep what she'd decided and done under the rug, or tell the person who—despite his misstep—was still the most significant person in her life at that precise moment?

Mitch nodded. "I've been thinking a lot about that too," he said. "I can't stop, in fact. I'm not quite ready to buy in though. But thank you, for forgiving me. I really am sorry."

"I know. And while I do forgive you, the hurt is still there, Mitch. Maybe I just need to process this more, or . . . I don't know. Forgiveness is one thing, but I don't know how we get trust back."

"Whatever it takes, I'm here," he said. "Unless you want me gone; then I'll go."

"I don't want you gone," she said, touching his arm again, then sliding her hand down to his. She squeezed it. "I wish we could go back to how things were too. Maybe we can."

"Whatever it takes," he said again.

"I just wish I knew what that was, where we go from here."

"I might have an idea on that."

She looked at him as he reached for his phone, swiped and tapped to a picture, and turned it her way. *Išimi.*

"You got a picture?"

"That was our reason for going. Figured it's as good as the real thing. I know we don't have all the answers, but we can get back to work, if you want. We've made it this far."

She dropped her head. "I don't know."

"Or I can send you the pic and you can work on it yourself, if you'd rather."

"It's not that, Mitch. I don't know about this search anymore. I've wanted to find the fountain for so long because I thought it could help me and my family, that there was something in the water that would enhance our lives."

"And now you have Jesus and don't need perpetual youth?"

"Something like that. I don't know. I'm still processing that too."

Mitch pursed his lips. "I can respect that," he said after a moment. "But this wasn't all about eternal or long life, was it? Weren't you also chasing history, chasing knowledge?"

She nodded in concession.

"You can still do that. And just because you have eternal life doesn't mean you can't still try to enhance this life, right? You never bought into drinking from some Florida stream would make you never die, did you?"

"Not really."

"So," he said with a shrug. "It'd be a shame to come this far and not finish the search, wouldn't it?"

She let the oncoming smile break forth. "Yeah, it would. If we knew where to go next."

"What would you say to grabbing some breakfast and coffee and trying to figure it out?"

"Coffee?"

"After an all-nighter, I'm desperate."

She nodded. "But not yet."

He waited.

Cameron looked out at the horizon. "I want to see the sunrise first. Somehow, it seems appropriate."

*   *   *

The sunrise was brilliant and beautiful, and when the new day had been fully born, Cameron suggested they "get out of here." They walked back to her hotel, and Mitch gave her half an hour to shower and change and freshen up, during which time he checked out of his hotel and exchanged the Nissan for a Honda Accord, explaining that he didn't want to take any chances that Olivia had put a tracking device on the Rogue. Then, for lack of any better direction, they headed north along the A1A after a stop at Dunkin' for some fuel. They had no destination, but both of them were ready to leave Miami and South Beach behind.

Hotels and condos and the typical tourist sprawl continued for mile after mile, until it was almost hypnotic. Fortunately, the coffee and an ocean breeze blowing in through the windows of the car kept Cameron awake and kept Mitch alert. Several times, he apologized again and tried to explain more about the last few days and his reasoning. Each time, Cameron said she forgave him but shut down any further conversation. She wasn't ready for that, not yet. Mitch and Olivia, her new faith, *Isimi* and the hunt for the Fountain of Youth were all too much to process, and she needed some time to think about nothing but the warm air blowing over her hand and arm as they hung out the window.

"You hungry?" Mitch asked as they drove through Hollywood Beach.

Cameron couldn't remember the last time she'd eaten, and concluded she was. They stopped at a seaside café that served some basic breakfast options. They ate on the patio, shaded from the morning sun by a retractable awning that flapped in the breeze. Neither said much, which was still okay with Cameron. She wasn't exactly sure how she and Mitch could rebuild their relationship—if it just took time, or if one or both of them needed to say or do something. Nor was she sure what to do about the Fountain of Youth in light of Jesus being *the* ultimate Fountain. Mitch was right, she figured, that her search could continue, and should continue. But something seemed to be missing. Maybe that wasn't so much motivation as a clue what to do next.

"So how do you want to play this?" Mitch asked as they were finishing eating.

Cameron picked up half a piece of toast with orange marmalade. "I'm not sure," she said before taking a bite. She chewed and swallowed. "*Isimi* seems like another dead end. I have no idea what to make of her, we still don't have a clue about the mission, and now the clock's ticking with Van Buren's people likely having the painting, but . . ."

"But?" he prompted.

"I think I need a break."

He drained his orange juice, not asking "From what?" orally, but asking it nonetheless.

"I need rest. I didn't sleep all night, and with the stress of everything . . ."

"How about this?" Mitch said. "We find a place to crash, relax, unwind. See how you feel tomorrow. If you're ready to get back at it, we get back at it. If not, we decide what's next then."

Cameron nodded slowly. "Yeah, I think that works."

Mitch got out his phone, scouted for a few minutes, and found the Marriott Harbor Beach Resort and Spa a few miles north in Fort Lauderdale. He booked two rooms, and they settled their bill and set out. It took nearly half an hour with traffic and with having to navigate the mouth of the Stranahan River leading to Port Everglades. They arrived at quarter to ten, and while Mitch checked in, Cameron wandered through the airy lobby, already feeling her stress level declining. Their rooms were on the fifth floor, with balconies facing the ocean, and as Cameron brushed aside the shear curtains and stepped out onto the balcony, the stress dropped even farther. A nap and a swim and she might be almost back to normal.

"There's something else you should know," Mitch said, leaning on the railing beside her.

"What's that?"

"About Erik."

She turned his way. "What?"

"He's been compromised."

Cameron frowned. "What do you mean?"

"I ran into him as I was leaving Primero. He said he'd been trying to steal *Iśimi* to beat Van Buren to it because Van Buren had kidnapped his girlfriend and was holding her as a ransom, making him spy on us."

"What?"

"Said her name was Jessie."

"Yeah, I've heard him talk about her. They kidnapped her?"

Mitch nodded. "That's how they found us in Tampa, how they found you at his villa, probably how they found out about the gallery in the first place."

"I can't . . . Wait, the villa? He sent them there."

"He said they promised they wouldn't hurt you."

She dropped her head. "I don't believe this."

Mitch placed his hand on her back. "Sorry, but I thought you should know."

320

She took a moment. "What's he doing now?"

"I don't know."

"I mean, that he doesn't have the painting. That was his plan, wasn't it, to trade it for her safety?"

"Yeah." Mitch shrugged. "In theory, Van Buren has all he needs and should let her go."

"In theory."

"Yeah."

She shook her head. "This is too much."

"I'm sorry."

She blinked away tears, then sighed. "I need to rest, Mitch. Can I call you later?"

"Of course."

She nodded and followed him back to the door. She placed a hand on his arm as he left, forcing a smile, and then locked and bolted the door behind him. She spent a moment digging through her luggage for the most comfortable clean thing she had, adjusted the thermostat in the room, and crawled into bed. At first she cried, and then she tried praying but found she didn't really know how. Then she got up and found the Gospel of John Kessler had given her. She started reading it again, making it through chapter four before sleep finally overtook her.

*   *   *

Mitch returned to his room, tried to sleep, and failed. So he unplugged his phone from its charger and sat down on the balcony, studying the picture of *Isimi*. A dark-haired woman, wearing a dress that turned into a waterfall, standing on two islands in the water, and looking back over her shoulder. Was the water the fountain? Was she the fountain? Was she looking back toward the fountain, or beckoning people to come to her as the fountain? Was it sunrise or sunset? And did it matter?

He replayed everything Cameron had said about Diego Figueroa and his search for the Fountain of Youth, the words of the Castillo de San Marcos carving, their chats with Kessler—none of it made any sense of the portrait. Frustrated, he put on a pair of gym shorts and headed down to the outdoor basketball court on the edge of the property. At ten-thirty in the morning, it was vacant, and he was able to blow off some steam shooting buckets. Then he took a walk on the beach. The sun was out in full force, but with the breeze, it wasn't unbearable. Already, puffs of clouds were billowing on the horizon, looking like the sails on ships of yesteryear.

Mitch was hot and sweaty when he returned to his room, and he took the day's second shower, dressed, and used the in-room pot to brew some coffee. Whether it was attributable to the long hours and stress or whether Cameron was rubbing off on him, his attitude toward the aromatic beverage was changing. He took it out to the balcony, now shaded, and resumed staring at *Iśimi* and thinking.

Was she walking into the sunset, as in heading to the afterlife and motioning for others to drink her water and follow to immortality? Was she walking toward a sunrise, symbolizing new life and eternal hope? It'd been a while since his last mythology class, so Mitch knew neither what stock the Greeks, Norse, or other cultures heavy on myths put in such things, nor what Figueroa would have believed about them. The Spanish weren't big on mythology, were they?

No, they were big on religion, Roman Catholicism. So what did east and west, sunrise and sunset, mean to Catholics? Other than a few childhood friends who had been confirmed, he knew nothing about the religion. He spent a few minutes Googling various combinations of ideas, but got nowhere. He laid his head back and closed his eyes, willing himself to think. Maybe figuring out the answer to the riddle could win his way back into Cameron's good graces. Even though she'd forgiven him, he couldn't help feel there was something between them still—something that needed to be erased.

Next thing he knew, his phone was vibrating in his hand. He shook off sleep and sat up. The display showed Cameron's smiling face, and he swiped to answer the call. "Hello?"

"Mitch? I think I have a lead."

"A lead?"

"Want to meet me for lunch?"

"Lunch? What time is it?"

"Quarter to one."

"Whoa."

"You okay?"

"Yeah, just dozed off for a while, apparently. A lead?"

"Yeah. Meet me in the lobby in, say, half an hour?"

"Sure."

He smiled as he put down his phone, having long missed the excited tone in Cameron's voice.

CHAPTER FORTY-FOUR

Cameron wore the sea-green sundress she'd worn back in Clearwater, and it looked as good on her now as it had then. Her hair was loosely clipped back, and there was a carefree smile on her face when they met in the lobby.

"I take it you're refreshed," Mitch said.

"A nice morning nap and a swim in the pool do wonders."

"Guess I should have tried that. About this lead?"

"First lunch."

"Okay. Got a place in mind?"

"There's a seaside patio restaurant and bar on grounds, but it looks a little pricey."

"At this point, what's a few more bucks? I'll buy."

"Okay."

She led the way through the palm-shaded pool area to the Sea Level Restaurant and Ocean Bar. They were seated across from each other in padded wicker chairs next to a railing looking out over the dunes at the beach. That view was almost as good as the one straight in front of Mitch.

They spent a few minutes looking over the menus, then ordered. When they were alone, Cameron sat forward. "I was just finishing my swim when Dr. Kessler called me."

"Kessler? Isn't he fishing in Naples?"

"Not yesterday—too many storms."

"I see."

"So he and his professor buddies sat around drinking bad coffee and swapping stories," she said. "One of them is writing the comprehensive history of Caribbean piracy, and Dr. Kessler said the conversation allowed for him to very discreetly ask if any of them knew much about Spanish missions in the seventeenth century. He said a colleague of his was doing some research for a project but had hit a dead end."

"Not untrue."

"No," she said with a half smirk. "None of them did, and the conversation moved on to other things. But this morning, out on the boat, one of these buddies—out of the blue—mentioned a colleague of his who might be a valid resource. As soon as they came back to shore for lunch, Kessler called me and gave me her name. She's a history professor at the University of Florida."

"Gainesville."

Cameron nodded.

"Another road trip?"

"Not yet. I'll give her a call after lunch."

"Well, it's something maybe."

"And it's something there's no way Van Buren can have."

"Unless they got to Kessler, or his phone, or your phone."

"You sound paranoid."

Mitch reached for his Corona. "With everything Olivia knew about us, with Van Buren's people getting to Erik, who knows anymore."

"Think we should ditch our phones?"

"I don't know, maybe."

"Really?"

"I doubt they've hacked our calls, but they might be pinging locations. Olivia seemed to have unlimited resources."

Cameron exhaled.

"Sorry. I won't bring her up again."

"It's not like you cheated on me, Mitch."

"I didn't. Whatever you saw at the gallery, it wasn't anything."

"Not on your end, maybe."

"She was running game. From start to finish. I'm just mad I fell for it, that I didn't figure out some way to fact check her sooner. And I'm sorry I ever doubted you."

"I'm sorry I doubted you too. I should have known you wouldn't ghost me."

"I wouldn't, Cameron. I wouldn't ghost anyone, but especially you."

She smiled.

Mitch shook his head. "I don't know exactly what we have here, or had until two days ago. I don't know what this mess with Olivia has changed, or what will happen once we finish our search. But, cards on the table, whatever it is between us, I want to pursue it further, see where it leads, where it can lead."

Cameron swallowed. "I feel the same way."

"I hear a 'but' in that sentence."

She exhaled. "It's like I told you earlier, there's a hurt from what happened. I'm not blaming you—I understand now, and I can see what a hard spot you were in. There's no hard feelings, I'm not putting you in the doghouse or anything—"

"But it still hurts."

"Yeah. I can't explain it, exactly, but the wound is still there, and it's going to take some time to heal. Until it does—and it will—but until it does, I don't think we should pursue anything."

"Okay."

"Let's do this. Let's go back to where we were Thursday morning."

"Which was . . . ?"

"Working together to find the Fountain of Youth, getting to know each other, having a great time. And when we're done, when we find it or run out of clues, we'll see where we are and decide what's next."

Mitch nodded. "That works for me."

*   *   *

Dr. Isabelle Botana, professor of Southern colonial history at the University of Florida, did not answer when Cameron called her a little after two. It was a Saturday in the summer, but Kessler's colleague had provided her cell number, so it shouldn't have mattered that school was not in session. Instead of leaving a message, Cameron opted to try back later. Deeming it too hot for a walk on the beach, and with the sky looking like rain, the duo decided to find the nearest shopping center. After more than a week in Florida, both of them were in need of some items, and Mitch said he was serious about new phones. So while a rain shower moved through, they picked up some extra deodorant and toothpaste, a couple T-shirts and tank tops, and two pay-as-you-go phones, what Mitch referred to as burners. While Cameron perused a shoe store for a new pair of flip-flops, he configured the phones. When she emerged with the fruits of a two-for-one sale, he handed her a bland, black smartphone.

"I programmed them with our numbers and only our numbers," he said as she sat down on the bench beside him.

"Are we going dark?" she asked with a raised eyebrow.

"It might not be a bad idea. You need to call your sister suddenly, go for it, but especially if we start moving again, at least for the time being, I think we should make our phones untraceable."

"Okay."

The rain had stopped, so they headed back to the hotel. On the way, they caught each other up on the previous couple of days. Mitch went into greater detail about the things Olivia knew about them. He'd gone from trying to convince Cameron of anything to analyzing the competition. She in turn told him about the man she'd seen at the pool during her midnight swim Thursday night and recounted each call or text she'd made to Erik, trying to pinpoint how Van Buren had tracked them down. They both agreed they were up against multiple foes with far better spy capabilities than they possessed, reinforcing their decision to "go dark."

By the time they returned to the hotel, the skies had cleared. Cameron placed another call to Dr. Botana, this time from her burner, and left a message when Botana didn't answer. She dropped the name of Dr. Kessler's colleague, Dr. Ambrose saying he had recommended Botana for some possible research help on a project, and asked her to call back when she had a chance. Cameron hoped she hadn't taken a post-schoolyear vacation and was sitting on a beach halfway around the world.

Then, with nothing better to do, Cameron and Mitch headed down to the pool and relaxed in the shade of the palms. The air was clear and less sticky after the rain, and with balmy ocean breezes floating onshore, it was a perfect, lazy afternoon. Eventually, Mitch went to get them drinks, and as he was returning, Cameron's burner buzzed. She looked at it for a moment until she recognized Dr. Botana's number, then quickly accepted the call.

"Cameron Leigh."

"Ms. Leigh, this is Dr. Isabelle Botana returning your call."

Her voice contained a trace of an accent, but was clear and crisp, as if she were standing next to Cameron.

"Thank you," Cameron said. "I hope I'm not disturbing your weekend."

"Not at all. I was doing some gardening, so I missed you earlier. I understand we have a mutual friend?"

"A friend of a friend, actually," Cameron said, briefly explaining how Kessler had put her in touch with Botana via his colleague.

"How can I help you?" the doctor asked.

"I'm not sure exactly how much Dr. Ambrose told you, but my friend and I are working on a project and it relates to Spanish missions in Florida in the 1600s. Dr. Ambrose thought you might be able to help us."

"Perhaps. What would you like to know?"

Cameron bit her lip and looked at Mitch, who had returned carrying a pair of sweating glasses. He sat down as Cameron said, "It's rather confidential. I wonder if you might be available to meet with us in person."

She and Mitch had discussed how much to say over the phone, even burners, and decided for multiple reasons that a face-to-face might be best, even given the distance from Fort Lauderdale to Gainesville.

"I guess I don't see why not," Botana said. "I have a dinner engagement this evening, but I'm free tomorrow."

"That would be great, thank you."

"What time works for you?"

"Let me check," Cameron said, and lowered the phone. "How far to Gainesville?" she asked Mitch.

"About five hours."

"Early start tomorrow?"

He nodded.

Cameron raised the phone. "How about one o'clock?"

"That's fine."

"Where should we meet you?"

"I'd say my office, but it's under renovation this summer. How about Gator Corner, just southwest of the football stadium? They serve brunch until two on Sundays."

"Gator Corner at one," Cameron said. "We'll be there."

"Look for a Longhorns hat," Mitch said.

"My friend is a Texas alum," she said into the phone. "He'll make it easy to recognize him."

"All right. I'll see you tomorrow at one," Botana said.

Cameron ended the call and reported to Mitch. He tipped his head to the side, closing one eye. "I don't think we've ever played Florida in football."

She nodded at the glasses dripping condensation on his hands. "One of those for me?"

He handed her a piña colada. "So what's on tap for the evening?"

"I don't know," she said, then took a sip. "Something relaxing."

"Hmm."

She sat up. "If I was just a girl and you were just a guy and we weren't on a quest but just hanging out, what would you suggest?"

"The Fountain of Youth museum in St. Augustine."

"Ha, ha."

Mitch grinned. "Actually, I think I have the perfect idea."

*   *   *

"So how'd I do?" Mitch asked several hours later.

Cameron turned toward him, the ocean breeze lifting her hair off her shoulders. "Very well," she said, before licking her ice cream cone. She looked radiant, as she had all day, but more so the last couple hours. On a whim motivated by a billboard, Mitch had opted for an old-school date—dinner, a movie, and ice cream. They'd eaten at a steakhouse, seen a cheesy romantic comedy that didn't live up to the reviews, and headed for the Hollywood Beach Boardwalk.

"Can I ask you something?" he said as they strolled and licked their cones. The hubbub of the Boardwalk was oddly relaxing in its normalcy.

"Of course."

"What changed your mind?"

"About what?"

"Jesus, eternal life, the things Kessler talked about."

"John," she answered matter-of-factly.

"The Bible?"

She nodded.

"What in particular?"

"It wasn't one thing, it was . . . everything. John said that he had written about the things Jesus did so that his readers might believe he was the Son of God. And the more I read, the more it—I don't know how to say it other than it made sense. It wasn't just that it resonated with where I was and what I needed. But it made sense logically."

"Anything especially?"

She thought for a minute. "He talked about the world hating the disciples because they hated Him first, or about how rejecting Him was actually rejecting the Father. It was a constant theme, the unity of Jesus and the Father."

"Who's the Father?"

"God. It took me a minute the first time too." She took a bite of ice cream. "Another time, Jesus argued with the Jews. They kept claiming that they were descendants of Abraham, but He stated that they were hostile to Him and He had come from the Father—who they claimed was their Father and Abraham's Father—which proved they were actually not the ones with the close relationship to God they claimed."

Mitch hid a frown, wondering if Jesus had said it as confusingly as Cameron had resaid it. He moved on. "And you trust the Bible? I mean, it's awfully old. You yourself said the farther you go back in time, the less credible documents and witnesses become."

"Generally, that's true."

"But you still trust the Bible?"

She licked and nodded. "I do."

"Mind if I ask why?"

"For one, because I trust Dr. Kessler. But mostly because it . . ."

"Made sense?"

"Yes. There was something about the words Jesus said, about the way he stated things, that—I don't know—I can't put it into words. His words had authority," she said with a shrug.

Mitch nodded.

"You can borrow my copy, read it yourself."

He nodded again.

Cameron looked at him for a moment. "That not the answer you wanted?"

"No, it's not that."

"What is it?"

He looked down. Cameron placed a hand on his arm, and he raised his eyes to meet hers. He decided a little vulnerability might go a long ways.

"You remember that verse in the Castillo de San Marcos, the one above the Figueroa carving?"

"Not exactly."

"Neither do I, but it was something about man being appointed to die and face judgment. When Kessler mentioned deserved punishment and penalties for sins, it got me thinking. Then I practically broke into a cold sweat driving over the Skyway Bridge again the other day. It's weird, a strapping specimen

329

like myself," he said with a grin, "but I can't stop thinking about death and what's beyond. I've never given it much thought before, the whole heaven and hell thing. But lately I've been wondering, and I thought maybe that was what changed your mind too."

"It certainly factored in. And I also started thinking, if he's wrong in what he believes, there's no real harm done. But if someone who doesn't believe in hell or in Jesus is wrong . . ."

She let her statement hang in the air, and neither said anything else as they finished their ice cream and walked back to their car. On the drive back to the hotel, they discussed what time they would need to leave in the morning, where to get breakfast, and the possibilities that talking to Dr. Botana might bring. When they got back to the hotel, Cameron lingered outside her door.

"Thank you for a lovely evening, Mitch."

"I owed you at least that much."

"What a difference a day can make, huh?"

He smiled. "Yeah."

She opened her door, then held up a finger. He waited, and she returned carrying a small book. "The Gospel of John" was stamped on the front in gold letters. She extended it to him.

"Give it a read," she said with a shrug. "Maybe it will make sense to you too."

He looked down at it.

"You've got nothing to lose, do you?"

He took the book. "No, I guess not."

She smiled ever so sweetly at him. "Good night, Mitch."

"Good night, Cameron."

She smiled one more time, then eased the door shut behind her.

Mitch read through the book twice before going to bed.

CHAPTER FORTY-FIVE

Cameron felt like a new woman after a good night's rest—albeit too short of a night. She had been up a little after six so as to be ready to eat breakfast and leave Fort Lauderdale by seven-thirty. On a Sunday morning, traffic was fairly light, and in no time they had left behind the sprawl of the Greater Miami Area and were cruising north on I-95.

"You okay?" Mitch asked an hour into the trip. "You're quiet."

Cameron shrugged. "I don't know. I feel weird, almost like I should be in church today."

"I didn't even know which day it was."

"They do tend to run together, don't they?"

"Where would you find a church around here?"

"I'm sure they have churches in Florida."

"I mean, don't you need to find the right one? Right brand or whatever they call it—Baptist, Catholic, Methodist . . ."

"I don't know," she said, leaning back into her seat. "I don't know how any of this works."

Mitch nodded.

"How about you?" she asked, turning her head. "You've been quiet too."

"Didn't get much sleep," he said.

"No?"

"Stayed up reading."

"John?"

He nodded again.

"What'd you think?"

"I don't know. It's a lot to digest, to reorient myself to a new way of thinking on everything. I'm not sure I'm ready for that."

"Why not?" Cameron asked. "Do you not believe it's true?"

"I guess I do believe Jesus said what John said he said. But the whole concept of eternal life, heaven and hell, is foreign to me. I've always been more of a here and now sort of guy."

"I get that," she said. "Until you're not here and it isn't now anymore."

He looked at her but said nothing, and they continued driving, mostly in silence. They stopped in Kissimmee, outside Orlando, for gas and coffee, and found everything busy in the proximity of Disney World. Some clouds had begun to pop up, but the sky was still mostly blue and the air was absent the humidity of recent days. Cameron didn't mind the heat, but the drier air—even by Florida standards—was welcome.

"There's something else that's been on my mind," Mitch said as they resumed driving.

"What's that?"

"The theory goes that Figueroa found what he deemed to be the Fountain of Youth, and let's just assume there is some water somewhere that has some quality to make a reasonable person think that."

"Okay."

"And then instead of telling anybody where it is, he creates two cipher disks that have to be properly decoded so as to interpret a secret message in a stone he carved inside a fort on one side of Florida, after painting a somewhat abstract portrait of an Indian princess he seemingly fell for and also leaving some message behind on the bell tower of a Spanish mission. Is that about the size of it?"

Cameron nodded.

"Doesn't that seem a little far-fetched?"

"If I were reading it in a book, maybe. But you saw the disks, saw the carving, saw *Iśimi*."

"Yeah," he said without conviction.

"You wake up with a case of the doubts or something this morning?" she asked good-naturedly.

"Just trying to figure out why he went through all the trouble."

"He was a complicated guy."

"I guess."

They drove a few miles.

"So what's your plan, when we find it?" Mitch asked.

"My plan?"

"Say Dr. Botana can pinpoint the mission, we go there this afternoon, hold up the picture of *Iśimi* next to a carving or a painting in the bell tower, and it gives us GPS coordinates to a hidden spring. Then what?"

"I take a drink."

"Seriously?"

"Well, yeah. And some photos, collect some samples."

"That's where I'm getting at. You're not going to keep it to yourself, right?"

"No, of course not."

"Not going to create a series of secret coded messages for others to follow."

"No."

"Even assuming it's just you and me, not Van Buren and the Hogans and Olivia and Hall Parker Cook, this isn't something you can just splash on Instagram and be done with."

"No, I've thought about that. It's like any other discovery. You document what you found and how, and then let the right people come in and do what they do—whether it's archaeologists to further uncover everything or historians or, in this case, scientists."

"Lawyers?"

She shrugged.

"If you want the credit for finding it, you'd better have a good attorney at the top of your call list."

"I don't care so much about credit," Cameron said. "I want to find it for myself, for my own credit, if that makes sense, same as someone might climb a mountain or run a marathon."

"To know they did it."

"Yeah. And I wanted some of the water, or what's in it, if indeed it had some health benefits."

Mitch nodded.

"I have some ideas," she said. "We'll cross that bridge if we come to it."

"Fair enough."

"*Splash* on Instagram? Cute."

He winked.

They made Gainesville by twelve-thirty, and then took a few more minutes to find Ben Hill Griffin Stadium, the home of the Florida Gators football team. As they drove past its brick-sided façade, Mitch informed her that a previous coach had nicknamed it "The Swamp," back in the '90s when it was one of the most formidable places to play in all of college football. As far as Cameron knew, Clemson had never played Florida in football either, and all she knew about the Gators was the name Tim Tebow. She doubted that was relevant to finding *Misión San Francisco de Sevilla*.

Gator Corner was located at the intersection of Gale Lemerand Drive and Stadium Road, immediately across from the football stadium and just south of another arena that Cameron figured was for basketball. True to his word, Mitch had worn his old Longhorns baseball cap, which was likely why a woman in a bright orange T-shirt approached them as they neared the front steps.

She was short, dark-skinned, with long black hair tinged with brown highlights. It was partially clipped back, the rest falling in curls around her shoulders, framing a giant alligator head on her chest. Cameron recognized it as the University of Florida logo. She wore white Bermuda shorts and tennis shoes with blue in them to accent the blue in the logo.

"Cameron?" she asked, extending a hand.

"Yes, you're Dr. Botana?"

"Please, call me Isabelle."

"Mitch," he said, extending a hand as well.

"Forgive the excessive school spirit, but I was asked last minute to conduct a brief tour this morning. Prospective students."

"No problem," Cameron said. "Thanks again for meeting us."

"Are you hungry?" Botana asked. "The food here is quite good."

"Starved," Mitch said, and they headed inside. Gator Corner had not only a wealth of fast food menu options, but also its own dining center. The brunch buffet was more than sufficient, and the trio sat at a table by the window with plates piled high.

"How can I help you?" Botana asked. She had propped sunglasses up into her hair, and regarded the duo with sober brown eyes.

"We're looking for a seventeenth-century Spanish mission," Cameron said. "*Misión San Francisco de Sevilla*."

"Here in Florida?"

"We believe so."

"Most of the Spanish missions had been destroyed or had fallen into neglect and disrepair by the end of the seventeenth century. Quite a bit before that, in fact. Many of them dated to the sixteenth century, which is a long time before the more well-known West Coast missions. Those in Florida were far more primitive, and unsuitable to stand the test of time." She took a drink of juice. "All that said, there were and still are a few surviving missions in the state. None of them, however, that I know of, were named Seville or *Sevilla*."

Cameron tried to hide her disappointment.

"May I ask why you're seeking this mission?"

"It's a rather long story," she answered.

"It is all you can eat," Botana said with a smile.

It was disarming, and despite the fact that Cameron feared this was another dead end, she briefly explained her years-long quest to find the Fountain of Youth, from her research that suggested Diego Figueroa had indeed found *something* he believed to be the fabled fountain to her and Mitch's recent expedition across Florida and the clues it had uncovered.

"All that brings us here," she said, "because until we find this mission, we are pretty much at the end of the string."

"You have certainly logged a lot of miles. You must be very passionate about this."

"I know most people laugh when they hear about the Fountain of Youth, think it's some fairy tale or whim. And I don't buy into all the legend, but I do think there is a fountain somewhere that has some life-enriching elements in its water. Even if it is just the purest most refreshing freshwater spring, Figueroa believed it to be more, and I want to solve the mystery."

"We've come this far," Mitch said. "It'd be a shame to fall short now."

Botana slowly swallowed a bite of pancake, almost as if debating internally. She took a drink, then said, "I should tell you two things."

Cameron nodded.

"First," she said with a glance at Mitch, "my brother-in-law is a student at Texas A&M."

"I won't hold it against him," Mitch said with a smirk. "Not everybody can get into UT."

Botana flashed a good-natured smile. "Second, I think we should take a walk, see some of the campus."

"Okay," Cameron said with a shrug. They finished eating, and with full stomachs, exited into the midday sun. They headed east, along Stadium Road. "The Swamp" was on their left, and a large brick building beyond a variety of trees on their right.

"I had a visitor last night," Botana said. "He was waiting on my front porch when I returned from dinner. He asked me if I knew where to find *Misión San Francisco de Sevilla*. I told him I had never heard of such a place and gave a brief overview of Spanish missions in Florida, similar to what I told you inside. I didn't tell him anything else."

"Why not?" Mitch asked.

"He was very friendly, but the way an, well, an alligator's smile might be friendly. Something made me not trust him, especially in light of our conversation on the phone yesterday."

"Do you trust us?" Cameron said.

"I do. And I called Drs. Ambrose and Kessler this morning, and Kessler assured me you could be trusted."

"Must be raining in Naples," Mitch said.

Botana frowned.

"Never mind, sorry."

She continued. "Which is why I'm going to tell you what I know." They had veered off Stadium Road and down a diagonal path leading between buildings. "In the mid to late 1600s, there was a legendary Spanish missionary in Central Florida. By this time, the Spanish had largely ceased their conversion efforts in Florida, due to an influx of European diseases and attacks by the English, primarily under Colonel James Moore in the early 1700s. But this missionary was not so easily intimidated. He was known as a fearless man of God, and many came to believe that he was divinely protected by God. In 1691, he commissioned the building of a new mission, in an effort to revitalize the Spanish efforts to share the gospel with the native people. He died just a year after it was completed, and his brother took over for him. But he lacked the same fervor, or, if you believe some, he lacked God's protection. He was killed around the turn of the century, and the mission was abandoned. It survived Moore's attacks and even the Seminole Wars. It was used as a hospital, an armory, and a prison, and stood until the late 1800s when, having largely crumbled and eroded, it was taken down."

"What was it called?" Cameron asked.

"It was named for the missionary, San Francisco de León—Francisco the Lion—so named because of his fearless faith."

"Not Seville?"

"No, at least, not that I know of. But de León didn't become widely known or popular until after his death, and so it is possible that the mission originally was known by another name."

"Any idea where de León came from?" Mitch asked.

"Like Seville?" Botana asked.

"For example."

She shook her head. "I don't know. I haven't delved thoroughly into his background, but what I know doesn't include much before his arrival in Florida in the 1670s." Botana shrugged. "Whether he or the mission are what you're looking for, I don't know. But they are the closest thing I know of to what you're asking."

"What can you tell us about the mission?" Cameron asked.

"What do you want to know specifically?"

"Did it have a bell tower?"

They had reached an open common area, and Botana motioned toward a bench. The trio sat down. "Yes, it did. How did you know?"

"The carving I mentioned said to 'reunify Iśimi with me in the bell tower of *Misión San Francisco de Sevilla.*'"

"Yes, it had a bell tower."

"Do you have any idea what the phrase 'with me' could mean?" Mitch asked.

"Keep in mind it was Diego Figueroa who carved the phrase," Cameron said.

"I do not know," Botana said. "But," she added quickly, sensing Cameron's disappointment, "that doesn't mean this is another dead end."

"No?"

"I told you the mission was taken down in the late 1800s, but remnants of it were preserved."

"Where?" Mitch asked.

"Originally, near modern-day Palatka, a small town east of here, near a bend in the St. Johns River. But there is nothing at that site anymore. The remnants of the mission that were preserved were, as I understand it, kept in various locations over the years, until they were brought together and put on permanent display at a church in 1960 in the then fledgling city of Orlando."

"Orlando," Cameron said. "Why Orlando?"

Botana shook her head. "I don't know."

"Do you know the name of the church?"

"Not Our Lady of Milk, is it?" Mitch asked.

Botana gave him an odd look.

"Ignore him, please," Cameron said. "He's from Texas."

As if that explained everything, Botana continued. "Church of the Redeemer. I don't know much more than that, other than it is in Orlando."

"Is there anything else you can think of that might be relevant?" Cameron asked.

Botana opened her palms. "You know all I know."

They walked back through the campus, grateful for the shade of several cumulous clouds. When they returned to Gator Corner, Botana regarded the sky. "I hope the rain holds off."

"Another tour?" Mitch asked.

"More gardening. There is always something that needs doing in a garden."

"Thank you very much for your time," Cameron said. "You've been a big help to us."

"I hope you find what you are looking for. If you need anything else, you have my number."

"One more thing," Mitch said as she turned to go.

"Yes?"

"This man who came to see you last night. What did he look like?"

"He was tall, probably a little taller than you. African-American, bald, like I said earlier, an alligator grin framed by a black goatee."

"Thanks," Mitch said.

Cameron contained herself until they were back in the Accord. "Mitch, Dr. Botana's visitor sounds exactly like the guy who met me by the pool the other night."

CHAPTER FORTY-SIX

The Orlando Church of the Redeemer was nestled on a piece of perfectly manicured lawn that appeared carved out of the hustle and bustle of Orlando. In addition to a small flower garden, the two-acre lot was covered with palm trees that insulated it from the city. So did gnarled oak trees, heavily cloaked in Spanish moss, that lined the cobblestone street leading to the church's driveway. Beautiful, they were also a little ominous in the darkness.

It had taken a long time for Mitch and Cameron to journey the hundred-plus miles from Gainesville to Orlando. Shortly after getting back on the interstate, the heavens had opened in a deluge. A result of that or not, traffic had been backed up for miles due to an accident that blocked multiple lanes of traffic. When it had finally cleared, the sun was back out, and the duo stopped for fresh peaches and tea at a roadside stand, and consumed both while pondering Botana's words and their implications. She hadn't specifically said that whatever clue Figueroa had left in the bell tower of *Misión San Francisco de Sevilla* had been preserved in the Church of the Redeemer, but it was worth checking out. To that end, they did some research on their phones and eventually found a contact number for the church's caretaker. He hadn't answered Cameron's call.

They had also speculated as to who Botana's visitor had been, if he had indeed been the same person to interrupt Cameron's swim at the hotel in Fort Myers, and how he had found her and them. Presumably, he was working for Van Buren, who had somehow interpreted the carving and known to find the mission. Perhaps Erik had been compromised again, or further. Cameron wanted to call him, to check in on him, but Mitch advocated for radio silence. As far as they knew, nobody else knew where they were or what they had learned, and it was best it stay that way.

They'd arrived in Orlando, found and driven past the church, then selected a place for dinner. After a lighter fare of fish tacos, they'd called the caretaker again, a man by the name of Edward Pickett, and he'd answered this time. Cameron had explained they were interested in the history of the old church and wondered when it might be possible for them to look around. The caretaker said he would be working that evening and suggested they stop by. So, after getting settled at a local hotel, they'd driven back to the church.

Done in the Spanish Colonial style, fittingly enough, its white walls were bathed in soft floodlights that only deepened the shadows of the oaks and palms around the lot. A short, circular driveway led under a carport and opened to parking spaces off to the side. Mitch parked next to an old Schwinn bicycle and they got out. Clouding skies had made for a remarkable sunset as the pink and orange light reflected off the clouds and colored the entire sky in a breathtaking panorama. The same cloud cover now bounced back the ambient light of downtown, which seemed to sparkle in the mist. Everything about the place seemed just a little eerie.

Mitch and Cameron approached the church. It was laid out in the shape of a cross, with the top of the cross being the carport. The arms were short and stubby, surrounded by ferns and palms and beautiful flowers. A bell tower stood thirty-five or forty feet over the ground, the brass bell visible in the open air. In front of the carport, in a small grassy circle inside the driveway, was a Madonna with a small fountain, lined with bricks. Hundreds of coins paved the bottom of the fountain, and Mitch wondered if they were there because kids liked to throw money into fountains or because heaving pocket change into the water somehow fit in with Catholicism.

Mitch rapped a brass knocker mounted on one of two oak doors (what kind of church had a knocker?) and, a moment later, they began to creak and groan as they were swung inward by a man in his sixties or seventies. He wore brown loafers, black socks, shorts that covered his knees, and a collared shirt one size too big. His white hair was combed across his head, and was almost as bright as a toothy smile he flashed.

"Are you Edward Pickett?" Cameron asked when doors had stopped complaining and the echo had died away.

"Yes. Are you the young lady I spoke to on the phone?"

"I am. I'm Cameron Leigh, and this is Mitch Owens."

"A pleasure to meet you both," he said, offering an arthritic hand. Mitch shook it gently, then followed as the man invited them inside. A small foyer was bisected by a hallway running right and left, into the arms of the cross. Dual doors like those on the front of the building were propped open to allow entry to a narrow sanctuary with wooden pews and a crucifix above the altar. It was lit with flickering candles, as was the foyer. On closer inspection, they were fake.

"I've been going through some of our old records, down in the basement," Pickett said. "Keeps my mind sharp," he added with a grin.

"What sort of records?" Cameron asked.

"Oh, church membership, births and baptisms and confirmations and marriages. Sadly, divorces and deaths too. But that's not a concern for young folks like you. What brings you to the Church of the Redeemer?"

"We understand that parts of the Francisco de León Mission are preserved here," Cameron said. "Particularly a mural? We'd like to see it, if possible."

"Ah," the old man said with a twinkle in his eye, "Francisco the Lion. A great man of God."

"You know of him?" Mitch asked.

"A little."

"Do you know where he was from?"

"Spain, originally."

"Seville?"

"Possibly. I don't know. Come, the objects you seek are in the bell tower."

He shuffled across the stone floor and opened a door near the front door. Mitch had assumed it was a coat closet or fake candle storage, but it actually led to a wrought-iron spiral staircase. Pickett flipped a switch and several bare lightbulbs came on to dimly illuminate the way. "Pardon the pace of an old man."

"We're in no hurry," Cameron said.

"Why were parts of the old mission brought here?" Mitch asked from the rear as they climbed.

"That depends," Pickette called back.

"On?"

"Whether you believe in the Providence of the Almighty or the whim of man." He climbed a few steps, the metal stairs clanking under his weight. "One of the founding members of the church was also part of the architectural firm that designed it, and claimed that he could trace his lineage back through the centuries, through several countries, to Francisco the Lion. When he

341

learned that a remnant of the original bell tower from the mission was still in existence, he incorporated it into the design of our bell tower. He arranged to have it transported here, restored, and built into the church."

They emerged at a wooden platform at the top of the tower. The bell hung over their heads, with windows on each side of the bell tower letting in air and, in the daytime, light. Now, it was provided by more fake candles mounted in sconces in the four corners. They even flickered, like real candles, adding to the aura as they shone on four murals, one on each wall.

"Three of the murals were designed and painted by local artists," Pickett said, "each depicting a 'hero' of the faith. Saint Francis of Assisi, Saint Augustine, Saint Thomas Aquinas." He turned toward the east wall. "And this is from the bell tower in San Francisco de León Mission."

Mitch and Cameron turned to face the mural. It covered almost the entire wall beneath the window, and the patchwork was such that Mitch could hardly see where the original slab ended and the new construction began. The mural itself, although faded in places, was evident even in the dim light. It showed a man, dressed not unlike those in the Conquistador drawings Mitch had seen (albeit without the morion Conquistador helmet), stepping across a crescent-shaped river. His front foot was lifted, as if to climb a step, only there was no stairway, but rather several tufts of cloud. His arm was stretched out, striving for something, perhaps the rising or setting sun that peeked through the clouds at the right edge of the mural. His other hand was empty, and trailing behind him were three items. Mitch took a step closer and bent down to examine them. A sword was obvious. A small brown bag was partially untied, revealing the tops of coins. The third item appeared to be a loaf of bread.

Mitch stood up and back, and looked at Cameron. Her eyes went back and forth as she absorbed the painting. Mitch turned to Pickett. "Any idea what we're looking at?"

"The theories are endless. No one knows."

"It has similarities to *Iśimi*," Mitch said. "Walking over water, outstretched hands, the sun."

"He's not dressed in a waterfall, though," Cameron said.

"Few men are."

She turned his way with a small grin. "Do you have the picture on your phone?"

He had sent the image from his e-mail account and saved it on his burner, and now called it up. He handed the phone to Cameron, and she compared them side by side. "She's beckoning him," she said. "He's following."

342

"Where?"

"Toward the rising sun or the setting sun."

"Either one of those mean anything, religiously?"

"I don't know."

"Christ is said to have arisen early in the morning," Pickett said. "And some believe He will return again at dawn."

"Eternity," Cameron said. "Eternal life."

"Is that why he's stepping into the cloud?" Mitch asked.

"I hadn't noticed that. Maybe."

"What's with the sword and bread and moneybag?"

"I don't know," she said, stepping over to look at them. "Maybe . . . he's leaving behind the trappings of life. Wealth, sustenance."

"He wasn't a warrior, was he? Figueroa, I mean. That is him we're looking at, isn't it?"

"I presume so."

"That's the belief," Pickett said, "that this was a self-portrait."

"He wasn't a warrior," Cameron said, "but the Spanish government at the time was consumed with conquest. Maybe it symbolizes that."

"Good a theory as any."

"'To find the Fountain of Youth reunify *Iśimi* with me in the bell tower of Mission San Francisco of Seville,'" she quoted. "How does this help us find it?"

"Is she the fountain?" Mitch asked. "Clothed in a waterfall."

"You mean the whole thing is symbolic?"

He shrugged.

"Then what would we need to find?"

"I don't know. His grave?"

"To what end?"

"I don't—"

"What?" Cameron asked.

Mitch ignored her and instead climbed a small wooden platform in one corner. It put him just within reach of the rope used to ring the bell, but also able, if he stretched, of looking out the window. A black SUV was parked beside their Accord, and four figures stood beside it. They were all dressed in black, head to toe. As they quickly approached the carport, he saw a streak of red hair following one of them.

"Bad news," he said. "We've got company!"

CHAPTER FORTY-SEVEN

"What is it?" Cameron asked.

"Hogans," Mitch said, then turned to Pickett. "Is there another way out of this church?"

"Fire exits in the sanctuary."

"Come on, we need to get out of here," Mitch said, reaching for her arm.

"Wait," she said. She pulled her phone out of her purse.

"Cameron, we don't have time."

As if to answer him, the heavy oak doors below them swung open on creaking hinges. Cameron hastily snapped shots of the mural and pocketed her phone. She looked to Mitch as the gravity of the situation hit her fully.

"There is an access door to the roof," Pickett said, his eyes wide. He too must have picked up on the intensity on Mitch's face and in his words.

"The roof?" Cameron asked.

"There's a maintenance walkway along the peak."

"The roof must be fifteen feet high at the eaves," Mitch said.

"In the southwest corner there's an old oak tree that overhangs the roof. You could climb down on it."

Mitch looked to Cameron.

"Sounds dangerous," she said.

Footsteps from below indicated the people Mitch had spotted were spreading out through the church. Maybe they could sneak down the stairs behind them and get out to their car. Then a second, much softer creak sounded. The door to the bell tower opening.

"It's our only way," Mitch said.

"Quickly," Pickett said, "it is on the half landing below us a dozen steps. The door is unlocked. Go."

"What about you?" Cameron said.

"I belong here. I will stall them."

"Thank you," she said, placing a hand on his arm and smiling. Then Mitch tugged her toward the stairs.

They descended as quietly as possible on the metal rungs, all while hearing footsteps coming up. Halfway around the circle, the stairs paused for several feet, creating a landing in front of a metallic fire door. Mitch turned the brass handle and it opened outward noiselessly, but immediately let in a breath of air. Mitch again led the way, stepping out first.

In keeping with the Spanish Colonial theme, the roof of the church was made of orange clay-tile shingles. At the peak, a corrugated metal walkway no more than eighteen inches wide ran from one end of the building to the other, stopping where the back wall of the sanctuary extended several feet higher than the roofline. The walkway had no railings, and flexed slightly as Mitch took the first few tentative steps. Far from sturdy, Cameron wondered how old it was and how often it was actually used for any maintenance, and whether it was ever meant to support two people at once. But as Mitch had said, it was their only way.

She closed the door behind them, wishing it would lock from the outside.

"Here," Mitch said, stepping back beside her. He quickly yanked his belt from his pant loops. He wrapped one end around the door handle and the other around the base of a light fixture beside the door. He was just able to fit the buckle's prong through the hole and latch it. It wouldn't hold anyone for long, but would hopefully give them time to make the shelter of the oak tree before someone burst through the door.

"Come on," he said again, then led the way along the catwalk. Mist had given way to rain, just a light, warm shower, but it made the metal surface even more tenuous—not to mention the clay shingles should they misstep. Cameron diverted her eyes for a moment and saw the oak tree Pickett had mentioned. It was huge, twice as tall as the roof and as wide as tall, a stately old tree draped with grayish green Spanish moss. Several branches hung over the roof, and looked sturdy enough to support their weight. If they could get there.

Mitch stopped three-quarters of the way to the end of the church. He turned and faced the oak, some twenty-five feet away and ten feet beneath them. Mitch looked down at his tennis shoes and at Cameron's flip-flops. "I'll go first. If I fall, turn back and negotiate surrender."

"Mitch."

He winked. "Wait till I'm ready, then I can catch you."

She nodded and watched as he began carefully descending, sidestepping toward the nearest branch of the oak. Cameron had seen some movie—she couldn't remember which—where someone had been climbing on a clay-tile roof and the tiles had kept giving way and slipping out from under the person. That didn't happen with Mitch, and his athletic ability and background served him well as he reached the safety of the tree. He took a moment to anchor himself, one arm around a stout branch and the other extended, ready to catch Cameron.

She reached down and took off her flip-flops, then extended one foot off the walkway. She stopped and nearly lost her balance when the fire door they had exited through shook and opened partway, catching on Mitch's belt.

"Slide," Mitch said. "I'll catch you."

"What?"

He waved his free hand slightly. "I got you."

She looked back at the door, then took a deep breath, and launched herself toward Mitch. Her Bermuda shorts protected her backside as she slid and bounced on the shingles, unable to keep a scream from exploding out of her mouth. She felt herself skidding to the side and tried to right herself, which only caused her to spin the other way and fall back onto her back. She just avoided banging her head, then looked up to see she was about to plummet over the side of the church.

Instead, Mitch's arm slammed into her chest and hooked under her armpit. He growled with the sudden strain, but managed to haul her toward himself and away from the edge. Like a drowning swimmer reaching driftwood, Cameron floundered for the branch and held on. She'd dropped one flip-flop, and now threw the other down toward the ground. Mitch was already backing onto the branch on all fours. Although it creaked once, it held with conviction. Cameron summoned her courage and turned to follow.

The branch was thick, almost a foot in diameter, but rounded and slick from the rain. It also had dozens of smaller branches and twice as many sticks and twigs, every one of which seemed to find a place to poke her. But she managed to keep her balance and follow Mitch until he backed into the main trunk of the tree. He took a moment to find footholds, and helped guide Cameron to a spot about eight feet above ground.

"Wait there," he said, just as a clang from the roof suggested the belt had given way and the door had slammed open. Cameron didn't look.

Mitch slipped and slid the last several feet to the ground, then extended his arms under her. "Okay, drop. I got you again."

She didn't hesitate this time, and Mitch's strong arms caught her easily. No screaming this time, either.

He set her on her feet and looked her in the eye. "You okay?"

She nodded.

"Let's go."

Forsaking her flip-flops, one of which she'd lost track of anyhow, she followed Mitch through the grass around one of the arms of the cross-shaped church. He peeked around the corner toward the parking lot. He turned back.

"What is it?"

"They've got someone by the car."

"Now what?"

Mitch turned around and looked toward the roof. She followed his gaze to see two silhouettes on the catwalk. Before she pulled her eyes away, Mitch took her arm. "Come on."

She again ran after him, away from the church and through a small grove of palm trees off to the side of the property. Beyond them was a low row of ferns and lilies, and then an eight-foot-high hedgerow. Mitch pushed through it and extended a hand back for Cameron. She climbed/was pulled through the hedges, suffering more scrapes and scratches. But they emerged on a sidewalk beside a four-lane city street. On the other side of it was a spacious park surrounding a circular lake, one of hundreds like it in Orlando. Beyond that was the downtown skyline, aglow in the rainy night sky.

Mitch paused just a moment looking both directions, then motioned for Cameron to follow him to the right. They jogged along the sidewalk, her barefoot, as a dozen cars released from a nearby stoplight whooshed past. At the next corner, they crossed the street and jogged for a block past an apartment building, a clinic, and a small insurance office. Then they crossed the four-lane street and went a block west before crossing the side street and venturing down a curving cobblestone street that wound around another small lake. The other side of the street was lined with a canopy of oak trees, all adorned with Spanish moss. Cobblestone driveways led to gated brick and adobe houses set back amidst their own canopies. The mist obscured the glow of a few streetlights, and the trees blocked any ambient light from downtown. Cameron wasn't sure if the darkness was comforting or scary.

After a couple of turns that took them deeper into the neighborhood and had her thoroughly lost, Mitch stopped. Cameron was breathing heavy, but he seemed ready to keep going.

"Mitch . . . what's our end game?"

"Live happily ever after."

She raised an eyebrow.

"Our short game is stay alive long enough to do that."

"You think they followed us?"

"No."

"So where do we go?"

"Let's keep walking," he said, and they did, turning onto another street around yet another lake, this one with a sidewalk meandering beside it, through a strand of palm trees. Several ornate, post-lantern streetlamps were spaced every hundred feet or so, and the duo could have passed for neighborhood folks out for a walk—were Cameron not barefoot, her shorts not a dirty brownish orange in the back, and the bottom hem of her shirt not torn in at least one place. And were it not still raining.

"Did your phone survive?" he asked.

She pulled it out of her pocket and brought it out of standby. "Yeah," she said, the glow of the screen revealing no cracks.

"Find us a hotel somewhere."

"We have a hotel."

"I'm afraid it might be compromised. I'll buy."

"Okay."

"And I'll get us a ride," he said, thumbing on his phone.

"All our stuff is back in the car."

"Find a hotel by a CVS."

Half an hour later, and thanks to a Chinese Uber driver who spoke hardly any English, the duo had checked into a Courtyard by Marriott. Given the circumstances, they had reserved only one room, and no sooner had they secured themselves in it than Mitch said he was headed back out.

"What?"

"I'm going to take a cab back to the church, check on Pickett and see if the Hogans are gone. If so, I'll drive our car back."

"And if not?"

"Have the cabby keep driving."

"I don't like it."

348

"I'm sure they're gone. The last thing they'll want to do is hang around there knowing we got away."

She sighed.

"You all right? You look a little the worse for wear."

Cameron paced to a mirror outside the bathroom. "Wow." He hair was a rat's nest, complete with a few sticks and twigs. She had numerous red lines on her arms and legs, and her clothes looked like they'd come off a homeless person. Add to that she was pretty sure her sternum and under arm were bruised from Mitch's hook-like grab as she'd been flying off the roof.

She turned back to him. "The good news is I don't feel any worse than I look."

"Take what you can get," he said. "I'll call you when I leave the church one way or the other."

Cameron nodded, then locked the door behind him. With a deep sigh, she collapsed backward onto one of two queen beds, now feeling the soreness and the pain of the evening's exertion. She wanted a hot shower, but not without something clean and comfy to change into. So she lay and stared at the ceiling, her mind racing with a hundred thoughts. How had the Hogans found them? What would stop them from finding them again? What had Diego Figueroa intended for those who deciphered his message to do, having reunified *Iśimi* with the mural in the bell tower? And what would happen if she and Mitch shared a hotel room for the evening, especially after all their adventures and the bond that was redeveloping between them?

Cameron didn't know all the ins and outs, but she was pretty sure traditional Christian teaching—which as a follower of Jesus she now felt obliged to learn and follow herself—wasn't too keen on sex outside of marriage. Not that she was anticipating her and Mitch doing anything of that nature. But they'd already come close a few times, and after the day they'd been through, sharing a room . . .

She decided not to focus on it and instead retrieved her phone. She accessed the pictures she'd hastily taken in the bell tower. She'd snapped three of them, and none were exceptionally clear in the low light, but they captured the particulars. A man, presumably Figueroa himself, stepping over a river and onto a cloud, while reaching outward with one hand and dropping a sword, a loaf of bread, and a bag of money with the other. Then she accessed a picture, sent from Mitch's phone, of *Iśimi*, depicting a woman clothed in a waterfall, reaching behind her as she walked on a pair of islands. Both were taking place at sunrise or sunset, most likely the former, signifying resurrection or eternal life. The symbolism wasn't hard to figure, but a location of the Fountain of Youth based upon it was.

Cameron got up and paced, studying the painting and the mural, trying to think outside the box. She remembered the translated message from the carving, to reunify *Iŝimi* with Figueroa, meaning the two had to go together. The outstretched hands of both, her beckoning him to follow, toward the sun. Was she the fountain, or had she passed through the fountain, as in had gained eternal life? And now he was leaving behind the trappings of this life—wealth, sustenance, his affiliation with the Spanish government—to follow her.

But where?

To the east. But east of where?

Islands . . . A bend in the river . . .

Cameron stopped. She remembered something Botana had said, and suddenly it all made sense. Hypothetical sense, but sense nonetheless.

She startled as her phone vibrated. She looked down to see Mitch's number, and quickly swiped the screen to answer it. "Mitch, I think I figured it out!"

"Cameron, we've got a problem."

CHAPTER FORTY-EIGHT

The church parking lot contained one Schwinn bicycle and one rented Honda Accord when Mitch's taxi turned down the cobblestone drive. The rain had stopped, but the stones were still wet. Mitch paid in cash, then approached the front door of the church. He knocked several times, and when no one answered, he pushed his way in.

"Mr. Pickett?"

No answer.

Mitch closed the heavy, squeaking door behind him and walked into the middle of the foyer. The church was empty, lit by the flickering faux candles. He stood and listened for a minute, also looking for any signs that anything was off. Nothing was.

"Mr. Pickett?"

Again no answer.

He decided to climb the bell tower, to where he and Cameron had left the old man. Halfway up, he heard a groan, and doubled his pace. When he reached the top landing, he saw Pickett slumped in one corner. His white hair was askew and stained with blood, the result of a large gash running from his forehead to the part at the back of his head. It had dripped all down the side of his head and onto his shoulder. His face was bruised and one eye swollen.

Mitch swore under his breath, then hurried over to the fallen man. "Mr. Pickett," he said, gently touching his non-bloody shoulder. The man stirred but didn't regain consciousness.

Mitch swore again as he stood, reached for his phone, then dialed 9-1-1. He spent several minutes with the dispatcher, then checked Pickett's vitals. He tended to the old man until the medics arrived, then stepped back and let them take care of things. He descended to the foyer and outside, then called Cameron.

"Mitch, I think I figured it out!"

"Cameron, we've got a problem."

"What?" she asked.

"They brained Pickett."

"What?"

"He's got a huge gash on his head, unconscious. Looks like they roughed him up a little too."

"Oh no!"

"Not sure if they beat out of him where we'd gone or punished him for helping us. I'll tell you this, next time I see them, I'm not running the other direction."

"Mitch."

"Look, the cops are here," he said, seeing the blue and red lights reflecting off the mossy oaks. "I'll tell them what happened, then drive back."

"Okay, be careful."

"I will," he said, then ended the call before asking what she had figured out. He spent half an hour talking to the police, explaining in as vague of terms as possible what he and Cameron had been doing at the church, how they had left Pickett via the roof, and that they were staying at a nearby hotel. The cops didn't seem suspicious and, after taking a thorough statement, moved into the church to investigate. By then, the paramedics had left with Pickett, who had regained consciousness. Mitch hoped there was no permanent damage, and couldn't help feeling somewhat responsible.

After being cleared by the cops, he walked back to the car and spent several minutes carefully surveying it, even getting on his hands and knees. He was rewarded when, under the inside of the rear bumper, he found a small black box with a stubby antenna and a blinking green light. It had been a little while since he'd been up on such things, but it looked like a state-of-the-art tracking device.

He didn't touch it, instead going back inside to get the police. They removed it, bagged it as evidence, and asked a few more questions about the Hogans. Mitch wasn't sure if anything would come of their having the device, but it beat having it attached to his bumper.

Almost an hour after leaving the hotel, he got into the car and headed back, taking a few misleading turns and side streets to throw off anyone who might be observing and to check for a tail. He saw no signs of either.

"I was starting to get worried," Cameron said when she unbolted the door for him.

"I found a tracking device under the bumper."

"So that's how they found us."

He nodded.

"But when did they plant it?"

"I don't know. Maybe they staked out Botana and saw us talking to her, since your bald friend didn't get anywhere with her. Or maybe they found us somewhere else. Who knows."

"Do you think we're safe here?" she asked.

"Yeah, we should be."

"Then I'm going to take a shower, now that I have clean clothes," she said, nodding at her suitcase that Mitch had brought in.

"You hungry?"

"A little, actually."

"There's a diner a little ways down. I'll go get a couple of slices of pie to go."

"Sounds good."

"Want a particular flavor?"

"Whatever."

He set out on foot, enjoying the cool but humid post-rain air. He felt a smoldering anger at what had happened to Pickett. In his mind, a line had been crossed. It was one thing for the Van Buren Gang to come after him and Cameron with any sort of violence. It was unacceptable, but it was understandable. But there had been no need to do what they'd done to Pickett, and Mitch was boiling. He tried to shake it off by breathing in deeply and thinking about pie, but it only mitigated the feeling a little.

He also was a little unnerved by the fact that things had escalated to this extent again. He wondered how this would all play out. The closer he and Cameron got to the Fountain of Youth, the more they seemed to cross paths with sketchy characters, as if all of them were being drawn inexorably toward a joint conclusion. Was there any way to avoid it, to avoid the violence and mayhem?

Fortunately, he reached the diner and had to contemplate which of a dozen types of pie Cameron would want. They'd had Key lime pie in Clearwater and peach pie at Dr. Kessler's house, so he choose French silk, figuring chocolate was a comfort food, and Cameron would be wanting comfort.

She was finishing drying her hair when Mitch returned. She had changed into jeans and the purple Clemson shirt she'd worn eons ago, back when they'd escaped from St. Augustine. He kicked the door shut behind him and held up two clear plastic containers. "Chocolate silk," he said.

"You mean French silk?"

"Whatever."

"Sounds delicious."

He set them down, then bolted the door. He turned back toward her. "Now, you said something about having stuff figured out?"

"Yes," she said, casting aside her towel. She walked over to take one piece of pie from Mitch, along with a plastic fork, then climbed onto the end of one of the two beds and crossed her legs under her. She waited until Mitch had pulled an office chair from by the desk, sat back, and propped his shoes on the other bed. "You're sleeping in that bed, by the way," she said.

"Fine. What'd you figure out?"

"Remember what Dr. Botana said about the San Francisco de León Mission, that it was by a bend in the St. Johns River?"

He nodded and took the first bite of pie.

Cameron got up to grab her phone, swipe to a picture, and hand it to Mitch. She stood beside him. "Look, there's Diego stepping over a bend in a river."

"Okay."

"He's reaching out for something, and in the painting, *Iśimi* is reaching back to him as she stands on a pair of islands in the middle of the water."

"Okay."

"Figueroa is leaving behind earthly pursuits and reaching for his love, clad in a waterfall, symbolic of the Fountain of Youth—"

"Which is located by two islands on a river."

Cameron nodded.

"Either east or west of the bend in the river," he said.

"I'm thinking east, based on what Pickett said about the resurrection and belief that Jesus will return someday at dawn."

"Have you checked a map?"

"No."

He took another bite of pie, then set it aside and drew out his phone. It only took a moment to call up a map of the Palatka region of northern Florida, some thirty miles east of Gainesville. The city was on the western banks of the

St. Johns River, which snaked back and forth, flowing from south to north toward Jacksonville. Two bends stood out prominently, one shaped like a slightly tipped over C, north of the city. The other, where the river was narrower to the south, was like a backward C. And upon closer examination, there was a third horseshoe bend in the middle, smaller and tighter.

"Which of these looks like the mural?" Mitch asked.

Cameron turned her phone to him. "If he's walking east," she said, "then it'd be . . . that one," she said, pointing to the lower bend, the inverted C.

"It is a pretty close match."

"Assuming the river hasn't changed course in three centuries."

"So now we need islands in a river east of here," Mitch said.

"Let's get out a computer and look at bigger screens."

Mitch nodded.

"I'll make some coffee," she said.

"I should have bought a whole pie."

*   *   *

Cameron and Mitch sat side by side on the same bed, a laptop in front of them. The laptop screen showed a segment of north central Florida from Palatka to the coast. As they finished their pie, they scanned the wooded terrain, looking for rivers or bodies of water that might contain islands. There weren't many.

The St. Johns River ran almost due north approximately fifteen miles inland from the coast until it reached Duval County, where it began its curve east toward the Atlantic. Between the river and the ocean there was very little water, other than the Intracoastal Waterway. The majority of the St. Johns' tributaries were farther south, closer to its headwaters. The water that did exist was mostly small little lakes and ponds or narrow rivers and creeks.

Painstakingly, they checked every one of them, considering the islands upon which *Isimi* trod might be little more than sandbars. After several promising possibilities failed to pan out, Cameron got up, taking their empty containers and forks to the garbage, then using the bathroom. When she returned, Mitch had zoomed in on a parcel of land several square miles across.

"Find something?" she asked.

"Look at this," he said, tracing the screen with his finger.

"What is it?"

"It's hard to tell from satellite," he said, then clicked to switch off the satellite view and add an enhanced terrain feature. It brought out the smallest ridges and valleys, and indicated the area he'd been tracing with his finger was a ridge running from southwest to northeast for several miles. It was jagged in places, especially at the bottom left, where it curved upward to look like a J.

"I was thinking more the Nike swoosh," Mitch said after Cameron voiced the thought.

"Okay. What's the significance?"

He tapped the screen where a very narrow thin blue line zigzagged away from the ridge. He scrolled on the map for several minutes until the thin body of water finally emptied into the St. Johns.

"Did you find any islands?"

"I can't even find a name for the creek."

She shook her head.

"As far as I can tell—and I've checked both the map and satellite—the river seems to start right at the ridge. As in, there's a waterfall or spring that is its source."

"You think it's the Fountain of Youth?"

"I think it's possible."

"Can we get a closer map?"

"I'll look."

"Want more coffee?"

"No."

Cameron again got up to top off her cup, then paced while Mitch checked the internet for different maps. After several minutes, he motioned for her to join him. He said he'd come up empty on finding anything better, but had zoomed in the satellite image as close as possible. It was grainy and indistinct, but he pointed at two darker spots in the river.

"I can't tell," he said, "but that doesn't look like shading in the water, not compared to other places in the river."

Cameron leaned in, tucking hair behind her ear and out of the way. "Islands?"

"Very small ones, but I think so."

"Mitch!"

"It's at least a possibility."

She leaned over and hugged him, then kissed the side of his head.

"It's just a possibility," he said, scrolling back out.

"But a good one. Islands in a river, next to a waterfall, east of the bend in the river."

"We don't know that it's a waterfall. I suspect it is."

"Wasn't there white by the islands, like foam or spray?"

Mitch zoomed back in.

"Wait!"

"What?"

"Zoom out again."

He slid the mouse over to Cameron. She zoomed out, then scrolled down. "Look," she said, revealing an area of the map she had glimpsed briefly when Mitch had zoomed out the first time.

"Espanola," he said. "That could be a coincidence."

"It could." She continued studying the map, and her eyes honed in on another name. "Mitch."

"What?"

She pointed. "Bimini."

"Remind me of the connection again."

Cameron stood. "Original Caribbean people referred to a place called *Beimini*, and it somehow became associated with the Fountain of Youth."

"In the Bahamas, right?"

"Yes, that's one theory, and it's where the Bimini in the Bahamas got its name. But what I just remembered is that the word Bimini, in its original language, means 'two islands.'"

"Are you sure?"

"Pretty sure. Look it up."

He did, confirming what she'd thought. He also researched Bimini, Florida, finding nothing more than a few blurbs about it being an unincorporated community. There was nothing about its origin or etymology. It could have been named hundreds of years after Bimini in the Bahamas, and have no connection to the river Mitch had spotted several miles north of it. But it was another coincidence, and they were starting to stack up.

"Okay," Cameron said, pacing again. "We've got a *possible* location. We could still have this wrong. Those may not be islands, they may not be the right islands, we may not even be right looking east of the river. But it's worth looking at more closely, don't you think?"

"I do," Mitch said. "I'm already trying to find out how to get there."

"First thing in the morning?"

"I'm thinking even earlier," Mitch said.

"Earlier?"

"No matter what we've done, we've been unable to stay far ahead of Van Buren and the Hogans. I have a feeling it won't be long before they know what we know."

"How?"

"No idea. Maybe they've bugged my shoe, 99, or maybe they're doing the same math we are and reaching the same conclusions. But I told the cops where we were staying, and if Van Buren has the connections to law enforcement Erik said he did and could somehow garner that info, the sooner we move the better."

Cameron looked at the clock. It was a little after eleven, although it felt much later. "How far of a drive?" she asked.

"Couple hours."

"And when's sunrise?"

It took him a moment to look up the answer. "Civil twilight's about six."

"Leave here at four?"

He nodded. "I hope this fountain of yours has magical properties that make up for lost sleep."

CHAPTER FORTY-NINE

Plans changed quickly. Mitch's online research had finally found a map that identified the narrow channel of water as Spanish Creek, which, given the wealth of Spanish influence in Florida, didn't provide an undeniable link to Figueroa but certainly strengthened the connection. However, Mitch had been unable to confirm who owned the land around the presumed waterfall. One map suggested it was public land, owned by Flagler County, but an online plat map indicated it was private property. While the duo was unlikely to encounter anyone, they didn't relish the idea of a potential discovery being marred by trespassing charges, not to mention the jurisdictional issues that could result from it.

To add to the trouble, there were no public roads anywhere near the believed falls. An old logging road ran within a mile and a half of the ledge where the river seemed to originate, but that was it. Given the uncertainty of who owned the land and the gear—hiking boots, bug spray, something to fend off snakes and other dangerous animals that might inhabit the area—they would need to purchase, Cameron and Mitch made the decision to delay a day.

They slept in separate beds until seven, took advantage of the hotel's complimentary breakfast, then drove their rental car to the airport and exchanged it for a Jeep with four-wheel drive. They saw no signs of a tail, and thus stopped at the hospital to check on Pickett. He had a concussion, some short-term memory loss, and external injuries that would take some time to heal, but was none the worse for wear ultimately.

From the hospital, they went to the police station, where Mitch asked if there were any updates on the attack at Church of the Redeemer. There were none, which wasn't surprising. He also made a call to a former girlfriend, Kellie, whom he assured Cameron wasn't a bad breakup for either of them.

She worked real estate in Forth Worth, and he hoped she would have some connections that could find out about the owner of the land in question, under the auspices of looking for some prime hunting ground. Kellie said she'd make some calls and get back to him.

"How long did you two date?" Cameron asked when he ended the call.

"I don't remember. Few months."

She grinned at him.

"What?"

"The 'aw shucks' recap of your football career, retiring at age thirty-three—it seemed like you were trying to impress her without sounding like you were trying to impress her."

"Why, Cameron Leigh, are you jealous?"

She looked away. "Maybe a little."

"Relax. She's just an old girlfriend, nothing more. I laid on the charm to get her to spend half an hour of company time to help us."

She nodded.

They spent the rest of the morning doing further research on Bimini, Espanola, Spanish Creek, and the town of Palatka, particularly as any of them might be tied to Spanish missions or Francisco the Lion. They turned up nothing, and found a Chick-fil-A for lunch. They ate on the patio, enjoying a cooler day than the last several.

"I've been thinking," Cameron said, dipping a waffle fry into her Polynesian sauce.

"About?"

"Van Buren and the Hogans and how we can't seem to shake them."

"Yeah."

"We don't know if they interpreted the carving, but they now have seen *Išimi* and the mural, so they could theoretically know where to look."

"You second guessing our decision to wait a day?"

"No. I'm just afraid we might not be the only ones descending on a particular piece of land."

"Yeah, I've been thinking the same thing."

"Any thoughts about what to do about it?" Cameron asked, looking into a light breeze. An idea had hit her earlier that day, but she didn't much care for it. She was hoping Mitch had something better.

"They don't know what we're driving," he said, nodding at the Jeep. "They don't know where we're staying."

"We don't know that either."

"Exactly. We're using burn phones, and not contacting anyone they might think to monitor for information. I don't know how they could possibly find us or follow us, or any other precautions we could take."

She reached for her drink. "So you think we're safe?"

"I think we're safe unless they can put the pieces together same as we did. There's not much we can do about that, other than be careful."

His phone chirped.

"Kellie?" she asked.

"No. I made another call while you were in the restroom." He put the phone to his ear. "This is Owens. . . . That's great, thanks. . . . Yeah, this number. . . . Thanks again. . . . You bet. See ya." He lowered the phone and Cameron nibbled on another fry while waiting for his explanation. He took a bite of his sandwich first, then slurped on his soda.

"Come on, Owens."

He grinned. "My freshman year I roomed with a wide-out who quit the team when he realized he was never going to see the field. Dropped out of school. Second semester, he was replaced with a kid named Nick who was studying geography, with the goal of one day working for the National Park Service. He and I were different people on different tracks, but we got along and stayed in touch. Last I heard, he was working for the BLM in Montana."

"Black Lives Matter?"

"Bureau of Land Management," Mitch said with a contained chuckle. "I gave him the same story about hunting ground and asked if he had any colleagues with BLM or the Forest Service or something in Florida who could find out if there were any access roads or hiking trails or anything like that around Spanish Creek, something not showing on a map."

"Even though it might be on private land?"

"If there's a road or trail it might indicate it is public land, or maybe a trail would get us closer. Trying anything and everything."

"What'd he say?"

"He called the BLM's Southeastern States office in Mississippi and talked with a woman there who confirmed there is a hiking trail that runs about a mile west of the river."

"West? Wasn't the logging road east?"

"Yeah. He's sending me coordinates, but said it's a long trail."

"We were going to buy some hiking boots," she said with a tip of her head to the side. She dipped another fry. "Good thing you're connected."

"We'll see," he said. "We'll see."

*   *   *

After lunch, they found a shopping center where they could outfit themselves with hiking gear. Mitch called a few of his former security buddies, inquiring about somewhere he could get a gun. Waiting periods made legal options untenable, even with his concealed carry permit back in Texas, and the semi-legal options weren't much better. So he settled on bear spray, which would be effective against Florida black bears, panthers, or bobcats—or Hogans.

While they were shopping, Kellie called back with good news. The land surrounding the headwaters of the river had been part of a large tract that was privately owned until 2014, when a third-generation citrus farmer died and his son looked to unload a few thousand acres. Flagler County had purchased them as public land with a goal of maintaining a wildlife habitat. Wary that Cameron was listening, he kept his charm at a minimum as he thanked her and agreed to keep in touch.

"We're a go," he said to Cameron after ending the call.

"Good deal."

"Celebrate with some ice cream?"

"We just ate."

"That was at least two hours ago."

"One and a half, max."

"Take a walk in your new boots, then cool down with some ice cream?"

"Sure."

Northeast of downtown they found a park that encircled a small lake, and went for a pleasant afternoon hike, enabling Cameron to break in a pair of hiking boots much better suited for a potentially long walk in the woods than anything in her luggage. Despite the cool breeze, the afternoon had warmed, and ice cream cones were a welcome break after the exertion. They sat and licked while overlooking the lake and plotting their strategy for the next morning. As had been their plan for the current day, they decided to leave early, hoping to arrive shortly after sunrise. It would be cooler then for a long hike, and given the chances of Van Buren and his people also honing in on the location, the sooner they found it the better.

To that end, they decided that instead of staying in Orlando, they should find a hotel as close as possible to the proposed site, and settled on a Quality Inn & Suites in Palatka, one of its defining features being a swimming pool overlooking the St. Johns River. They made the two-hour drive north, first on I-4 to Daytona Beach, then north on I-95, and then on a series of U.S. and state highways that led them through the "towns" of Espanola and Bimini. Espanola contained a few dozen houses, a fire station, and a Baptist church. Bimini was nothing more than a couple of buildings and a dirt-road intersection. There was absolutely nothing in the geography that would suggest islands or fountains or anything related to their search in either locale.

They continued on to Palatka, even though staying somewhere on the I-95 corridor might have put them a little closer in the morning. Cameron had argued that maybe there was a small museum or information center or something in Palatka that would reference Francisco de León or the mission. And there was that pool. Mitch doubted any such place, if it existed, would be open, but Cameron was quite persuasive.

After checking into a pair of second-story rooms overlooking the river and freshening up, they met down in the lobby and decided where to eat dinner. Cameron had changed into a pink cascade blouse and denim shorts, and looked cute as ever, her hair in a loose ponytail.

Since it was a beautiful evening, they decided to walk the nearby St. Johns Avenue, through the old downtown. They didn't find any information on old Spanish missionaries, but they did find a hole-in-the-wall Mexican restaurant that served delicious fajitas. Afterward, they walked along the river through Riverfront Park.

"So, I've been thinking," Mitch said.

"What about?"

"When we finish our search," he said, pausing and making eye contact, "I'm going back to Texas."

Cameron said nothing, just marched along beside him.

"I know we talked the other day about figuring out us after we find the fountain, but . . ."

"You've figured something out?"

"No. But I think we need some time to process everything. We're either going to make a huge discovery and become famous or we're going to crap out. Plus we've been on an adrenaline rush for a week, and I've been on vacation since I can't remember when. And I'm sure you've got obligations back home. Before we decide anything, we need to come down from the mountain, think things through, see how we feel when life is a little more normal."

Cameron nodded.

"And I thought you should know that now, so I don't spring it on you later."

"That actually makes a lot of sense," she said at length. "And you're right."

"All that said, I kind of hope we have a few more clues before this all ends." He leaned over and pecked her on the forehead.

Cameron looked up and grinned. "I don't. I want to find the fountain."

Mitch turned and looked toward the orange glow in the sky where the sun had just dipped below the low skyline of Palatka. Then the other way, at the river and the Memorial Bridge that spanned it. He thought of *Iśimi* and the mural at Church of the Redeemer, of Diego leaving everything to follow his princess to eternity. That made him think of Cameron's newfound faith, a belief in the afterlife, which brought to mind thoughts of mortality and the danger that could await them if Van Buren's people somehow tracked them.

He shook off all thoughts other than the beautiful woman beside him, and how, even though his head told him it was the right thing to do, leaving her to go back to Texas was going to be awfully hard.

CHAPTER FIFTY

Sunrise in Putnam County, Florida, in the middle of June was a little before six-thirty. Wanting to beat the heat—and possible competition—Cameron and Mitch had planned to leave around five-thirty, which would put them on the trail by the time civil twilight occurred around six, when it would be light enough to see. Cameron, however, was up long before five, giving her ample time to ponder what the day might hold. She also read the last three chapters of John by the light of her bedside lamp, marking her second pass through the book. She was torn between starting it again or picking a new book of the Bible, and decided to leave that decision until the following day.

Mitch knocked on her door at 5:25, and the duo headed down to their rented Jeep. It was covered in a thick layer of dew, and the same moisture hung heavy in the air. Even before sunrise, the temperature was already warm, and Cameron had a feeling her outfit of hiking boots, blue jeans, and two layers of shirt would become unbearable before long. But so would scrapes and scratches and bugs out in the woods.

"How'd you sleep?" Mitch asked as they got into the Jeep.

"With anticipation."

"Meaning not well?"

She nodded.

"I dreamt I was being chased down an unending waterfall by an Aztec warrior who looked like a cross between Johnny Depp in *Pirates of the Caribbean* and Johnny Depp in *The Long Ranger*."

Cameron frowned. "The Aztecs don't have anything to do with the Fountain of Youth."

He shrugged.

They crossed the river and stopped at a McDonald's that was serving breakfast. Then they headed east toward the brightening sky, first on the highway, then county roads, then a backwoods dirt road that tested the capabilities of the Jeep's four-wheel drive. Using the GPS on his phone, Mitch found a location approximately two miles west of the falls on Spanish Creek. The hiking trail his former roommate's colleague had identified would take them half of the way there. At least, that was the plan. But Cameron spotted no trail.

"It intersects with this majestic thoroughfare a couple hundred yards ahead," Mitch said when she mentioned her observation. "Runs at an angle, so we can cut through the woods and save some time."

"Oh can we?"

He nodded, and they got out. The sky was a hazy orange above and to the east of them, and the woods were already alive with the croaking and chirping of various insects and birds. The woods themselves were thick, full of hearty trees and abundant scrub and underbrush that would make going slow. Mitch's efforts to locate a machete had not borne fruit.

After dousing themselves in bug repellant, they set out. Each of them carried a backpack with bottles of water, some energy bars, more bug repellant, Cameron's camera for documentation purposes, and a couple of vials they had purchased the previous afternoon for collecting samples. Mitch led the way, quickly finding a sturdy fallen stick to use as something of a bushwhacking device. Cameron kept an eye out for wildlife or signs of wildlife, especially snakes.

With one more thwack of his stick, Mitch pushed through some brush and onto a rudimentary trail. It was little more than consistently beaten earth, wide enough for them to proceed single file, but no more.

"So far so good," he said, reaching for Cameron's backpack and a water bottle. He took a swig, then offered it to her.

"Almost as if you knew what you were doing," she said with a wink, then took a drink.

Mitch looked at his watch. "Four minutes till sunrise."

Cameron looked up. "You'd never know it." The canopy was thick, a combination of oaks, maples, and pines. While it kept out the light, it did nothing to mitigate the heat. Cameron's outer shirt was already soaked, but that might have been from dew passed on from branches and bushes. Mitch's T-shirt—orange with that dreaded Longhorn on the front—was wet too, and sweat was beading on his forehead.

They followed the trail for fifteen minutes, seeing nothing but woods and a pair of deer that startled when they saw the duo. The terrain was mostly flat, but a few small undulations and rocky ledges—only a foot high or so—suggested the ridge that caused the waterfall wasn't far away. When they stopped to rest and drink again, Mitch checked his phone and said they should veer off the trail.

"Already?"

He nodded.

Cameron surveyed the woods to their right—to the east—and shed her outer shirt, tying the sleeves around her waist. She concluded getting scratched by bushes beat drowning in her own sweat. Mitch smirked as she tucked hair loose from her ponytail behind her ear.

"What?"

"You know what sounds really good right now?"

"I'm hesitant to ask."

"A swim in life-giving waters."

"After we get some photos," she said. "Lead on."

The woods off the trail were thick but navigable. Several times, the tree cover overhead parted enough to allow a ray of filtered sunlight to penetrate the forest floor. Twice Cameron stopped, thinking she'd heard something moving the same direction off to their right. Both times, neither she nor Mitch saw or heard anything. A few minutes later, they came to a ridge. It appeared that the woods had overtaken a rock ledge, and now the slope was more gradual, the twelve-foot ledge half covered with dirt, grass, brush, and tree trunks.

They stopped for a minute, contemplating following the ridge to the falls. It meandered at an angle, whereas Mitch's phone indicated a path straight east would take them there directly. So they carefully picked their way down the slope, paused for water, and were surprised themselves by a deer that darted over the ledge not far behind them, perhaps explaining the noise Cameron had heard earlier.

The deer turned and headed east, and Mitch followed it for a dozen paces, then signaled for Cameron to join him. "Game trail," he said, pointing to where the faintest indication of a path led east. "Toward water."

"Makes sense," she said.

"Let's go."

They hiked for another fifteen minutes, including skirting a rattlesnake. When they paused for more water, Cameron held up a hand.

"What?" Mitch asked.

"Hear that?"

He listened for a moment. "Water?"

She beamed as she took the bottle from him and drained it. He stuffed it back into her backpack for her, and they continued on, still keeping an eye out for dangerous wildlife, but with increased pace. The sound of water grew louder, and when Mitch paused again, he did so to allow Cameron to step beside him. He pointed toward the far bank of a river some fifty feet ahead of them, through the woods. Cameron took the lead, approaching the near bank. As she stepped around a large bald cypress tree, she turned and saw it.

Tumbling out of the ledge was a ten-foot plume of water, about four or five feet wide, and broken into several channels so that it almost looked like three separate waterfalls, each at different levels as they dropped like a veil. Half of the water fell into the river, which flowed lazily to the northwest. The other half fell on a rocky, mossy spit of land. With Mitch following, Cameron advanced and saw that the spit of land was actually a small island in the river, no more than a couple dozen square feet in size. Just downriver was a second island, a little smaller, a little rounder.

On either side of the falls, the ridge was well-defined, mostly wet rock with a few stubs of trees growing out of it. On the far side, a large oak stood beside the river, its roots dropping over the bank into the water or being intertwined in the ridge. Its boughs towered high over the falls, Spanish moss draping them and seeming like a shroud over the river's origins.

Cameron slipped out of her backpack and walked up to the edge of the bank. She stared at the waterfall for several minutes, marveling at the fact that the water did indeed flow out of the ledge. There must have been an underground river that flowed to the ridge, then emerged "above" ground at the falls. That would explain why they hadn't seen the headwaters on any map, and why these falls had been dubbed a fountain.

She felt Mitch's hand on her back, and turned toward his smiling face. She stood up on her tiptoes and kissed him, then wrapped him in an embrace.

"You did it," he said. "I don't know that I ever believed it until right now, but you did it."

She pulled back and looked at him. "We did it."

"I came along for the ride."

"You did more than that," she said.

He shrugged, then removed his backpack. "You should get some pictures."

"Yeah."

"Or, I should say, I should get some pictures. You go stand over there like Captain Morgan."

"What?"

"Leg up on keg, a great conquest pose."

She nodded, helped him with the camera, and then approached the falls. She was about to turn back to face Mitch so he could get a shot of her in front of it when something caught her eye. To the right of the falls, an outcropping of rock formed a small ledge, just out of the immediate spray. As Cameron drew closer and got a better angle, she saw that the face of the ridge actually receded behind the falls and a second ledge a step away from the first extended behind the water.

She edged to her right for an even better look and saw darkness behind the falls. She turned back to Mitch. "I think there's a cave back here."

"What?"

"A cave, behind the waterfall."

"You mean a regular old cave or a secret treasure trove?"

"Let's find out."

CHAPTER FIFTY-ONE

Before exploring the cave behind the waterfall, Mitch persuaded Cameron to pose for a few photos—"moment of" shots of her finding the Fountain of Youth. She looked the part, hair in a somewhat disheveled ponytail, shirt wrapped around her waist, in a tank top (even a Clemson orange one), denim, and hiking boots. He took a dozen photos at several angles, posed for a cell phone selfie with her, and then suggested they take "contingency samples" of the water.

"Like when they landed on the moon," he said. "Before Buzz came down the steps, Neil Armstrong took a few contingency samples."

"How in the world do you know that?" she asked, hands on hips.

"I watched the Fiftieth Anniversary re-air," he said.

"Then let's get some contingency samples."

Using the vials they had purchased, they collected some of the water from the river, just down from the falls. They secured the lids and stowed them in Mitch's backpack. Then, they approached the ledge beside the falls.

Though relatively small compared to most waterfalls of note, the Spanish Creek falls was quite noisy up close, and kicked up a fair amount of spray. Mitch let Cameron go first, but urged her to be careful. She tested every step on the slick rock before taking it, and did the same with handholds higher up on the ridge. There was just enough room for her to fit between the rock and the falling water, and she disappeared behind the falls.

Mitch ducked in behind her, and found himself standing in a dark, narrow cavern. The waterfall was like a curtain behind them, and they retrieved pocket flashlights to light their way. The ceiling was only inches above Mitch's head, which made sense given that the river had to flow over them and yet underground. The rock was jagged and there was nothing to indicate anyone— or anything—had been in the cave recently.

Cameron went first, at times having to squeeze between the walls on either side. Mitch sensed they were angling slightly left, and perhaps down. In several places, the rock was wet with dripping water, likely oozing through the ceiling above them. Not prone to claustrophobia, Mitch was nevertheless not thrilled with his environs.

If Cameron had any apprehension, she didn't show it. Instead, she followed the beam of her flashlight farther into the cave. She stopped suddenly, and Mitch bumped into her. "What is it?" he asked.

"The end?"

The cave had widened to a small chamber, several feet wide and deep. Mitch slipped around Cameron and joined his flashlight with hers, first illuminating no hibernating bears or coiled snakes in the crevices of the chamber, then panning the walls. The rock was rough and seemingly untouched by human hands—this was indeed a natural cave, and a dead-end. No crevices or fissures led deeper into the ground or to an alternate exit.

Cameron's light had stopped moving, and she breathed his name. Mitch turned to see what she was looking at, and couldn't believe his eyes. Etched into the rock at eye height were a series of crude letters and numbers. The writing was in Spanish.

"What's it say?" Mitch asked.

"*Yo Diego Figueroa reclamo esta Fuente no para el trono español sino para todos aquellos que tienen ojos para ver. 7 de junio de 1698 en el año de nuestro Señor.*"

"I caught Diego and fountain, but that's about it."

"Roughly, it says 'I Diego Figueroa claim this Fountain not for the Spanish throne but for all those who have eyes to see. June 7, 1698, in the year of our Lord.'"

"Dang, you've been scooped."

She turned to him with a budding smile.

"But, that does eliminate any doubts as to whether this is the right place or not."

"Do you think you could get the camera in here without getting it wet?"

"I've got my cell."

"Me too, but I want a better camera for this."

"I'll be right back."

He left her panning around the chamber again and squeezed back to the opening. He picked his way across the ledge, hopping down onto solid ground.

He took a couple steps toward where they'd left their backpacks and stopped as a man emerged from the woods.

He wore a black shirt, sleeves pushed up to the elbows, and dark camouflage pants tucked into black boots. He looked more commando than party stiff, even with the frosted tips, and the pistol in his right hand added to his menacing visage. So did the fact that he was not alone. A second man appeared, like an apparition from the mist behind him, and a flicker of movement caused Mitch to turn left. Like the tail of a darting fox, the red ponytail extending from under a dark baseball cap gave Lora Hogan away. She wore all black, as did the man—Kevin Stuart/Charles Calvin—behind Shay Hogan. Stuart/Calvin and Lora both held guns as well, and instead of smirking like evil villains, their faces were cold as steel.

None of them moved or spoke. A crunching sound indicated the arrival of a fourth person, and Mitch watched as a man appeared between Shay and Stuart/Calvin. He was old, judging by the full crop of white hair and the walking stick he held, despite a jaunty pace. His khaki pants and matching safari jacket were almost white, and gave him the appearance of Colonel Sanders. That is, except for the fact that a down-home Southern smile was absent and, in its place, a dour mouth and dark eyes regarded Mitch evenly. He didn't need introductions to know he was looking at Harrison Van Buren.

The man walked and stood beside Shay, then stopped as well. His eyes never left Mitch as he tapped the walking stick into the dirt in front of him, casually placing both hands on top of it. His lips finally parted. "Where is the girl?"

"She's not here," Mitch said. "I came alone, in case we ran into hoodlums."

With lightning fast motion, Stuart/Calvin brought his gun up. Before Mitch realized it, he squeezed the trigger, and a fiery burst of pain knifed through Mitch's arm. He looked down at the rip in the sleeve of his T-shirt and saw blood oozing from the wound.

"Mr. Stuart only winged you," Van Buren said in a gravelly voice, as if he was discussing the weather. He took several steps forward and stopped. "There are two backpacks over there on the ground, and two sets of footprints in the earth. So, please, don't insult me with your games. Where is Ms. Leigh?"

Mitch looked from his bloody sleeve to the sneering Stuart with his gun raised and back to Van Buren.

"That shot was no accident; Kevin is an expert marksman. If you don't answer me in the next five seconds or if you don't tell me the truth, I assure you, his next shot will go right between your eyes."

*   *   *

Cameron didn't know exactly what she was looking for or hoped to find. Maybe some hieroglyphics or cave drawings that matched, roughly, the portrait of *Iśimi* and the mural in the bell tower of *Misión San Francisco de Sevilla*. It didn't matter; she had confirmation that this was the Fountain of Youth. Whatever that meant, whatever it ultimately was, she had found it!

A gunshot interrupted her excitement, echoing through the narrow cave. Forgetting carvings or drawings, she hurried through the passage and back to the ledge behind the waterfall. She couldn't see Mitch, or much of anything. She thought about calling his name, or stepping out from behind the falls, but if someone had been shooting in the area, staying concealed might be prudent.

There was not a second gunshot, and she wondered if it was possible that there was a hunter or poacher out in the woods. But if so, where was Mitch? She strained to see anything through the water or hear over it. At first, there was nothing, but then a gravelly voice shouted over the din of the falls.

"Where is she!"

Cameron didn't know what she would be facing, but the gunshot, the loud demand, and Mitch's absence gave her a fair guess. She didn't wait. Extending her hands, she edged out onto the ledge. "I'm right here," she said at the same time as her eyes took in the scene of three dark-clad figures holding Mitch at gunpoint while a fourth, dressed in white, stood directly in front of him.

The man in white, two of the figures in black, and Mitch all turned Cameron's way. The last man with a gun kept it trained on Mitch. She recognized him as her old acquaintance Charles Calvin, and the other two as Shay and Lora Hogan. That meant the man in white was Van Buren, and that Dax Wilder was unaccounted for somewhere. She scanned the ridgeline and the woods around her, but saw no one.

"Ms. Leigh," the man in white said, "please join us."

"What's going on?" she asked, not moving.

"Now," he said with a nod at Calvin, who took a step closer to Mitch, his gun aimed at his head.

"Okay, okay." She eased further onto the ledge, then down onto the ground. Lora Hogan was there to meet her, grabbing her by the arm and jabbing a gun into her ribs with the other hand. "There's plenty of water to go around," Cameron said.

"That's very cute," Van Buren said. He nodded at Hogan, who pushed Cameron down onto her knees in front of him. Calvin was less gentle in forcing Mitch to his knees.

"Are you okay?" Cameron asked, noting Mitch's bleeding arm.

"Not so much."

"Where's your fourth man?" she asked Van Buren. "Wilder?"

He smiled. "Being clever won't save you now."

She said nothing.

He took a few steps closer, and she thought he was going to strike. Instead, he lowered his head to growl into her face. "You were given ample opportunity to quit, but you don't listen. Now, you will pay the price. But," he said, straightening up, "I'm not a cold-hearted man. I'll give you a chance to drink of the water of life before I shoot you."

Cameron shook her head. "Why do you want this so bad? You don't even believe in it."

"As a magic elixir, no. But what I believe isn't nearly as important as what millions of people will believe if properly convinced. Not to mention, the rumors that Diego Figueroa hid a rather substantive cache of smuggled Mayan gold at the source of the fountain."

"Just an empty cave," Cameron said, following his look toward the waterfall.

"It could be elsewhere," Mitch said. "In the area. You kill us, you'll have to find it yourselves."

"We have sufficient manpower for the task," Van Buren said.

"Might take more than shovels," Cameron said. "You've been following us for a reason. Are you sure you want to dispense with us now?"

"As a matter of fact, I am. Like I said, you should have cashed out when you had the chance. After all," he said with a malevolent grin, "after we found your boat, found you at your friend's house, found you in Tampa, found the gallery and the church in Orlando, did you really think we wouldn't find this as well?"

"In fact, I did," Cameron said. "That's why I took out an insurance policy."

*　　　　*　　　　*

Mitch turned his eyes to Cameron, wondering what game she was playing. He was desperately thinking of anything he could use to stall, but she seemed less desperate and more . . . conniving.

"What insurance?" Van Buren barked.

Cameron merely grinned.

He slapped her with a meaty backhand, and Mitch made to get off his feet and plow into Van Buren. If he was going out, it would be with a blaze of glory. But being on his knees, he was slowed, and before he could even get up, Stuart had placed his gun into Mitch's neck.

"Don't think about it," he said, squeezing Mitch's arm—right where the bullet had winged him—with his other hand. Mitch gritted his teeth and bit off a curse that he feared might only get Cameron more abuse.

"What insurance?" Van Buren asked again, practically spitting.

Before Cameron could answer, Van Buren stood up straight. Mitch turned his eyes fully to the man and saw a small red dot had appeared on the white of his jacket. The gun moved from Mitch's neck, and he turned to see a similar dot appear on the neck of Stuart/Calvin.

Mitch craned his neck farther and saw that, behind Cameron, Lora Hogan had already dropped her gun. To Van Buren's right, so had Shay Hogan. Mitch was only distantly aware of a pulsing sound in the distance, growing louder by the moment. It was not yet loud enough to drown out Cameron's voice as she softly said, "You too, Charlie."

Stuart/Calvin dropped his gun in the dirt, and Mitch looked from it to Cameron to the top of the ridge just above the falls, where two figures in black stood like wraiths under the dripping Spanish moss on the oak tree. They were backlit by the hazy morning sky, the light of which reflected off the barrels of two AR-15 rifles, their laser beams pointed at Van Buren and Stuart/Calvin. Mitch turned to the left and saw a third figure in black behind the trunk of the oak, his rifle aimed at Lora Hogan.

The beating grew louder, and Mitch realized it was a helicopter, shortly before the tops of the trees began to sway in the breeze of the chopper's rotors, and then it appeared hovering no more than a hundred feet over the tree tops, the thup-thup-thup-thup now almost deafening.

"What'd you do," Mitch shouted, "call in the National Guard?"

"Not exactly," Cameron said with a half smirk as she turned her eyes to the ridge. Mitch followed them and saw a fourth figure appear between the two original black-clad people he'd spotted. Like them, the fourth figure wore black—boots, leather pants, and tank top—to match the long, wavy hair. She too carried an AR, but loosely in her hand. She stopped at the edge of the ledge, surveyed the scene, and finally brought her head around to make eye contact with Mitch.

Then Olivia winked at him.

CHAPTER FIFTY-TWO

Mitch was underdressed in a clean, untorn, unbloodied T-shirt and a pair of shorts. Most of the other guys passing through the Lobby Bar of the Hammock Beach Resort wore loafers, chinos, and collared shirts. Even the golfers coming in off the course for post-round drinks put him to shame. So did the two women on the couch adjacent to him.

Cameron had clearly taken the time to shower and style her hair, and looked marvelous in a purple sundress, her hair flowing onto her shoulders like a, well, waterfall. And Olivia had shunned her lady bartender look for a light green blouse and white skirt and matching heels, her apparel professional yet accenting her figure. Cameron and Olivia both held cocktails from the bar, whereas Mitch was content with a beer. He needed one.

The moments after Olivia and her private army had come to the rescue had been chaotic to say the least. In addition to a duo of black-clad figures rappelling from the chopper, Oliva had been surrounded by a total of four gun-toting rescuers. Two more had radioed in from the road a few miles west, where they had apprehended Dax Wilder, the getaway driver and lookout man. Olivia had placed Van Buren and his cronies under citizen's arrest and tasked most of her team with walking the five criminals back to the road where the local authorities would meet them. Then she'd directed another of her team to provide Mitch with immediate medical attention. She and Cameron had then examined the waterfall, talked privately, and signed papers that had materialized from nowhere.

By then Mitch had been thoroughly intrigued and confused, but unable to get answers because Olivia's medic had given him something for the pain, even though he hadn't been in that much pain. It had also served as something of a sedative, and Mitch had started to wonder if he'd been set up and would wake up in a Guatemalan prison camp. Instead, he'd been transported against his will to a hospital in Palm Coast while Cameron, after assuring him she would explain everything when she returned, had driven back to Palatka to get their things.

He'd checked out fine, been bandaged and given a prescription for pain meds he had no intention of using, and been chauffeured by one of Olivia's people to a room at the Hammock Beach Resort on the coast. Cameron had texted and said to meet in the lobby at four, which had given him a couple hours to rest, and he had taken advantage. After a shower and some clean clothes, he'd felt like a new man. And been ready for answers. Cameron and Olivia had both been waiting in the lobby, looking beautiful as ever, and the group had ordered drinks and adjourned to a private corner of the lobby.

"How is your arm?" Olivia asked with her sultry accent.

"Babied. Now will one of you please explain what's going on?"

Olivia looked to Cameron. She took a sip of an orange crush, then said, "After what happened in Orlando, I started thinking about how Van Buren kept finding us everywhere. Whether they were tracking us somehow despite our vehicle and phone changes and constant movement or they were just figuring out the same clues we were, I had this feeling they might show up at the fountain too. So, like I told him, I took out an insurance policy."

Mitch glanced at Olivia, who gave him one of those top-of-the-eye looks, but said nothing.

"I also started thinking about some of the things you said about Olivia," Cameron continued, "about how much she knew, how connected she was, how powerful she was."

Olivia again remained silent.

"Go on," Mitch said before tipping up his longneck.

"Once I was thinking more clearly, I researched Hall Parker Cook and generally liked what I found. They are a powerful company, but respected and responsible."

"I told you," Olivia said to Mitch.

He said nothing.

"After we checked into the hotel yesterday, I called Olivia, told her I had a deal for her. I said I believed I knew where the fountain was and that we were going to find it. I also told her about Van Buren and the Hogans and the danger I anticipated. I asked if she had the resources to take care of something like that."

"Meaning her own SWAT team?"

Cameron shrugged innocently. "Then we merely hammered out a deal."

"A deal?"

"If we found what we deemed to be the Fountain of Youth, we would cede rights to it to Hall Parker Cook with a provision that you and I be listed as discoverers and that any actions taken by Hall Parker Cook or any drugs developed required my approval. I even had a lawyer look over it and help me with it."

"When?"

"Late last night. I know a guy back home, and I was able to e-mail him a copy."

"You know a guy?"

"A friend of a friend. We had drinks once."

Mitch raised an eyebrow. "And I thought you went to bed early because we had a big day ahead of us."

Cameron shrugged playfully.

Mitch stroked his jaw. "And you went for this deal?" he asked Olivia.

"She can be very persuasive."

"I told her if she said no I would make the deal to someone else, and Hall Parker Cook would be left out in the cold."

"Just like that?" Mitch asked.

"What can I say," Olivia said, "it was a good deal that made sense for all parties involved."

"How'd you know where to find us?"

"I texted her in the drive-thru at McDonald's to let her know we were headed out, and then updated her with coordinates before we started hiking. Then I just had to stall Van Buren until they arrived."

"We heard the shot and were still a little out of position," Olivia said. "We apparently made it just in time."

"And I'm glad you did," Mitch said. He took another drink. "So where do we go from here?"

Olivia reached into her purse and withdrew several sheets of paper. She handed them to Mitch, and he proceeded to scan a signed contract between Olivia, representing Hall Parker Cook Pharmaceuticals, and Cameron, detailing the provisions Cameron had just described. It was even notarized by one of Olivia's men, she explained, who was a notary public in addition to a trained paramedic.

"Were those all Hall Parker Cook employees playing commando out there?"

"No," Olivia said with something of a grin. "I told you, we have a lot of connections."

"And did I recognize one of them from Fort Myers?" Cameron asked.

"Geoffrey," she said. "He was following you in case Mitch was lying to me," she said with a sideways glance at him.

"How did he find me? And why did he scare the crap out of me?"

"We knew your connection to Erik Diaz, and had someone monitoring his movements. As to scaring you, it wasn't meant to scare you so much as get in your head a little, as insurance, again in case Mitch was being untruthful."

Cameron frowned, but said nothing.

"And you sent him to Dr. Botana too?" Mitch asked.

"Yes. We figured out there was more to finding the fountain than deciphering the painting at Primero, so we ended up doing what we'd hoped to avoid all along and actually analyzed the Castillo de San Marcos carving ourselves."

"How?" Cameron said.

"Well, we'd long known about the disk at Morgan's Pirate Den in Clearwater—"

"You were the ones who called him a few weeks ago," Cameron said.

Olivia nodded. "We knew it was part of the puzzle, but until we had the rest, it didn't do us any good. So we sat on it with the fake insurance agency. Fortunately, the office next door was vacant."

"How'd you get the Figueroa Cipher? It's never been out of my possession. And don't tell me you just happened to stumble upon the solution like we did?"

"Do you remember how long you were swimming before Geoffrey showed up?" Olivia asked with a smirk.

Cameron's eyes widened. "He was in my room?"

"Took photographs of the disk. Then, from there, it was a series of computer algorithms until we 'stumbled' upon the solution. It did take our experts a while to figure out how to play the two off each other."

Cameron shook her head.

"Once we cracked the code," Olivia said, "we realized we needed to find *Misión San Francisco de Sevilla*. A little bit of research led us to Dr. Botana as one of the foremost experts on the subject, so I sent Geoffrey there to question her. He made no headway. So he staked her out, figuring you'd show up sooner or later."

"He put the tracker on our car?" Mitch said.

Olivia nodded and stirred her drink.

"You people are incredible," Cameron said, slack-jawed.

"You're sure you want to partner with her?" Mitch asked.

"I am."

Olivia took a drink of a margarita. "As to your question of what's next, a lot of tests and verification will need to be done. First, we'll have to corroborate Cameron's research and discovery to prove this really is *the* Fountain of Youth of legendary fame. Then, after all the required permits and licenses are taken care of, we'll begin testing the water to see just what is in it—what benefits it might have."

"Let me guess, Hall Parker Cook can cut through that red tape pretty quickly?"

"Another benefit to us working together," Cameron said as she lifted her straw to her lips.

"The falls are on public land," Olivia said, "so the county and state will both likely claim jurisdiction, and, who knows, the federal government may wish to make this a national park or historic monument or something of that nature. Per our agreement," she said with a look at Cameron, "Hall Parker Cook will handle all the regulations and permits and whatnot, as you said, and all the negotiations, with Cameron having approval rights."

"People will flock to it," Mitch said. "As soon as word gets out. You have a plan for that?"

"Hall Parker Cook will take care of all the PR," Cameron said. "As for securing the land, determining who gets to see it and how, that falls under what Olivia was talking about with government involvement, the licenses and permits, red tape . . ."

"We're already mobilizing," Olivia said, "but of course, we don't do anything without Cameron's approval."

Mitch turned to Cameron. "And you're sure of the legalese in all of this?"

She nodded.

"Why, don't you trust me?" Olivia asked, batting her eyelashes.

"Last we talked, you were blackmailing me by threatening to release a mugshot of her sister—when she was in college, by the way—claiming it was

Cameron and insinuating that she'd stolen some Civil War colonel's letter from an old man. Yeah, I'm working on trust."

"Not my finest moment, admittedly," Olivia said like a scolded schoolgirl. "I was desperate and I went too far."

"It's water under the bridge, Mitch," Cameron said.

He raised an eyebrow.

She nodded reassuringly, and he tipped his head. "Okay. It's your call." He took a drink. "Any word on Van Buren? He has friends in high places."

"So do I," Olivia said, "and so do the execs at Hall Parker Cook. Our friends look down on his friends. Cameron and I both gave lengthy statements to the authorities and sworn affidavits, and when I checked a few minutes ago, the State's Attorney has already filed charges and applied for warrants to search phone and e-mail records, search through Van Buren's many financial holdings and business dealings, and toss his numerous homes and office buildings. My brother happens to know the State's Attorney, and she's relentless. She'll pick him apart."

"Erik also will testify, and his girlfriend," Cameron said.

"You heard from him?"

She nodded. "He and Jessie are both fine now. Jacksonville PD found her 'locked' in a penthouse of an office building owned by Van Buren."

"How?"

"I told you, the State's Attorney is relentless," Olivia said with a sip of her margarita.

"So that's it then?"

Olivia nodded. "Hall Parker Cook has reserved rooms for each of you tonight, and you're welcome to dine on us this evening. I'll be driving back to our office in Jacksonville tonight, and will be reaching out to Cameron in the near future—as soon as we get the various permit applications and filings underway. Oh," she said, reaching into her purse, "an Agent Alonso asked you to give him a call." She handed Mitch a business card. "I presume he wants your statement too."

Mitch took the card.

"And other than that," Olivia said, rising, "I'll leave you two to your evening." She had also pulled a couple of twenties from her purse, and tossed them on the table. "Drinks are on me."

Mitch and Cameron also stood, exchanging handshakes with Olivia. She winked at Mitch as she shook his hand, then turned on her heel and strode for the exit. As she left, Mitch couldn't shake the feeling that Cameron had signed a deal with the devil. But the deed was done now.

They both sat back down on the couch.

"You sure you're okay?" Cameron asked, touching his arm below the elbow.

"It really was just a scratch."

She dipped her chin.

"Relatively speaking. I'm fine."

"Are you going to stay the night before flying back?" Cameron said, sipping the rest of her orange crush from the glass.

"Yeah."

"Well, I'm exhausted. I could use a nap. Wanna meet for dinner in a few hours?"

"Sure."

She looked at her watch. "Make us reservations for seven?"

"Okay."

Cameron leaned in and pecked his cheek. "I'll see you then."

He stood again as she did, but didn't move, instead watching her across the lobby and to the elevators. Then he drained the rest of his beer, trying to make sense of the last half hour. Of the last day, or even the last few days, for that matter. He got the feeling there was something Cameron still wasn't telling him, but didn't let it bother him. They had not only found the Fountain of Youth but also survived a near-death experience and, apparently, worked out all the logistics with Olivia. And now, he got to have one last dinner with Cameron before their adventure officially came to an end.

*   *   *

Cameron and Mitch savored entrées of chicken carbonara and a bone-in veal chop on the candlelit terrace of Delfino's, part of The Hammock Beach Resort. The sun set as they dined, coloring the seagrass a magnificent amber hue while the ocean beyond it darkened until it matched the dimming sky. Cameron's two-hour rest had recharged her batteries, and the mental break had allowed her brain to finally process what had happened—what they had done. She was overwhelmed with a sensation of pride, excitement, and awe. The only downside was that she and Mitch wouldn't be together much longer.

After dinner, they took a moonlit stroll on the beach. The soft ocean breeze, the balmy night air, the rhythmic sense of sand beneath her feet, and Mitch's arm in hers soothed Cameron into a relaxed state that made her wish the night could continue forever. Or that she and Mitch could.

"Can I ask you something?" he said, snapping her from wistful thoughts about their parting.

"Of course."

"Why didn't you tell me about Olivia?"

She looked down, plodded a few steps. "I knew how upset you were with her, how personal you had taken what she did. I didn't think there was any way you'd agree to it, that you'd have talked me out of it."

"I'd have probably tried."

"Are you mad at me?"

"No."

"You think it was a mistake?"

"Depends on whether or not you trust her."

"I do. And I trust Randy, who helped me draft the contract."

Mitch nodded.

"And I trust the *other* insurance policy I took out."

"Other insurance policy?"

"I recorded my conversation with Olivia, as proof, in case she double-crossed us. And I also overnighted a vial to a friend in Atlanta, someone I could trust to have the water tested and identified if things didn't pan out."

"You are full of surprises."

"I promise that's the last of them."

He nodded.

"Something else bothering you?" she asked.

This time it was his turn to plod for a few steps. He looked up, and into her eyes, the moon glinting off his. "This morning, when Calvin put me on my knees, I thought for sure I was going to die. And . . . Cameron, I was panicked. I kept thinking about that verse on the wall of the fortress about facing judgment, and thinking about all the things Kessler said and that you now believe, and I couldn't help wondering, what if they're right? What if I was seconds away from eternal judgment?" He shook his head. "I still don't know what to think, what to believe. I don't think I'm convinced, like you are, about Jesus. But . . . I think I'm ready and willing to be convinced. I hope to never face a moment like that again, but I want to be ready."

She clung a little tighter to his arm as they continued walking.

After several minutes, he stopped. She did too.

"So what's next for us?" he asked.

"Aren't you going back to Texas?"

"I fly out of Orlando tomorrow at one."

She shrugged. "I'm going back to Atlanta, at least for a few days, while Olivia and her people handle some of the logistics. Then . . . I don't know."

"Talk shows, lecture circuits, a book deal?"

"I doubt all that."

"Anyhow, that's not what I meant."

"Then what?"

"What I said yesterday, about going home and taking some time to think and evaluate . . ."

"Yeah?"

"I still think it's the right thing to do. But Cameron, I don't think it's going to change anything. I don't think it's going to change that I'm falling in love with you."

Cameron couldn't contain the smile that broke out. "I don't think it's going to change it for me either."

"So, what's next for us?"

"I can't wait to find out."

She leaned forward and kissed him, and he kissed her back, slow and soft, with the waves lapping against the sand paces from them. Cameron's heart was full of peace, of satisfaction, of delight at the future—and for the first time in her life, that peace, satisfaction, and delight was both temporal and eternal—and the latter had nothing to do with a spring of water in the wilds of Florida.

EPILOGUE

Eight Months Later . . .

Warm, salt-tinged air washed over the windshield of Mitch's rented Porsch Boxster. He looked through his shades at the gleaming glass skyline of downtown, Jacksonville Landing at the foot of the blue steel Main Street Bridge, and in the distance at TIAA Bank Field, home of the NFL's Jaguars. He brought his focus nearer, to Cameron, blond hair flowing around her shoulders in the passenger seat. She too wore sunglasses to fight off the February sunshine, and a beatific smile graced her face.

That quickly, they were across the St. Johns River, and Mitch was navigating downtown streets. Compared to several of the city's more prominent buildings, Hall Parker Cook's headquarters didn't stand out, but the gleaming white exterior and reflective glass were still impressive as they towered a dozen stories over the pavement. Mitch found parking on the street a block away, and soon he and Cameron were zipping to the top floor in a glass-paneled elevator that looked down on the lobby and through an atrium at the skyline.

Before the elevator doors had closed, a smiling receptionist led the duo into a sleek office overlooking the same sights Mitch had seen on the bridge over the St. Johns. She offered them a seat on one of two leather loveseats, served glasses of water with lime, and apologized by saying their host was running just a few minutes late. She left, and a minute later, the President and CEO of Hall Parker Cook Pharmaceuticals, G. Hayden McNight, entered and immediately apologized for his tardiness.

With a three-piece suit that fit him like is own skin, silver glasses that gave him an air of intelligence, and a smile as warm as the Florida sun, McNight cut an impressive figure. But he was overmatched by his counterpart, a tall, caramel-skinned woman with smoky eyes and jet-black hair. It was

386

wavy and short, chin-length, and offset by a sleeveless ivory blouse and maroon knee-length skirt.

"Ms. Leigh and Mr. Owens," McNight said, offering handshakes and a wider smile. "And I believe you both know Ms. De la Cruz."

"Good to see you again," Olivia said with a sincere smile and handshakes of her own. The foursome sat back down, and McNight asked if he could get them anything.

"We're fine, thanks," Mitch said.

Cameron nodded.

"Good," McNight said. "Thanks for coming down. I trust your flights were okay?"

"Good as ever," Mitch said.

"It's forty-five in Atlanta right now," Cameron said. "I'm happy to be here."

McNight nodded as if this pleased him greatly. "Well, I'll get right to it." He set two clear-covered presentation binders on the table between them. "After exhaustive analysis, our R&D department has concluded that the water in Spanish Creek is slightly higher in PH levels than your typical central Florida spring, which, according to some studies, has some minor health benefits. To a . . . how can I put this delicately—more primitive mind, the water could be seen as healing or restorative. To us in the twenty-first century, it is no more beneficial than what's in those glasses," he said, nodding at the two tumblers with wedges of lime floating at the surface. "Probably less so."

"It's just water?" Cameron said.

McNight nodded. "No cures for cancer or aging or saggy skin. No health benefits whatsoever. The details are there," he said, pointing at the two binders. "Hall Parker Cook is closing the books on the Spanish Creek project. Per the agreement you and Ms. De la Cruz signed, Ms. Leigh, we are dissolving our partnership and ceding any rights to or claims on the water. I'm guessing there will still be a number of people who will be interested in the falls for health reasons as well as historical ones, so the State of Florida will have to decide how to proceed with its plans to create a historic monument there. We'll be releasing our findings to them Monday, but I wanted you to know first so you can decide how you want to proceed."

Mitch sat back and looked at Cameron, who reached for her tumbler and took a slow drink of water. Then she smiled thinly. "Thank you, Mr. McNight."

He pursed his lips. "Are there any questions you have for me, or us?"

"Not me," Cameron said. "Mitch?"

"Me either."

"Well, then, like I told you on the phone, your expenses for the weekend are on us, as one last gesture of goodwill. It has been a pleasure working with both of you."

"You as well," Cameron said.

The group stood, shook hands again, and McNight exited as quickly as he'd come. Olivia hung around for a moment. "I'll echo what Hayden said, it has been a pleasure, Cameron. I'm going to miss working with you."

"We made a pretty good team, didn't we?"

"For what it was worth, which wasn't much. Mitch," she said, turning his way, "we'll always have the Fountainbleau."

"Better luck on your next miracle drug," he said with a smirk.

"I'll show you out," she said, and led them to the elevator, down to the lobby, and to the front doors. With a final handshake, they parted ways, Mitch and Cameron exiting onto the sidewalk. It was then that he broke out laughing.

"I take it you're not disappointed," Cameron said.

"Not in the least. I feel like I sold a perfectly good house a week before a sinkhole opened under it."

She looked at him.

"I'm sorry," he said, controlling his laughter. "Are you okay?"

"I am."

"Not disappointed?"

"Had I still been expecting long or improved life from the water, maybe. But I completed the historical quest. We found the Fountain of Youth, such as it was. No, I'm not disappointed."

"So you're still up for a romantic dinner?"

She took his hand and leaned in. "I am."

"Good. I promise, you won't be disappointed by it, either."

*   *   *

Mitch was right; Cameron was not disappointed.

Not by the slow private dinner cruise down the St. Johns River on a private yacht, nor the magnificent sunset, nor the four-course meal featuring an assortment of seafood, with fresh strawberry cheesecake for dessert. As they floated leisurely back toward downtown and the last vestiges of daylight, Cameron scooted her chair around the table closer to Mitch. The two-person crew consisting of a captain and steward had catered to their every need and now left them alone on the stern deck of the yacht, candles flickering and ends of the tablecloth fluttering.

"Tell me," Cameron said, "how did you arrange this?"

"Easy, with a few properly placed calls and a little planning ahead," Mitch said. He reached for his glass of wine. "But you're not asking the right question."

Cameron sat up. "The right question."

"It's not how but why."

She stared into his eyes for a moment. "Why?"

"Yes. Why arrange something so, well, extravagant?"

"Being romantic isn't reason enough?"

"Well, it is, but I also have a few things to tell you."

She leaned her elbow on the table, resting her chin in her palm. "What things?"

"First, as you know, I've been really studying the Bible, examining everything it says, all the evidence—the prophecies Christ fulfilled, the authority and unity of the various books, the evidence for the resurrection. And remember what I said that last night back in June, about being willing to be convinced by the evidence?"

"Yeah."

"Well, I have been. Just last week, I reached a verdict. I realized the evidence was convincing, and I decided Jesus was who He said and was worthy of my trust and obedience."

She took his hand. "That's great, Mitch."

He licked his lips. "You know, it's weird. Ever since I did, I feel at peace mentally, like I weighed my options and know I made the right choice. But isn't there supposed to be some feeling that washes over me, some sort of spiritual something?"

"I don't know. I don't think so, not necessarily. I've gotten involved with a church in Atlanta, and from what I understand, some people come to Jesus and are flooded with emotions and can *feel* a transformation. Some are more like you, where it's more their head that needed to be convinced than anything else."

He nodded. "I have a lot to learn, I imagine."

"Don't we all?"

"So there's something else I've been convinced of."

"Okay."

He took a deep breath. "I love you, Cameron. Every time we're together, I know it more and more. But, this long-distance thing is hard. A weekend in Atlanta, a long holiday in Austin. It's taking its toll. Frankly, it's not working."

Cameron's breath caught in her throat, and all she could do was nod.

"I think it's time for a change."

She couldn't even swallow. Before she knew it, he had reached into his pocket and withdrawn a small box.

"So what do you say we end the long-distance part of the relationship? Cameron, will you marry me?"

Words still wouldn't come, so she vigorously nodded. "Yes," finally found its way out, and the dam broke. "Yes, of course I'll marry you. I can't stand the thought of another goodbye."

"You haven't even seen the ring yet."

"I don't need to see the ring," she said, clinching his face in her hands and kissing him. "I love you too, Mitch."

They kissed again, and when she sat back, she looked at the box. "Okay, now I want to see the ring."

He smiled and opened the box, revealing a large gold ring, inlaid with diamonds and the number 1.

Her eyebrow raised.

"Oh, sorry. I had that along in case my long-distance pitch didn't work. I was going to bribe you with my past fleeting fame."

She slapped his arm, and he lifted the championship ring and its tray out of the box to reveal a diamond that sparkled as it caught the flickering candlelight. He took it off and eased it onto Cameron's finger.

"It's perfect," she said, and they kissed again as the yacht cut noiselessly through the waters of the St. Johns River.

"So, big news comes in threes," Mitch said at last.

"Does it?"

He nodded. "How do you feel about a June wedding?"

"June? This June?"

"I know it's short, but if you think it's manageable, I say why wait?"

"Four months? Why not, Mitch? I don't want to wait either."

"Good. Then your school year will be over and give us a couple months for our honeymoon."

"A couple months?"

"Well, I've been thinking, as much as lounging around on the beach with you will be great, it's a little low-energy compared to our last vacation together."

Cameron waited, admiring the twinkle in Mitch's eyes.

He leaned forward. "Have you ever heard of the Caribbean Cross?"

"The alleged eight-foot high cross fashioned out of Incan gold by conquistadors and then lost somewhere between Mexico and Spain? Yeah, I've heard the legend. Several versions of it, in fact."

"How would you like to try to find it?"

"Me?"

"Us. I've done my research, and I think the legends are legit."

"You're serious?"

"I am. I already have a couple leads and four months to find more."

"You want to go on a treasure hunt for a honeymoon?"

He shrugged. "Why not? I'm sure we can find plenty of beaches and sunsets and relaxing dinners too. What do you say?"

Cameron leaned forward and spoke just before kissing him again. "I say I can't wait for June."

Author's Note

As usual, I owe great thanks to the people who helped in getting this book published. Their contributions in editing and proofing, as well as listening to ideas, have been noted before and deserve to be again.

Far more invaluable are the people, many of them the same ones, who have supported and encouraged me through writing and through life. The last few years have been stressful in a variety of ways and for numerous reasons, and their presence in my life means more than words can express. But here are some:

Sierra, my wife, has been an unwavering rock in stormy weather and a warm companion on sunny days. Mom and Dad laid a foundation over the decades and continue to build on it with guidance and reinforcement. Tiffani and Mark, my sister and brother-in-law, are true friends and confidants I can always count on. And Caleb, Gabey, Chloe, Sophie, and Laynie never cease to make me smile and provide a welcome escape from the trials of life.

Speaking of escapes, I hope that's what *The Fountain* provides you. I hope the story takes you on an adventure, on a "vacation," from the stress or monotony of everyday life. More than that, I hope *thee* Fountain receives your trust and thus gives you an escape from death.

ALSO BY NATHAN BIRR

Last Resort Series:
Fire & Ice
Broken Trust

Standalone Novels:
God, Girls, Golf & the Gridiron
(Not Always in That Order) . . .
A Love Story

The Douglas Files:
Overnight Delivery – Book One
Three's a Crowd – Book Two
All an Illusion – Book Three
Shot List – Book Four
Chasing the Wind – Book Five
Blood and Treasure – Book Six
One Life to Lose – Book Seven
Golden Key – Book Eight
Mine to Avenge – Book Nine

All is Calm? – A Christmas
Novella

The Book of Levi

Augusta Whispers

Black Male – Short
WinterKill – Short
Short Sale – Short

www.nathanbirr.com